Kainaz Jussawalla is the author of the bestselling novel *Coffee Days, Champagne Nights and Other Secrets.* A university topper from St. Xavier's College, Mumbai, she has worked as a journalist with Magna Publications and the *Times of India* among others. Her storytelling ranges from bold and humorous to dark and edgy.

Kainaz, better known as Kai, is a former international cabin crew. This gave her the opportunity to travel extensively and meet people from different cultures and backgrounds from around the world.

A Reiki Master and a mental health activist, Kainaz has spoken at various forums, including AIIMS Delhi and Health First UK, on body positivity and self-acceptance.

She has won awards, including the Shiksha Ratna, Asian Literary Society Award and the Fuzia Woman Influencer of the Year, for her contribution as a micro-influencer on social media.

Kainaz hosts a celebrity chat show *Break Free* on her YouTube channel 'Chai with Kai'.

She is the founder of the social initiative 'Be a Friend' that supports, engages and entertains senior citizens.

Kainaz firmly believes (courtesy Katherine Hepburn) that if you obey all the rules, you miss all the fun.

Connect with Kainaz on Facebook and Instagram at Kainaz Jussawalla. She can be reached at kainazj@yahoo.com and kainaztheauthor@gmail.com.

Advance Praise for the Book

'This book is a tribute to the new age feisty, powerful, actually invincible and highly charismatic female figure…in the futile search for the ideal man…Self-deprecating, candid, honest and always hilarious is the only way to describe the trajectory of the protagonist…Go on then sit back, belt up and enjoy the bizarre, the brazen and beautiful. A refreshing tale in an increasingly stale society. Men, you have been warned.'
Cyrus Broacha, TV anchor, comedian, podcaster, author, political satirist, columnist

'Just what the world needs. A bit of hope, light, love, mad humour, positivity and passion. The Parsi characters kept me in splits. A mind-blowing book. Couldn't put it down.'
Sonu Sood, actor, film producer, humanitarian and philanthropist

'Kai's book I am sure will spread smiles and laughter and yet bring to fore issues many young women deal with. She will be their inspiration….'
Priya Dutt, ex-Parliamentarian, social worker-Nargis Dutt Foundation

'Breaking every stereotype! The author delivers a fun-packed, witty, heartwarming and honest account of her super eventful life.'
Jitesh Pillai, editor, *Filmfare*

Who Wants To Marry KAI JUICEWALLA?

One life, Many loves, Endless (Mis)adventures

Kainaz Jussawalla

Om Books International

First published in 2023 by

Om Books International

Corporate & Editorial Office
A-12, Sector 64, Noida 201 301
Uttar Pradesh, India
Phone: +91 120 477 4100
Email: editorial@ombooks.com
Website: www.ombooksinternational.com

Sales Office
107, Ansari Road, Darya Ganj,
New Delhi 110 002, India
Phone: +91 11 4000 9000
Email: sales@ombooks.com
Website: www.ombooks.com

ISBN: 978-93-94547-86-5

Printed in India

10 9 8 7 6 5 4 3 2 1

To

My reader

I hope my life story inspires you to love yourself a little more and believe in the power of your dreams.

I hope it gives you the courage to live life on your own terms and never let anyone make you feel less worthy.

Most importantly, I hope it lights up your day!

This book is from my heart to yours.

contents

Me: In a Nutshell ix

Aborted Take-off 1

1. The First True-blue Nazis 3
2. Ambushed by Dragon Dolly, Pervy Polly and Vampire Veera 19
3. Bawa Beckham and Kai Juicewalla Get Hitched! 30
4. Touching Base with My Jhansi ki Rani Avatar 47
5. Getting My Mojo Back with Great Gusto 54

Fasten Your Seat Belts 71

6. Battling Bullies, Bulges and Badmash Company 73
7. Close Encounter of the Ethereal Kind 87
8. Bonding over Batata Vadas and Nimbu Pani 98
9. Fabulous Four: The Whackadoodles 108
10. Starry Days, Kinky Nights 121

Mile High Club 139

11. It Took a Parrot to Change My Destiny 141
12. Moody Crab Meets Two Lionesses 158
13. Krish, Deewana Tujh Sa Nahin 169

14. Our Barcelona Catch:
Hugh Grant, Brad Pitt and Colin Firth 182
15. A Very Happy Birthday to Me 200
16. A Trip down Gangsta Paradise 213

Joyrides and Parachutes 225
17. Met My Knight in Shining Convertible 227
18. I Saw Someone Kissing Santa Claus 245
19. Kamasutra to Karma-sutra 257
20. Messiah Clooney to the Rescue 269
21. Fake It till You Make It? 280
22. Birthday Bumps and Royal Dumps 292
23. From Man-eaters to Born-again Virgins 302

Smooth Landing 313
24. Experiencing Joy Down Under 315
25. Margaritas and Matchmakers 326
26. The Strange Case of
Dr Jekyll and Mr Hyde 334
27. Kahani Mein Twist 349
28. Romancing King Khan 359
29. The Wall Crumbles Like an Apple Crumble 369
30. I Am Friends with the Monsters inside My Head 378

Acknowledgements 390

Me: In a Nutshell

I am

A junk food-aholic.

A love-aholic.

A coffee-aholic.

A borderline alcoholic (was).

A complain-oholic.

A shopaholic.

A perfect friend, granddaughter, daughter, cousin, aunt (or so I would like *them* to believe).[1]

A Parsi by birth, crazy by right.

A chick with a clean heart, but with a f**ked-up mind.

In a constant limbo between doing what is good for me and what *feels* good to me.

Never going to learn my lesson(s). *Ever*.

Shallow most of the times. Deep when it matters. (Profoundly profane, profanely profound.)

Going to accept that being full-bodied, hefty and chubby is a past-life punishment for causing a brutal world war. Take your pick. (Or, *why else*?)

Not going to let others control my peace of mind.

---

[1] Why not a perfect lover? You may ask. Well, that is a long story, dear reader, one page or a footnote is not enough.

Getting hotter and weirder by the day and nothing can stop me.

A jaded lover yet a hopeless romantic.

A Sex Goddess in the middle of an endless parched spell. (Though I would like the world to think that I am 'a wanton sex goddess with a very bad man between my thighs', just like Bridget J.)

Diva but a hustler. (Hat tip to Beyoncé, the diva of all divas.)

Proud to age disgracefully. (And waste gracefully.)

I want

A desi boy! A desi BOY! (Ain't nobody like our desi boys…)

A Nobel prize for enduring *thadkees, thakelas* and *taporis.*

Enough money in the bank to spend on charity.

A chance to tell King Khan aka Shah Rukh Khan aka SRK, how I really, *really* feel about him.

To be stuck on a remote island with my best friend Krish (with high-speed internet of course). '*Ek ladka aur ladki kabhi dost nahi ho sakte*, Madam?' (A boy and girl can never be friends, Madam?)

Well, it is a long story.

A love so powerful, so boooooombastic that the dusky, midnight sky turns into one massive rainbow and the heart explodes into an SRK love song: '*Tujhe dekha to yeh jaana sanam*'.

My family to live infinitely. And Zoya, Simran, Coco, Danny and Aliya around me forever. (Our friendship is built on a solid foundation of alcohol, sarcasm, inappropriateness and shenanigans.)

Free food coupons from Michelin-type restaurants and all fast-food chains, FOR LIFE. (My mind says 'flat abs' but my heart says 'cheesy fries' always, without fail.)

A slimmer waist, smaller butt, slightly bigger boobs and *only* one chin without exercising or mindful eating.

Revenge, retribution and respite. (An eye for an eye is never enough. Never, *never*, NEVER.)

To go back in time and stand up for myself.

A law to be passed with immediate effect that allows drooly therapists, lawyers, doctors to get amorously involved with their clients, if they so wish.

The government to declare a public holiday (NOT dry day) on my birthday.

To walk into functions/gatherings without being judged for my mindless choices.

An ageless liver and eternal youth.

To be the only single woman in a room full of hot, sexy, *single* dudes, whenever and wherever.

A wish-genie at my disposal, with endless belly rubs.

A killer story for my next bestseller. (This is certainly one. Thank you, dear reader.)

To reach '1000 XXXs' on my kissing marksheet with or without the opposite party's 'consent'. (I am all for the MeToo Movement, but I am harmless. Really.)

I believe

Lying about her age is a woman's prerogative. (After all, age is just a number. It is totally irrelevant unless you happen to be a bottle of wine. And I am vodka.)[2]

Men are perhaps from Mars, but women are *definitely* from a planet that even God did not know existed. (That proves God is a man. Ladies, I know, I know. But *think*!)

[2] Timelines in this book are changed for obvious reasons.

There should be a zoo where eligible men of all ages, shapes and sizes should be on display, with placards outside the cages that evinces information about their vital stats and results from their individual lie detector tests.

'A thousand half-loves must be forsaken to take one whole heart home.' (Thank you Rumi, you could not have put it more aptly.)

If eating greens and walking all day made one thin, cows and pigs would not be obese.

Love handles are God's way of showing, 'I gave you more than you asked for'. (So be thankful ladies, and wear your girth with mirth.)

Everyone needs those friends who say, 'F**k it! Get ready. We are going on an adventure.'

'We are all just thunderstorms wrapped in beautiful flesh, looking to be felt and understood in a world that loves sunny days.' (Courtesy the internet. Forgot whose quote.)

If you could believe in Santa Claus for eight years, you should be able to believe in yourself for eight minutes. *Try.*

'Behind every crazy woman, there is a man who made her that way'. (Some random quote from somewhere.) Count me as one…

My soulmate (and playmate) is carbs. (Because, dear reader, carbs always have the answers no matter the question.)

It is a short life, so there is no reason to not go after what sets your soul on fire, not pants on fire.

'Women are meant to be loved, not to be understood.' (Oscar Wilde, who else?)

Some people age like fine wine. Others age like sour milk.

Falling in love can be more dangerous than jumping off a boat without a life jacket or more foolish than petting a hungry crocodile. (Trust me, I have tried the last two to gauge the risk factor.)

Ten regular people are sacrificed at the altar for one *insane* Parsi to be born.

Men are like French fries, one is never gonna be enough!

If you do not do a lot of stupid things when you are young (or not-so-young), you will not have funny things to talk about when you are old (with or without grandchildren).

There is a special place in Hell for me—it is called The Throne.

I have learnt (believe me I try...)

Nice girls certainly do not create history. That my friend is an established fact. Bad girls, on the other hand, create both history and mystery.

What you need to become to survive is not always who you really are. (Yes, this is deep. Read that S-L-O-W-L-Y one more time.)

That we all crave the deep waters of intimacy, which is created when the rivers of friendship and love become one. (Corny but true.)

If wedding vows came with a five-year renewable licence clause, marriages will become much more successful.

Sometimes we keep hope buried, just to keep it safe because sometimes that is all we have left. Hope is the best dope. (I am no *charsi* but this rhymes so well.)

There are some people who open your heart; others open your eyes.

You may believe in true love, but true love may not believe in you. (Hard, cold facts, bro.)

When you have a good heart; you help too much, you trust too much, you love too much and it seems like you are the one who gets hurt the most. ALWAYS.

The less you give a damn, the happier you will be.

It is never too late to go after what you have always desired. However, do read a few of the Ten Commandments just in case… (My twist to the original.)

Thou shalt not kill (even if it is a son of a gun, womanizing, romantic partner).

Thou shalt not commit adultery (tempting exceptions to every rule. Ahem.).

Thou shalt not steal (chips from a friend's plate and ideas for my Instagram reels, do NOT count).

Thou shalt not covet thy neighbour's house (unless it is AB's Jalsa or SRK's Mannat).

It is important to have a loyal bunch of friends. PERIOD. ('They say nothing lasts forever. Dreams change, trends come and go, but friendships never go out of style.') Thanks, Carrie Bradshaw for always getting it right.

Timing in life is EVERYTHING.

Singing Gloria Gaynor's '*I will survive*' on the top of your voice can get you through mostly every achy-breaky heart kind of a scene. (Especially these lines: '*And so you're back, from outer space, I just walked in to find you here with that sad look upon your face…Go on now, go, walk out the door…Did you think I'd crumble? You think I'd lay down and die*?')

'Life can only be understood backwards, but it must be lived forwards.' So said the famous existentialist philosopher Søren Aabye Kierkegaard. *Sigh.*

In the end, 'tis not about who you loved, why you loved and where you loved. It is how faithfully you loved that truly matters even on Tinder…

ABORTED TAKE-OFF

1

The First True-blue Nazis

17 March 2019, 7:35 p.m.
Seth Jeejeebhoy Dadabhoy Agiary, Colaba, Mumbai

March is a great month for an outdoor Parsi *lagan* (wedding) in Mumbai.

It not only marks the lucky month for the Parsis when one of their biggest festivals of the year Navroz synchronises with the spring equinox, but also does not have the humidity that April and May bring.

Lagan is just the right occasion for budding *bawi* (as a Parsi lady is called) fashionistas to wear their body-hugging or slinky attires with just a golden Asho Farohar (Guardian Angel) hanging around their necks as a style statement and for the rest of the lot to show off their exquisitively embroidered, traditional Parsi *gara* saris. *Bawas* (gentlemen) not to be left behind would be in sync, garbed in neatly cut tuxedos or smart semi-formals or custom-made *daglees* (a white attire with bows in the front worn by Parsi men).

That evening, the grounds of the fire temple Seth Jeejeebhoy Dadabhoy Agiary where the Shanbur (Shanaya+Burzin) wedding was taking place could have easily been mistaken for an extravagant Bollywood film set. It was lavish, impressive and buzzing with excitement. And as I soaked in this ambience, I almost expected SRK to magically appear from nowhere, break into his trademark romantic posture—à la spread-eagled—and scoop me up like an ice cream in his arms before I melted under the scorching blaze of his twinkling eyes and devilish dimples. *Sigh.*

Filmy, I know, I know. But it has always been my favourite fantasy that has kept me going on confusing days like that. On the one hand, I was an emotional wreck and on the other, I was this elated puppy, prancing around in joy for my cousin who had just tied the knot. Why wreck? Well, the feeling was an offshoot of one gut-wrenching déjà vu after another and with every step I took deeper into the celebratory function, the unpleasant flashes became even more intense.

The last time I felt this tensed was when I awaited the results of my pregnancy test. Though I was not really pregs this time either—but I was still a f**kin' mess.

'Let's rock
Everybody, let's rock…'

No, there is nothing to celebrate about my messy state of affairs.

Contributing musically to my distraught state of mind was self-acclaimed 'Bombay *ka* Elvis Presley' Eddie Paowalla and his *koyla* and *besura* rendition of '*Jailhouse rock*'. With burnt orange-hair, middle-aged Paowalla was no Presley (more Trumpish if I may add) for he played everything under the sun, from *dhinchak* filmy numbers to the soul-stirring Beatles. Whether he sounded like a cat with diarrhoea or a chalk across a blackboard, it mattered little to the excruciatingly delirious Parsis who were a few pegs down, already.

Several aunties and uncles were setting the floor on fire with their trademark, old-school dance moves and some newly self-choreographed grooves, much inspired from Malaika's glorified booty wiggles and Hrithik's pelvic thrusts. I felt like I was attending an audition for '*Jhalak Dikhhla Jaa*' or 'Parsis Got Talent' except *jhalak* of any talent was missing from there, sadly.

For several years, tbh (to be honest), I had deliberately kept myself away from Parsi weddings, *navjote*s and community fêtes, spinning out one excuse after another while RSVPing, which covered a rather broad spectrum of illnesses, from food poisoning to sprained ankles to urinary tract infections.

It was easier for me to squirm out of such social obligations because I did not live in a Parsi colony, and so my family's network of fellow bawas was limited, and so were the invites. *Thank God*! But that did not mean we were un-Parsi-like in any way whatsoever. The characteristic eccentricity ran in our veins as much as the next Parsi's. Maybe more so.

But that evening of March, I had gathered enough courage to show up for Shanaya Billimoria, all of thirty-three years and three months old, my dearest and nearest cousin. The Bride. Shanaya provided a tiny ray of hope for single women like me in their mid-/late-thirties, who often got slagged off for appearing in public without a significant other or a 'suitable *var*', that a happily ever-after was possible, at *any* age.

Not that a happily-ever-after should have made much of a difference to me if I did not let it. As my soul sister Carrie

Bradshaw of *Sex in the City* reminds us, 'You know marriage doesn't guarantee a happy ending, just an ending.'

I fancied myself to be a mature woman with mild traces of teenage impulsivity. But I had lots to give in the right relationship, if I chose to. But it had not happened for whatever unearthly reason. Cosmic mischief? Karma? Maybe my soulmate was hibernating with polar bears in the Arctic region and had forgotten to wake up? That only time will tell.

But yes, I was as single as the last autumn leaf in Hyde Park and had been so for a while. And yes, I was looking for love. '*Real* love. Ridiculous, inconvenient, consuming, can't-live-without-each-other love', the Carrie way.

Whatever may be the cause, I had made a solemn promise to myself and The Fab Four aka TFF (I shall introduce them later) that I would try my best to not let 'the Nazis' (my monikers for a few Parsi mischief-mongers) frazzle me with their *faltu* opinions on my single status, this time. I refused to be under anyone's microscopic scrutiny. Husband-less or not!

Even though they were in the minority, these *jasoose*s and *khabaree*s, would bombard us solos with a zillion questions about our personal (read sex) lives, as if it was their goddamn business, and then add masala and *tadka* to the freshly squeezed juicy bit of gossip to feed to their own uninspiring, starving tribe. Very *saas–bahu* soap opera- type. I was familiar with their drill which had got under my skin almost a decade ago when I had sworn off attending any events where these right-wing characters showed up. Those days I was barely in my mid-twenties, and they had not spared me even then, jealously judging my new, hip job and my carefree lifestyle as an international flight attendant.

I shuddered to think what they would do now, considering that I was heading towards a freaky 40 in a few years and still without a two-carat sparkle on my left ring finger. And to make matters worse, I was the only member representing the Juicewalla clan and Shanaya would hang me by my ears if I feigned yet another headache or a stomachache on the most important day of her life.

My parents were in Auckland for their closest friends' 50th wedding anniversary bash and my younger brother, Ashtad, was sunbathing with his family in Goa. So, I was left to hold the Juicewalla torch (and burn myself with it).

And for the sake of my beloved Shanaya, who had always come through for me since childhood, I had to don an impostor costume with a spirited bounce and a bubbly smile to get through the evening, which to me was as painful as a root canal done without anaesthesia so I felt like a sack full of twisted nerves.

And so there I was, holding the neat pleats of my deep red gara, draped almost perfectly (thanks to my house help Mangal *tai* who had pinned it like a nappy on a baby) and embossed exquisitely with the obligatory Birds of Paradise. To complement my glam look was a blingy, golden, oversized clutch bag. (It was a special occasion, c'mon!)

So in my bestest Parsi babe avatar, I was desperately screening the grounds in search of my rescue team to free me from this self-inflicted anguish I had called upon for myself. (Blood is thicker than water…blah, blah.) Even my knockout cousin Parizad or her charming younger brother Jimmy would do, as long as they were carrying my favourite poison.

But no one was in sight. *Gaddars.*

'Where the f**k are these guys?'

I mumbled to myself as I removed my phone from my purse to call them. I had already placed a 'reachin' in five' call, from my car. They should have been waiting hand and foot for me. They knew how I hated walking in alone, it made me feel naked and lonely.

I could almost hear the predators, sneering and pointing at me: 'Look, there she is, Kai! Always a bridesmaid, never a bride.'

My comfort cushions had ditched me. Shanaya had invited the rest of TFF, my besties from college, whom she had met on and off over the years. But Simran was playing the dutiful daughter in law-to-be with her future in-laws visiting from Delhi, Krish was on his way back to Mumbai from a shoot with Miss R and Posh Zoya was on her way to the venue but fashionably running late and would then make a grand entry, gliding in her Porsche and carrying off one of her Sabyasachi's or Abu Jani's with her usual flair. Though *she would like all to believe* that *a queen is never late, everyone else is simply early.* By then, I would be probably oscillating between drunken oblivion and hypoxia, depending on how the evening metamorphosed.

When I had left my Bandra pad, I began listening to a 15-minute video on express healing, meditation and chakra balancing on YouTube endorsed by one of the many blonde healers from the West Coast. I was, after all, concerned about how the day would unfold. I had to sort myself out before the Nazis unleashed themselves on me. Halfway through my arduous journey, I switched to affirmations of gratitude, confidence, courage and neat vodka. (Always, *always* keep one handy.)

Ram Singh, my ever-reliable chauffeur, had pretended hard not to notice me doing shots in the backseat, from the hip flask that I *almost* always carried in my bag, but I could tell by his incessant throat clearing that he was not approving of it at all. Well, he did not have a vote now, did he? What did he know about being a single woman battling an eternal belly bulge and a nonexistent sex life (leave alone love life)?

Drinking numbed the pain of being left behind on the shelf. Professionally, I may be a well-known columnist, a popular vlogger with a decent YouTube following[1] and a cool, composed, safety-driven, well-groomed (with great effort) flight stewardess for a leading international airline, but my personal life was in the pits. The incorrigible romantic in me was shattered from inside. The paranoia of being left alone without a permanent man-candy on my arm had increased with each passing year, throwing me into panic attacks, awkward situations and a gloomy state of affairs more often than I wanted to remember. It was almost as if I ran a signature club for losers.

The few graces that had saved me from enrolling myself into a mental institution were the strong support system of TFF, doting grandmothers, a few good friends and the fact that I belong to an extremely rare and rapidly dwindling community called Parsis known to be a harmless and endearing minority who could get away with just about anything, including walking around the town in a bathing suit if they so wished.

It was normal for our bawas and bawis to hear, 'Oh, he is a mad Parsi!' 'She is a crazy bawi! What do you expect from them?' These allowed us exemption from following protocols and 'socially-approved' behaviour, thus excusing our quirkiness, idiosyncrasies and extremities.

---

[1] Check out my YouTube channel 'Chai with Kai'. Please like and follow it. Yes, I never, ever miss the opportunity to plug it. Thank you.

When I had finally (read reluctantly) accepted my jinxed love life about four and a half years ago by following a 'no guy–no cry' ideology of male abstinence, I had become a more contented person, or so I thought. Can't help humming that famous Bob Marley number, '*No woman, no cry…everything's gonna be alright*'. (Though the reason for her crying could be different.) Becoming a globe-trotting, glamorous sanyasin could easily be my next occupation.

For now, I had found a new version of self-love in the past two years away from relationship *jhamelas*—validation by social media, primarily Facebook and Instagram. As they say FakeItTillYouMakeIt and I had, well *almost*. My lifestyle vlog 'Chai with Kai' was doing reasonably well, and my selfies of wolfing down gulab jamuns and kachoris at Brijwasi Sweets and stroking SRK's neck at Madame Tussauds had gathered quick likes and heart emoticons.

And above all, I had written a bestseller, almost! *Coffee Days, Champagne Nights and Other Secrets* is the book. My baby. My first novel which 'is a complex take on duality of the human mind with hair-raising twists and turns' as one reviewer would have it. Hmm, how could my second baby be less complicated? (Now buy it and make it a bestseller too!)

Yet, the niggling fear of bumping into past tormentors who had more awkward questions for me than Karan has on *Koffee with Karan* for his guests caused my heartbeat to accelerate with every step I took towards the bewitchingly lit-up arena.

The world has changed, Kai. You have redefined your boundaries. People now value a woman for her achievements rather than her wedding band or her waistband. A familiar inner voice chided me. Sometimes you need to have these stern conversations with yourself. (Though they never led me anywhere.)

Simran and Zoya had pumped me on our TFF WhatsApp group earlier with their *yeh dosti nahin todenge* type of texts, 'Go get 'em tigress. We are rooting for you.' 'Sway in like a ramp model with a crown on your head. You got this.'

And so on, accompanied by half a dozen 'Boss girl' gifs.

Maybe they were right, I had to stride with pride, like the high value woman I was though the last time I had tried to swish my hips differently and maybe a tad seductively at my book launch event, just for effect, I had almost tripped over a step and a loose wire. Thankfully, I had missed landing atop the chief guest, poet and lyricist, Javed Akhtar.

But I must have done something right that evening, for I could not help but notice the admiring glances thrown my way from a few strangers as I walked the red carpet, deeper into the human forest. Maybe it was my bright lip colour that was drawing attention or the immaculate root touch-up and the perfectly blow-dried hair neatly executed by Matalyn, my hair stylist. I felt lightheaded and empowered with all my fears fading away.

'Pari! Finally!'

I almost stumbled in relief.

Parizad looked bloody awesome. Lucky bitch. She had shot out two little menaces and still owned washboard abs. It was in her DNA, she had her mother's genes. Unlike me, who neither had slim-genes nor skinny-fit jeans.

Though that evening, I had smartly covered my untoned (and ever-spreading) torso with a sizable portion of the gara, held in by a pair of M&S peach-tinted, high-waisted granny panties (sacrificing my lucky red bikini cut ones for a change).

She held my Absolut vodka tonic lime wedge against her dazzling smile.

'Kai, *late-latif*, how are you?'

She kissed me hard on my right cheek.

'I thought you had gotten lost in some pub or mall along the way.'

'Almost...'

I giggled, feeling buoyant.

'Ooh you wearing J'adore, *mon* fav! And I so luvvvv what you've done to your hair, so RAD. You look freakin' lit! Glad you're crushing it after two imps.'

She laughed, throwing her head back, and said, 'You've really become so zillennial. Jimmy had warned me. I hardly have time to see your lively posts and stories, but he swears that if he didn't know your age, he would guess it to be twenty.'

'Flatterers and liars, all you cousins.'

I played along, secretly pleased. I hid my age well (and have kept it well under wraps). And that is known to everyone who knows me well.

'I try hard to keep up with these trends and tags, Cuzzy, but we both know, dahling, that I am getting more hag than swag.'

We had no facades between us.

'You certainly are not!'

Pari objected vociferously.

'You have the chutzpah of a cool twenty-something with a funny bone to match. In fact, I was just discussing this with Cy.'

'Talking about that pain in the neck, Cy, where is your worse half?'

'He's chatting up some gals from Burzin's side.'

She rolled her eyes.

'My idea. After two kids to drive you around the bend, nagging in-laws, waking up at six a.m. every damn day of your precious life to pack dabbas, checking on homework, and making tea and brekky for your entire *khandaan*, you just hope your hubby finds some distraction and there is one less person to manage.'

I was enjoying our banter, so I let her vent. She had gotten married to the first guy she had laid eyes on—a typical case of young sweethearts (or fools) rushing in—and I had begrudged Cyrus ever since for taking our Pari away from us way too soon.

We moved in slow motion, savouring our catch-up time, Pari yapping away whilst I was in an Alice in Wonderland kind of a mood. Entranced by the different elements of the evening playing themselves out, drawing in sharp breaths now and again, and mesmerised by the impressive transformation of the Colaba Agiary grounds.

Unlike the garish grounds I remembered from many eons ago, it roared with grandeur and class this time! More tasteful and à la mode, lesser pomp and show. A reflection of the well-heeled and well-travelled power couple with no shortage of sophistication.

The entrance was decorated with orchids, tulips and camellias; the sit-down arrangement on the lawn showcased chairs dressed up in cream-coloured, rich, satin upholstery with neatly tied golden bows; round tables were embellished with red candles and soft, yellow roses in elegant, crystal bowls; and mid-Eastern-moulded vintage coppery lamps dangled over arches and trees.

There were waiters hovering around in beige uniforms, carrying heavy silverware. Parsi ladies of all ages strutted around flaunting their ancestral jewellery and a bunch of fine-looking men walked around in well-styled jackets. Everyone seemed to be in high spirits. Or was it just me? *Already*!

Gen Z were catching up at their separate tables, probably scouting for new dates or discussing the OOTD (outfit of the day). The baby boomers and Gen X too had formed their own cliques, some doing *khus pus* in each other's ears probably trashing the newer lot's brazen fashion statements and unexplainable haircuts.

Though it was all swanky and swish, the mantra of a Parsi function always remained the same: *Khao, daru piyo, maja ne masti karo*! *Aapre tau evaach chaiye*. (Eat, booze, have fun. We are like that only.) I had always been proud to be Parsi, and that day even more so.

'Oh, I am so chuffed for Shanaya and Burzin! What a kickass venue!'

I shouted, taking another big swig, celebrating my happiness for our cousin who had earned every quantum of this marvellous day.

Pari grinned as we headed towards the bedecked stage about 250 metres away, where the dazzling duo stood in front of their throne-like velvet burgundy chairs, set against a backdrop of an aesthetically created floral arrangement with two massive red foil heart-shaped balloons at its centre, greeting their guests with welcoming grins though Shanaya seemed tired already as I noticed her subtly switch from one foot to another under her Gulshan Kolah sari.

So far, so good. Pari's blend was definitely working for me because I found myself winking unabashedly at a drop-dead, handsome guy, sporting a navy blue three-buttoned blazer, possibly an Armani, leaning against a column in conversation with a bearded gentleman.

Drrroooollll! He returned my spontaneous candour with a provocative once-over.

'If only I wasn't a devoted mother, I would beg for a ride in his Rolls Royce. Hey Kai, would you like to swap lives?'

'Hell no!'

I pulled my tongue out at her.

'But isn't he dishy? *Ek dum* David Beckham *lagech*! Where the hell has he been all my life?'

'Biceps *jau nee*...just look, man! He's ripping out of his clothes.'

Pari gripped my flabby arm tightly, almost making my glass drop.

'Eh *gheli,* silly, careful.'

I chuckled as we walked past Becks. I tried to look behind, wondering if he was still checking me out.

'Mrs Parizad Marker, I didn't know you had a squint. FYI, his biceps are not between his legs.'

We burst into silly giggles almost toppling over each other.

Becks cut a tempting picture, clean shaven under his slickly done salt and pepper hair, an endearing mole below his lips but that could be my boozy illusion though overall he was just enough to whet my appetite for a long, passionate snog.

'I am two short of 1,000...and the kiss count had been at a standstill for way too long.'

Pari rolled her eyes.

'You are still *counting*?'

'Yeah, I know, I know that I have been on a love-sabbatical remember? But now I am seriously thinking of saying "screw you" to the "no guy–no cry challenge" and going for it.'

I was barely audible over Paowalla's '*Disco*'. (A popular song at functions.)

'And smooching Becks would be like having a spicy triple burger after years of prison dishwater soup—worth every satisfying, juicy morsel.'

I was salivating now, literally and metaphorically, wondering if I could convince Burzin to introduce me to him.

'Are you horny or hungry?'

'Good question, boring married cousin. It's never a choice dear. Can't I be both?'

Moreover, 'first lust then love'. (Thank you, Jackie Collins, for your inspiring philosophy of life.)

Our lady (who else but me) was turning out to be quite immature for a woman in her mid-thirties, which was good actually. Every woman needs to revisit their inner girl once in a while. Now all I had to do was wish the cosy twosome on stage and then make a beeline for another drinkie before I finally get acquainted with Mr Delish who had revived my happy hormones. (Dopa is mine…) I was so charged up with the vibrancy of my immediate surroundings and caught up in our energetic exchange that I almost forgot that every silver lining holds in it, a looming, dark cloud.

There it was. A tsunami emerging from the far west, best described as my spookiest and eeriest nightmare coming true, which paralysed me into immobility each time it struck, making my stomach gnarly with intense panic and mouth dry as a bone.

I speedily tried to assimilate fragments and bits from the books of the revered spiritually intelligent authors, like Deepak Chopra, Robin Sharma, Paulo Coelho and Dalai Lama, that had recently been added to my minuscule book collection—a last-ditch attempt to keep some sort of perspective in sight before my fighting spirit thawed out as quickly as a snowman in a desert.

But I drew a blank. I contemplated a quick, quiet exit, but my feet seemed nailed to the ground. The raging bull was honing in on me and I was no matador.

I am a self-assured and beautiful woman. I am in control of my emotions and my reactions. I am attracting only wonderful people today who love me and accept me completely. I am…

Positive affirmations only. They always work. They *have* to. Pari must have gauged from my colourless face that I was freaking out.

'Ohhhh! I know she is the last person you want to see Kai. Just chillax!'

'*Nahinnn!*'

I let out an unhinged cry but it was too late.

Busted. Roasted. And that was putting it mildly.

'Oh, Kai *jaaaaaan,* you are here, finally. Yoo-hoo!'

Dhak dhak, dhak dhak —no, not the magnificent Madhuri Dixit kind. Obviously.

It was my heart racing at the speed of lightning. The unmistakable shrill voice made me cringe (and pukish), as she wrapped her petite frame around me like a viper, refusing to let go until I began coughing hard.

Dragon Dolly.

The first, true-blue Nazi in her true intimidating element, reeking in sheer gaudiness from head to toe, had ambushed me. And she was not going to let me out of her sight until she had written the first sentence of my obituary, etched in her blood orange nails. (Always introduce people with thoughtful details.)

She belonged to the tribe of the Bawa Nazis who seemed to be at every Parsi function, appearing out of thin air and activating a cyclone that leaves behind irreparable damage. They had these invisible choppers and daggers and their primary POA on any gathering was to seek out those who had not found 'suitable marriageable boys/girls' and shame them to tears.

'*Bechari ni train chutigayee* (poor thing she missed her train)', being one of the classics from the The Nazi Manifesto of Insults.

2

Ambushed by Dragon Dolly, Pervy Polly and Vampire Veera

'Kai, *maari mitthi*! (My sweet one!) How lovely to see you after ages. Been waiting for you. Oh *Khodaiji, pag nathi mukyo ne pachu peevanu saru thaigayu*? (Lord! You have hardly stepped in and have started drinking *again*?)'

Her taunting, nasal tone, laced with the aroma of golden, fried prawns and Black Label, pierced into the air, loud enough to startle even our *behra* Banoomai who was seated at a fair distance with a hearing aid.

Aunty Dolly Lalkaka with her floppy mahogany dyed bun loosely held together by her bawa *Adam zamana nu* (ancient) hair net and mismatched bobby pins, and protruding eyes that reflected the same conniving gleam under her bifocals, which I remembered only too well from our last encounter. She was a family friend-cum-distant relative (all bawas are related some way or the other) and a permanent fixture at every social gathering I had ever been to since I was a kid.

I could have sworn that Dragon Dolly was wearing the ditto brassy aubergine gara with the tacky bronze ducklings when we had collided into each other almost a decade ago at Eric's lagan, where she had made a huge fuss about my backless blouse and had showered me with sarcastic remarks—the cattiest one being about my childbearing hips, which in her manifesto had only 'one good use'.

Pointing below my waist around my vag zone, she had badgered me in public, 'If you do some good for our community, *dikra* (child) by marrying a 100 per cent pure Zoroastrian boy and not some *altu-faltu parjaat* (useless non-Parsi), then maybe Almighty will bless you. *Hara-bhara chokreeyo* like you are the last hope left for us. You are 25, *na*? So, you have at least 7–8 good years to remove *ardha dajan bakalyas* (half a dozen kids) from there.'

'I'm not a yogurt that comes with an expiry date.'

I had protested mortified by her audacity, before getting wasted on white wine and whisky that night in quiet retaliation.

Pari lightly touched my arm as if to say, 'Be calm, Kai. Breathe. Detach. This is all maya'. That brought me back to the soiree.

'Nice to see you, Aunty.'

And followed it up by taking a large gulp of air and Absolut.

SILENCE.

We let the heavy silence settle down for a while as we stared at each other in mock amicability. I contemplated asking about her sons, Yohan and Pakzad, 40-something swindlers who had recently gotten caught in some money-laundering scam. Putting her on the back foot would make my day.

But as usual, she beat me to it, maintaining the upper hand.

'*Tumhe tau ekdum eski meski lagi-rayach*! (You look totally stylish!) But you are still as *gol gol* as a rasgulla, *haan*!' (The gist being I am stylish but still round as a rasgulla.)

Trigger alert: The fat girl in my head had been living outside the box for a long time now. She had not busted her ass to come back to square one. She was not going to crawl back inside. Not today. Not tomorrow. *Not ever*.

My eyes dropped to my feet like my podgy, hapless, embarrassed 10-year-old self.

I should have gone with my intuition—attending this wedding was a huge, sick mistake. I had dug my own grave by doing so. And despite all the inner strength and zest I had tried to muster, I felt myself slipping down a bitter memory lane. My gaze remained transfixed on my golden, glittery sandals.

I had always liked blingy shoes. Mommy had bought me my first pair from Metro Shoes when I was nine—pretty pink flat sandals with delicate silver bows. I had worn them to several grand parties hosted by our family and friends, including The Readymoneys who lived in a five-bedroom ritzy manor at the upscale Carter Road area of the chic suburb of Bandra and a five-minute drive from our own tastefully-done modest apartment at Perry Road.

Daddy had brought me a turquoise dress from an authentic German local brand store on one of his business trips to Frankfurt, and the shiny pink pair was such a lovely contrast. Or so I thought until The Readymoneys' brats, a couple of years older than me, brought negative attention to my couture effort by squealing over my shoulder, 'Piggy, piggy, pink flats! Too fat to walk in heels?' as soon as I entered their whopping mansion.

All I could recall was rushing out of the door, tears burning down my heart-shaped face as I plonked myself on a swing, swollen-eyed and shaking. They had the ammunition to reduce me to nothingness. It had not been the first time I felt persecuted by bullies and it certainly was not going to be my last. My weight issues had been the touchiest and sorest point of my life.

'Kai, let's go and congratulate our Shanu and Burzin. Aunty, we'll be right back!'

Pari had learnt from her experience that this ordeal was about to go up in thick, black smoke *très très* shortly. So, she chose the flight over fight mode.

But just as we were about to flee from the guillotines, Dragon Dolly's semi-balding husband, the potbellied, stocky and whisky-loving, 'Pervy Polly' magically shot out from behind her, almost like a second head, in a jazzy, fluorescent green, velvet coat with haldi-stained high-waisted pista green and peach checkered *patluns* and chalky white shoes, with two-inch heels. His outlandish attempts at youthfulness and a filter-less mouth reminded me of a certain US president though Pervy's wardrobe seemed to be stolen from the one and only Ranveer Singh.

There had been several stories scuttling around about Polly Lalkaka's *badmashgiri*. Right from the blatant passes he had made at trainee nurses during his sponge baths at the Parsi General Hospital after his hernia operation to flagrant hanky-panky with his best friend's wife, Naaju Battiwala, from Kharegat Colony. His badmashgiri had earned him the reputation of a serial Baira Master (Ladies' Man).

Predictably, Pervy's slimy right hand had already found its way to my bra hook under my blouse, moving his wiggly fingers up and down my back in 'paternal affection', but lingering a pervy-second too long, giving me both the chills and the creeps.

'*Jau ni*, Dolly dear! If it isn't our little roly-poly pudding and pie *jevi*, Kai Kai, and she still hasn't won the first prize in husband hunting.'

He purred like an evil cat, making sure his eye contact with my chest did not falter, slugging a king-size measure of whatever crap he was having at the same time.

He was on a roll, his hoarse jeering tone increasing my palpitations as he dished out more scoops of unsolicited advice, 'Now look dear, you are no spring chicken. *Peti tight kareene su faido?* (What's the point of locking your modesty?) You may not be as pretty as *aapri* Zorabian and Penty, but I am sure some mama's boy is waiting for you in one of our *baugs* to grab your Amul *maakhan jeva gaal* (buttery cheeks). Uhhh, not in the Adar Poonawalla or Ness Wadia category, of course, but…'

I was this close to punching his absurdly long nose or poking the sharp end of one of the safety pins from my pleats into his sticky digits that had now made their way to my smooth right cheek in light caress. I just could not decide which would be more apt.

Okay so, I was on the plump side and there were many places in the world where 'voluptuous' and 'curvy' were considered very exotic. Let us see, Kuwait, Fiji, Jamaica, Samoa…).[1]

Just then, the eldest of Pari's kids, little Anahita, appeared, howling because she had lost her friends in a game of hide-

---

[1] Suzy Duvall, 'Top 10 Countries Celebrating Female Obesity', TopTenz, https://www.toptenz.net/top-10-countries-celebrating-female-obesity.php. I do my research well, dear readers.

and-seek. The mother–daughter departure was my cue to pull myself away from the Lalkakas before I threw my half-empty glass on one of their heads.

But then things plummeted even further. Vampire Veera from DPC (Dadar Parsi Colony) came striding towards us in all her noxious splendour, a peacock blue gara with the famous Chinese men embroidery, waving her flabby left hand and holding on to three bite-sized quiches in her right. I hastily dug out my phone and managed to quickly send a text to the TFF group: 'Deep shit! SOS. Z where r u?!'

I had made it this far to the function only because I was counting on Pari, Jimmy and Zoya to make it through. But the first had vamoosed, Jimmy was nowhere to be seen and Zoya I am sure was still getting her toes painted by her personal assistant.

'Kai, *aapri madam ni mai*, come and give me one, big *kotee* (hugs)–kissy, Miss hoity-toity. *Wah re wah,* very nice sari but the cut of your choli is too deep, *nai*? *Jara,* over the hill, Barbie doll *jevi lagech;* don't you think?'

Veera Sopariwala, life critic-cum-investigating cop, had kicked off with her expected *chavitrapanu* (mischief). Her curly, unruly mop reminded me of a honeycomb I had once seen as a child, hanging from the branch of a banyan tree. It was a shame the bees were missing.

'At our age, we sag like old cows and oh, *mari jaoo,* I will die, just look at those freckles on your face and dreadful lines under the neck? Tch. Tch. Maybe cover such marks with your *pulla,* my love?'

'Marks? At my age!'

I was as wrinkle-free as the 120-pound worth of Lancôme Absolue revitalising moisturiser from Boots pharmacy,

Piccadilly Circus, London had promised. And freckles were adorable, as certified by my very with it-gay friend Dan.

I tried smiling it off. If I did not let her get under my skin, maybe I had the smallest chance of coming out of this mental torture unscathed? But I got no such breather. Vampire Veera and her matt-finished purple lips were not planning on giving up until I slit my wrists or cut my throat or both.

'And *Khoda re Khoda* (God oh God), why so much *charbi* on your tummy-tum-tum? You must be careful with the junk food. Remember that time you swiped two dozen *sarias (*sago chips) off the *paatru* (three banana leaves used as a plate) before anyone else got their turn to even try them? It's all catching up now, *ni*?'

Polly and Dolly gave gleeful snorts as Vampire Veera pinched her own unflattering saggy stomach below her sleeveless silver choli for a demo. She took a big bite of the savoury and continued on her rampage: 'Oooh Miss *hawa ni pari* (air hostess) your bracelet! Wah! Wah! Is this from your Mumma's *khazana,* or have you finally found a sugar daddy? A *phoren* pilot perhaps who is showing you his *cock*pit?'

Tickle. Tickle. Laugh. Laugh. Such wit!

Jabbing her chipped off claws into my diamond and emerald wristlet, she glanced around for affirmation to her dig at the word 'cockpit' from the posse of old cronies who were seated around. They snickered in solidarity, some adjusting their hearing aids, others their dentures—raising their whiskies, colas and fresh limes to an eager toast at my expense.

'Excuse me?'

I took two steps behind as I shrugged off the blood-sucking Vampire Veera's palm over my wrist. A little too aggressively, I admit.

I was barely 45 minutes into the function and already burnt out. I had sashayed in there trying to forge the exuberance and oomphiness of a groovy *Sex and the City* gal, but was mutated into a *makhee* on a wedding gateau.

After countless years of emotional ups and downs, I had managed to make peace with my weighing scale and my star-crossed romances, pacifying my heart into the quiet acceptance that being '*patlee* and *fatakree*' (thin and a perfect 10, respectively) were as impossible a feat for me as having the breathtaking romance depicted in almost every SRK film.

I cursed Zoya under my breath. Why could she not be on time just this once? I would have been spared from this *mastak maari bimari* (feverish headache) if I had got myself a strong ally. And Zoya was definitely one. Simran too. Being super defensive of me, they would have smacked the three, impudent villains back into shape.

I looked around for some usual suspects to rescue me. Nada. I seem to have been ambushed forever. I settled for a passing young waiter, pleading with my eyes, to rescue me from my misery. My desperate smile must have confused him, for he almost dropped the tray of kung pao paneer on a nearby table.

New plan. I could dunk all their despicable heads into the kung pao, which smelt heavenly.

Finally, after scanning my surroundings twice over, I caught a glimpse of another potential victim. I began waving at him furiously, almost knocking off Polly's precious tumbler; soon realising that he had turned his head away to put his arm around some PYT in the bar area, much to my dismay.

'Damn you, stupid, flirty cousin bro, Jimmy, with an overactive sex drive.'

Vampire Veera, who was now gobbling a handful of chicken lollipops, was being as pushy as a telemarketer selling insurance, not ready to buy into my 'I need to visit the washroom' story.

'I hope you are not minding us, sweetoo. We are your well-wishers only. We all had great regard for your wise *bapaiji* (paternal grandmother). We also want what's genuinely best for you only, ni?'

Mentioning my Granny B was a BIG mistake.

'Yeah, you sound as genuine as a profile on Tinder.'

I hissed back at her, but she was too immersed in her own blah blah to acknowledge my metaphoric brilliance.

Pausing for a cough and a gasp, she continued slamming me, '*Marere dharere* (oh golly), unless you are what they call these days…what's that word, Dolla? *Uffo!* I forget …Oh *haan*, a lebbo—Lebanon?'

Dragon Dolly, who was caught up in chugging down a piña colada and adjusting her husband's hideous pink bow, quipped in an equally brutal tone as her infuriating counterpart, 'Lesssssbian, Veera dear! It's l-e-s-b-i-a-n. *Aaj kal* it's a big fad, you know!'

The sexism and preposterousness of it astounded me. If a woman was not married by a certain age, did that mean she had given up on cock and embraced pussy? Would smacking Dragon Dolly with her tacky embroidered potlee bag be counted as self-defence? Worth a try, na?

Before I left my pad, I had instructed myself that I would not let their jibes get under my skin. I had even fooled myself into thinking that with the passing years the Inquisition Squad would have found another distraction or mellowed down or even fling a praise or two my way. But the chances of being hit by lightning that evening were higher than that.

I just had to break free before I passed out in suffocation or fury, or both, so I began pushing past the semi-circle that they had formed around me. I was almost there.

As kismet would have it, Veera Sopariwala's husband, Toupee Tehmtun, a Mr Bean clone, known to be a real *jhoroo ka ghulam* floundered into the loop of madness. Which circus had lost its clown? Faux leather, crotch-hugging, tan trousers, red silk shirt, sunshine yellow suspenders, red ankle high boots—seriously? Straightening his ridiculous ginger-bleached wig, he dug into his unusually wide nasal cavity, then wiped his finger on Polly's shirt and put his hand out for a shake. If there was ever a time to pretend having a stroke, it was then.

Polly, who did not seem to mind his sniffle buddy at all, blabbered on, '*Eh gadhera ka marigailo? Pela kewab try keedha ke—bilari na maatha jeva motta motta? Joine-ach maara mona maan pani avigayu.* (Where were you dying, you donkey? Have you tried those kebabs—the size of a cat's head? My mouth began watering by just looking at them.)'

Taking a gigantic glug from his short tumbler, Tehmtun retorted, '*Nahin re, mad**ch*d,* Polly! That social activist, *naak ni tichki* (snooty) Daisy Limbuwala bumped into me near the toilets and began *bheja*-frying me about that baby making scheme she is promoting. That *jiyo* Parsi funda. She says we bawas will be as extinct as dinosaurs, if we don't buck up.'

Polly opened his mouth wide and countered, '*Su bolech?* That Daisy Duck caught you too. Beware! Nowadays with this MeToo and all *nu chakkar,* one must be careful. *Kaun jaane, apune bhi koi fasavee kare tau*? (Who knows, someone will trap us too?)'

I looked at them in disbelief, were they just being senile or pissed drunk already?

Tehmtun Sopariwala rambled on, 'I *tau* told her, "Oye Daisy, don't be crazy, we are 75-year-old dinos, so why are you doing this *dahi dochaan manjan* (unnecessary conversation) with us? Find some youthful *porya* and *poreeo* to *gyan maro na*"'.

Polly shoulder-thumped his buddy, 'Good one, Tehmu. What is this *jiyo jiyo*? At our age, we boys are only interested in *piyo aur so jao,* ho ho! But Kai Kai. Better late than never for you *haan?* Like we say in cricket, *ek wicket tau maar.* BURRRRRPPP!'

Letting out an enormously disgusting belch and bringing the rest of the nags to howl like happy hyenas, they returned to the table that they shared with their *chaplooses,* leaving me standing there seething like a volcano waiting to erupt.

3

Bawa Beckham and Kai Juicewalla Get Hitched!

How dare they? *Pani matha ni upar avigayuch.* (The water has gone above the head.) I am up to my tits with their lack of empathy and overdose of *lavaro* and *koylagiri* (nonsense and stale humour). Am I bulletproof?

I strode angrily and bumped into Jimmy who was lounging in the verandah adjoining the bar, already *pee ke tunn* (happily drunk). He broke into a goofy grin as he enveloped me into a bear hug. He had witnessed my butchering session from a distance, and held two huge flutes in each hand, knowing pretty well what I needed the most. Responsible drinking? Now that is an oxymoron. Getting *talli* was perhaps the only way to get through this tragedy. He looked dapper in a salmon pink linen blazer and distressed jeans, clearly not adhering to the formal dress code. I wish Shanaya had allowed me to wear one of my short skirts or bootcut jeans. The sari did nothing for me, in fact it was a bit of an inconvenience, for neither did I look like a dandy peacock (as one usually does at such galas) nor was

I able to carry it off as fluidly and elegantly as the beautiful Vidya Balan, whom I seriously adore.

'Seemed like a near bloodbath from where I was. I wanted to be your knight and rescue you from the slaughterhouse but Pari was there, so I kept an eye on you from a distance in case your Swiss Army knife showed up at any point.'

'Ha! I was this close. BTW, your sis is quite useless. She leaves me on my own to endure the maniacs. As are you, falling over that 18-year-old while your hottest cousin is conjuring up ways to end her life.'

Keeping it breezy was an effort because I was fuming.

'Oh don't be so dramatic, Kai.'

He was well aware that I would disintegrate into dust if he did not say something that I needed to hear, so he immediately set the record straight.

'Kidding! Actually, they are burning with jealousy, Kai. Haven't I always told you that?'

'Why?'

'Coz you have everything they don't—a cultured upbringing, the prettiest face I have ever seen and class. The Lalkaka kids are SSC failures and *chors,* and just the other day, Mom mentioned that the Sopariwalas haven't seen their children or grandchildren since they moved to Singapore, five years ago. So how sad their lives must be.'

His lips were twisted into a snarl, his hand was on my shoulder like a protective brother.

'That doesn't excuse their bad behaviour but Kai, you've gotta start giving a rat's ass to all this. *Laat maro* yaar! You have a flying job that anyone would kill for and the freedom to live life on your terms. Don't forget—you are an author too. That's another blow for the haters. They must be wetting themselves with envy and exasperation whenever they see you. Stay classy, sassy and a bit bad assy.'

He beckoned to a passing waiter carrying yummy-looking tandoori aloo and corn nuggets, neatly stacked them for me in two paper napkins and held them out to me, saying nothing as he watched me gobble the grub in ravenous vengeance.

Why?

Because I just do not want to look back and think I could have eaten that. Good food has always been the answer to any challenge life threw at me. And everyone dear to me knew that.

'It's amazing how some people have this great need to stereotype and compartmentalise everybody...'

I trailed off, a tornado of emotions churning inside me, finding it tough to keep a heroic face when all I wanted was to bawl my eyes out.

'C'mon Captain K. Fire those pistols.'

He drew me closer, covering me up with his 5 feet 11 inches frame, mindful of my past record with assorted intimidators and bullies that had brought out the waterworks in me. Unable to keep up with the charade of Wonder Woman any more, my emo-dam broke.

'They are just beastly, man. So judgmental, despicable and hateful. *Paaki ne poro thaigauch maru*! (I am overfried like an omelette!)

I was trying not to sound hysterical though in vain.

'It's not *ke* I haven't tried praying for the right man, you know...I have been venerating our Iranshah Atash Behram almost every year since 2009. But my efforts have been *ekdum bhunkus* (completely useless)!'

Jimmy was all ears.

'Yeah, we went there together. Somewhere in 2014, was it? It was after that America-returned disaster you were almost engaged to? You even chatted up the sanitorium owner, I forget his name, a seedy-looking chappy who sat at the welcome counter in his white legha, remember? His jealous wife almost kicked us out when she found your number scribbled in the guest register. But full marks for the efforts, I must say.'

We both gave a short laugh. It had been quite a trip to Udvada, a sacred site for the Parsis situated in the Valsad district of Gujarat and home to one of the oldest fire temples in the world.

After an hour of praying at the Iranshah for good health of my family and tragic personal life, I had walloped 10 scoops of the local mango ice cream all the way up to my three-star lodging, and I was as sick as a dog on the way back.

It was a fact that I could neither control my food habits, nor my flirtatious overtones.

'Maybe Swiggy should have a soulmate delivery app for late bloomers like me.'

Jimmy clicked for another top up of his rum and Coke.

'Kai, I really think that your guy is out there. You've just gotta hold on. Though there is nothing like a perfect dude.'

Let my sweet cuzz say what he wanted. He was a free spirit (and a typical guy) and thought of me as an *overacting ki dukaan*. I believed that 'Mr Ideals' existed in the world, perhaps like needles in haystacks, but they still did exist. Most of my girlfriends had found them.

Weren't Laila–Majnu, Radha–Krishna, Ram–Sita all about true love?

It was just that a stroll into the sunset with my one true love was not written in the stars for me and my Venus seemed to be in a perpetual retrograde. I was forced to surrender to my destiny of infinite spinsterhood, clutching on to the last straws of youth for dear life.

Not that singledom was bad by any standards but the mere thought of not having someone to wake up to and get spooned or forked by (pun intended) had squashed my morale and faith in love. And in spite of having endured more heartbreaks than all my close friends put together (with the exception of Simran), I could not masquerade being as one of those alpha feminists who were fine with even marrying *themselves*, if they had to. I yearned for attention, devotion and passion from my Mr Right. Neither sologamy nor polygamy was for me. And I was not going to be apologetic for it. Period. Just like I was not going to be sorry for being comfy in my own skin. It had taken the power of ten thousand elephants to get me there.

Self-love was all very well said and practised, but I needed love from that one special person. I craved love, drank love, ate love, pooped love. I was in love with love. My latest and lengthy sabbatical from romantic entanglements was only to avoid pain and misery that came with most relationships and not because I wanted to be less needy or more independent. I was not afraid of new love, I was afraid of the old pain.

And whatever said and done, I believe we all are ready to fall in love at the drop of a hat, the most jaded and cynical too in spite of toppling like ninepins a 100 times over; we all want to nurture that secret, sacred, passionate and ambiguous feeling in the core of our being, even if it is unrequited or challenged or guaranteed to blow up in our face. Yet, we buy into its promise.

'To be brave is to love someone unconditionally, without expecting anything in return. To just give. That takes courage because we don't want to fall on our faces or leave ourselves open to hurt.' Madonna the original diva could not have been so spot on!

Whatever lessons the universe wanted to teach me had gone *phutt.* I refused to learn them. They say the journey to evolution can only be covered by yourself; if that is the case, I would settle for being an emotionally stunted, fun-loving chimp for the rest of my life than be a wise, old, lonely owl.

The idea of being whisked away to Le Paris for a moonlit dinner or a clichéd Eiffel Tower proposal electrified me as much as Disneyland exhilarated children, and a few adults (count me in).

However, secretly I had aspired for all of it with just one, unattainable guy. A guy more cryptic and complex than the game of Cluedo. Krish Aryan aka Confused.com aka Thick in the head—*gaandu* of the first order. Even though we may look like Laurel and Hardy when we stood together, he was my best friend in the whole wide world. A man who had kept the doors to his soul open for me, but the window to his heart firmly shut.

But hope floats, and in my case, it had for almost a decade and a half.

'My chemical clock is ticking bro and no amount of yuppie hashtags and lying about my age is going to reverse it.'

I signalled for another replenishment.

'Not the biological one though. You know my aversion to kids. Smelly diapers. School run. Art and craft. Drainage of resources...'

He muted me with his finger on my lips, casting a fleeting look of admiration my way.

'Hush, don't worry so much. You are our hero, just the way you are. And why would you want to be like the rest? You are one of a kind.'

And followed it with his *jadoo ki jhappi*. He was right, I needed to remove my cloak of victimhood and simply celebrate myself for all the odds I had overcome to get where I was.

'Now let's get you up there to wish our gorg cousin and her frisky bunny with whom I am irritated with, by the way. She emotionally blackmailed me to get here early and watch the full thing, ya. From the *nhaan nhaavanu* to the dasturji's *ashirvad* ceremony (holy bath and priestly blessings). And to make matters worse, the bar was shut. I almost died. Lucky you, missing the tedious part with your *hazaar bahanas*.

I managed a weak smile. Jimmy's set of life and death problems paled in comparison to mine. But one thing was true, my job was a blessing. I had landed that afternoon from London and had missed many (read tiresome) rituals, making it just in time for the *khana–peena* and *naach–gaana*.

I had not made it to the pre-functions too, the Madarsaro, where a sapling is planted as tradition as a symbol of fertility, at the bride and groom's house in individual ceremonies, a few days prior to the main shaadi. Just as well, since unwedded girls were not permitted to participate in key formalities and it also gave me enough time in London to prepare mentally for the main day.

Shanaya did not mind what I did as long as I showed up and made it in time for the four-tier wedding cake-cutting ceremony. An eight-kg fusion of rich Belgian chocolate and buttercream, topped with a creamy layer of white chocolate fondant and a cute porcelain bridal pair, which I had picked up from TK Maxx, London; all selected under my expert supervision, preceded by a two-day-long cake-tasting marathon starting off at the plush Café L'Amore, Colaba, and winding up in Coomi Aunty's Jer Baug kitchen, where a fresh tutti fruity cake from her Baby Bell oven, awaited our reviews.

We got lots and lots of free gâteau that week! And that for me was the best part of the celebrations.

Shanaya, Pari, Jimmy and I—we had been quite close as kids. I was the eldest, followed by Shanaya Billimoria, a corporate lawyer and a CA, my *masi*'s daughter and clearly the brains in the family.

The youngest among us, 29-year-old Jimmy Engineer, my *mama*'s son, had switched six jobs in the last five years, but had a natural flair for trading in stocks and ladies. He was always loaded—a BMW, a girlfriend every season and a swank condo in Parel.

Parizad, a year younger than Shanaya, had married her college squeeze, Cyrus the friendly Virus, named so because she had caught the love bug too soon and was a mother to two *dudh malai-jeva* toddlers (milky cream-toned kids). Even though life had become busier for us in the last decade, we effortlessly picked up from where we had left off whenever we all met.

Funnily enough, the other first cousins had never been a part of our gang. Ashtad had always preferred the company of his few handpicked friends. Shanaya's younger sister, Roxy, owned her own fashion label and had found this thick cousin bonding and fussing too juvenile and not worth her time since the very beginning.

'Oh, look who's here—our very own serial gate-crasher Bomi Daruwala, living up to his surname.'

Jimmy pointed to a chubby, flushed, middle-aged man in a maroon-striped waistcoat.

'Just look at him tanking up on the most expensive *daru* like a rebellious adolescent with a healthy liver. Couldn't care a pickle who's watching or judging, so long as he gets his freebies.'

'If only one could be like that—but I care too much, feel too deep, cry too hard, live in unpredictability and give too much. This has turned out to be both a blessing and a curse.'

I was very aware that I was being a complete buzzkill that evening with my nonstop *rona dhona*.

'Sometimes I wish Dad and Mom had decided to live in a Parsi baug. The odds of hooking up with eligible bachelors would be greater if I had a wider range of choices.'

'Bollocks! Look at Shanaya. She resided in one all her life but finally married Burzin who owns a beach penthouse away from any baug.'

Jimmy who probably needed another fix to get through the mind-boggling verbal cruelty I was inflicting him with, when he would rather be dallying with some size zero chiquita, summoned for another round of double quenchers for us.

Either the Paowalla band was sounding better than before or the heady concoctions were doing their job because it gave me the much-needed thrust to get back into the game and enjoy the rest of the evening—the earlier catastrophic feelings dissolving slowly.

As if on cue, I heard my name crackling on the speakers. At first, I thought it was my *daru-sharu* talking. For me to drink responsibly means do not spill it. I had to pinch myself hard to get back to reality.

It almost sounded like an announcement that is made while paging for a missing passenger on a flight: 'All you good-looking bawas and beautifoool bawis! There is a special song dedication for Miss Kai Juicewalla coming up after our little break. So, grab each other and don't miss the fun. Miss Juicewalla, kindly join us soon, *aavi jao*.'

'It's that *ghelsappo* Eddie Paowalla whining for you.'

Jimmy said, winking at me.

'Drunk punk!'

I was not hearing a word though.

'There is a song dedicated to *me*? From whom?'

'It's got to be the sharp and suave Beckham twin who your sister and I were ogling at a while ago. And I just knew he felt the same, from those hot vibes we shared. You know Jimmy, I bet he is from the Tata or Wadia dynasty…he has that pedigreed look. Oooh if that's the case, then I might as well bid ta-ta to my job. Yippee! Lets' toast to that!'

I raised my fourth drink, falling over my own puns and phrases though Jimmy did not look convinced at all.

As much as I loved being an international flight stewardess, the aches and twinges after a hectic and strenuous 15-hour day bespoke a different story and recently my body had started to feel like an old, rusty car. Ideally with age, wisdom should follow but that is a different story…

'Sis, you just stay put with me…let's not get ahead of ourselves, something's not right here.'

Jimmy held my hand tightly, a bothered look clouding his calm face.

'Oho bro! Always such a cynic. See, this is what they call the Law of Karma. A sudden generosity of fate falling on my lap just in time, giving me the perfect opportunity to show off to those villains that I have a hot and loaded guy bestowing undivided focus on me and I am not this big, fat failure that they labelled me as.'

Jimmy looked unimpressed with my analysis.

I ignored him. My priority was to be in the spotlight and claim my moment of glory. A cheek-to-cheek dance with Sexy Becks was Dadaji's (Parsi Prophet) way of apologising to me for all the inconvenience and dejection the heavens had caused me thus far. I just wanted to walk up to him and say, 'Marry me. Because I'd like to date you', à la Andrew Paxton way in *The Proposal*.

A warm glow dispersed inside me; Becks and I would soon be chasing each other like love-starved bunnies. I shut my eyes for a few happy moments, imagining the inevitable with my latest conquest:

You are cordially invited to the wedding of
Bawa Beckham and Kai Juicewalla

Date: 1 January 2020

Venue: Mauritius

We seek your blessings for this union that our
All Mighty Ahura Mazda has orchestrated.

Followed by an article in the newspaper:
Bombay Times, 1 July 2020

The Lifestyles of the Rich and Famous

Kai Beckham, who lives in an eight-bedroom mansion in South Mumbai hosted the coolest and hottest party of the year when she brought in her half-year wedding anniversary with her dynamic and dashing new husband. Attended by the Who's Who of the country, from socialites to tycoons to film stars, the event was an absolute showstopper.

Kai's old gang of friends were seen having a ball except for one young man, a musician and alleged best friend of Kai, who had a remorseful look on his face all through the evening. But Kai was too busy sharing her joys with her guests to notice anything or anyone…

Spotted on her left hand was a seven-carat sparkly which complemented her Donna Karan ensemble to perfection. Kai's devoted husband gifted her a silver Lamborghini for their anniversary which cost a whopping two cr and the flamboyant couple are rumoured to be hosting the future King Charles and Queen Consort Camilla at their majestic residence situated in the Mayfair district of London at the end of the year. This new power couple of India will be continuing their six-month celebratory bash in Rajasthan at a maharaja's palace (in an undisclosed location) before they jet set to their sprawling estate across the French Riviera.

'*Sheikh Chilli*, can you please get back to reality?'

Jimmy snapped at me as he lit another cig.

'Okay okay, but fantasies are like potato chips, you can't stop after just one.'

Jimmy, who was usually an embodiment of calmness, appeared disturbed, as he urged me with his eyes to take another slug from my glass.

Just as I was about to embark on yet another flight of fantasy, my thoughts were interrupted by another broadcast over the mike, 'And now for that special request, we promised to deliver for a Misssss Kai wherever she may be…Ahem. *Are you lonesome tonight*?'

Jimmy shot me a staggering look, horrifying clarity finally shadowing both our faces.

F**kity F**KS!

And just like Jack and Jill, it all tumbled downhill from there upon…

I could not believe my ears. Yanking the glass from Jimmy's hand, I swallowed half of his R and C in one swig and then ending the binge with my leftover quart, not caring about the fatal repercussions of mixing almost every noxious fluid into my system, I dashed to the scene of crime with my fists clenched, flushed out of colour and infuriated beyond words. I crossed the Just Marrieds hounded by aggressive photographers who were behaving like they were shooting at Chopra and Jonas's shaadi, capturing every fart of the newlyweds.

Jimmy strut right behind me, my clutch bag tucked under his arm, mumbling, '*Pani* Kai *pani,* don't be impulsive', holding a tiny Bisleri bottle in one hand and a tumbler of daru in the other. I took one swig of water (yes, sometimes I drink water to surprise my liver), but it was too late for any sort of rational dialogue; moreover, 'Life begins where fear ends.' Osho got that right.

The Nazi cult seemed to have multiplied as I watched Dragon Dolly, Vampire Veera and several old fogies from their *paltan*, semi-circling around the stage, pointing at me, bobbing their heads up and down in glee as if that was the most fun they had had since the summer of '69.

Their extended entourage had left their seats in a hurry lest they miss the act of humiliation, making me wonder whatever happened to their various hip transplants and knee replacements? A miraculous recovery on the sanctified grounds of the Colaba fire temple, perhaps? *Khodaiji ach jaane* (only God knows)!

Commanding the bogus and frightened Presley and his chamchas to buzz off the stage, I stood on the podium amid the four hundred plus invitees.

All eyes were on me now. My heart was in my mouth. (Swimming in the aftertaste of the tiny veg nugget Jimmy had discreetly handed over.) A surreal silence enveloped the earlier jaunty mood. They all seemed to be waiting with bated breath to see how the spectacle would unfold, wide-eyed and curious, trying to figure out from my mixed expressions what I was doing in place of their beloved Paowalla.

Many began to applaud and hail as though expecting me to break into one of Gulzar Saab's delightful *shayari* or sing an ABBA song to entertain them. Predictably, a few requested '*Dancing Queen*', and I swore I heard a couple of '*Choli ke peeche*' demands drifting through the air.

Jimmy cleared his throat, a signal that he had my back, no matter how it would all pan out.

I recognised some permanent fixtures that managed to get invited to most of the Parsi shindigs. On my far left, were the middle-aged 'powder-puff sisters', Zenobia and Lily from Gamadia Colony, Tardeo, too engrossed in fluffing up their make-up and combing each other's hair.

And Dad's third cousins, Rohinton (Ronnie) Uncle and Roda Cama stood a couple of feet away from the Nazis, but not a part of their frat by any means. Sensing the undercurrent of the tense ambience, good ole Ronnie Uncle sent me a flying kiss in his usual affable manner. He and his wife were one of the *mitthas* (sweethearts) who never failed to be nice to me whenever we met.

Before I could decide which route to take—a sweet melody or high-octane drama—I heard the dreaded voice of Pervy Polly, 'Take it with a pinch of salt, Kai Kai. We are only doing *g**nd masti.* No need to become a Kai Gussawalla.'

'There she is, our *rari paroo podru* (cry baby), who can't take a joke.'

I heard the familiar Dragon Dolly jibe.

A few sniggers stunk up the air.

I am sure there were plenty like me who had put up with a similar type of character crucifixion in such community jam sessions. Mostly the female lot; gender bias existed everywhere. A 40-something guy would still be commended for taking his time to find 'the perfect wifey', while we were admonished for being 'difficult and unreasonable'.

My situation, on the other hand, was a double whammy of sorts. Not only had I been signed off into the ineligible coffins for the over 35s, but I was body-shamed too. Nobody should get away with such brutality akin to the cold murder of the soul, but yet there they were in front of me, having a field day. If I was going down that night, I would make sure that I took each and every one of the Nazi-shebang with me.

*No, Kai, no. Su karech? Shame, shame poppy shame on you! How can you even think of causing a scene? Shanaya loves you—she's stood by you through so much crappity crap and even volunteered to be your surrogate if you ever changed your mind and decided you wanted a baby after all because she knows you could never go through the vagina-tearing exercise. And just look at her, radiating like ten thousand sunrises in her champagne-shaded sari, with the man of her dreams. Finally. Would you really want to f**k it up for her on the most important day of her life?*

While I was oscillating between creating a scandal and swallowing my pride, I was interrupted by a crude voice, '*Baap re baap! Koi var sodhwa stage per chadigayi hose*! (She must have climbed on stage to find a husband!')'

Savage!

Bepsi Berjorji Chotia aka BBC, an omnipresent entity at most bawa lagans, and the most acclaimed Parsi matchmaker in town, was infamous for crossing all parameters of decency, humanity and civility with her caustic comments and profane barbs. She had positioned herself at a 45-degree angle from where I stood with arms akimbo enhanced by the A-line cut of one of her characteristic flowery frocks she often wore—an unadulterated smile of satisfaction written all over her smug mug below her flaring nostrils.

I had locked horns with BBC a couple of years ago when I had accompanied the then groom-hunting Shanaya to her Cusrow Baug residence in Colaba, where she had hammered me about my overweight disposition being the cause of my spouse-less misfortunes.

Do not get me wrong. I respect elders, but not when they drill holes into my soul and suck my last ounce of sanity. If the Nazis were vile, then BBC was their ringmaster. And to prove my point, she addressed the gobsmacked crowd, 'Kai Juicewalla, a matchmaker's nightmare, comes to my house one day and lectures me about my values. Imagine! The *bechari* is under the illusion that a line of suitors is awaiting at her doorstep. But *chaalo ni,* let's find out today once and for all.'

I felt my arteries tightening under my snug blouse and heard Jimmy cussing from behind.

'So, anyone out here brave enough to marry this not-so-young lady? Come on, speak up. Who dares? *Chalo, haath upar karo*! (Come, raise your hands!) Who wants to marry Kai Juicewalla?'

Barbaric BBC never to miss being in the limelight, gave a whoop and a shout in her glass-cracking opera tenor, sending several muffled chuckles my way. I caught a glimpse of dear Ronnie Uncle from the corner of my eye, giving me a sympathetic look. Chatter and titters polluted the air. And that was precisely when the BADASS in me was born.

Intoxicated by fury and with neat daru cruising in my belly, I adjusted the mike, raised an imaginary glass of wine and toasted, '*Cin Cin*! *À ta santé*! *Salamati*! *Tandarosti*! Cheers! It's showtime folks! This party has just begun…'

Because 'courage is a love affair with the unknown', and I was ready for mine.

4

Touching Base with My Jhansi Ki Rani Avatar

Jimmy, my bodyguard for the evening, handed me a real flute which could have been a Smirnoff-Red Bull, which he had managed to snatch from a passing tray.

The murmurs and whispers began to grow louder and fiercer among the onlookers breathless with anticipation. They knew they were about to get much more than they had paid for.

'*Chup*! Shhhhh! You spoke and I listened all evening—now I will talk, and you will listen! I have lots of *purana hisaab* to sort with all of you.'

'Cause, darling, I'm a nightmare dressed like a daydream.

I could have easily passed the *Devdas* audition with flying colours if SRK's role was up for female grabs.

The crowd went quiet.

'Let's start with you, Vamp…hmm Aunty Veera. Didn't you just say something about my wrinkles that looked like chains? Makes me wonder, do they remind you of the gold chains you stole from your sister-in-law's locker to pay for your husband's gambling addiction?'

An uncomfortable stillness scratched through the crowd, which was then broken abruptly by a gruffy, male voice in a satin leopard print shirt, 'Oh, *maree mai karu* (oh sweet mother) Tehmtun, is this true?

'And uhhh, where are you? Ah there, the one and only Polly Uncle; Casanova's Parsi avatar! Ummm, I'd rather put my neck into a cheetah's mouth than go through these so-called fatherly back rubs from you. And I am sure many other women share these sentiments.'

There was a collective gasp.

An unrecognisable voice from the crowd pitched in, 'Oh, Dada Hormaz (Supreme Lord)! *Eh chokree tau Dhoni ni kaani, sixers marech!* (This girl is hitting sixers like Dhoni!)'

Dhoni or no Dhoni but I was clearly on a roll.

'And, of course, dear dear Dolly Aunty, how can I ever steal your moment of fleeting fame?'

Dragon Dolly was now sweating into a flood; she put her hand under her sari and quickly unfastened the last three buttons of her ill-fitting blouse to gulp some air.

'Aunty, thank your stars we are in India; I could easily sue you for mental torture if we were anywhere else.'

A tetchy, male voice from below the stage shouted, '*Gelch**yao*! *Talli gaandi ne chup karavo, nai toh aapra badhao ni ijjat ni faloodo karse.* (You bloody fools! Shut the crazy drunk or she will make falooda out of our self-respect.)'

'*Jamwa chaloji, jamwa chaloji*...(Come to eat, come to eat...)'

A voice boomed at a distance, which I ignored and continued.

'You should all hang your heads in shame. *Saakar ni vaani ne karela nu dil*! (Sweet talks but a bitter gourd-like heart!) This is your golden age of retirement. You should be planning yatras to our beloved Iran, spoiling your grandkids with toys and planning their navjotes. But no. You have only one mission in life: to make life miserable for others. Judging the world by your narrow-minded standards…'

I paused for breath and muttered half a *Yatha Ahu Vairyo* (our short prayer for strength) before launching on my final comeback: 'And you, BBC, are you Parsi community's top matchmaker or an A Class troublemaker?'

BBC's eyes squinted like Lalita Pawar's and her *fulela puri jeva gaal* (puffed up puri-like cheeks) turned crimson red. The terror-stricken Nazi coterie had taken a few steps backwards in awe of the crazy freak. (Taking a bow.) They had asked for it. Character assassination and killing someone's joie de vivre should be a punishable offence under IPC.

A few zillennials stood staring open-mouthed, and were filming the whole thing. I quickly combed through my hair with my fingers to make it worth their time, in case it went viral. (It BETTER!) If there was one thing worse than creating a mess, it was looking like one.

I know, I know, good words, good thoughts and good deeds are the crux and the sine qua non of Zoroastrianism but what did our predecessors know about *Kalyug ke dukh*?

Just then I noticed two figures marching towards me; one looked a tad mad and the other a wee bit lesser. Automatically, the haze began to fade, and the tension in the air cut like a knife. It finally dawned on me that I was not filming one of my YouTube vlogs—this was a family function for crying out loud!

Oh Khoda, I've ruined everything for my sister. I hate myself. I should've just eaten humble pie, gone home, put on the aircon, made myself a stiff tipple and thrown my legs up and watched a replay of The Big Bang Theory or MasterChef or both because the night could be long.

Granny B, the epitome of self-control and composure, would not have been proud of me if she had lived to see that day.

A thunderous voice added to my shameful realisation.

'*Eh mui, nicche aao*! This is not Adi Marzban's *natak* company!'

A clammy gent with large pupils, a thick, grey moustache, wearing a creased faded khaki jacket, was swearing at me, waving a humongous ladle angrily.

'Now stop all your *faista fajeta* (tantrums and howling) at once. Your *nautanki* has delayed my second sitting! And nobody comes late for Dinshaw Goliwala's *paat*. Nobody!'

Paat is a dinner seating arrangement of banana leaves laid across long wooden tables with traditional delights, like sarias, topli na paneers, lagan nu achar (sago chips, soft cheese balls in baskets, tangy spicy sweet pickle with raisins, respectively) sali per eeudus (egg on potato wafer strips) kid gose (thick, white mutton gravy), dry rotlis, kharee marghi (salted-braised chicken in gravy), lacy marghi na farchas (egg-battered fried chicken) saas ni machchhis (fish and sauce), mutton pulao daar washed down by cool raspberry and mango drinks, served on them.

The furious caterer and his ladle meant business. He may be renowned for his lip-smacking variety of *bhonu* (food), but held a notorious reputation of mixing castor oil in his food that set off loosies, if one dared to complain about it.

Goliwala looked me up and down crossly as though he was contemplating between knocking my head off with his kitchen tool or playing pie-in-the-face with me with his velvety *lagan nu custard* (popular Parsi dessert).

'*Oye,* Mister Goliwala, today you gave us a real *goli. Ramakrao* (toys) *maan haddi jasti, ne maas ocho uto.*'

An old bawaji on a walker aired his grievances about less flesh and more bones in the mutton dishes.

Now even more agitated, Goliwala took a step closer to the old man and thundered, '*Khaadrao, khai peene boom barara karoch*! (All you greedy ones are creating a ruckus after hogging and enjoying!)'

The godsend interruption gave me the opportunity to vanish. But just as I was about to scramble off the dais, I felt a firm hand on my shoulder. Shanaya, Burzin and Pari were standing behind me now in a line like a squad of soldiers.

'So sorry...'

I barely managed to whisper.

'I'm so sorry guys...'

Poor Shanaya and Burzin were simply not prepared for a LIVE telecast of *Big Boss* whatever, on their wedding day.

My cousin had waited long enough to find her perfect other half—someone genuinely dedicated to her; who did not live with his mumma and dadda at 38 or spoke in a classic bawa accent. The couple had even gone out of the way to arrange the vegetarian menu to my liking: an entire spread of *eeda* (eggs) preparations (Parsis consider eggs to be completely vegetarian) to be served only on my paatru. This day was to be the most memorable day of their lives, so I decided to banish myself really quickly before Burzin's family forced him to divorce Shanaya on the grounds of 'whacko, boozy first cousin' in the family.

But then something downright mental happened. Dr Burzin grabbed the mike from right under my nose.

WTF!

Oh no! Burzi don't publicly fire me, I promise I meant well. Okay, do what you want but please don't leave our Shanu. Not today, not ever. I will never show my face again. But don't make her lose face. She is nothing like me. She is sane, stunning, responsible and balanced. And I am half-goddess, half-hell.

Too late. The bridegroom went into action.

'Ladies and gentlemen, thank you all for coming; my beautiful wife, Shanaya, and I are very appreciative and grateful. Now I would like to have my first dance with my new wife. But I can't do it without your help because I am a terrible dancer, a total klutz and Shanaya my love here is as graceful as a swan. I will need your support and some fake cheering, so I don't look like a complete idiot.'

The tall and unaffected neurologist stood there, beaming at his guests as if nothing unseemly had happened a few minutes ago.

'You slayed it.'

Shanaya squeezed my hand and whispered, 'But before I become bridezilla, can you please buzz off the stage, so that I can have my moment back, you thunder-stealer?'

Thank heavens she was not as mad at me as I had expected her to be. I chuckled, before I turned into this giant ball of mixed emotions.

'Yeah, of course…damn sorry again.'

I got off the stage, and I willed myself to hold my head high like a queen would under any circumstances as I brushed past the baffled spectators. The plan was to stay classy, sassy and a bit bad assy. The band jumped back on duty and without wasting time, followed the orders of their host and hostess. Of course, I should have stayed like a good cousin would, to watch the love birds twirling like waltzing angels on the floor on MJ's '*I just can't stop loving you*', giving us couple goals but I did not. Staying a breath longer would be like tying me to an electric chair, stark naked.

Besides, I could not trust the aggravated Goliwala with my dinner. A bout of *julaab* was the last thing I needed that night. Sensing my acute discomfort, Jimmy put an arm around my waist, hissing gently in my ear, 'Come on, Jhansi *ki* Rani, let's get you a teeny-weeny quickie and then drop you to your *gaddi*. Baby steps…'

Fifteen minutes later and another 30 ml down, I pinged for my car.

Exaggerated screeches poured in the backdrop, a clear indication that it was time for the traditional shimmy, clicks and claps, which in colloquial lingo was 'The Birrrrrdy Dance'. All the *Parsaaon* (Parsis) were back in good spirits. Except me. Who felt like the scum of the earth in spite of giving them a good beating. *Almost*. I would rather have heard '*Killing me softly*' and called it even.

But then as someone once said, 'If you have enemies that means you've stood up for something, sometime in your life.'

Still that night would haunt me forever…

5

Getting My Mojo Back with Great Gusto

Colaba to Bandra

Law of attraction, my ass! All I had intended and chanted for on my way to Shanaya's was a fun, stress-free night, but the so-called law of the universe had mucked this one up, BIG time. The entire bloody universe was conspiring against me.

Rummaging for my phone inside my purse, I breathed a sigh of relief as Ram Singh zigzagged our Fortuner away from the *jhol jhamela, shor sharaba.*

I furiously texted on our group:

'So f**ked. Left the venue. On the edge. It was ghastly—same shit, different year. Worse than being attacked by 5 Alsatians. Hammered. Acidic. Lost control of reflexes. Caused a big scene. Anyone has valium?' (Two flat-faced smileys.)

'Late again your Majesty Z? Thanx a ton. But FYI, Burzin's younger brother Farhad is as delish as Lonavala Cooper's coconut fudge—do check him out!' (Four heart-shaped-eyes smileys.)

Without waiting for a response, I noticed the time on it, 9.40 p.m., before flinging my phone back into its hut. That would be two hours of my life, I would never get back.

I shut my eyes; the events of the evening were echoing in my mind, like a broken record. My head felt as if an excavator had run itself over it.

Tumhe zyada chad gayee hain Kai. (You are too drunk Kai.)

I started speaking to myself in Hindi, which meant I was beyond buzzed. Yes, I was single, but it was NOT my first choice or second or *even* fifth. I was not one of those protesting burn-the-bra-type of women activists (more power to them) who could find happiness in support groups. In fact, the only time I had come close to burning my lingerie was when I had cast my bra over the deck of a ship in a drunken episode (yes I know, way too many of them and this is just the beginning), and it had almost got caught in-between the Captain's cigar and his nose. (To follow later…)

The universe was supposedly 'abundant' (listening to way too many podcasts, bro) and the cosmos was drenched with over gazillion eligible men carrying a billion dating opportunities, then why had I been the sole beneficiary of handpicked toads disguised as boyfriends and lovers?

Why God why? Am I supposed to die alone with only Teddy Pookie shedding make-believe tears for me?

The Nazis had been bang on. I was lonesome that night and *every other night…*

Ignoring the Whatsapp notifications that seemed to be coming in swiftly, I looked out of the car window instead. The shops on Colaba Causeway were shutting down for the day.

Why don't they have night markets in this city like they do in Hong Kong or Bangkok? Some retail therapy sure wouldn't hurt. Raaste ka shopping is cheaper than any psychiatrist. Any day. Mumbai sucks. This country sucks. All men suck without a doubt. Weddings especially sucked! I might as well hold on to those who cared just a wee bit for me…

I finally opened the TFF chat window.

Simran: 'VictoryforKai. (Trophy emoji.) Sounds v Bridget Jones. Always told you that cougar is the way 4ward 4 u. Did you speak to fudgy new brother-in-law? Any potential there? Sry gotta scoot. Playing house-house with future in-laws. Huggies.'

Zoya: 'Uffo Kai (angry emoji)! I should've known u would do a number again. I'm here now and barely know a mosquito ya. Sum elderly folks are eyeing me as though I've descended from an alternate reality. It could be the solitaire on my belly button.'

Zoya: 'Acha yr cuz Jimmy thankfully recognized me and I'm chilling with him. Showed me his new gothic tattoo. I think we missed each other by a sec.'

Me: '(Eye roll emoji.) Yup, u should've come in a l'il later, u cud've helped them clean up the place. Lol.'

Zoya: 'Sarcy and catty r we today? Btw just been shown a clip that's doing the rounds here. Quite a dhamaka-wala performance, must say. ROFL. (Two claps emoji.)'

Me: 'I don't GAF (give a f**k).'

Zoya: 'Acha Miss Crabby, got it. But if u must do a show-shaa at least don't have yr red bra strap sticking out babe. N what's with the tarty scarlet lipstick smeared all over yr face? So attention-seeking.'

Me: 'Okay Lady Z, so much time to write? Must be dead bored. Well-deserved, u ditcher.'

Krish: '(Five smiley emojis.) Just catching up on all my msgs. Landed from Goa 50 mins back—sounds like my Whackadoodles are having a real blast.'

Me: 'Feeling slightly nauseous peeps. TTYL. DND.'

My phone beeped again. It was on K to K private this time.

Krish: 'Hey Bawi, where are you?'

Me: 'Dark night of the soul. In Jahannam. Hell.'

Krish: 'That bad, huh? Bawi, listen! Align yourself. Keep it all in your orbit of stillness. Think positive. Inhale the life force. Exhale negativity. May the force be with you. Remember our discussion before I left? Don't let anyone mess with your head.'

Me: 'But I'm very upset, Krish.'

Krish: 'You have to rise above this BS—look how far you've come!'

Me: 'I need u to listen…'

Krish: 'I am here, Besto. Always. But can we connect in a bit? Just got into the city, so need to return some calls. Ruby is dropping me off —I'm on her way. Hugzzz. BRB.'

The tears began to slowly descend as a million questions hijacked my mind.

Is there a taxi strike in Mumbai? Can't he take a bloody Uber or Ola? Has Goa and its plethora of beaches not been enough for them? Did she make him massage sunscreen lotion all over her smooth, young, blemish-free back, shoulders, toned thighs… ughhhhh, BITCH!

Of course, there was the entire crew of the production unit travelling along but still…

*Wakey, wakey Kai. Smell the coffee. Miss bee-stung lips has put Krish Aryan's 'no woman–no stress' f**k-ology in grave danger.*

Picking up my vibes as he usually did, Krish dinged again: 'I'll give you a shout in an hour and a bit. Go home, have a warm bath, meditate. And please, stop guzzling like it's your last day! It imbalances all energy within and derails the chakras.'

Take your chakras, your wannabe starlet friend and your spiritual f**kwittage and shove them where the sun does not shine, *saalo naalayak*, I almost began punching it all in and then deleted it.

Krish *halkat* my best friend since 2001, had always been ignorant to my womanliness and *irresistible* feminine presence. This ball-less, heartless hottie with ribbed arms, bow-shaped lips, smouldering eyes and the cutest butt in the history of mankind, had friend-zoned me for eternity, and that had made me want him so much more. He was not only forbidden fruit, but also that fruit on the highest branch of the tree that was unreachable and unobtainable.

Not seeing me as more than a friend was still bearable but hanging out with this 20-something aspiring singer Ruby Razzle was simply unbearable. Even though he had labelled their relationship as strictly 'professional', I was certain something was brewing between them. He belonged lock, stock and cock to her.

Booby Ruby, as baptised by me, was a proud owner of a plastic smile as fake as her jutting rack. You could serve coffee using the rack as a ledge. She boasted of 1.5 crore subs on YouTube (as opposed to my 519), not surprising though, for what she did not have in talent, she made up with long legs, a gym-toned bod and a ridiculously obscene dress sense. And, of course, by strutting and slutting on TikTok where she has a fandom as large as any of the Kardashian sisters.

And here I was suffocating in a rib-breaking spanx and indulging in a psycho-babble monologue. How UNFAIR can the world be?

Krish was composing music for one of her albums and was making a special appearance with her in one of her music videos which is why they had been shooting in Goa over the weekend. We had last met on his birthday a fortnight ago at Novotel, but it was touch-and-go because he was on an exceedingly tight schedule and Zoya was late to pick Naseem up from karate class.

What I could not comprehend was why the female leech had not found somebody else to bikini around with and make sweet music with on sun-kissed beaches? Why was she after 'my friend'? Yes, he had this raw, rugged and lost musician thing going which many women would find attractive, but he was no Greek God.

And the flying solo, workaholic Krish, unimpressed by even a Katrina Kaif or an Angelina Jolie seemed to be following her everywhere like Mary's little lamb. In fact, nowadays whenever we spoke, it was 'Ruby said this and Ruby did that'. It was a hard kick to my ego and heart. Hated them both. Loved him too but hated him more. Sometimes (very rarely I swear) I wondered if I should try some paid witchcraft, there were so many 'get him to love you back', 'removal of third-party situation', kind of pages on Instagram nowadays. Just because he had the voice of an angel speckled with hypnotic eyes, a cool piercing in his left ear and had proved to be a devoted best friend to me for ages, it did not make him more of a stud and less of a douchebag in my eyes.

A black drop fell on my sari—*shit*! My waterproof mascara was leaking. Now, not only was I super pathetic, I was a super-pathetic, obese panda. Desperately needing a distraction before the lump in my throat turned into a full-fledged Niagara Falls, I began fidgeting with my iPhone.

'Siri, will SRK ever fall for me?'

I had to know. It is now or never.

No response.

'Siri, will I ever meet Shah Rukh Khan?'

'I don't know.'

'Does Krish like me?'

'Don't count on it.'

'Why are all guys such assholes, Siri?'

'I am afraid I don't have an answer to that.'

Having such deep conversations with Siri was something that my nephew Rehu and I thoroughly enjoyed. I could hear Ram Singh behind the wheel let out a huge sigh. Understandable.

Dang. SRK, had always been my eternal aphrodisiac and heartbeat, all rolled into one. He looked super sexy even in his fifties. If only we could cross. Just once.

Just one kiss, God. Sirf ek baar. And I will forget all injustices you have dumped upon my love life. I will die happy as a lark after that.

'Gusto.'

I almost pleaded to Ram Singh who could drive me to my favourite South Mumbai pub with his eyes closed. I was not ready to go to an empty Bandra flat and cry my eyes out, just yet. If my six-and-a-half-year-old nephew had been around, I could have considered it for he was the only one who could hug me back to normalcy.

Besides, I was dehydrated and famished. I needed a pit stop at the Peddar Road hub because an empty stomach is the Devil's playground.

The car came to a jerky halt and I staggered out, almost tripping over a sari pleat, which was now lengthier than the rest. The six yards of fabric, smothering me like an Egyptian mummy, was certainly not my choice of OOTD.

I gestured to the usual bartender as I almost tripped inside the bar. He winked back, smiled and gave a thumbs up. I mouthed a few phrases and he at once connected the dots, making me wonder if expert lip reading skills were a mandatory requirement for a job in the hospitality sector.

Twenty minutes later, I had washed my face to a semblance of its usual attractiveness and claimed a corner table at a safe distance from a coochie-cooing couple and a lone soul perched on a bar stool who seemed to be a new arrival. DJ Kenneth as usual was lost in his music, with his headphones in place, quaffing a beer and playing with different keys in front of him.

Feeling a sense of comfort in the four walls of the joint I knew so well, adorned with murals and posters of prominent bands, musicians, pop artists; actors, both retro and avant-garde, I gratefully slurped on the Long Island iced tea that Bryan had promptly delivered with a plate of spicy potato wedges, extra sour cream on the side and their house nachos with gooey cheese sauce.

'Hey Kai, how was uhh Shanaya's uhh, isn't it? How was the wedding?' he asked, leaning towards me.

We had all been acquainted only last week. It had been Shanaya's bachelorette pub crawl which we had inaugurated at Hard Rock Cafe. We joined the young, enterprising restaurant staff there on the bar top as they did their traditional dance routine to the peppy beats of '*Y.M.C.A.*' by Village People and then scrambled over to Gusto's, the finish line for our drinking marathon. Bryan and team would never forget us. We had literally set the house on fire.

It had begun when we had coaxed Shanaya to tear open her presents right in the middle of the pub; curious onlookers had borne witness to a variety of naughty hen party gimmicks including nipple clamps, a leather whip, provocative playing cards and fruity flavoured condoms that unintentionally coasted into the bowl of onion rings on the next table, almost getting us thrown out from the pub.

We climbed atop the bar ledge (if you have not yet, you must try it at least once in your life. It will empower you faster than anything ever will) and started singing '*Mamma Mia*!' precisely 10 minutes after knocking our fourth shot of The Flaming B52 each and even though it was not karaoke night we had howled on top of our voices, cooking up a storm for the staff at Gusto and their patrons.

'Oh, the function was awesome! So much fun! Nice to see you again, wazz up?'

He was my official bootlegger for the rest of the night, so I had to be super sweet.

'Hmm. Been a quiet Sunday. You chill, we ain't shutting until one tonight. If you need anything, just gimme a shout.'

As soon as he left, I sipped my LIT and started chatting with the Marilyn Monroe fresco on the opposite wall.

'Man, you are so glam and perfect. Giving men that come-hither sexy look in your short sexy, white dress. Maybe if I was as voluptuously enthralling as you, things would have been different in my life. That Champion of Morons aka Krish would have been all over me like *maska* on a bun.'

I was tired of the BFF title 'Besto' he had given me. I wanted more. Much, much more. I had lingered around him for way too long, hoping for an epiphany to thwack him, but to no avail. What stopped Krish? Why was he behaving as daft as a bush? Or did he expect me to make the first move and finally gotten fed up and gave in to the phony allure of the awful Booby Ruby? I almost hoped that Marilyn would jump out from that wall and share some handy seduction tips that would work on my man.

'See, it's not my Laughing Buddha tummy tiers or JLo bottom (if one saw hers with a magnifying glass). Nah! He never fails to tell me that I am the prettiest girl he knows. But isn't 13 years enough time for a man to know what he wants? I bet your admirers didn't take 15 seconds to desire you.'

Even though DJ Kenneth kept the volume to a tolerable scale, he seemed to be as high on emotion as I was.

For just a few ticks ago, he had bounced from Ed Sheeran's '*Shape of you*' to '*Deewangi deewangi*' and was now on some remixed version of an incredibly familiar soundtrack.

Three genres in extremities? Brave.

It took me a few seconds to place the number and then it hit me like an avalanche. Oh praise be, Dadaji! It was a pop-rock remix of the old Doris Day classic, yet the words were as clear as day. All I had expected from my solo night out at Gusto was to sozzle myself into numbness and binge on comfort food until I had massacred all my demons. But this one had come as a bumpy surprise:

'When I was just a little girl
I asked my mother, what will I be
Will I be pretty, will I be rich?
Here's what she said to me

Que sera, sera
Whatever will be will be
The future's not ours to see
Que sera, sera ...'

Granny B's wrinkled and kind face gleamed before my eyes. The first time I had heard her sing it was when I had returned from a dreadful Easter wingding at the Readymoneys' house. I was an innocent 10-year-old going on eleven. I was a stout, lonely and insecure kid with robust cheeks that hid my eyes when I smiled, so I had stopped smiling.

I was desperate to be a part of the Readymoneys' snobby circle. Those kids shared secrets with code languages and passwords so had formed a closed clique, shutting me out and leaving me with only the fish in their aquarium for company. When I had grovelled slightly to be accepted or greeted warmly at the very least, they sniggered, calling me names like '*Dudh Puff* (Milk Balls)' and 'Double Bubble Chin' to my face.

It was during this phase of life that I made a special haven for myself—an imaginary cardboard box which protected me from the monsters. In between my sobs in the box, I could smile as much as I wanted without being ridiculed. I could also gorge to my heart's content without being answerable. And I could tell the bullies to go rot in hell. The happiness in the box was often short-lived for it showed me my place in the larger universe—a tiny nobody and an isolated and derided child destined to be unhappy.

So that Easter night post another Readymoney-disaster, Granny B had held me in her arms and hummed '*Que sera, sera*'. Little did I know back then that it would stick to me like an anthem, for life.

'Am I a big, fat Easter egg like they teased me?'

I had asked her with tears in my eyes.

'No, my dikra, you most certainly are not. You were born to be a princess and the brightest star in the sky.'

'*Sacchu boloch*? (Are you telling the truth?)'

I looked up at her from the cushion that she gently laid under my head. I always believed Granny B more than anyone else in the world. She made all my fears redundant.

'Scout's honour.'

Her eyes were filled with unconditional love as she whispered. Granny B had been a girl guide, so it was a significant part of her memory bank. She then enchanted me with the same tune until I fell asleep in her arms, dreaming of twinkling stars, kinder people, a better tomorrow and all things bright and beautiful. Since that day, it had become my feel-good mantra each time I would plunge into crisis, emotional or otherwise.

As the song paled out, I was slowly guided back to Gusto craving another glass of LIT and a portion of sun-dried tomato bruschetta and hummus and pita chips. My next full body check-up was three months away, so I could afford generous helpings of everything.

Yumzzy!

I kicked off my heels and pulled my feet up on the magenta suede couch that would be my retreat for the next few hours. (Days, if they allowed it.)

'This is going to be one f**ked up, nostalgic night, my dear Mariluuuu.'

I warned Marilyn.

'No Facebook, Insta, Twitter, WhatsApp or phone calls. *Sirf main aur meri tanhai—aur tum*.'

And just as I had begun digging into the appetizing spread that was served before me, I was accosted.

'May I join you?'

A foreign voice rumbled over my head.

Who has the guts to enter Kai's territory without a permit?

It was that lonewolf on the barstool who had been stealing occasional stoned glances at me, which I had been completely ignoring. (I forgot to mention.)

So, there he was around six feet tall, probably in his early fifties with a sophisticated edge around him. He cut a charismatic and towering persona in his smart evening rust-coloured jacket over dark khakis, a salt-and-pepper ponytail and a neat shave. Not my type at all.

Before I could respond, he pulled out one of the large chairs opposite me, flung his jacket on the other, stretched his long legs, rolled up his sleeves and made himself at home. And before I could protest, he started to whine, 'I've had a very rough day, hit rock bottom. Almost suicidal, a real damp squib, if you know what I mean?'

Okay. Articulate. Perfect English. *But, why do I care*?

He was free to go home and do whatever the f**k he wanted. I just needed a quiet evening to myself, drinking my sorrows away. Was that too much to ask? As Humphrey Bogart had wisely said, 'The problem with the world is that everyone is a few drinks behind.' And I had a lot of catching up to do.

I had wanted to scream all of that across the table but managed a shrug instead.

How should I put it across without sounding like a Class A bitch that he needs to vamoose?

'Look, I don't know you and I don't want to know you, either. I am certainly in no mood to play Agony Aunt tonight. I could give you a number of a good psychologist even though you seem as happy as a dog with a bone.'

It was true, on the first impression he did not come across as rock-bottom types. But then again depression can sometimes be smokescreened with sufficient ease, *ask me*! I could be the life of a party one minute and down in the dumps the other.

'Don't worry, I have no intention of yowling like a baby all over your grub.'

He scanned my astonished face with his piercing eyes, making it clear he was not going to budge.

'And you know what they say, misery loves company so I just need something or someone to divert my mind before I do something stupid in a weak moment.'

Cock and bull.

Even if he was faking the whole *khudkhushi* story, which I was sure he was, I was too shit-faced to summon Bryan and have security to have him thrown off my table.

'I overheard Bryan calling you Kai when you entered—I assume that is your name?'

I grimaced.

'Perhaps. If it's a mood-changer you are after, you are barking up the wrong tree. Go join those two lovesick birds who will be plotting each other's murder soon after the honeymoon *nasha* goes kaput. Through thick and thin, my ass! The moment she puts on a little weight after popping out his sperm produce, he will be banging his seccy or nanny, or both.'

Okay agreed, I have been carried away lately by this recent web series *Boom* which is turning into quite a fad. But he laughed uncontrollably at my rather bad joke.

'Ah! Gotcha! That hellacious, huh? A lovers' tiff? Problems in lovers' paradise, Miss Kai?'

'It's always the case, isn't it? Expectations lead to disappointments—with or without a lover. But why do you care?'

Why is he so suited and booted if he is planning his own death? Have I seen him before? Nah! No recollection of that.

I tried studying him closely. Not because I wanted to, but I did not want any more trouble. He could be an escaped convict looking for a place to hide (in that case he may follow me home, shit), or Cyrus Broacha in disguise doing a MTV *bakra* on me. My author brains seldom rested despite being pretty pissed drunk.

Froggy watchful eyes, tiny creases across his face, lightly stained teeth, a costly timepiece on his left wrist—a Rolex likely. I could not see his shoes (a smart way to judge anyone's character, I tell you), but there was no mistaking his designer dice-shaped cufflinks and a yellow sapphire on his right ring finger. Loaded.

That reminded me of my own heirloom jewellery, weighing down my neck and ears which was as out of place in a pub as his accessories. So, I started to remove them one by one, starting with my neck piece.

'Oh, for Christ's sake! I am not going to mug you.'

He chuckled, throwing his hands behind as he leaned back further into the comfort of his soft chair.

I glared at him.

'*Ghelo che ke su*? (Are you nuts?) This is not about you, Mr Intruder! I can't bear having this crap wrapped around my neck. Adds another kg to my own 71.'

He laughed aloud, gesturing to Bryan who came over at once, he said, 'Bring Boss Lady anything she wants. I am smitten.'

I had been with enough male company to know who emitted an asshole-looking for a quick make-out sesh vibe and who did not. This one was the latter. Mostly.

'What else can you not bear, Miss Kai?'

A roguish smile played across his face.

Sigh. That was the trouble with meeting people in real life vis-à-vis social media. They never came with verified profiles attached. But so far so good. He had not demonstrated any signs of being an axe murderer, rapist, thief, psychopath, *sadak chhap* or an ex-boyfriend with a face transplant.

Touchwood!

Surprisingly, I was not really as uncomfortable as I should have been; maybe getting painfully wasted was building up my mettle, or I was secretly longing to throw up on someone's shoulder after the third degree I had just endured.

'So, I am all ears my Lady. Give me the dope. And let's give sexy Monroe a break, shall we?'

'Hmmm. You saw…?'

He smiled.

'And don't fret, nothing will leave this table unless you want it to.'

He had a mischievous glint in his eyes as he took a nip of his JD and coke, signalling to Bryan for another.

Whatever does, 'IF I wanted to', mean?

He was behaving oddly. And was being suspiciously pushy.

'I'm an attentive and a patient listener. Besides I need a strong distraction, remember? Who knows, your story may just save my life.'

He blinked his eyes playfully, appealing for a refill for me to one of the other waiters, an attempt to bribe me I presumed.

Sure. Jhootto.

'And in the end, we only regret the chances we didn't take.'

Wah! Mister is quoting Lewis Carroll. Impressive.

I do not know what it was. Whether it was the SRK dance track, '*Where's the party tonight*', over the amps that was completely out of sync with the mellow ambience, or an overdose of spirits purging through my veins, I was summoned for an emotional striptease to a total stranger whose antennas were up and ready. And who seemed more interested in my late night soap opera (Balaji Telefilms and Ekta Kapoor are you listening?) than any of the TFF's had been that night. The *Nikammas*!

No harm in giving him some spicy meat and some sweet juice from a few chapters of my life, considering it to be a free therapy session for both of us. And strangers rarely judge. That I learnt 35,000 feet above sea level, when flight attendants swap their entire Ram *kahanis* with each other without even knowing first names, sometimes.

It was almost 10:30 p.m. and I had nowhere more exciting to be. My phone had not rung even once. And the wanker Krish must be wanking off for all I knew. Also, the chances of crashing into this Mr Anonymous ever again were slim. So, I took a sizable gulp of my lethal LIT and announced grandly.

'Okay, Mister Whatever-your–name is. Let's kickstart with Season One of the Parsi version of the *Game of Thrones*. There will be hate, war, betrayal, revenge, defeat, loss, heartbreak, tears, anger, suffering, violence, soul-shredding; some joyfulness, love and laughter here and there, thrill, madness, passion and utter chaos. Have you heard of the Kingda Ka in New Jersey?'

'Oh yes! One of the world's scariest and fastest roller coasters, if I'm not mistaken? I am petrified of them.'

'Atta boy! Now imagine you are on one for the next two hours. DON'T say I didn't warn you!'

FASTEN YOUR SEAT BELTS

6

Battling Bullies, Bulges and Badmash Company

Childhood to 2001

It was the final year of the 1990s and school was finally winding up. The only thing I felt was a deep, *deep* relief because going to school was like attending a constant party at the Readmoneys. The Readmoneys, Sherry and Shapur, and their monstrous offspring had made my pre-teens and part of my teenage years miserable. Ash and I were forced to tag along there as kids because our parents were friends with them.

The three Readymoney brats were vicious, mean and borderline abusive. Perhaps it was their affluent status and the elite schools they went to or the four ayahs and three *mistris* (cooks) massaging their egos that brought out an obscene level of arrogance and haughtiness in them.

Along with their extended clique of co-conspirators, they sought sadistic pleasure in hurling malicious comments at me, from my choice of clothes to shoes to the tubby tyres that stuck out from under my flat chest to my penguin walk. Their jeers had been doing the rounds since I was around nine years old. And these continued till I was old enough to threaten to run away from home if my folks insisted on lugging me with them to their place.

My parents, loving as they were, never acknowledged my plight, pushing it off as 'childish behaviour'. Not wanting to rock the boat with their so-called old as gold friends, they simply advised me to 'be nice' whenever I raised an alarm.

As years went by and our visits to the House of Hell increased, I had learnt to cope as effectively as I could. As soon I sensed danger, I would crawl into this imaginary cardboard box I had constructed in my head and wait until the coast was clear. Sometimes I had imaginary friends in there too, mostly a different Enid Blyton character each time, either from the Famous Five or the Five Find-Outers and Nancy Drew dropped by once in a while. Responsible Julian, brave George(ina) and Fatty (Fredrick) being my faves.

Unless it was dinner time, of course, when we went through diverse gastronomical experiences that included stuffed turkey in cranberry sauce, corn and mushroom vol-au-vents, pot roasts, braised oxtail, Wiener Schnitzel (Austrian veal dish) with dollops of butter, Yorkshire pudding, beef Wellington, well-done steaks, barbequed lamb chops, mutton pan rolls, lobster thermidore, all kinds of crusty pies, mini-chocolate éclairs (tiny drops of heaven that melted in the mouth), which brought me back in form. And how!

Then even their disdainful comments about overloading my plate and shoving it all inside me until the hooks of my dress ruptured, did not make an iota of a difference to me. I was a hardcore foodie and as much as their snide remarks on my weight hurt me, I was not going to let that stop me from doing my most comforting thing in the world—eating!

But one could not fault the kids alone for being such crap bags to me. Aunty Sherry and Uncle Shapur Readymoney, the decadent hosts, were no less conceited than their awful prodigies. They walked around with an extra chip on their shoulders, gloating about their endless vacations to foreign destinations, including luxurious cruises, first class flying and being invited by some prince or baron of some f**king land for supper and a polo match.

'Oh Sherry dear, remember when we went to Wales once with the Count of (f**kville) ...' the pompous Shapur would swirl his costly cognac in a round-mouthed glass in front of his envious guests, attempting to appear classier and more well-honed than he actually was.

Sherry's acquired British accent was even more ridiculous than her fables.

'Oh yes, Shappy dear, have we told our friends about the Baroness of (hell knows where) who gifted me such an exquisite charm bracelet on our weekend to Monte Carlo that summer of '92? What a precious little heart her tiny puss was. Gosh I tell you folks, being a cultured Parsi and light-complexioned, at least gets us a foot in the door of the crème de la crème.'

Suffering them and their predictable gobbledygook, as they stood at the centre of their massive living room demanding all eyes and ears on them, drove me up the wall.

'Better live abroad. Canada and Australia are thirsty for us bawas. This India of ours is going to the dogs, filthier than a dump yard, I say. And the potholes? Our imported cars are not made for these roads. It's like riding on a pregnant camel.'

The worst was when they began enquiring about everyone else's lives and vacation plans. Luckily my parents had travelled around in Europe a bit, so they always had something to contribute though humbly. My father, a shy, soft-spoken, clean-hearted sort of a man, believed in letting his successful business speak for itself and my mother a home-maker who even though enjoyed the occasional fuss and a well-heeled life, charitably gave her time to the mentally challenged and the needy kids and remained grounded and eloquent in her replies.

Shapur Readymoney, the most *pakau,* hands down, would miss no opportunity to *lapet sapet* (tell fibs) at any given opportunity. Here is one such gem:

'I tell you folks, our family certainly has a close connect with the Rani (the Queen of the United Kingdom, God bless her soul) herself. Did you all know that the childhood photos of the Queen Mother, and my great grandmother Lady Mehroo Dhanjiboy Readymoney are like xerox copies? They could be twins. They even took their tea in the same way, I believe so.'

It was a known fact that most bawas were madly in love with the Royal family.

One day, unable to digest the absurdness and pretentiousness of it all and having heard the insane twin story for the hundred and eighth time, I butted in, 'Yes of course, *eleko Kumbh mela maan ghumai gaya hose* (they must have got lost in the Kumbh mela).'

That cheeky and unexpected statement cost me a tight slap from my embarrassed mother and another doze of nasty soup from the snooty kids. The only silver lining to this woeful ordeal was that I had to endure them once in a couple of months, which was far more acceptable than getting bullied almost daily for those 10 years of my torturous convent life.

Cara, Jo and Michelle. Cinderella's evil step sisters reborn in the 20th century, had taken an oath to destroy my school life.

From pulling up my PT training skirt and showing my flabby legs to the rest of the school in my fifth grade, to using cruel nicknames like Humpty Dumpty, Lazy Hippo, Potato Head and Thunder Thighs for me, they were the insufferable trio.

Their message was loud and clear: I was an ugly, repulsive and a misfit wherever I went. Even the two sweet friends I had managed to partner with initially soon joined the bandwagon of body-shamers, leaving me gasping for clarity.

I hated school; appealed to my family every second month to pull me out of it. Extreme anxiety would turn into panic attacks at the end of every summer vacation before another school year of body shaming began in June. I had a strong suspicion that even the teachers got carried away by the so-called cool kids, doling out certificates and good grades to a chosen few and rejecting the ones with issues of colour, size and beauty. My suspicion turned true when in spite of giving a stellar performance at the auditions for *The Pied Piper*, I bagged the role of the squeaky, fat rat.

I journalled everything: my joys few and far between and the moments I wished I had not been born. When you pour you heart out on blank pages about your traumatic life, the wrongs and the anguishes do not go away, but the urge to smash your bully's face into a wall diminishes slightly.

'Are they not the same friends who have attended my birthday parties year after year, enjoyed Mommy's mouth-melting crunchy chicken puffs and luncheon meat sandwiches? I even pack extra portions of ham rolls and frilly kheema na cutless (mince cutlets) in my school tiffin to share, you know.'

I bawled to my neighbour-cum-pal Delna Guzdar (Dellu) who went to a different school but we caught up with each other over our balconies or during short walks around our small complex compound.

'You know what they say, Kai, *kutra ni puchri koi divas siddhhi nahi thai* (a dog's tail never straightens out),' Dellu used to reply wisely.

'But I have this gut feeling that someday you will leave them all behind and have the sky at your feet.'

Really? *Me*? I did not think I had it in me.

The only things I had and welcomed at my feet were salami and eggs, aleti paleti (gizzard and kidney masala prep), delightful pork chops in pineapple jus and tarela boombla (fried Bombay duck) made to perfection by my darling mother. Like most Parsis, her initial solution to all unhappy experiences was food. But it did not really help my cause, for every school year I would gain 9–12 pounds more and a new uniform had to be stitched.

By the time she realised that, I was in 10th grade and on the cusp of college life. Mom and Dad began to stress out about how tough my college life would possibly be if history repeated itself, so they prodded me to exercise and Mom diligently dished out healthier meals by cutting out bread, sweets and rice from my diet. *Imagine.*

No wonder, I was confused and angry all the time. I suffered from terrible carbs-sweets withdrawal symptoms.

***

One more year to the millennium. School was alas, done. I would begin junior college soon and I would not have to see the ugly faces of the sisterhood any more. It was a no-brainer that I was made for Arts, so Bachelor of Arts it would be. Commerce and Science were completely out. The only accounts I was pro at keeping, was counting the fries on my plate and the only chemistry I wanted to pursue was one that came hand in hand with boy-ology.

It was time for renewed hope, new friends, a chance to start all over and a few new additions on the to-do list—I wanted to be a world-famous writer some day, and explore every nook and cranny of the whole, wide world.

Granny B had predicted that all of these things would happen, and she never lied to me. Also, she had read parts of my diary over the years and she would often say, 'You have such an interesting way of telling a story, dikra—mark my words, you will be a bestselling author someday'. Still I always had only one question for her, 'But what about a sweetie pie boy, Granny B?'

Like any teenager gorging on Mills & Boon novels and battling a thousand complexes about my awkward appearance, it was all I could think of.

'*Sabar kar,* bachcha. They will soon be falling in your lap. And if I've ever taught you something, let it be this: Never ever run after a man or a taxi, as there will always be another one coming your way.'

As if on cue, the summer break before junior college began at St. Xavier's College, Mumbai, brought the tender temptation of my first romance. It was a distraction from my miseries—of the very best kind.

Not only was Jehangir Nanavati aka Jangu a good Parsi boy or rather a young man from a small Parsi colony, he was also much older than me and unlike other boys (so I had heard) he was not in it for, 'just the flesh'.

Cupid had struck us both as soon as Jangu had gotten off his bike to apologise to my father for scraping our Maruti Alto at the Turner road, Bandra junction, and despite his heavy moustache and beady eyes, he had caught my fancy. Initially, we shared nothing more than a few kisses on the rocks of Bandra's Bandstand and sodas at Café Seaside situated at the tail end on the same road. Though the kisses tasted bitter, I did not know any different.

Happy to be basking in the attention of a man older by 11 years, I ignored the attention of the few boys at St. Xavier's, as I found them to be childish and brainless. It also made me feel superior to the rest of the giggly pack of airheads in skimpy clothes, who were still trying hard to adjust to their first year out of school.

We were the perfect Parsi couple and I could not wait for the proposal he promised me when I turned 18, two years hence. In fact, we had even decided names for our kids, Nazneen, Monaz and Rayomand. We would live in his two-bedroom flat in Tardeo where he had grown up with his overbearing mom, an early-retired daddy, a good-for-nothing brother and Naughty Dotty, his spoilt pom.

'Will you be my fluffy pillow for life?' he once asked me one Valentine's eve, as we sat on the sea-facing parapet, swinging our legs, chewing on *ganna* sticks.

'Forever and ever and ever, Jangu,' I replied, lovestruck.

There was not a doubt in my mind that I would marry my first and only love.

'I will meet your parents, Pumpkin Pie Kai, and ask for your hand the day you turn eighteen. Hope they will accept a simple, junior store manager.'

'I love you Jangu Mangu and so will they.'

I had kissed him zealously, even bravely touching his inner thigh, intrigued by what I was not shown yet, carried away with the rising throes of sweet love in my heart.

'We're in public,' he recoiled, 'and you are still a minor. I could be arrested, you know.'

'*Pyaar kiya to darna kya* (if you loved someone then why to afraid), ' I challenged him and he grabbed me in his arms and kissed me harder, his thick moustache making my face all prickly, but I had gotten so used to it by then that it began to feel *soooo* good.

'As you say, my love...' he said, running up my pedal pushers with his hands and ignoring the wide-eyed passersby.

I had spilled the beans to my family about us, a year into the relationship. And I had made up my mind that if they objected to his lack of good looks or a decent bank balance, I would elope. There were no two ways about it. I wanted to be Mrs K. J. Nanavati *badly*.

But they handled it surprisingly well and told me to graduate first, before deciding what I wanted to do. But I was adamant on making it happen before that, precisely on the day following my big 18th birthday.

So a couple of months later, Mom understandably took me to a baba who read faces. One look at J's photograph and he quickly shouted, '*Behenji, kya bol rahein aap?* (Behenji, what are you saying?) *Yeh to shaadi shudha hein.* (This guy is married.)'

'*Jhootto*!'

I hit the old dude with my sandal and stormed out of the room; furious that he put such a dire accusation on my future-to-be.

Five weeks later, I received a call from one Mrs Freya Nanavati asking me to lay off her husband. When I confronted him, he gave me an icy stare and said calmly, 'I would divorce her and marry you. Why are you making such a big deal out of it? You should have trusted me rather than send the CBI after me.'

'But I wasn't the one to do it. I trust you, I love you…please don't be mad Jangu Mangu.'

I apologised profusely for his wrongs, scared my only shot at *true love* would end, if he left me. I looked at him, pathetically, hoping that he still loved me. And just as I was about to kneel in front of him (to beg forgiveness, you dirty minds—I still did not know then, there are other reasons to kneel) as the last resort, he hugged me.

Playing with my frizzy ponytail, he said, 'My Pumpkin Pie Kai, always jumping to conclusions and listening to others. Now listen to your boyfriend instead.'

I nodded hard.

'Anything you say, *jaanu*. Shall I leave my home and come to you?'

He looked alarmed.

'No no! You see my wife is mentally unstable and she gets violent too. Sometimes she beats me and other times she harms herself. I am in such a bad marriage. What should I do? And I didn't want to worry you.'

I stared at him, my mouth open, waiting for further instructions.

Oh Khodaiji, he's been through so much. Have mercy.

I vowed to myself that I would go to the ends of the earth to help him.

'Oh Jangu, we will look after her, don't worry.'

I rested my head on his shoulder, comforting him.

'I have a small boy too, he's three.'

I swallowed hard. I was not prepared for that.

(You see, love is not blind but it leads to blindness.)

'Okay, Jangu, but how will we all live together in your two-bedroom flat? I mean, your pet, brother, parents, wife, son, me?'

I was maturing into a fine, young woman by the minute.

'If you can convince your rich daddy to buy us a house somewhere in your posh Bandra, where his pampered little girl and I can make our love nest… maybe even two flats on the same floor? That way Freya and Jehan can be monitored too. What say, *jaana*?'

Jangu replied with dead seriousness.

Just like the atom bomb that dropped over Hiroshima and demolished it, this one fell on my head with almost the same impact. And shattered me into pieces that no God could fix again. I do not know how I managed to straighten myself out and walk away, unable to stop my big rolling jilted tears until I reached the curb where his motorbike was parked. A steel rod next to it was simply a stroke of providence.

Woosh! Boom! Clang! CRASSSSHHHH!

That was the last the financially and morally bankrupt Jehangir Nanavati saw of me. Or his Hero Honda. I stopped replying to his calls and after a while he gave up. I despised him, but I disliked myself more. I had been so gullible and desperate to squeeze out some kind of interest from the opposite sex that I walked straight into a trap.

'*Bh*******d*. It wasn't your fault, please!'

Shanaya, 15-year-old then, spat when she heard of my recent encounter with deception.

Being a resident of Jogeshwari's Malcom baug, she had picked up some unfiltered vocab from her colony friends at a raw age. Cussing had never been part of our sober Juicewalla gene pool who considered themselves a refined version of the community but as time passed by, I came to realise that there were some BC's who truly deserved their titles. But the deep cut in my heart did not heal that easily; your first love is like your first Godiva chocolate, unforgettable.

Few days later, I found myself crying on Granny B's shoulder; this time at her Lonavala mansion the 'Juicewalla Chateau', which had always been my hideaway.

'God has a bone to pick with me. *Why*? WHY?'

Granny B had no answer for me but looked equally shaken up as we sat in her verandah facing the backyard, staring into the vast fauna, her eyes fixed on a bamboo tree. I am sure that if Jangu was in front of her, she would have made him *nangu* and beat him unconscious with a *bumboo*.

'Nobody loves me, Granny B. *Nobody*! He used to call me Pumpkin Pie Kai. I even wrote his name in *my* blood in my journal. Why did he do this to me? Was it because I am so plumpy? You think his wife is prettier? Thinner? You think, I should take your kitchen *ni chari* (knife) and cut off my charbi? Maybe then he...'

My incessant howling must have caught her off guard because she grasped my hand tightly across the low cane table between us, where an open tin of my favourite condensed milk was perceptively kept aside for much needed occasions like these.

'*Eva kharab manaso* (such bad men) should be put in jail. *Khodaiji ni meherbani* (God's grace), that we discovered the truth on time. Or else, that badmash would have swindled you off your virginity and your finances.'

'But, but...I wanted to marry him Granny B! And he was Parsi and you told me that all Parsis are good people.'

I burst into tears, as if my dalliance with Jangu the Cheat had been her fault.

'There are always exceptions to every rule, even with us.'

She extended her right arm to pat me whilst lovingly pushing a triangle of Kraft cheese into my mouth with the other. The fragrance of Pears soap whiffed from her, lulling me into that familiar sense of well-being and security within her cosy nest that prevailed since I was in my diapers.

'I will never trust a Parsi boy ever again!'

I announced, knowing it made no sense but I had learnt way too many lessons already in my rather limited years on this planet.

'*Sarosh Yazad, maari dikri ne Raakshaso thi raksha karjo.* (Archangel Sarosh, protect my child from demons.)'

Granny B adjusted her maroon, geometrical print scarf on her head and began flipping through her thick, blue *Khordeh Avesta* prayer book. This was her only way to deal with the crisis.

'People envy you my Persian Princess, your skin is as soft as a baby and you are a sensitive and clever child. All this *buri nazar* (evil eye) will go away. I have just the correct *nirang* (a prayer of invocation for this sort of thing), don't you worry, dikra.'

She started to mutter, stroking my palm, but I could see that her usual calm disposition was shaken by my recent catastrophe. After a few minutes, she spoke, 'Princess, as a child, you have done potty on my bed umpteenth number of times. I know you better than you know yourself. Do you remember what I've always quoted to you?'

Granny B had this proclivity to quote from Shakespeare to Kipling to Keats. Though I could not then see the relation between that and poo poo, I let her enlighten me.

'One man in a thousand, Solomon says, will stick more close than a brother. And it's worthwhile seeking him half your days if you find him before the other.'

'What it means, is that good things come to those who wait, so wipe those pearls, forget this Jangu and have a mango.'

She hugged me tightly and then began slicing a ripe alphonso for me. The tin of condensed milk was almost empty, the cheese had vanished into our stomachs and three alphonsos were wiped out in six minutes.

She looked upwards and said, 'Thank you Dada Hormaz that her appetite has not been affected with all this romance-shomance.'

Like all grandmothers, and most bawas, she believed in the power of fatty foods to solve life's problems—the cheesier, creamier and sweeter they were, the better.

Gently caressing my cheek, she assured me in her usual soft voice, 'There will be a boy for you, dikra, but what's the hurry? But whoever he may be, remember this, he must respect you and place you above all things and be your best friend when things fall apart. But sadly, you'll have to kiss lots of *derkas* (frogs) before you find him.'

'Did you also kiss many?' I asked, interested to know more about her and my late granddad Eruch whom I had never seen, wondering whether I should make a small note about my XXX (kissing) experiences in my diary.

'Oh in my days, we could not do all that.'

She was blushing profusely now.

'When will I have that knowing?'

'Que sera sera, Princess. *Chaalo, aaje aapre saathe gaaye.* (Come on let's sing together today.) 1, 2, 3—When I was just a little girl, I asked my mother what will I be...'

XXXSCORE = 99

7

Close Encounter of the Ethereal Kind

In June 2001, I marched into senior college, determined to put my heartbreak behind me.

The Lonavala summer with Granny B had been exactly what my counsellor would have recommended if I had one. We had nursed my emotional injuries with spoonfuls of *malai*-infused breakfasts, lavish midnight feasts and crooning old melodies over long drives to Bushi dam in her old Ambassador, which was in mint condition (We bawas treat our bikes, cars, furniture, steel dabbas, showpieces, etc., like family).

Our traditional mango-eating marathon became even more lively when my 12-year-old brother Ash was dropped off by our parents on their way to Pune. Of course, I won; a dozen mangoes in one sitting. I broke my own record every year.

As a first-year senior at St. Xavier's College, pursuing Sociology major, I had resolved to slither into one group or the other. Anything was fine—as long as they let me tag along. Yep, my standards were that low. But over a month and fortnight into the new academic year, I was still friendless and bloody panicking. I would constantly hear weekend plans being hatched around me, but without me in the picture. Sometimes, I pretended that people were talking to me and laughed along. It was all so pathetic, but really, what choice did I have?

But I simply could not give up that easily. Once, I even tried to chat with one of the girls from the distinguished 'Pink Ladies' a gang of seven spoiled brats born with silver spoons stuffed in their mouths—daughters of business tycoons, film producers and a politician. They wore tonnes of pink and glitter and most of them stayed away from us common folk as though we would contaminate them. The brat threw me a 'Did I just step on cow dung?' glare and dashed in the opposite direction,

It was simply not fair. Everyone had found their place under the sun and I had to suffice with my green teddy Pookie to entertain myself, yet again. *Want to know a tiny secret*? Once in a while, I carried him to college well-hidden in my red canvas haversack. Of course, I still had Dellu and my cousins Shanaya, Parizad and young Jimmy all of whom I met rarely, but it was not the same as having a 'St. Xavier's hip and happening group' to hang out with.

During those days, my only weekly companion on that side of the town close to my college at Marine Lines was Amy Ma who resided a few metres from the Charni Road Station in an old Parsi society, made up of several 150-square feet apartments clustered together in a two-storied building.

Amy Ma was my maternal grandmother who had got the rawest deal from God. Separated from my grandfather for more than a decade, short-changed by an unfair divorce settlement, she lived on her own in somewhat ramshackle conditions, which was a far cry from the copious lifestyle she had been bestowed with in her formative years as a wife.

She was a simple woman with a heart of gold and a childlike fascination for special occasions and celebrations. She was an adorable little lady who often wore a small *amora* (bun) and mid-calf length inexpensive frocks with velvet hair bows and silk ribbons tied to her hair, perhaps in a bid to appear 20 years younger. Yup! It runs in my blood.

Though my mother and my maternal aunt (Shanaya's mom) tried keeping her comfortable in every way they could, even inviting her to stay with them, she flatly refused to be a burden on anyone. One of her deepest wishes was to travel to a foreign destination, just once in her life.

'*Manne phoren javuch. Manne lai jasse?* (I want to go abroad. Will you take me?)' she would often ask me.

'How will I, Amy Ma? I travel only to Lonavala or Pune and made one disastrous trip to Kashmir when I was in school, remember? I had fallen off the pony.'

She solemnly nodded; of course, she remembered that I had blubbed my eyes out on my return to Mumbai; the below average size horse was not able to take my body bulk whilst crossing an icy stream on a Palghar excursion and crumbled under pressure. It was obviously funny to the rest and extremely heartbreaking for me.

'But the world is this big,' she held up her fingers like a gullible kid, pupils shining in wonderment as she made me pinky swear, 'someday if you get the opportunity to see it, you won't leave it, promise?'

I always agreed, watching her enjoy the mutton chop or the egg mustard roll or RTI's dal ni pori or patrel I picked up for her from the little pocket money I had. It made me feel very proud that I could give her small joys of life. But Amy Ma had a secret desire which was far more important than globetrotting—it was to meet her estranged son, Nariman (Parizad and Jimmy's father), who had drawn a distance from her years ago (following in his father's footsteps) for reasons best known to him.

'I can get you the moon my darling grandmother, but this I can't.'

I would often tell her, wishing I could shake up my mama and bring him back to her at gunpoint. Okay, so maybe not that extreme but in my book, disowning a loving mother or mistreating a loved one is a crime worse than homicide.

'That's why I have insisted many times that only marry for paisa and *dabbau* him under your *anghoota. Ghanto*, this *janam janam ka saath*. (Nonsense, this togetherness for life and after.)'

Amy Ma would often advise me or more like warn me.

'All *bairas* (women) must make their *matidas* (men) sign property papers before the lagan or else they will end up in a chawl like me. Remember my words. Tell my other granddaughters too.'

These were her usual homilies.

***

A short hike from Amy Ma's residence was the Banaji Atash Behram, one of the most revered Parsi fire temples in the country. Going there had become a ritual of sorts, making it a weekly sanctuary for my despondent heart.

It was the day after Parsi new year in August 2001. Parsis celebrate two new years: March is the new year in Iran and August is according to our calendar. I sauntered into the compound of the holy shrine armed with my red polka-dotted umbrella and hundreds of questions haunting me. I kneeled on the blue carpet in front of the *atash* (the sacred fire) and offered the customary sweet-smelling *sukhars* (sandalwood sticks) in surrender.

The recent incident from one of the Psychology classes played in my mind again and again—a page straight out of the book of 'Kai's all-time bloopers'. And the mortification raged over me. As luck would have it, Cara, Jo and Michelle, the evil sisterhood from school, managed to get admission to my college in senior year, enrolling in similar classes to mine. That meant another three years of putting up with their repulsive *guar jeva* (owl-like) mugs. A fate worse than not eating potatoes for the rest of my days.

I was shaking like Rex (strawberry) jelly in front of the glowing flame—at the edge of an inevitable meltdown.

I became the butt (quite literally) of their cruel gags once again. The oldest trick in the book was played on me—a fart cushion was slid under me and unknowingly I had plonked on it. And the rest I would like to be long-forgotten history, but that was sadly not the case. I soon became a laughing stock in college too.

As the ethereal, golden, pristine fire burned leisurely, sloppy tears rolled down my face.

'Why Khodaiji *why* (sob), do I have to go through this total eclipse of the heart?' (That Bonnie Tyler song Lord, have you heard it?)

'Once upon a time I was falling in love
Now I'm only falling apart
There's nothing I can do
A total eclipse of the heart

Once upon a time there was light in my life
But now there's only love in the dark
Nothing I can say
A total eclipse of the heart...'

'Will I never be accepted as a human being with *feelings?*'

Now, not only will I be known as the fat one but worse, I will be "the fat one who farted like a beast".

There was a stir near the low podium. Maybe this was not the right place to mention toilet etiquettes. Last thing I needed was to upset my spirit guides, if any. An elderly gentleman with a healthy, dark beard, wearing a white robe and headgear of priestly character stood above me. I assumed he was the *panthaki* (chief priest) or a senior dasturji of the Atash Behram. I leaned to the left to make way for him to enter the inner sacred sanctorum which was separated from the regular prayer room/hall by a low step platform.

Holding my gaze for a few seconds as I glanced up at him, he touched my head lightly with his fingers, he felt oddly familiar. A tiny current passed through my body, it was not like me to let a stranger this close.

'*Su baila ni kaani rarya karech?* (Why you sobbing like a coward?)' he asked, his voice cracked like a whip into the silence.

Taken aback by his candour and sudden question, I replied after a few seconds, 'No, I am not a wimp, but I can't tell you the reason I am crying.'

'You can tell me anything, dear.'

His stern voice changed to a more amicable one.

Well, he was a priest, wasn't he? Catholics confessed to theirs, so I saw no harm in doing the same with mine. Besides who knew, he might take my grievances directly to God.

Maybe it was not such a bad idea to decant myself into the chalice of a holy man; he could have some useful tips on how to survive my oppressors.

'You see, I turned 17 last month but I am still so fat. The puppy fat is simply not cute any more. The only guy I ever loved was dishonest to me. I don't have a single, good friend in college. And Dellu, uhh Delna, my only close friend is migrating to the States. And Amy Ma, she's just sinking…'

I tried holding back my surging emotions, but the lump in my throat gave it away.

'Some have the gall to call me Humpty Dumpty Eggy and Kaddu ka Laddoo. It's sooooo demeaning. School was already a nightmare and college was supposed to be my turning point and it's anything but that.'

My knees felt a bit sore. Very soon my neck would be too if I kept straining it to look up at him.

He stood listless.

Was he even listening to me?

Dude, I am drowning here.

'Should I just quit college?'

He moved. *Finally*! He shook his head slowly and suddenly his face appeared to shine, reflecting deep compassion; there was a surreal energy around him.

'Observe our magnificent and never dying Atash Padshah closely. The lessons we Parsis have always learnt from this sacred flame is to be proud of our strength and our roots. We never gave up then when we escaped from Iran and we should not give up now.'

His voice was as soothing as a raspberry duet ice cream. I gave him one of the sweetest smiles I could manage.

'But these are far worse than those Arabs who chased us out; these are "she- devils" who need to be punished.'

My smile melted away like an ice cream.

'Good and evil are two sides of the same coin and that's why we have the three tenets "*Humata Hukhta Hvarshta* (Good Words, Good Thoughts and Good Deeds)" to keep us on the right track. We can't control others, but we must choose how we react to it.'

'This is a journey of faith and of victory, Kai. You have to chase your own dreams. Make your own mistakes. Trust the process, Kai, for everything happens for a reason. Life will change for you, but for that, you will have to first learn to follow your own heart and most importantly believe in yourself, even when nobody else does. You have just one life; own it, Kai.'

I felt myself submerging into an infinite sea of wisdom and love. *Did he just say my name*? *Not once but thrice*!

I tried to rise from my knelt-down stance so I could meet him at eye level and soak in his aura a while longer, but my legs seemed frozen like slabs of Parsi dairy farm kulfi and words failed me. There was a lady in a bright yellow *mathabanu* (scarf) in the far corner of the room, reading from a prayer book, giving me obscure looks and clearing her throat constantly. And then a terrifying thought ran through my head: *Oh Khodaiji, tumharu bhalu thai.* (Oh God, praise be you.) *Am I the only one who can see him*?

If that was the case, it meant only one thing: I was dead and en route to meet my ancestors. I had complained to God so much that he had sent this ethereal being to fetch me. He did mention about my life changing forever, hadn't he?

'No, no, please, Sir. I beg you. You can't take me yet. Not before my last ham sandwich. Or my final mango. And certainly not before I'm done with my top-of-the-Eiffel-Tower kiss dream.'

I folded my hands, begging him to spare me.

His thoughtful eyes turned into confused ones. He bent over, planted a protective kiss over my moist forehead, took a few steps back and vanished. Into thin air! Pooooof! Or am I in heaven *already*?

'Wait, you can't just leave me like this!'

I gave a blood-curdling scream that seemed to scare the poor, old lady for she threw her handbag over the carpet and fled from the prayer room. But her mental state was not my biggest concern then. I had to follow *him*. *He* had to explain himself to me. *He* was NOT allowed to add to the day's turmoil. I was already lugging around enough baggage of my own.

Thobo! *Thobo*! (Wait! Wait!)

I finally managed to stand up somehow in spite of the cramps and dashed out.

I spotted a caretaker in a round red cap, cleaning the window panes of the adjoining room.

'Where did he go? *Bolo jaldi, jaldi*!'

I almost barked at him.

'*Kaun*?'

He snarled back, not wanting to be disturbed from his constructive pursuits of delivering the windows spotless to his employers.

'Spiderman! The dasturji, who else? He was just talking to me inside.'

'*Gheli che ke su?* (Are you mad or what?) Dasturji will be coming at *pauna chaar* (3.45 p.m.).'

'No, no, the one who just left! You must have seen him!'

'Are you high on ganja? He left an hour ago—to meet his girlfriend. Nobody is here.'

This guy had gone bonkers. The noble 60-year-old dasturji had a girlfriend?

I stood there, looking at him incredulously.

'*Arrey*, Dilshad from the sandalwood shop, who else?'

He pacified me and resumed sweeping.

I knew Dilshad; she was a decent and hardworking girl in her early twenties and helped her parents run the tiny *sukhar* shop, adjacent to the premises.

I have just had the ultimate paranormal experience, oscillating between divinely sublime to downright bizarre. How dare he ruin it with visions of the old, pious dasturji pursuing the lovely, young Dilshad?

'*Tu sharam kar.* (Have some shame.) Talking rubbish about such a holy man and an innocent girl. I will report you to the trustees of the Atash Behram, you *fekuchand*.'

I was almost shouting now. I lost my temper at the cleaner, wearing a cheap copy of RL Polo and lying through his buck teeth. He put his mop down with a loud thud and kicked the bucket angrily, making the water spill out over the brown carpet and over my feet, creating one fine mess.

I stepped back, half-scared. This was turning into a feud.

'But why are you so interested in him, *haan*? He already has a girlfriend, I told you, *na*? And also, you are not Farokh's type. He likes thin and beautiful girls. Not fatsos like you,' he said, leaning closer.

Unable to process the incongruity of it all and pinching myself to make sure I was not in some deranged dream, I stomped off, throwing at him my dirtiest look, determined to conduct research on the mysterious priest who had dissolved right in front of my eyes, a few minutes ago.

After checking every nook and corner of the premises, I finally gave up. It was official now. I had turned mad, thanks to my lonesomeness.

I placed Rs 50 into the steel box for the *divas* I had lit, when my eyes almost missed the copper oblong frame, hanging above it. I felt my body shrivel into a ball of wool, as he peered at me through the thin glass exactly the same way I remembered him last. I was rendered speechless. I could feel my fingers tingling and lips quivering. That specific rainy Wednesday had been the *roj* (the day) of the Parsi archangel Bahman who protected and nurtured animals, and somewhere in my own naive way, I made an ambiguous celestial connection. Maybe if I stopped hurting animals, the world would stop hurting me.

And so from a 'chicken-loving, bacon–devoted, marrow-sucking pure bred Parsi', I donned the hood of a committed eggetarian, even if it meant falling in the graces of my Zoro community, who devoured their luscious meats with arduous passion. And little did I know back then that my tryst with mystical inexplicability would be a beginning to a trajectory of extraordinary twists and turns in years to come.

8

Bonding over Batata Vadas and Nimbu Pani

2001

The senior year at St. Xavier's was an amalgamation of merit holders, middle class nerds, the Malabar Hill/Walkeshwar snoots, suburban commuters, a handful of teenage delinquents and some campus crashers. While some focused on the curriculum, others preferred to be extracurricular in their approach by kindling the early trickles of romance with their classroom crushes in-between library bookshelves, on cafeteria benches, under foyer arches and behind the trees at the infamous 'woods'.

My 'cosmic connect' no longer confused me instead it gave me a lot of confidence, so the following day, I paraded into my Socio class with a bounce in my step.

Why?

Well, if I am worthy of a sublime shower of angelic grace, then I must be some kind of special. So, I bravely donned my micro denim skirt before I left home.

It was something I never dared to wear to college until then, knowing the ragging that would follow, but I no longer cared a hoot for anybody's approval. As the wise Dorothy Parker once said, 'If you wear a short enough skirt, the party will come to you.' And I was in the mood to party.

I finally owned my title of 'Thunder Thighs' proudly and if the Evilhood messed with me, I would simply show them my middle finger and march off. And just when I had learnt to become my own best friend, I was in for a surprise at a morning lecture on cultural segregation a few weeks later.

'I hope this spot isn't taken.'

A cheerful voice interrupted my undivided concentration from the blackboard. Not waiting for an answer, she slid next to me, a little too close for comfort.

I studied her closely. She had attempted talking to me a few times before but I had ignored her mostly because she was a bit too tomboyish—her braces, youthful t-shirts and pixie haircut cutting a rather unconventional appearance. Hypocritical? Shallow? I know, but I was not very different from the average teen. There was no end to the depths of my shallowness. But that day, I liked her. Maybe because I had started liking myself a teeny-weeny bit too.

I had not seen her hanging out with many friends either, but she did not seem to mind because she came across as a happy-go-lucky sort with hands in her jeans pockets, sometimes whistling and skipping around, jingling a set of keys around her fingers and flashing her endearing dimples to the rest of the world. More original and refreshing than the haughty, tight-assed, entitled Pink Ladies who actually had embossed pink denim jackets too. Clones!

The Pink Ladies moved almost everywhere in a single group, verbalised their opinions with easy authority and were completely self-involved. They were meticulously groomed with evenly painted nails, glossy lipsticks, colourful tank tops, low-waist jeans and brands that screamed *phoren ka maal* (foreign goods). Except for one who did not seem to really fit. At first I did not pay much attention to Zoya Hussain, but there was something different about her.

Zoya smelt different. She walked differently. And there was an equanimity about her which I could not quite put a finger on just then. I had noticed her helping Mahesh, the visually challenged boy up the staircase to his class at the end of the corridor and feeding the stray cats that rolled in the mud on the sidewalks outside the academy.

Back in the classroom, Ms Dimples was shuffling her feet impatiently and fluttering her eyelashes, expecting me to make the next gesture which I eventually did.

'I'm Kai.'

I whispered cautiously, afraid of being ticked off by Professor Namita Desai who was engrossed in explaining the differences between urban and rural lifestyles.

'I'm Simran.'

She was beaming, as she extended her hand to shake my hand and knocked off the water bottle between us. Thanks to my carelessness, the cap on it was loosely sealed. Almost a litre of water gushed out and flooded the front row. As luck would have it, the she-devils parked on the bench in front of us were the unlucky recipients of the clumsy spill. They let out piercing shrieks, jumping out of their seats and wriggling as though mice had crawled under their chuddies.

Malevolent Michelle was the first to go, 'What else can one expect from Lazy Hippo?'

Catty Cara sniggered and asked, 'You mean, Potato Head from school?'

Spiteful Joanna was close on the heels, 'Humpty Dumpty fell off the wall...boo hoo!'

And they burst into laughter.

My eyes filled up and my heart pounded miserably. I looked down. I cut a sorry figure in front of my potential new friend. The Obnoxious Sisterhood had done it again; they had taken away that last ray of hope from my otherwise doomed existence.

Now I had lost Simran for good.

Why Khodaiji? WHY?

Obviously there will not be any life-changing miracle that the mysterious priest had hinted about.

'Girls! Either settle down immediately or get out of my class!'

Professor Desai shouted in her trademark, clear-cut voice. She was giving us a disdainful look, adjusting her golden rimmed square glasses, with a duster in hand; she looked ready to fling it towards the five of us.

And just when we were about to get back to our respective textbooks, the miracle happened. Simran dug into her Adidas backpack and brought out a thermos. Before I had a chance to even register things, an entire 750 ml flask of water was emptied on the heads of the she-devils.

'Are you NUTS?!'

Cara was flapping her arms like a rattled sparrow, squealing, yelping, jigging and running around in circles. Michelle and Jo were too stunned to react, but their hairdos were all botched up.

Simran giggled through her silver braces.

'*Aaj bach gaye*! (Today they got saved!) Usually, it's *garam* chai in there.'

My mouth opened and closed like a goldfish.

Professor Desai immediately banished all five of us from her class that morning and suspended us for the whole of next week. So, Simran and I had no option but to hang around the canteen that week.

One day, as we sat sipping tea in tiny, plastic cups, Simran gave me a brief lowdown of her life.

'Look, I am a simple girl from Grant Road. You are a kinda cool chick from Bandra. I have a silver scooty, you probably have some Maruti-type car, but we have a lot in common—identity crisis and boy troubles!'

She said it all in one, long, unassuming breath.

I tried to suppress a grin for she had obviously done some in-depth research on me. But how I loved her and wanted to squeeze her senseless in gratitude until her cheap sunglasses fell off. Battling those bullies was like pouring water (in the literal sense too) over years of unresolved anger and injustice. Watching the trio drenched in sheer agony in front of an uproarious class was the best thing that had happened to me since winning 100 rupees in a game of Housie at a Bandra club a fortnight ago.

'Now listen carefully. We've both taken Psycho-Socio combo this year, right? That means the same timings, same classes, same breaks, same bunking options and same time-pass. We're both fish out of water in this college, but things will get better once we join forces. What say?'

She was a firecracker this one. Now I had no excuse for dropping out from uni.

'Besides, what option do you have? I am your pragmatic

choice, so think about it. Oh and one more thing, don't you dare short form me to Sim, Simi or Simo. It's Simran, get it?'

Cute, candid and crazy! This girl was the real deal.

'Yes. I choose you Simran and even if they paid me, I wouldn't have it any other way.'

I finally replied, wanting to hug her but was hesitant, as I had not hugged a whole lot of friends before. And then it happened, my first proper friendship hug which I returned readily.

'I was around when the fart cushion happened.'

She gritted her teeth, disengaging slowly.

'Pretty shitty thing to do. And it's not something anybody should get away with either.'

I nodded.

'My tummy is rumbling, wanna share a plate of hot batata vadas? Then we can sit *aaram se* in the woods and talk about those boys from the third year.'

My eyes shone on hearing the magic words, 'batata vada'. And boys, of course.

As we sat wolfing down the vadas, I said, 'Govind has a cute smile.'

'Who's looking at the smile *re*, have you checked out his ass?'

'Oh yeahhhh totally, as *kadak* as a brun pav.'

I said sighing as I munched along.

She laughed.

'You are my first Parsi friend, you know? A bawi, as they say, right? I've always wanted one of you in my life. I've heard that you guys are such a riot that even Charlie Chaplin looks sober in front of you.'

'Oh, that's just a myth! I'm anything but wacked out.'

'We will see about that,' she retorted with a wink, 'we will see.'

And within no time, as if it was all just meant to be, 'saucy and sassy Simran Khanna' became my reason to wake up effortlessly and jump on to a fast local to college every single day without a fuss.

***

Simran and I were so relaxed and in sync with each other that the next few months passed by in a flash. We were busy making memories. We did not need anybody else to make it more perfect, but life, of course, had other plans.

It initiated with both of us having this creepy feeling of being followed by this nameless lad wearing a P cap and a brown guitar case slung over his slightly droopy shoulders. He seemed to be everywhere we turned. At the dosawala, at the campus gate, the scooter parking lot, the chapel too. He was not in our batch, so we presumed that he was a year or two senior to us.

One fine day, Simran and I were lounging around the foyer on the ground floor when Simran turned around and confronted him, 'What's with you? Why are you lurking around us always? Shall we report you to Father D'Souza?'

Upon hearing the name of our college principal, the boy looked quite terrified and I noticed drops of perspiration running across his gullible face. Avoiding our gaze, he removed his cap and started to fan himself with it. I could not help notice his soft brown eyes, a tiny silver stud in his left ear and a tiny mole on his chin.

He was cute but in an ambiguous sort of way. (Go figure!)

'Dude, find your own friends and stop stalking us!'

I wanted to remind Simran that we too were stalkers, snuffling around every half-decent guy across the campus like

German shepherds on drug trails.

He appeared harmless and lost, bearing an uncanny resemblance to a 'Pathetic Kai' not so long ago, shadowing her batchmates, hoping to get a tidbit of curosity thrown her way.

'Hey, you have something real neat on you. Could you play us something?'

I asked him, feeling sorry for him.

His face lit up though he still remained tongue-tied.

'Are you a dumbass too?'

Simran continued relentlessly.

I pinched her arm.

'So, I'm Kai and this is Simran. Nice to meet you.'

But he turned around and walked away, leaving us a bit confused.

He returned 30 seconds later.

'Sorry, I had to chuck my gum out.'

So, he had a voice.

'Hope it was in the dustbin.'

Simran had all the makings of a crusader and I could already see her changing the world, if given the opportunity.

The guy gently brought his guitar out, gave it a strum and shyly asked, 'Are you sure you have time to listen to some bad music?'

Not giving us a chance to reply, he launched into the groovy Rod Stewart number:

'Keep smiling, keep shining
Knowing you can always count on me, for sure
That's what friends are for
For good times and bad times
I'll be on your side forever more
That's what friends are for...'

Hearing him sing was like watching a caterpillar metamorphose into a butterfly. Our jaws remained dropped in rapture. Soon, an audience gathered around him mostly infatuated female fandom.

Simran and I glanced at each other, voicing similar thoughts, *He is our discovery and by default he becomes our property. We shall never let him out of our sight again.*

And that is how Krish Aryan played his way into our hearts.

From that day on, Krish skipped most of his Science lectures to hang out with us and bombard us with life's (not so) serious questions on and off.

Krish turned out to be quite an open book as he spoke about his parents' messy divorce, which he had found out on his 13th birthday (inhumane), and although his well-off Kashmiri father, a well-known musician in the country, had set the mother and kids up pretty nicely before fleeing off with a girl half his age, his Parsi mother, Rashida, never quite recovered from the betrayal and had been on mood stabilisers ever since.

Rashida wanted him to pursue Medicine or Engineering but since he lacked interest in both, he chose Physics and Botany as a middle path to please her. She was ready to let him explore anything except music. But Krish wanted just that. Even though he had tried convincing her about his true passion more than once, she was so jaded by her ex-husband's infidelity that the mere mention of "music" made her go ballistic. He was quite protective of his younger sister, Ishika, more so because the atmosphere at home was so harrowing for her that she had become aggressive and violent in her school, which almost got her expelled.

His story made us both realise that what we had been complaining about—no admirers, not enough pocket money and the mixed pakoras chappy charging us two rupees extra for chutney—was all irrelevant and resolvable.

One afternoon, while we were indulging in a glass by three of nimbu pani, we asked him why he had been tagging behind us for all those weeks.

'To write a tune on your undying friendship.'

Gosh! He was so matter-of-fact about it.

'Right!'

'You just wanted to check us out. Admit it!'

Spitting his last drop of lemonade, he guffawed at Simran's statement and then drawled in his deep voice, 'Pllllease. Are you kidding me? No hard feelings but a mad bawi and a male exterminator?'

'Hmph!'

'Like all the rest of the girls in this college are dead.'

He muttered loud enough to make us chase him around the campus. Like sprinkles of sugar on French toast and luscious maple syrup on waffles, Krish Aryan completed us. The first year of senior college came to an end too soon and I was more than grateful for the two friends I had. Simran and Krish had found a beautiful spot in my diary, which was now expanding slowly with happier narratives fast replacing disappointing ones. And just when we thought that nothing could come between our self-contented trio, we were in for a shocker!

9

Fabulous Four: The Whackadoodles

2002

It was a scorching May afternoon of 2002; pretty much in the middle of summer vacations and I had skipped my time-honoured Lonavala trip with Granny B. I was roasting my butt on the bottom two stairs of Marine Line station's footbridge where Simran was supposed to pick me up for a Malhar volunteer meet at our college. Malhar the most talked about college fest in Mumbai was just a couple of months away and Simran and I had enrolled to assist in the catering committee with an ulterior motive of tasting free food samples and meeting boys from various colleges.

'Sorry Kai.'

I heard a brake and a squeak from behind, Simran and her bike were both panting and puffing.

'Baby Boo is PMSing majorly today. She let me down again. I had to park her against a tree and fix her. You have no idea how we managed to make it here.'

The burning sun had made a black toast of me, thanks to her old scooter that seemed to shutdown more often than it worked. So, I was far from feeling sorry for her.

'Please Boo, start na. Take us on time... *izzat ka sawal hain,*' she said, giving light kicks to her baby (that was a toxic relationship there).

'We already late, let's just walk to college, dump it here on the pavement.'

I begged her; tempted to end the sentence with 'forever'.

'Are you mad? Leave her alone in the middle of the road? What if someone steals Baby?'

'No one is going to touch her.'

Oh Khodaiji, can someone please tell her that she would have to pay someone to rob this?

Simran continued fiddling with her two-wheeler, resuscitating her damaged junk was clearly far more important than honouring a commitment. So, I was about to hail a cab when a fancy white Mercedes slowed down next to us. Pink cat frames under a dark brown, wavy mane, popped out of the window. We blinked twice. Zoya Hussain was waving her well-manicured hand at us. We looked around, wondering whose attention she was trying to get.

'Late too, eh?' she asked in a slightly accented voice.

Simran's forehead was dripping like a leaking faucet and my hair was tousled into a nest. *Be bhootrio jeva lagela.* (We looked like two unkempt sprites.) And she looked like an angel.

'Yes, for the Malhar meet.'

We took a step back, fearing that our questionable odours might drift across to Lady Zoya's aristocratic nostrils.

'Thought so. I think I spotted both of you munching chips in the back row of the last rehearsal.'

She quipped genially.

Red as beets, we nodded in sync like a pair of busted juveniles.

'If you are having bike trouble, why don't you park your bike near that corner wall and hop in? I'll get Arif bhai to pick it up and get it fixed as soon as he drops us.'

She smiled as she spoke directly to Simran.

Simran looked unsure. I gave her a furious once-over. It was not every day that a Pink Lady lets sweaty, grubby hitchhikers ride in her Merc.

'Kai, I will come but in one condition.'

I could not believe that she was bargaining! I contemplated jumping into Pink Lady's chauffer-driven beauty and leaving her alone to pamper her Baby Boo, if she fussed ever so slightly.

'WHATTTTT?'

I growled back, not wanting to upset Zoya who was waiting patiently.

'It's Cutie Pie's birthday in November and you will have to come with me to wish him.'

Simran had a fan crush on this world-famous Indian cricketer. Actually, obsession was a better word for it. She breathed, yakked, ate, drank and maybe even burped him.

'Simran! Seriously ya! Don't bheja fry me again. Take Krish.'

Realising that she would not budge unless I complied with her insane demand, I said, 'Uhh okay, I can't promise but I will try.'

(Hoping she would forget by November.)

We slid through the open door Miss Hussain's chauffeur was holding out for us.

Wah! I was 'VIP of the month' or what?

The air-conditioning and sweet lavender scent exuding from inside the sleek maiden, made us feel human again.

'*Bhai saab, yeh chaabi rakhlijiye aur mere bacche ko sahi salamat college pahuchaye* (Arif bhai, take the keys and make sure to bring my baby back to college, safe and secure),' Simran said, leaning over to the front seat.

Zoya caught me rolling my eyes and tried hiding her smile. A few seconds later, both of us burst out laughing uncontrollably, much to Simran's displeasure.

***

We saw Krish standing at the gate, looking displeased. He was late for practice. He was to play in the festival band and we had instructed him to wait for us at the rear entrance, near the rehearsal area. His eyes almost fell out of their sockets when he saw us tumbling out of a swanky vehicle rather than stumbling out from a rickety scooter, which he had gotten used to. But soon enough Krish and Zoya surprised us by chatting easily, it turned out that Zoya's second cousin and Krish were lab partners.

Simran and I exchanged fearful looks, voicing each other's thoughts yet again.

Is Posh Zoya planning to steal our simple, sweet Krish and make him the mascot for the Pink Ladies?

Thankfully no such thing happened, but Zoya started to hang around more and more with the three of us when college reopened.

What could be her hidden agenda?

Had she scrapped with her snooty club and was using us to kill her loneliness? Or did she truly enjoy our company?

'I adore my Pink Ladies but I need some unpretentious friends, you know, to keep me grounded,' she said one day in passing though we considered ourselves a brief fling in the life of Zoya Hussain.

Gauging our insecurities, she invited us over to her house for a chaat party, on the last Saturday of August, calling it 'an *alvida* monsoon party'.

Zoya lived in a palatial four-storey mansion overlooking Chowpatty Beach. As the three of us ambled in awestruck into her lush garden, we were immediately greeted by her sister and mother who hugged us warmly and welcomed us like their own family. The outdoor area had been converted into a mini chaat street with tiny stalls being tended by half a dozen of their staff members with soft Indian classical music in a background. There was a canopy in the centre of the green patch where four chairs and a round table were set up for us. We dug into chatpata sev puris, dahi batata puris and ragda patties.

Zoya baptised us 'The Fabulous Four' as she took a giant-sized pani puri and held it up like a wine flute. We stood and held up our respective puris and cheered, more like bumped them together. There was no ting-glassy sound but a splash and crackle, as our puris broke open and the khatta–mitha pani spilled all over our clothes.

The next thing I knew, I had tripped over the chair leg trying to salvage my clothes and to avoid losing my complete balance, I caught Krish's hand for support. Bad idea! Because before we both realised what was happening, we were rolling on the grass atop one another, Krish wiggling beneath me for breath; my A-line knee-length tangerine skirt flying up, revealing my white cotton panties and my fair, fat thighs to the entire Hussain household, including Zoya's 70-year-old *chachaji* who was enjoying his hookah until then.

The scandalised, old man shot off his chair and hobbled away in the opposite direction mumbling to himself, while Zoya's sister tried distracting the staff. But it was too late. Simran who was trying to bend over to pull my skirt down on all fours, ended up straddling one of Krish's legs by mistake;

he let out a piercing scream, making Zoya rush towards him to help him get up. Unable to pull him up but not wanting to be the odd one out, she dropped to the ground too and we all lay on the grass for the next five minutes entangled in one fine mess. A mess that would carry us in its womb for decades to come…

***

Simran being Simran made sure that I lived up to my promise and somewhere around mid-November, we were standing under Sports Turf Apartments in Worli with a large hand-baked double chocolate cake.

'Should we send it through the watchman?' I asked her, unsure how she planned to deliver it to 'cutie pie' that day.

'Nope. I have an idea. I was thinking…'

Oh no! I don't want to hear it, you little blackmailer.

'We pretend we know him and enter the elevator, confidently.'

'Are you crazy? We will get hurled out, see how tight is the security here.'

Zoya and Krish had been right. We were inviting serious trouble.

But Simran had not toiled and steamed from dawn to 10 a.m. to be denied access by the Nepali guard who refused to buy our story of being the dark and handsome cricketer's long-lost relatives from Delhi.

'Come on, let's get back to your Baby Boo and make it for Keith Sir's class.'

I could not believe that I had let her talk me into cutting two morning lectures, including a small test, for this nonsense.

'No. Not until I see him and wish him.'

She stood her ground firmly.

'Simran my *jaan*, it's past 11a.m.! Since he has not surfaced yet, maybe he is not in town.'

I tried reasoning with her, but in vain. She was almost grovelling.

'Kai please, please. I have waited all year round for this. You know how it is to love someone so much with all your heart… It's like you and Shah Rukh Khan.'

'Hmm.'

Simran Smarty Pants had caught me there.

I decided to take matters in my own hands otherwise I would be stuck there all day with this over enthu cutlet. I looked up and attempted my loudest shout, hoping the second-floor apartment facing the road was his as my mad friend claimed and he would hear the helpless cries of two young college kids.

Simran was even more psyched up and screamed, 'CUTIEEE!'

Two guards came charging towards us. Simran panicked, her only chance of meeting the love of her life was going to be vanquished. Just then, two heads popped out of the first-floor window. Then another from the second.

'Kai, is that someone from his house?'

Simran could not help squealing. Her window of opportunity had opened.

A minute later, the Nepali guard informed us rather sullenly that we had been summoned by '*Memshaab*'.

An elated Simran eagerly pressed 2 on the lift panel while I prayed not to be handed over to cops or worse still Father D'Souza. A door was left ajar of the only flat on that floor and we stepped in. A woman with long, wet hair and a light pink bathrobe greeted us with a smile and said, 'Good morning, it's the left room at end of the corridor, you can wish him in person.'

'Thank you very much,' I replied politely.

'She is his wife, I've seen her in mags,' Simran affirmed, confidently.

'Okay Einstein!'

She was so excited that I was afraid she would pee in her jeans.

We found the nation's pride lounging on a lime green low settee in the shortest of red sports shorts, sipping a beverage. I was afraid Simran would pass out, as she handed him the cake garbling a barely audible, 'Happy Birthday, thank you for being born.'

He appeared chilled out as he opened the heart-shaped box and voiced his gratitude, 'Oooh! I love chocolate. Nice.'

'She baked it with lovvvvvve.'

I updated him, wondering what he must think of us barging into his house like that.

'So are you those cool college daredevils?'

We blushed.

'I call you too, a blank phone call almost every day.'

Simran was unable to hold her dark secret any more. And blushed again.

'Ah! So it's you, my secret admirer. We thought it was the Press harassing us. You should just talk the next time.'

'I will. I will. I will!'

Simran nodded her head furiously. My friend was clearly clean-bowled!

***

The Fabulous Four soon became a force to be reckoned with. Our friendship was real, the camaraderie was electrifying; the laughter was nonstop. Sometimes I had to pinch myself to make sure that it was all really happening to *me*. It was!

One of the grand plans designed by The Fabulous Four was to witness the spectacular waterfalls and the breathtaking views of Lonavala in the monsoon. My 19th birthday provided the perfect reason to visit the hill station in July. And the doors of Granny B's chateau opened for everyone. Usually, Granny B shuffled from her Bandra residence to Lonavala a few times a year but this time she had extended her summer visit to relish the rains and keep her home ready for us, excited about meeting my fun gang for the first time.

Mommy dearest had conjured up an award-winning mixed fruit brandy trifle for my big day and had given its guardianship to Krish, whom she believed was the most responsible of the lot. We spread ourselves in one of the train coaches out of the Victoria Terminus, throwing dirty looks at anyone who dared to trespass our space.

As the express train left the station, we tried to match the tempo of our vibrating hearts with our croaky melodies. Raindrops danced on the rusted circular bars of the coach windows as we got out of the busy city and soaked in the scenic beauty of the mountains and valleys, dreaming about happy days ahead. Of course, the three-hour journey would be incomplete without Simran, Zoya and I discussing the elusive and enticing world of sex with our limited awareness.

Simran brought out an old anthro notebook and pen. She started scribbling something on it, making us wonder if she had gone a bit potty. On a normal day, the notebook gathered dust, surely she was not going to start studying now? Zoya peeked over her shoulder and her face lit up into a naughty grin.

'This is what the male pecker looks like, let me educate you, in case you *gavars* have never seen the real thing unlike me,' Simran showed off, flaunting her drawing under our noses.

'Are you kidding me? This mouse *ka poonch* (mouse's tail)?' Krish shook his head.

'Simran, you're bonkers. It's not even close.'

'Correct me, I dare.'

She waved the sketch between his eyebrows.

He pushed her hand away.

'I'd rather jump off this train than…'

I grabbed the pen and book from her hand. Shutting my eyes, I tried to remember the adult movie that I had watched as a teenager with Delna, which she had stolen from her parents' videotape collection.

'Are you sketching some type of a carrot, Kai?' Zoya enquired, clearly the most clueless of us all. The closest she had come to expressing any male interest was crushing on a cute professor.

'My ex didn't oblige, so I can't get the correct proportion, but it's as close as it gets from what I felt.'

I informed them.

Krish sighed again.

'Bawi, it's not a vegetable.'

Resigning to the fact that he would have to save face for his male frat, he provided us with a few outlines.

'Oooh!'

'Aha!'

'Reminds me of a shrivelled-up sausage.'

'Looks like a cobra.'

'A *bhutta* I had just yesterday.'

'Dracula-like.'

'With awful fangs.'

'Wait is this you?'

He threw us annoyed looks.

'What are the semi-circles?' Zoya asked innocently.

'Really Zoya, you gotta watch porn, man,' Simran said, screaming.

'Shhhh!'

Krish hushed us.

The ticket collector had just walked in and his eyes went straight on the page of the book which we tried pushing in between Krish's thighs.

Hiding a smirk, he left our section, after checking our tickets.

Clad in colourful windcheaters and sporting broad smiles, we sang popular English and Hindi tunes all the way to Juicewalla Chateau, which was a 20-minute walk from Lonavala station, where we were welcomed by an enchanting garden laced with mauve and white bougainvilleas, pines, peepal, eucalyptus and gulmohar trees swinging in the monsoon wind.

It was the best time of the year to be there when the fragrance of fresh, organic, monsoon mud melded into the aromatic richness of garma-garam bhajiyas, sabudana vadas, chaapats (sweet crepes), batasas, tarela kera (banana fritters) chocolate sandwiches, devilled eggs, home-grown mulberries, fresh fruit jams, stringy cheese pancakes and Parsi mint *choi* from Granny B's bountiful kitchen.

It seemed just yesterday that I had been there as a child and a teenager, lying in her lap and sharing dreams; crying and aching for one thing or the other; throwing stones at our marvellous mango tree in the backyard to catch the falling ripe fruits while she watched and clapped; chasing pet hens that laid fresh eggs, which she would then go on to prepare in 10 different ways for breakfast.

Simran explored the garden, generously feeding her share of bhajiyas to Granny B's doggies that she had made friends with at once. Zoya was enraptured in Granny B's vivid handmade paintings that adorned the cream-coloured walls of the house. We were a picture postcard of easy warmth and mutual affection.

My heart felt warm and fuzzy as I watched Krish hold my 89-year-old grandmother's hand and give her his exclusive time and consideration while she narrated some of my embarrassing childhood antics. In turn, he told her about his newly acquired love for poetry and *purana zamana* sayings (one of the few things they had in common) and recited a few poems, including 'Waiting' by John Burroughs.

'Serene, I fold my hands and wait,
Nor care for wind, nor tide, nor sea;
I rave no more 'gainst time or fate,
For lo! My own shall come to me

I stay my haste, I make delays,
For what avails this eager pace?
I stand amid the eternal ways
And what is mine, shall know my face.

Asleep, awake, by night or day,
The friends I seek are seeking me;
No wind can drive my bark astray,
Nor change the tide of destiny.

The stars come out nightly to the sky;
The tidal wave unto the sea;
Nor time, nor space, nor deep, nor high
Can keep my own away from me.'

He kept referring to us as 'Whackadoodles', emphasising that I was mostly responsible for the tag. Granny B and Krish spoke of me with immense pride, which struck a tender chord. He seemed to fit into my intimate world. Almost as if he were part of it from the very beginning. There was a fleeting flicker that made me feel both unnerved and snug.

The pitter-patter of gentle drizzle on our old window panes that overlooked the waterfalls across flowy mounts and misty peaks and the downpour of a multitude of intense emotions—brought back a distinct memory: 'Trust the process, Kai, everything happens for a reason. Life will change for you.'

Had Cinderella's steppies not existed, perhaps Simran and I would have never clicked and so on…Come tomorrow, maybe the sun will shine again or maybe the fog will not clear. It did not really matter. Connections mattered. Family mattered. And I mattered to others. Maybe someday I will matter to a special someone too. A soulmate, so to speak.

A love so powerful, so boooooombastic that the dusky midnight sky will turn into one massive rainbow and the heart will explode into an SRK love song, '*Tujhe dekha to yeh jaana sanam*'.

But for now I was content in the certainty of the moment and the aroma of Granny B's freshly baked date and walnut cake that was seducing my nose.

10

Starry Days, Kinky Nights

2004–2006

After graduating in 2004 and acing my college in Sociology, the terrifying days of 'what's next?' arrived. While Zoya had made up her mind to pursue her Master's, Simran's fiery and no-nonsense attitude made her the perfect candidate to join an NGO that gave jobs to underprivileged women and enrol in a law college at the same time. Krish inaugurated his ghazal–hip-hop fusion band, first of its kind in India, or so he claimed. His mother had finally realised that she was being unreasonable by holding her son back from pursuing his musical ambitions and that he was nothing like his father in personality or appearance, and the only common thing they both shared was talent.

I was confused. As usual. I loved theatre but acting in films was a distant dream because my Hindi was comical. That is when Mom had a brainwave, 'Kai, you are constantly scribbling in that diary of yours. You even wrote mystery books as a child. Maybe you can get paid for writing.'

'Yes! It's not a bad idea at all but I don't want to spend another couple of years studying Journalism. I need to explore life outside the classroom,' I replied like any fresh graduate would, though wondering how I would get my first break at a news desk without a degree in Mass Communications.

One day, Granny B's bridge partner, Nargis Kanga who overheard me discussing my predicament with my grandmother, recommended this miracle bird-human duo Rustom–Sohrab who with their supreme skills of clairvoyance and extrasensory perception (ESP), had proved themselves as one of India's greatest soothsayers.

So I went.

'Call me Rusty,' the feathered African grey greeted me when I visited them at Panthaky Baug in Andheri West, somewhere mid-2004.

Sohrabji's wife, a pleasantly plump middle-aged lady Hooty (short for Hutoxi) with an oversized bun made from plaited hair, a yellow and orange-striped day gown that reached the floor and two cabbages in hand, had opened the door, looking fed up.

'We don't have any privacy any more,' she confided to me, offering me a glass of *kalakhatta* sherbet, as I waited for her astrologer husband Sohrabji to finish his bath and prayers and come out to meet me.

'*Muo aakho time vachma padech, daar ne dodhi maan eni choch nakhse.* (The dude keeps coming in the middle and pokes his beak into our business.) It's our fault, I suppose. Spare the rod and spoil the child.'

I gave a half-nod, assuming she was talking about the parrot and not her hubby.

'And do you know the *jabro* (cunning one), sniffs around our liquor cabinet all day long and doesn't shut up until we pour him a peg too. Not any peg. A Parsi peg! Sometimes it's hard to tell if he is a bird or a human.'

Listening to her never-ending list of grievances and that too at our first meeting, gave me the urge to ask for a nip of Johnny myself, which was lying on their side table.

Hooty enlightened me further that when Sohrabji, a simple bank clerk, had brought the African grey bird home, she was delighted. Childless Hooty decided that she would bring him up with all the maternal affection flourishing inside her. She even named him Rustom after her beloved great granddad. But within a few months of overpampering and doing lots of '*Maro nallo* (my baby)', Rusty's wings spread further than his large cage. He began to have an opinion about everything. He even detested bird food like grains, chana and fruits and had to be fed authentic Parsi cuisine, every other day.

As I sat in front of Rustom-Sohrab that day, I noticed the scrawny man's devotion to his son as he stroked him lovingly and spoke to him tenderly while he removed him from his cage.

'What's this sheeeeet?' the feathered creature asked, screeching in my ear as I placed my *kundali* quickly between his two thin legs, petrified that he would bite me.

Sohrabji started shuffling a pack of whisky-embossed playing cards.

'He is moody and doesn't believe in horoscopes. Only our magic cards.'

Rusty looked at me sharply, his piercing eyes scrutinising me, head to toe, making me very, very conscious. He bent over and pulled the king of spades from the pack when I told him about the top media houses I had sent my CV to. Magnum Opus Publications drew an extra heart, confirming that not only would I be successful in acquiring a job there, but also have a new love interest around that time. I was not ready to believe him that fast; after all, trusting a bird with your fate is hardly the brightest idea under any constellation.

But when a week later I got the job as a rookie reporter at *Starry Buzz* a popular film tabloid at the Magnum Opus house in Prabhadevi, I called the psychic duo to share the good news.

It was not long before I realised that I had struck gold. The opportunity was a dream come true for someone who had struggled to fit in all her life in the realms of the cool and hep circles. I was now sought after by the rich, privileged and famous, thanks to being hired at one of India's top entertainment magazines.

My office was infested with senior reporters, mostly stuck-up and dismissive.

Few even questioned my ability to woo celebrities whom they had spent years establishing a rapport with.

'Don't you worry your pretty, little head for me, I will be just fine,' I finally had it out with one Miss Know-It-All, a snooty correspondent who got threatened by any newbie, I could tell. She had drawn attention to my lack of journalistic experience to handle a cover story for the fifth time at an editorial meet.

'We Parsis are known to get along with anyone with a pulse. Haven't you heard the folklore of my great, grand ancestors and Jadi Rana, the Hindu king?' I asked her.

My college soul seeds had played a great role in building back by punctured confidence and I was not going to let anyone throw me off course any more.

My editor, who was the only good thing about the patronising team, looked rather impressed at my satirical throwback.

'No, we haven't. Spit it out! Make it quick, we don't have all day,' Ms Snoot's counterpart, senior copy editor, a male chauvinist to boot, stated haughtily, tapping his five-rupee pen on the table like a headmaster. I would have ignored him, but I was damn proud of my lineage and these ethnic narratives were an important part of world history.

'Well, in a nutshell, we fled from Iran our original home from the hostile and violent Arabs and landed on the shores of Sanjan in Gujarat. Jadi Rana, the Hindu king was hesitant to take us refugees into his kingdom, so he asked us for one good reason to give us protection. Holding a glass full of milk and mixing sugar crystals in it, our head priest through one simple action relayed the following message to the king, "like this sugar mixes in the milk, we shall do the same. Parsis will blend with your society and not cause any problems in your country."

That made Jadi Rana open the doors of his land to us and eventually his heart. Just like all of you will do for me…soon, I hope?'

Phew!

'Sounds very Bolly masala-type but whatever!'

Ms Snoots commented though I could see from all their reddish faces that the ice was broken.

I started attending many star-studded premieres and events and soon the glamour and flirtatious bug bit me hard enough to get any 20-year-old carried away. An ordinary boyfriend with a 9 to 5 job was not going to be good enough for me, so if Rusty's prediction included a fellow reporter, a businessman or a factory manager, I would have to pass on that.

I needed a fanatically passionate Shah Rukh Khan-type of hero, who would climb summits and swim across the *saat samundars* for me.

So, meeting Siddharth in the beginning of 2005 at a film mahurat party at a five-star was a prayer answered. Even though he was a struggling actor, he was handsome, flashy and charmingly Punjabi and hence easy to fall for.

On being introduced, I was sucked in by his overconfidence, unpretentious behaviour and cheesy one-liners. He had S-R-K as his initials, I hardly needed a bigger sign from the universe than that to keep dancing and chatting him up through the night. My very own Paulo Coelho moment, 'And, when you want something, all the universe conspires in helping you to achieve it.' Or closer home, '*Kehte hain agar kisi cheez ko dil se chaaho, to puri qayanat use tumse milane ki koshish mein lag jaati hai.*' SRK's dialogue so could not resist.

So anyway, we flirted a lot, our similar sense of humour and colourful wisecracks eventually got us into the ladies' restroom of the hotel where we made out in one of the toilets until the cleaning lady caught us red-handed, with our pants down, literally.

I wrote it off as a one-time lustful escapade in my diary (which I was not very regular with those days). Hence, I was flattered to receive a four-foot tall bouquet from Sid, the day after next, at my office. We began dating and he seemed near perfect and our sexual vibe was unbelievable.

'Jangu the Jerk' had been a kltuzy bawa boy, trying to find a ripple over the nipple; my new squeeze knew the *Kamasutra* by heart. And he was well-hung!

If Jangu's amateur kisses had been like plain white rice (cheap quality), my filmy lad's were like spicy egg biryani (basmati variety).

Jehangir Nanavati had flattened my self-esteem, Siddharth R. Kaushal made me feel like a billion bucks with his pet phrase, 'I worship your body'. Four words I had never in my wildest dreams expected from any human being, dead or alive, let alone from a hottie who had smooched his way into my hopeful heart and become my second Mr Right, rather effortlessly. Of course, I was now an unapologetic and bindaas 72 kgs. What I have realised over the years is that if I did not care about labels, others did not either.

And having Siddharth as a boyfriend helped a lot. Ten years older than me, with beefed-up arms like Sunny Deol's *dhai kilo ka haath*, his dress sense was classier than some of his more successful counterparts and his romantic dialogue delivery (to me) could give SRK a run for his money. And even though we turned eyeballs wherever we went, his career graph had never been on a rise and besides giving one hit film in eight years, he was constantly on the prowl for good work from the industry.

Though a bit over the top and vain like most actors, my Punjab *ka puttar* boyfriend provided me with never-ending excitement and passion, in the form of risqué escapades involving going down on each other in his Baleno, making out in random car parks, quickies in the car under airport flyovers, club swimming pools and skyrise elevators.

Our relationship mantra was higher the stakes, greater the glory.

'You are the best!'

I would scream at the pinnacle of every love-making session, pulling the wavy hair on his head and chest even though I had no one to really compare him with.

'You are my *jannat*.'

He would reciprocate, making me feel like the most loved woman in the world. (More filmy the better, in my case.)

Life had become one big carnival. And my glamorous career brought out the best in me. I was a natural writer and was already creating waves among the tribe of scribes, with my flair for conducting candid interviews of celebrities and penning bold articles for the magazine.

Sid-Heart my self-proclaimed superstar boyfriend often insisted on gluing himself to me, on my visits to film sets and starry events, which were part and parcel of my work.

'Sweets, it is important that you don't go alone to such places and you need a *chak de phatte* bodyguard like me to guard that hot body of yours,' he would joke in his usual upbeat style.

Initially I was amused by his overprotectiveness but I realised soon enough that he was piling on to meet producers and directors through me, in the hope of being offered lead roles. He kept me entertained with his uproarious Hindi and Punjabi jokes and anecdotes, and I was a bit awestruck by his striking good looks, so I did not really have an issue with his motives. Besides what is better than having a handsome guy who is head over heels in love with you and reminds you of it, almost every hour? Nothing, right?

'Are you sure he is not using you?' Zoya's voice over the phone cut through like a dagger soon after she had asked me all the relevant 'how's your relationship going and where is it heading?' questions during one of our weekly chats.

I skirted around the topic, changing the subject to her recent alliance with the son of a business mogul from the Gulf. Last thing I needed was a *bhashan*. I was in love and love is blind. He could come out with no teeth and I'd still kiss him on the mouth. After all, love that does not turn you stupid, is no love. Being with him had made me a more positive person;

he helped me laugh away life's smallest problems with his infectious optimism and impeccable comic timing.

And if there were any doubts about his intentions, the mind-blowing passion we shared sterilised them all. So even if I was being used, it was a small price to pay for smashing chemistry and of course, louuvvveee…

***

We had all gotten busy in our careers after college, so the years slipped by quickly and it was only in September 2006 that we managed a Fabulous Four reunion after a long time. It was a few days before Zoya's engagement.

Simran had just broken ties with her six-month-old boyfriend, the famous *kavi* Subroto Sen. 'I called it quits. The murderer!'

This is all she announced one day. We did not ask her much. Apparently, he had pissed her off one fine day by eating a chicken kathi wrap behind her back. Our firebrand was extremely vocal about her dos and don'ts in her human equations and this time, animals were her new cause, or was it recycling of the foils of the kathi roll too? It was hard to keep up with saucy Simran's verve.

Zoya would continue with her PhD even after tying the knot. The immensely wealthy Hussain's had been determined to strike a stupendous transnational business deal with the multi-billionaire clan 'Malik And Sons', hoteliers from Abu Dhabi, and were aiming at killing two birds with one stone by marrying off their graceful daughter into the high-profile Malik family.

Zoya was no babe in the woods though; she respected her parents enough to agree to the collaboration but she was not going to give up her freedom for nothing. So, she made a clause: her fiancé Mustafa Rizwan Malik must move to Mumbai.

Zoya may have had little firsthand experience with the opposite sex as compared to other girls her age, but she was sharper and more eloquent than all of us put together. And she could not bear the thought of being more than a few streets away from her family and her Fab Four. Mustafa, smitten by her beauty and authenticity, was convinced in no time and immediately got down to setting up offices in Mumbai.

We had smuggled booze into Zoya's bedroom that day though it was not the first time we had broken rules at her plush residence. Her mother smiled as we entered, she obviously knew what we were up to— just like the old times. Our reunion was mainly to discuss the pros and cons of Zoya's upcoming nuptials to a stranger and to address the elephant in the room—the *suhag raat*!

Zoya was still a virgin. We had to train her. It was our foremost duty as self-assigned bridesmaids.

'I think you should test drive first.'

Simran was completely against arranged situations like these.

'Sure. Should I send him an invite?' Zoya shot back, suppressing a chuckle.

'Come on, you know what we mean. Abhishek and you only went up to second base,or was that just for our benefit?'

I ribbed her.

'I don't keep secrets,' she said, emptying her glass of rum and coke into her mouth before drifting back to us, 'yes, as hard as it is for you two sexomaniacs to hear, I fought to save my virginity for my husband.'

'*Like a virgin touched for the very first time…*'

Simran yanked the empty tumbler from Zoya's hand, and sang holding it like a mike, torturing us all with her *besura* voice.

'Who only gave head…in bed. '

I joined her, keeping up with Madonna's original tune.

Zoya began throwing ice cubes in our direction, aiming inside our t-shirts.

'You nymphos make me sound like an old maid. One is a serial dater and the other a ghostwriter for *Debonair*. How can I ever top that?'

'That's not be said aloud!'

I shushed her.

Okay, so I had scrawled a few porn articles for some adult mags under a pseudonym, but it was not public knowledge. Mostly because I was moonlighting.

However under all the light banter and fun, we were actually a bit paranoid for Zoya; not only because she was choosing a conventional style of wedlock, but also because we were seriously concerned about her long-term (read boring and lacklustre) sex life.

She would never know about the greener grass on the other side if she got roped into marital compulsions that early.

'What if he is impotent?'

Simran drove straight to the point.

'Worse still, what if he plucks your precious flower and turns out to be a pathetic gardener, what will you do then? Have a whirlwind affair with a real gardener?'

'I think both of you nutcases have been watching too many American soaps.'

Zoya appeared cross, not wanting to be grilled further.

But Simran refused to back down.

'Zoya, all we are trying to say is that why invest in a vehicle without checking its mileage first?'

'If only Simran had done that with Baby Boo, it would have saved us a lot of sweat.'

Krish broke in, determined to change the topic as usual, before we had a blowout.

It worked, as Simran began punching him playfully.

Krish, immune to our tomfoolery and outrageous girlie conversations, had been sluggishly lying across Zoya's lazy bean bag, barely batting an eyelid. Sometimes we suspected that he took cat naps on a few occasions, while we yapped away.

Zoya shut her ears.

'Guys, please! What should I tell the man whom I have met less times than my dentist?'

'At least the dentist stages an oral.'

Simran's always had a way that cracked us up.

Krish mock-fisted his head.

'You Whackadoodles!'

I had tried meeting his eyes a few times that evening, wondering if anything in him had shifted since our unplanned rendezvous 10 days ago. I had been assigned to cover the engagement party of a famous starlet at the Hotel Sun-n- Sand. Krish lived a few blocks away from the Juhu hotel and he had swung by as we had not met in quite a while. He seemed even more endearing as he excitedly chatted about rock ghazals that he had recently written.

'You must think I'm such a dunce. Look at you, a high fly journo and I'm still trying to find my feet.'

'You already have, and you'll make it someday. I am just a social climber disguised as some fancy correspondent.'

I comforted him with the truth.

I was glad I had left the mind-numbing do; I planned to catch up on the tidbits from an ally from our rival magazine, in exchange for a crate of beers.

Krish and I had jabbered on easily as we walked around Juhu beach, sometimes gazing over the silver ocean, lost in thoughts in between our short exchanges. It was past 9 p.m. and there were very few hawkers on that part of the stretch.

'It's nice to see you doing what you love and I am so relieved that you have stopped obsessing about your weight issues.'

'Are you nuts or blind? They will always be there. I am just in a better place, thanks to you guys.'

'That's what besto-friends are for, right?'

For a brief moment, I thought his fingers were moving sideways to touch my hand. For a second, they might have. I was not sure. It could have been the wind. My hair was blowing fiercely over my face and my glittery, red, off-shoulder flary dress and black heels was not an ideal choice for a walk. Heavy pellets of rain enveloped us, making us grasp each other's hands and run for shelter under a tiny shanty at a reachable distance, my soft palm entwined in his sturdy one for a moment too long as we stood under the shed, in a kind of inexplicable silence.

I was not sure if it was the bolt of lightning that had struck over my head or the sudden rumble of the last of the monsoon thunder that shook my heart cage, but it felt as if a higher force was pulling me into a direction that I did not want to go and was never a part of the plan. And it was goading me softly to cuddle my best friend, not in the usual group hug sort of way but in a meaningful embrace.

No, this is not correct or normal, Kai. It's the Screwdrivers you consumed earlier playing nasty tricks.

'I have a cool idea.'

His caramel eyes (they turned into several shades of brown in the years I have known him) twinkled in the nocturnal surroundings as he disengaged his hand abruptly and purposefully, taking two steps away at the same time.

We had ventured away from Sun-n-Sand and were now dependent only on some floodlights from nearby houses and hotels for vision and we could easily be mugged if our luck ran out, but somehow I knew no harm would come to me as long as I had Krish by my side, even if it was a rather secluded part of Juhu beach.

And for some incomprehensible reason, I found myself expectant and I was not really sure about what. This had never happened before and it even took me by surprise. Yes, I had always nurtured a soft corner for him but he had really not been my cuppa tea. I adored him, respected him and cared for him as much as I did for S and Z. But was I attracted to him?

No. Never. Maybe…

Mari jaoo, Kai. Krish- Besto? You like him?

Yeh! Kind of!

What's kind of? Yes or no?

Oh Khodaiji, where am I going with this?

'You know Bawi, we seem to all have flitted away and hardly ever meet; like from hanging out every single day for three years, it's not even thrice a year any more, isn't that strange?'

Krish seemed more melancholic about that than the other two Fabs who were immersed in their respective lives.

I half-nodded, wondering what he was getting at.

'Why don't you and I baptise this as our very own secret spot? So whenever we both really need each other, we dial each other to meet right here in this shack.'

He sounded as earnest as a school boy. I blinked. Did he hear my thoughts or what? The Shack?! Of all the names! Oh, goodness gracious!

I looked around the tiny booth-like structure made of bricks and uneven cement, it must have been someone's chai or toy stall once upon a time but was now in ruins. Surprisingly, the tin roof was fully intact. I gave him a half-hug, I dug the arrangement; it sounded rather clandestine.

'The Shack sounds perfect Krish.'

Yes, we need to shack up.

I did not ask him why he had chosen something so out of the ordinary, rather than a coffee shop or a park. But Krish was a free spirit and his moods fluctuated like the ebb and flow of the sea in front of us. He enfolded me in return soothingly, as if I was some delicate flower which would fall apart. His body scent fused with CK's Eternity lured me in like a moth to a flame. Instinct told me to not jump to the bait but simply keep still and let Nature (or the universe) take its course.

A kiss, a touch, a caress…anything would suffice. But nothing happened for two whole minutes which made me wonder if I should dare play the game of seduction that I was well acquainted with—a skin graze, a weak spot, an indirect move.

Chaalni gadhera, kiss me.

I sent him a non-verbal message, the uncertainty destroying my peace, hoping telepathy would work. This guy seems to have a serious dilly-dallying disorder.

Tujhe dekha to yeh jaana sanam…

I heard Raj of *Dilwale Dulhania Le Jayenge* prompting me to take the leap.

'So, how's that Punju hero of yours?'

Krish broke into a cough as he dropped his hands into his back pockets, avoiding my wanton gaze.

'Who?'

I asked aloud, without thinking.

Krish frowned. I smiled.

'Kidding! He's fine but we're not going anywhere.'

I replied as honestly as I could.

For even though Sid-Heart kept me in good spirits and was a beast in bed, and the midnight sky elicited a rainbow when we kissed, he just was not hubby material. And recently he had been dropping hints about those ill-reputed casting couch offers from lady producers and even male ones who had propositioned him to 'take care' of their wives in exchange for a decent role in their movies.

An overdose of Bolly debauchery was a bit too radical for me especially when I was not really a secure person and an open relationship was not what I had signed up for. Maybe sleeping around was a great way of knowing people, but my raunchiness was limited to monogamy. So, it was only a matter of time before the actor and I would stop dancing around trees and part ways.

I felt it in my gut. Punjabi *munda* may be my yummy egg biryani, but the boy in front of me was that bowl of crispy French fries I could rely on for comfort and taste always.

But the bubble of what could have been a beautiful moment to take home with me, had burst.

Or maybe Krish was only being his usual amazing, amiable self and it had just been my excellent imagination, after all.

I would always be confused about what exactly had taken place inside The Shack but chilling at Zoya's that evening in the comforts of her room overlooking Mumbai's magnificent Queen's necklace, it was all coming back to me.

And even though my heart was tempted to explore this unforeseen twist with my besto, my sixth sense told me that this lost soul popping fried moong dal in his mouth, behaving as cool as a cucumber, passionately explaining one of his new compositions to his three Whackadoodles, was not going to be my boyfriend soon or in the near future.

Krish Aryan was a boy of many layers. A true Piscean. Dreamy; spaced out; hard to read; tough to understand though easy to trust, if that made sense. Peeling them off would take a lifetime. And I did not have a lifetime to try and fail, err and learn.

Alas! Our beachy tryst was destined to be washed away in the sands of time. Life is such a tease!

XXXSCORE = 410 (Jangu + Sid)

MILE HIGH CLUB

11

It Took a Parrot to Change My Destiny

2007

Over two years of being a special correspondent at *Starrybuzz*, I felt less special with each passing day. The measly 15,000 rupees that splashed into my bank account each month trickled out quickly on shoes and bags and by the 18th of each month, I was left trying to save the last few drops from evaporating.

Besides the glam sham of any job eventually wears off after some time and then what is left is routine and, in this case, my conscience. Did I really want to fill my pockets by digging around people's lives and flashing them as headlines to feed idle minds, especially lives that were dotted with extramarital affairs, drug overdoses, plastic surgeries and eerie loneliness?

My boss Aparna believed that if I stuck around, I would be an editor some day but that did not excite me as much as it would have in my early days of journalism. I was hungry for more. I needed to see more of the world than the current peripheral vision of it which mainly rallied around chasing evasive VIPs, organising glossy photoshoots for our monthly featured celebrities and keeping tabs on their scandalous liaisons.

And to be honest, I was also getting a bit exhausted putting up with most of the celebs who were as sweet as 10 candy sticks on your face just so they could bribe you to be written about in a favourable light. There were exceptions too and the job had its perks, like some fun press junkets, fleeting friendships and pastimes over a period of time which would make their own headlines if I was a star too.

Like a healthy acquaintanceship with Chunks (an actor known more for his witty one-liners than his films) which led to me overfeeding him almost every second Sunday with dhansak straight out of Juicewalla kitchen for almost a year.

A brief yet electrifying rendezvous with V.K. an actor known for his rugged good looks and suave appeal; also known as one of India's sexiest retro superstars of the 70s and 80s. It was one of the few times, Zoya accompanied me to a movie set which I was visiting to interview a new actress. On spotting the much older V.K., my controlled and composed friend had almost slipped into a coma. For there he was, lounging on a settee, top three shirt buttons unfastened, teasing, suggesting and luring us towards him (in our minds of course) knowing only too well, the deadly effect he had on the opposite sex, never mind the age group. Every raunchy pore of our respective skins breathed fire as we managed to get ourselves seated next to him, tongue-tied at first but then as the conversation flowed, we summoned the courage to ask him if we would ever have the pleasure of seeing him 'totally bare chested'?

May the dishy veteran actor be at peace wherever he is, but be rest assured that his racy reply stole our peace and our sanity for nights to come…

Wink! Wink!

But if there was ever a night to remember it would be this: An irresistible and super *se bhi upar* hot (think triple chocolate sundae topped with sprinkles, marshmallows and extra whipped cream level of drool-isciousness) film star-turned-TV star-turned film star whose naughty boy image and cocaine addiction preceded him back in his days. A welcome add-on to my body confidence, upping my XXXSCORE by a whooping 10.

Of course, I would love to gloat about this one of the who, where and how but there are some secrets, if I do not take with me to hell, will end up taking me to court.

Though the most memorable part of being an upcoming correspondent was my unique connection with the legendary Dev Saab (whom I nicknamed DA with his permission and complete agreement). In spite of having an age gap of more than five decades, we had built a rock-solid friendship based on mutual admiration, long conversations on life and sometimes about the women he had loved and lost, all this taking place at his penthouse-cum-office, which was our private sanctuary.

***

In those couple of years, I had held on to my job and tried saving up for two business class tickets and a five-star hotel stay in Singapore with only one goal in mind, fulfilling Amy Ma's dream into reality. But it was taking longer than expected and I was frustrated.

I could have easily borrowed from my folks, but I wanted to do this for her on my own; in gratitude for all the times she listened to my never-ending lamentations. And then as really shit luck went, Amy Ma toppled down a few stairs and passed away. I was heartbroken. The only consolation was that she was now part of a much kinder and more welcoming dimension where the angels would treat her profusely better than the earthlings ever did.

So on a sultry May afternoon, I found myself knocking on the door of C203 once again, hoping to get some clarity on life, career and love.

Hooty opened the door, flushed-faced and panting, the mehendi on her hair unevenly done, haldi stains smeared over her dull pink apron. I did not ask her what was wrong, afraid I would get a litany of complaints when I had enough problems of my own.

But Hooty seldom needed an invitation to rant. Waving her hands animatedly almost whacking my face with her wooden spatula, she moaned, 'You won't believe what he did last Sunday, the badmash! He broke open his *pinjra* and flew all over the colony, disturbing our *aaju-baaju padosis* having their siestas. Our Lord Falkland in spite of overstuffing himself with seven bheja na cutless (brain cutlets) in our house, created a ruckus on their windowsills, demanding food and stealing leftovers from their kitchens. This parrot has the appetite of a buffalo!'

Poor Hooty. Weekend siestas are sacred to us Parsis after they walloped a huge afternoon meal made up of meat-based dhansak, curry-chawal or ras-chawal and shandy. Life stopped for the next three hours at least and other than a Martian attack or another culinary-rich function to attend, nothing would get a *pait bharailo* (full stomach) bawaji out of his bed.

She offered me khari biscuits that her sister Farida had brought a week ago from the Dotivala bakers in Surat. She informed me that the bird was territorial about his space that he even chased her sibling away.

Sohrabji appeared in his *sudrah legha* (muslin vest worn by Parsis under their clothes) munching on a nankhatai, looking rather sheepish as he informed me, 'My Rusty bachcha is in detention in his cage. Go to the verandah, I will join you in a minute.'

'Hi sexy Kai, lookin' good,' Rusty greeted me jovially, showing off his acrobatic skills in his fairly large hutch. He seemed to be in a rare mood of *maska maroing* me.

Usually, he scowled at his visitors, making it clear that he hated his job. He felt he should not be working for a living at all. But that day, I was his get-out-of-jail card.

'You know I can't go against Sohrabji and Hooty's wishes,' I told him.

And he proved me right.

'*Motu* Kai, *Golgappa* Kai!' he squeaked. 'Kai Kai big thighs, too many fries. Bye bye. Die.'

Luckily, an apologetic Sohrabji appeared on time and started shuffling his playing cards. Unlocking the cage, he let out his prized possession who nuzzled his ear in fondness. It was obvious, Hooty had come in-between this affectionate connection and not the other way around.

Rusty drew three cards and then stared at me. Yes, the damn clairvoyant bird was staring at me.

'Not possible,' he squawked. 'Impossible! How? When?'

Sohrabji whispered something to his accomplice and Rusty cackled back in their secret code making me all hot and bothered.

Do I have some life-threatening disease? Shit! Or worse than that, NO SEX EVER?

Crappity crap, am I pregnant? I don't want a baby. Not now, not tomorrow, not ever.

When were my last periods?

Sid and I were done around five months ago and though we had met three weeks ago for that 'one last goodbye kiss and some more', we had been careful. But then there must be a reason why every Durex packet has '99 per cent effective only' *chaapod* on it.

Oh God please. Not a baby with my weight issues and his IQ. What a guaranteed disaster!

Sohrabji, oblivious about scaring the living daylights out of me, took a slow breath before he spoke, '*Velaat* (abroad). It's your destiny to travel to the unknown.'

Huh? *Travel where*? *Virar*? *Nalasopara*?

The only place I could afford to go at that moment was Panchgani or Matheran. Maybe Goa if I dug really, really deep into my savings. Who was going to pay me for globetrotting? A rich lover, perhaps?

'Ahhh. Perhaps you are seeing that holiday to Singapore that I was planning for my Amy Ma?'

'No. No. No. New job. Newwwww boy.'

Rusty was fixated on his prophecy, bobbing his head up and down and then sideways.

'What new job? I haven't applied anywhere.'

'I guess what *aapro* clever Rustom is trying to say is that not only will you have a new career, but also a boy uuhh friend. Probably the love of your life. A different road awaits you, dikra, professionally and personally.'

Sohrabji comforted me kindly though I was perplexed beyond words by his words.

'The last time, you told me my actor boyfriend could be "the one" and then what happened, eh? Is this some game for you?'

I pointed out emphatically, blaming the parrot. As much as I knew it was inevitable and necessary, I had been gutted with the break-up. Nothing further happened with Krish either since The Shack episode, though no surprises there. I was on my own. Again. And it kind of sucked. That meant no flowers on Valentine's from a boyfriend, no monthly anniversary date nights and definitely no midnight calls of sweet nothings on private bedroom phone. Did I lose my one and only chance at love by dumping Sid?

'Bloody mishtake-mishtook, shit happens. Sheeeeet, bad girl Kai, bad.'

Rusty pierced back, swinging fiercely on his perch.

Humbug!

The *popat* (parrot) had now become overconfident!

'Good luck, Miss Juicewalla,' were Sohrabji's last words as he opened the main door for me.

An international trip? *A potential Mr Right*? *Such a load of bull*!

As I climbed down the stairs, the heady scent of Hooty's chumna (pomfret) fry lingered all the way to the ground floor, but I felt as directionless as I had arrived.

Firstly, I was in a job that I did not much care for any more. I had rubbed shoulders with almost every Khan, Kumar and Kapoor except the elusive SRK who was the real reason I had hung on for so long.

Second, I had recently rejected Nawaz *Fui's* (a distant cousin of my dad's) matchmaking attempt with *sojjo Parsi chokro* (a good Parsi boy) 'Dicky Junglewala', more so for his incongruous name.

Third, the small development with Krish at the beach had got my hopes a teeny-weeny bit high though the truth was that I had scarcely heard from him since.

Lastly, I had no Plan B or C. Personally or professionally. There were a few interests here and there but none that were worth pursuing.

And just when things could not get more convoluted, the psychic birdie was sending me on some wild goose chase.

As I flagged down a cab and settled into it, I opened Mom's neatly packed omelette sandwiches. Hungrily, I haphazardly tore the piece of newspaper which had been placed over the silver foil as extra protection to keep them from drying out. On my third bite into the soft bread, my gaze fell on the section of the ripped paper that I had carelessly chucked across the seat. I would have almost missed the advertisement had it not been in bold:

Air International

The world's most preferred airline

We are arriving in your city this winter!
If you have the wings, we will help you fly.
Interested candidates with a graduate degree may apply before the 31/10/2007 for the position of Flight Stewardess.
Height: Min 160 cms.
Weight: In proportion to height.
Age: 21–29 years old.
Gender: Female
Freshers and experienced are both welcome.

Successful candidates will be informed
via telephone call. No enquiries please.

Oh Khoda, what if the whacky bird is right? What if I actually get the interview call for the job? But me, a Trolley Molly?

It sounded almost like Monica Lewinsky was being elected as President of the United States.

But just imagine Kai, you will be flying across exotic locations and meeting handsome firangis with every third one looking like a Hollywood actor?

I would not even have considered it, thanks to my oversized disposition for the said job, but the loony bird had planted the seed of temptation in my mind and suddenly I had goosebumps all over my body, as I visualised a career in flying and swimming in dollars and pounds.

And just when I was about to dismiss myself for nurturing such unrealistic ambitions, Amy Ma's kind face appeared in front of me and her sweet voice echoed, 'The world is big dear and some day if you get the opportunity to see it, you won't leave it, promise…?'

And it was in that moment that I made up my mind to 'be realistic and plan for a miracle' as the wise old Osho once said. I folded and tucked the advert into my Bermuda pockets carefully. I did not say a word to anyone expect Shanaya and Pari about my new plan. They are needed for a reality check now and again to keep me on my toes and follow through with my decisions.

Not wanting to give myself the time to change my mind, the following week, I simply drove myself to a photo studio located at the end of my road, got a few pics clicked in formal wear, paid the studio a thousand extra to make me look the slimmest possible by tampering the originals with some new-ass technology and posted my photographs and biodata to the address mentioned in the advertisement. Then I got down to the Herculean task of getting my weighing scale to stop groaning by knocking down more than 25 kgs in five months and getting rid of my double chin so that my neck and jawline have better visibility.

I took leave from work to do a four-week weight loss crash course at a retreat in Uruli Kanchan, which had the reputation of making chihuahuas out of hippos. After shoving a few enema tubes inside my butt and four cucumbers, three carrots and two bowls of skimmed *dahi* a day in my mouth, I was ready to strangle the specialists, helpers and yoga teachers.

It was around the fifth day there that I met my *jodidar* Navika Ahuja who like me had arrived there reluctantly and forcefully to fulfil her long standing dream of being a size 6.

We were roughly the same size and age and it seemed like we both were equally unhappy with our weighty circumstances and the current scenario had made her almost suicidal too.

'I want *khana-peena* and *mauj-masti*, yaar!' she said, grumbling.

She was studying engineering but she wanted to pursue a career in the entertainment industry.

'Seriously man! We are so not meant for this *jhanjat*.'

I was in full agreement with her, delighted that I had found an ally with whom I could share my woes with.

Deprived of what we considered 'oxygen', a week later we both went into a state of borderline depression, realising if we did not take necessary and timely action, we would start to hunt and eat the humans around us. So, we did what was the most sensible thing to do: climb the boundary walls of the retreat and fill our tummies with pav bhajis and chole bhaturas from a food joint outside the premises.

We got caught on the fourth day of our misconduct and were asked to leave. We went out with our heads held high though, waving to those who were still around, happily munching a huge Cadbury's dairy milk each and watching with sadistic pleasure the ravenous faces of the residents, scornful authorities and envious staff who had probably not seen a chocolate in decades.

I reached home five kgs heavier, an additional tummy tyre and a new friend in town. Alas! There is no elevator to thinness. You have to take the stairs. So, I ventured on a diet of sorts—greens of all kinds, protein shakes, watery soups, selective fruits. Strictly no whole fats, processed sugar, comfort carbs or junk food.

Since dieting is as unsettling to bawajis, as sugar is to diabetics, I was falling apart. What was worse is all that exercising. The huffing and puffing on treadmills and exercycles at a local gym and brisk walking at Jogger's Park was the cruellest form of self-inflicted torture. However, I did manage to drop three dress sizes (and a pound of hair) in four months.

Voila! I achieved the impossible. And my new body felt so powerful that I suddenly felt this instantaneous energy to rule the world. Now it made sense as to why the she-devils and Pink Ladies walked around like the sun bounced off their asses! It was all about revelling in a positive body image.

My efforts were rewarded, I received an interview call in mid-November from Air International. I was over the moon. And then things began to fall into place at a breakneck speed.

I was shortlisted from the 700 interviewees, despite my pathetic make-up skills that even a party clown would refuse to be subjected to. Neither did I tick all their purrrfect boxes, nor was I as immaculately groomed as many there but for some deluded reason, they selected me in all my misfit glory.

A few weeks later I, along with 17 new aspirants, was en route to Switzerland for a six-week learning period at the training institute in Zurich—in cold, cold December. Once we passed the practical and theory exams, we would be sent back to Mumbai where our official flight routes would commence—Mumbai to Zurich, Mumbai to London and Mumbai to Dubai.

Never in my *khayali pulaos* had I imagined romancing the the land of roestis, fondues, snow-peaked mountains, Yash Chopra films, pristine lakes and inconceivable natural beauty. I was in a trance.

I? Me? On the threshold of being a globetrotting flight stewardess? The haathi mere saathi who could not fit into the sack at the sack race in school? The one who auditioned for the part of the alluring Snow White in middle grade but got the role of Dopey the Dwarf instead?

It was almost as if a wish-fairy had spun a magic wand over me. Maybe she was aiming somewhere else and the wand slipped. My parents were thrilled when I broke the news to them—they had no idea I had been plotting this all along. They had assumed the sudden weight loss was to cajole some guy into proposing or something ridiculous like that.

This was an unimaginable career path for me and a first in our family. Shanaya was delirious with pride and Jimmy and Pari sent me congratulatory cake and flowers. Simran and Zoya hovered around my Bandra pad the day before I was to leave. Every few minutes, we snatched tissues and dabbed them over our runny eyes and red noses.

'Whatta filmy scene! You aren't going to Kargil to win a war, and will be back soon enough to torment us all,' pronounced Ash drily, wriggling away from a cuddle like a typical younger brother.

The following week, he was taking off to Australia for further studies so could not understand the fuss.

Granny B bid a heartbreaking goodbye to me which spread over 10 days. We had never been geographically separated for that long.

'Who will give you nourishment, dikra? You have become so thin, *sekta ni sing lagech* (you look like a drumstick). I should have never let you out of my sight.'

I smiled, knowing I looked nowhere close to any kind of a stick. I gracefully accepted a gigantic jar of vasanu, a winter prep of mixed dry fruits and spices in a thick, paste-like concoction, which was '*khauraak*' to keep me warm and my bones strong.

'Don't share with anyone,' she ordered.

On the eve of my departure, she wrapped Parsi poro rotli (omelette roti), for the journey ahead, afraid that the food on the plane would run out.

'Whenever you fly to England in the future and visit Buckingham Palace, please give my regards to my dear Lizzy.'

She addressed Queen Elizabeth II as Lizzy or Aapri Rani because like most Parsis, she believed that we were all byproducts of blue-blooded lineage. In fact, she had three Godrej steel cupboards filled with British royal paraphernalia that dated back to the late 1800s.

'Do your Yatha Ahu Vairyos whenever you encounter evil and your *sudrah kusti* (holy thread ritual) regularly, our Parsi prayers are immensely powerful,' she counselled me a few hours before I took off to Zurich, convinced that the world outside Bandra and her beloved hill station was filled with thugs and despos.

'Granny B,' I rubbed her hand reassuringly, 'I am with an extremely safe and well-placed airline. I am sure I will only have good people around me.'

'And what if the aeroplane stops working in the air? What will I do? Alone in this world... *ovaryu ovaryu,*' she sounded frantic, as she hobbled to the fridge and pulled out a raw egg and began circling it superstitiously over my head 11 times to remove any trace of negative energy.

'Why do you have to be a waitress, dikra? We have enough money, if you don't want to work. Just sit at home with me and we will listen to the radio and play rummy and carrom all day.'

'I want to explore the world, Granny B. You know how much you loved England when you visited it.'

I did not have the heart to tell her that it had been one of Amy Ma's visions too. That would not go down well with her. She had always wanted to be acknowledged as the only grandparent on whom I showered my undivided time, love and attention.

'Okay, but will you at least ask the *velaiti* pilot to fly the plane slowly?'

As one of my favourite authors Paulo Coelho observed, 'If you think adventure is dangerous, try routine; it is lethal.' I wanted to tell her that, but she looked at me with such innocence that I simply wanted to embrace her tight.

'Yes, before we fly I will knock on the cockpit door and convey him your message, don't you worry now.'

I had called Krish a week prior but he had the flu, so he was not able to meet me.

'Last thing you need is to catch some bug before you set off on the most important journey of your life. And you are so fragile, anything gives you a cold, even a melted ice cream,' he had mentioned.

I still hoped he would come to bid me farewell at the terminal, at least. Or perhaps stop me.

My disappointment lessened when I heard the slight wistfulness in his voice, 'I am so proud of you, Bawi, but hey, we're all gonna miss you. Merry Christmas in advance.'

We? Why couldn't he simply say 'I'?

And then he dropped a nuclear bomb. He was leaving for a backpacking expedition across India for an indefinite period, something he had been planning for years.

'But what about your work? How can you just quit?'

I argued, though it was not my place to decide. The music business was highly competitive and ever-changing and he was still to find a permanent foothold in it.

'Bawi, I need new ideas and a different rhythm in my life. I need to find myself. Turnovers, profits and losses I will deal with later. This might help me. Some retrospection and reinvention, a rehab of sorts. Will be back with better lyrics, compositions, poetry…I don't get space at home to even think; you know how it's been.'

Of course, I did. His life was more complicated than a Parsi bharuchi akoori (scrambled eggs prep with dry fruits). A semi-depressed mother, a rebellious sister and the memory of being deserted by a father. I could not even imagine how tough it had been for him to keep it all together while growing up. Even though I had struggled with weight issues and approval all my life, I had a loving family who catered to every whim of mine. Touchwood!

It then struck me that I would not get to see him when I returned from Zurich and that was a bummer.

'How long, ya?' I asked him, feeling a bit knotted up that he was zipping off like that into deep dark forests and who knows where else.

'A year at least, Bawi, maybe more but I will call you wherever you are in the world, from wherever I am, every time I find a pay phone. I have to do this—for my sanity. Luckily my Baroda Masi, you know Zarine Masi, right? She agreed to come over for the next few months to help out at home. She just lost her husband, so it will be a good change for her too.'

So, he was not even taking his old Nokia with him? I could foresee the year ahead already.

Me clicking photos with my new Canon gifted by my dad, atop the London Eye and the Alps; shopping my heart out in ritzy malls and designer outlets in Dubai; guzzling overpriced wine and flavoured aperitifs in some trendy al fresco dining place overlooking Harrods or the Canary Wharf, and Krish nestled in a snug sheet under the expansive Milky Way at some remote location, happy and content in his solitude. I guess a certain 'darkness is needed to see the stars'. (Nod to Osho again.)

Pick me, choose me, love me.

But he did not and as per destiny, I joined the rest of the enthusiastic recruits on the flight to Zurich.

The gang at Starrybuzz had been elated and a tad envious, when I put in my papers—I was living their dream.

'Your dearest SRK, we believe, travels by Air International all the time. Drop us a note when you pop open a bottle with him.'

My sub editor Andy had teased.

And as the Airbus kissed the runway goodbye and propelled into the air at 12:06 a.m. sharp, my heart gave a huge leap.

If the cards happen to be correct again, then maybe a foreign city will bring me brighter luck in love. If not in Zurich, then London or Dubai. My very own SRK—my real-life hero. And then this ridiculous one-way fixation for the pain in the ass—Krish Aryan will end, once in for all.

I thought to myself as I wiped a suspended salt drop off my face, watching the Mumbai vista disappear. As Coelho aptly puts it, 'If you're brave enough to say goodbye, life will reward you with a new hello.'

Farewell, old friends and flames. Hello, brand new beginnings and adventures.

12

Moody Crab Meets Two Lionesses

The night flight to Zurich, on which the entire lot of the crew was booked in business class, held the promise of a good rest before we landed at our destination the next morning.

Fortunately, I had a window seat. I had never taken such a lengthy flight journey before and hoped to sleep through it all, so I could give my best in the upcoming classes and courses.

After take-off, I scanned around the lively group of strangers who would be my batchmates for the next few weeks and probably my colleagues for life. There were 18 in all, including me. I hoped and prayed that they would be a nice bunch. I recognised a few faces from the interviews. One was this absolutely gorgeous looking, below shoulder length, wavy, auburn-haired girl with God-carved features, perfect eyebrows and shapely legs.

I remember her sitting next to me in the group discussion round and carrying herself with such finesse and poise that I looked like a baked potato in front of her. Surprisingly, we had been the only ones in that group that had got through the final round of interviews with nothing in common between us except a red scarf.

She had even waved at me and smiled brightly as she settled down on her seat in the same row but the other side of the aisle. Dolled up like a Hollywood star, in white palazzo pants with a baby pink waistcoat over an off-white ribbed tube top, she could pass off as a dusky Julia Roberts easily. I was a bit intimidated and awestruck all at once.

There is no way I could be her friend.

I liked her though.

I wondered if anybody in that herd could be a friend, they all seemed so stuck up and pencil thin!

A far cry from what I was even though I had lost oodles of fat to rise to the occasion, size 10 if you please from a 16 plus but I was still a lot curvier than most.

The fullest bodied in every room, like always, why Khodaiji? Why couldn't you have blessed me with better genes?

Pulling my shirt lower over my black trousers, afraid of someone noticing my flabby anatomic structure and passing a catty remark or two, I sipped a Virgin Mary and continued to observe the hustle bustle around me. The flight attendants were getting ready for the midnight service, distributing sleeper suits and small bottles of water and making beds for passengers who wanted to grab a few winks without dining, and patiently answering the call bells. They were grace under pressure.

A shiver ran down my spine.

What have I got myself into? What if the pounds pile back on magically and I don't fit into any uniform size? What if I spill scorching coffee over a passenger and get sued?

What if my heels give in under my weight like that yellow swing in that play area had when I was eight? What if I'm not cut out for this life at all and writing is my only true calling?

Self-doubts. Self-sabotage. Self-damage. I seemed to be on this permanent trial mode.

While writing, I could be anything without thinking twice about squeezing into fitted skirts, wearing push up bras, owning a pair of toned legs, setting a perfect hairstyle and sliding gracefully through narrow aisles.

Writing was a natural gift conferred upon me, serving others skilfully was going to be a different ball game altogether.

'Snobs? Like the rest of 'em huh? '

A voice cut through the quiet cabin.

We were destined to be co-travellers that night; her elbows occupying more space than they should, almost scraping mine, but I had tried not meeting her eyes when she tried to start the conversation.

Her insolent smile was enhanced by high cheekbones and a curly ringlet hairstyle suited her petite frame and thin neck. A bit too spunky for my taste and to be honest, slightly daunting too.

Just as we took off, 10B had removed gum from her mouth and stuck it under her seat.

Cringe. CRINGE.

Now 32,000 feet up in the air, she was nudging me hard to get my attention almost making my juice fall out of the glass.

'Are you impaired? I'm talking about that snooty bootie at 10D. Her name is Coco. Behaves like she's fallen from cloud nine. Attitude!'

She was pulling a sour face at the beautiful girl I liked.

'Aliya Sood.'

She shoved her right hand forcefully into my right one, and jostled it hard.

'Kai Juicewalla.'

It was hard to ignore her, though I drew my hand back in a hurry, almost elbowing her in irritation.

Too direct and sprightly for me, not my cup of coffee.

Are you serious? *Juicewalla?*

She began to laugh aloud.

I glared at her.

Who does she think she is?

'Sorry,' she put her hand on her heart, 'I mean you are having juice and then you said Juicewalla, so it's funny…'

I did not know whether to be offended or simply go along with her warped joke.

I noticed that she had swiftly downed a beer already and was flagging for another—the night was young for this l'il spontaneous weirdo.

'So what do you think about hoity-toity Paris Hilton with her pouty lips, out there?'

I snubbed her again. This girl Coco was poetry in motion and even though she was way out of my league, she had this positive vibe about her and had been the only decent one who had thrown a genial glance my way when we were settling in.

I stared through the window, lost in thoughts, wondering what my family and friends were doing. I was missing them already. Mommy would be teary-eyed as it was my first Christmas away from home and Daddy had mentioned that he would look out for my airplane and wave from our balcony, before calling it a night. (I swear I saw him through my tiny window.)

I had got in touch with DA the day before, promising to bring him one of his vibrant neck cravats from my first trip abroad.

He had sent me a huge farewell bouquet with a tender note:

Dearest Kai,

We discover our best life when we are willing to step outside our comforts.

We can make our dreams come true only when we are willing to leave the shore.

You may have not been the leading lady in my movies but your million-dollar smile always captured my heart.

But now it's time for you to fly, learn new things and explore unchartered territories.

Never forget this—that we are only as young as we feel.

And who knows it better than me?

Yours,

D A

Sigh!

He had set the bar of charisma way too high for all my future heart-applicants. He had the spirit of a 21-year-old lad with countless dreams to achieve despite his age.

Our MAD (mutual admiration) society had always been a big question mark for those who knew of our unconventional friendship, but there are some bonds that are too precious to be labelled. DA's and mine was one of those.

'And we have another mega bitch in the house. A Miss Juice-Wall-Ahhh.'

I heard my neighbour gripe again.

Now she got my goat.

'An attention disorder?'

I turned to her and gave her one of my snappy one-liners, which I saved for such occasions.

'Well, now you talking! Finally! Sorry. Actually I am a nervous flier, yeh I know, how ironic, but I am gonna be pissed drunk by the time we reach Swaziland and I may need someone to carry me off…and since you are the lucky one stuck with me for the night, who better than you?'

'Geez, how big-hearted of you to pick me.'

Her uncanny resemblance to feisty Simran kept popping into my mind.

Coco got up and opened the overhead bin, a Hermès tote popped out while she tried to remove a set of clothes, which I guessed was her PJ's for the night.

'Ufff! Miss Fancy Pants needs another change, look, look!'

Junglee Aliya was even louder than the last time.

I closed my eyes, hoping Hermès gal had missed it. I did not need a hater on the trip, being away from loved ones for the first time was hard enough.

Coco returned from the washroom, in deep red wine-coloured velvet tracks and a matching hoodie, even in her night suit she could pass off as one of *Vogue*'s cover girls.

I had not even thought of carrying a change for the night like most had, which was a big mistake because I would meet our airport welcoming committee looking shabby and grungy under my thick black overcoat.

Aliya voluntarily vomited out several details about herself in less than 12 minutes. She was a tenacious Leo, originally from Bengaluru but would live as a paying guest in Mumbai once we returned; she was madly in love with this jobless photographer called Amrish Grover and planned on tying the knot with him as soon as she made some bucks with her new job.

Did I look *interested*? Hell NO!

Our cabin lights were set to a notch lower, so the business class passengers who had paid a pretty package for their seats earned maximum rest before they disembarked eight and a half hours later. A couple of attendants tiptoed across to the ones who were awake, asking them if they would like a quiet dinner and another bevvy.

Just when I was trying to make up my mind between an eggplant lasagna or a paneer makhani from the menu, a tall figure loomed over us and she did not look happy at all.

Damn! It was Paris Hilton, uhhh...Coco.

'Don't you two hellcats have anything better to do at this hour of the night than take potshots at me?' she asked, her hands folded in front of her chest.

I was about to open my mouth and tell her that I had been dragged involuntarily into the one-sided conversation and that I did not even know this batty, catty chick next to me but Aliya swooped in.

'Actually it was me. This holier-than-thou Parsi girl wanted to change the topic each time I had something tactless to say about you.'

Coco stood there, not knowing what to do.

So, this nut job Aliya Sood could be trusted after all. *Hmmm.*

Coco must have had the same thought as I, for she plopped herself on Aliya's footrest, whispering to us, 'Actually I am damn bored too, can I join you girls? We can find another target. How about Miss Peaches and Cream two rows ahead of us? She rammed into me in the security queue at the airport and hit her *sasta* purse on my head.'

Aliya stared at her open-eyed.

'No way! Will smack her hard before we get off this jet with my cheaper luggage. Promise you.'

Coco and I burst out laughing and I was transported to my years in college, not that long ago, where such predestined friendships had been designed around the most unlikely of odds.

'But seriously is Coco like your real name, not some pet name like Monu or Babloo?'

Aliya was not sparing her either.

'What's with both your families, man? Did they hate you?'

She looked at us, rolling her big brown eyes, which actually were very pretty.

Coco did not seem to mind, she seemed easygoing, now that we were all some kind of a gang.

An older, large-framed blonde attendant marched towards us, curtly instructing Coco to return to her seat.

'But the seat belt signs are off,' Coco pointed out, 'so am gonna stay put.'

The crew member turned her back and stomped off, mumbling something derogatory about Indian passengers being 'menaces on board' or to that effect.

'Will sort out "Blondie" later too!'

Aliya barked again, thankfully Blondie was out of range; making Coco and me both chuckle.

'So do you want to hire me as your hit man, Madame Coco Chanel? You so need one; you seem to have pissed off the entire humanity today.'

Aliya jibed, downing her third or fourth beer.

We spent the next few hours staying up, chattering like excited school chums and giggling, much to the irritation of our fellow passengers and crew around us, but there was no written law that could stop us. We made grand plans 'to dissect the steamy pilot's ass-ets' as he had strolled out of the flight deck for his hourly security walk around the plane, which was more like a catwalk. He gave us a liberal view of his taut butt in his tight trousers amplified by a narrow slim waist. We had to physically stop Aliya from subtly grazing his bottom, as he went past us, eyeing Coco for a few extraaa secs.

'You will get the sack, idiot!' I said.

'I want him *in the sack*,' she countered.

'What about your toy boy back home?' Coco asked.

'Oh, for Christ sake, he is like only 20 months younger to me dude and no harm window shopping, right?' Aliya declared, 'but did you see him check you out Coco? I observed that he trotted straight to the lavatory after that. Probably for a quick arm workout…'

I lightly punched Aliya on her shoulder to tone it down. I had not had *palak* juice (yucks) for lunch and one *katora* of dal only for dinner for the last two months, just to be fired that quickly from the job.

Coco seemed unaffected by any of the male attention around her.

'That fine piece of ass is mine for grabs too,' I said, as if the pilot was a giant Toblerone bar, who had no say in the matter.

'All yours, babe. He could be your first mile high casualty,' Coco teased, winking.

'Huh?'

She shook her head.

'Kai, don't tell me you don't know about that. Anyone who fools around on a plane, they then automatically get upgraded into, "The Mile High Club"!'

'*Achcha*!'

This was fresh gravy to my ears.

A romp in midair? Risqué but tempting.

'Another one to add to my bucket list of fantasies then,' I said, beaming.

Rumi's wise words echoed in my mind: *Forget safety. Live where you fear to live. Destroy your reputation. Be notorious.*

These two newbies were right up my alley.

'What else do you have in your *baaldi* (bucket)? ' Aliya asked, yawning loudly.

'Hmmm, let me think, I guess Paris, Spain, Italy, an Alaskan cruise, writing a book, a romance of a lifetime, a 36-24-36 figure, a Booker or a Pulitzer prize. An endless night of passion with SRK.Yum-yum!'

They listened carefully to my blabbering, agreeing to most but scoffing at the SRK bit.

(Bollywood was 'too pretentious' for Aliya and Coco was a fan of the 'intellectual Aamir'.)

They shared their To-Do dream lists too. Italy, Spain and finding true love were common for all three of us.

'Someday we shall have it all...' Coco said, clinking her champagne flute to ours.

Not wanting to summon the cheesed-off crew members once again, she had swayed over to the galley earlier and brought back three glasses of bubbly with her in a tiny tray.

I use the word swayed because Coco, in Aliya's words, had a natural '*jhatak* and *matak*' when she walked. Another lioness. I was amused. Two Leos completely poles apart and I, an unpredictable, moody crab, right in the middle of this crazy duo.

'Someday...' we chorused back, as Steamy Pilot passed us again, very stoked.

Tightening his belt purposefully and strutting like a pompous peacock, he brushed against our seats and leaning over our heads, hissed in a throaty voice, 'Someday, my dazzling Indian beauties, someday. I shall be waitin'...'

We cracked up so hard that the passengers in the back row threatened to get us off-loaded.

Steamy Pilot vamoosed of course and Coco finally went back to her seat. It felt as if we had been separated at birth and reunited on an aircraft.

As we landed effortlessly into Zurich airport a short kip later, I felt like a zombie barely having caught a wink. Coco had redone her hair, switched back to her designer avatar, touched up on the greasepaint, immaculate foundation, two-tone blusher, Christian Dior lipstick, the whole enchilada. (A far cry from the blotchy blush and flashy silver eye shadow I applied with my fingers.)

Aliya was peppier and sprightlier than ever, as she declared in a booming voice, 'You know what they say, right? A man is judged by how he drives. And it's been one smoooooth landing.'

I could already envision a frisky reindeer prancing over the Alps.

13

Krish, Deewana Tujh Sa Nahin

2009

Being a flight attendant kept me very busy but flying off to fast-paced Dubai, eclectic UK or picture-perfect Switzerland made the insomnia, erratic family life and the sore muscles worth it.

Everything goes like clockwork in the airline industry, not a minute here or there. From leaving your residence for the airport at inhuman hours to reaching your hotel at destination, every second is accountable. There is no room for any late-latif excuses, unless you got abducted on the way or there is a serious technical delay (even then you walk to the airport to catch the flight, if you have to, kidding).

I was not used to that kind of regimentation and discipline, so it took me a while to adjust. And I thoroughly disliked the cosmetic ambush on me. It is probably easier to teach a crow to sing than to trust me with an eyeliner.

Ever since my first official flight in March 2008, I had nurtured the ambition of bumping into SRK.

I had memorised almost every filmy dialogue of his and had them ready to recite, lest my boon got granted.

My foolproof plan of action: The superstar would enter the aircraft, I would greet him at the boarding door, then chaperone him to his First Class seat where I would accidently (read intentionally) touch my fingertips over his back, whilst assisting him to remove his jacket. Then tripping over an imaginary obstacle, I would fall over him and apologise profusely.

Cut To: We would both be locked in a tight embrace.

He would croon, '*Tujhe dekha to yeh jaana sanam…*' or something close, his sweet breath tickling my sensitive ears, his stimulating aftershave driving me to the edge and back.

I would lower my eyes and try hard to act my coyest.

He would fall in love with my cute persistence and mesmerising persona.

Nothing after that would stop us from being 'One' until the end of time.

***

Aliya, Coco and I caught up in Mumbai as and when our calendars synchronised or one of the three cities, if our layovers overlapped. Whenever and wherever we met, it was always a gossip fest: who had the hots for whom; who got skunk-drunk in crew lounges; who got laid at layovers; who failed the preflight breath analysers and got bumped off the plane or grounded from the job or both.

Our favourite topic of discussion was our 'all gals' fun holiday that we had been planning since our training days but something or the other had stopped it from materialising. If it was not poor Aliya coping with an unfaithful boyfriend, it was Coco dealing with her parents' divorce. I was in a rather foul and sulky state of mind most of the time too, mostly because Krish seemed to have vanished from the orb without so much as a trace. And without a mobile phone on him, I could not call him up and I had missed a couple of his calls, as I was always travelling.

The only good news was that Navika had *daaka maroed* the ad world and was now seen in almost every fifth ad on television. I could hardly recognise her. I called her up at once, wondering if she would acknowledge me, now that she was this hotshot model and all.

She at once invited me over for lunch at the Madh Island location where she was shooting for a toothpaste ad. We sat in her powder room, toasting with lassis and stuffing jalapeno poppers in our mouths for old time's sake.

'Who says health camp fugitives with severe food rage can't be victorious?' she asked, brushing her teeth quickly before her next shot. 'Damn it's a paste advert and I have stuff between my teeth!'

'I am so happy for you Navs. Kudos to you! May you achieve all your goals.'

'Ditto, my food buddy Kai, ditto!'

***

2009 stormed in under pressure with some heavy duty coaxing by my parents to attend a family friend's son's wedding. For me, dressing up and enduring such functions is more painful than sitting on a cactus plant, butt naked. But Mom and Dad had their usual unoriginal dialogues ready, '*Kharab lagse, ne log su bolse?* (It looks bad. What will people say?) These people have graced us with their presence at all of ours.'

'We haven't had many. Moreover, they come for free food. Get real.'

'Two navjotes, four anniversaries…'

'Ughhh. Stop counting, Dad! I will come, but don't expect me to be fake-nice to people or all smiley–smiley.'

Of course it had been one of the greatest mistakes of my life where I had to face the music in the form of Parsi snoop dogs who spoke ill about my career, all the while making jealous and audacious probes into how I had bagged such a coveted job when the stereotype around air hostesses being 'slim beauties floating in the sky', indicated otherwise.

'No doubt you have lost weight, *jhootoo su kanu bolu?* (Why should I lie?) But air hostess? Tch Tch. Aren't they supposed to be more shapely, taller and more beautiful? You know what I mean no, my pet?' purred our good old Dragon Dolly, blowing off my morale and self-worth in a single verbal karate chop.

'Did you pull some high power strings, those Mallya–Wallya types or was it your daddy's purse strings?' Vampire Veera served the next round of venom.

'My G-strings! You know those tiny chuddies we cool youngsters where, na?' I retorted, making them and a couple of others around very, very uncomfortable, much to my mirth.

That evening after I had exploded to dust, I swore to stay clear of such functions and tyrants or The Bawa Nazis.

Soon after, Coco, Aliya and I were chilling in a hotel room with cold beers, on a warm April Dubai day. I had just landed from Mumbai and Aliya and she were on the second day of their three-day Mumbai–Dubai schedule.

'It's been over a year since we first met and if we don't vacay this year, we never will. So let's stop overthinking and just head off somewhere. Kai, your 25th is a couple of months away. We all have got some leave left. You girls shout out a destination each and let's peg those. Now!'

Coco decided to take charge.

Aliya and I were quick to agree, she was right; there was never a more perfect time to have a blast, than the present moment. Who knew what tomorrow would bring? Or worse, what if tomorrow *never* comes?

'I think it's an awesome idea and we are all single and ready to mingle, this time…'

Aliya was heartbroken but it was nice to see her try to keep her spirits high.

We were all a bit listless, burnt-out and jaded. Yes, we travelled much more than an average Joe would in their lifetime and explored the curves and corners of three extremely popular and exciting destinations, but flying on duty and going on a holiday were two completely different things.

Coco reminded us, 'Achcha listen. We are not doing this to pick up guys, we are travelling to broaden our horizons.'

Aliya and I looked at each other and burst out laughing.

'Blah blah blah….'

'Sure Mumma…'

How we ragged her.

'Yeah, we shall leave our vags back in India in an iron vault,' Aliya said, winking at me.

'We will need Schengen visas, you tarts. Our crew ones won't work. So, let's get that done asap,' Coco said, rolling her eyes, shaking her head and giving us both one of her admonishing stares.

'Ding Dong! We're gonna rock until our knickers drop!' Aliya sang.

'Bingo!'

Maybe our girlfriends are our soulmates, and guys are just people to have fun with. Carrie Bradshaw could not have been more right.

Our plan to escape mundaneness was finally on! The sexy city gals from sweltering Mumbai were gonna get those temperatures rising in Barcelona and Rome, desi style!

***

A day before we were all set to leave for my birthday adventure I visited Granny B's Bandra house on my Parsi birthday. It was a stone's throw away from ours. She was busy baking *bhakras and popatjees* for my journey, even packing a dozen of each for the girls. I was not surprised at how perfectly round they turned out despite her trembling 95-year-old hands handling the oven rack. She was in a wheelchair nowadays but still rocked in the kitchen.

'You are a priceless treasure, who is even more beautiful than that heroine, *kaun uti, peli? Jeh pani maan kudi gayee*? (The one who jumped into the water?) *Arrey haan, Kaytayun*! Oh yes, Kaytayun!' she reminded me, pointing to half a dozen chikki boxes of Lonavala's navratan chikki she had kept aside for me to pack.

'I can't take so many. There are weight restrictions. And that actress is Kate Winslet, she played Rose in *Titanic*,' I said, chuckling.

'And no, she didn't jump into the water Granny B. The actor Leonardo DiCaprio did and drowned.'

'Achcha. Achcha. Good it was a man only. But what I am trying to say to you, dikra, is that anyone will be lucky to have a fair and smart *chokree* like you. *Tau koi majano gora ne pakadje, duniya farje, ne hasti, ramti sukhi rheje*! (So catch a nice foreigner, roam the world and smile, play and be blessed!)' she said, as if finding a man on a vacation was as easy as stumbling upon a chair in the dark.

I was surrounded by goras for the last two years and had not managed to click with anyone really. (Barring a coupla naughty kisses with a Greek stranger on a train to the enchanting city of Lucerne on one of my many days out in Switzerland and the harmless passionate snog with a Latino bouncer at a club in Chelsea, London. (Both men, delectably divine.) But on the whole, I had kept my raging hormones in check. I would wait for 'The One', where the midnight sky weaved rainbows and all that jazz.

Doesn't every single living creature have 'a soulmate'? A twin flame? The pop culture had been promoting it loud and clear. And I was sure if I waited long enough, they would show up in some form of transportation, if not racing in a golden carriage, then at least dangling from a hot air balloon.

Unlike most other bawa families, mine was the least conservative of the lot, thankfully. They did not expect me to get hitched 'with a Parsi only'. Maybe because we did not live in the stereotypical Parsi baug, so it was less clannish than let us say Shanaya's and Pari's who were surrounded with folks of the same community.

Granny B was clearing her throat impatiently for she had a small ritual planned. Steering me to her bedroom and making me stand over the chalk (rangoli) in the auspicious shape of seven small fish, in front of the frame of our prophet Zarathustra, she reached out for the *ses* (the silverware set on her prayer table) and pasted a tiny wet kumkum *tilli* (a red dot) and some chokha (uncooked rice) on my forehead. Handing me a dry coconut (a good luck symbol), she pushed a small, white envelope with '*Saal Mubarak* for the 19th July. Best of Luck' written on it in red ink. I bent over to her wheelchair, to receive her kisses, squeezes and hugs.

Suitcase and *bhakras* packed, the only two things left to do was to place a quick call to DA to wish him adieu (we had hardly caught up in recent times, I assumed he was busy with his usual youthful projects and I was following a tight roster) and meet Krish, who was finally back; the day before; just in the nick of time.

We met around 5:30 p.m. at The Shack on the eve of my departure. I had feared that our shack would be occupied by hawkers but it was still empty.

My heart skipped unnumbered beats as I watched him stride towards me with a long, black umbrella cross-bodied around him like he did so with his guitar, whistling a random tune.

I had missed him terribly in the last year and half. I had missed his lopsided grin that played around his bow lips; his slight cleft; his melting chocolate fondue eyes; his playful teasing; his simple ways. I felt his void when I saw budding musicians rocking Covent Garden on a British summer day, or as I revelled in Arabic music admiring the belly dancing of the Middle Eastern beauties of Dubai. I had even imagined singing corny filmy songs and flinging snowballs at him, across ski slopes and having hot chocolate dates that never ran out of conversation as we snuggled together in a cosy log cabin on a soft couch opposite a fireplace atop St. Moritz.

He had a healthy tan and his hair was longer than I remembered, the silver stud on his left earlobe was now a silver ring and he was leaner, as though he had not been eating at all. Suppressing my desire to take him home at once and have my zealous Parsi family overfeed him, I enveloped him with a hearty hug instead and asked in the most casual way I could, 'Hey stranger. Howz it going? You mentioned something about sharing some news?'

Truth be told, my stomach was doing woozy summersaults. I was even wearing one of the many 'lucky' denim mini skirts I owned, that Krish was more than familiar with. They had been used generously to *patao* some guy or the other during college days, and it was a standard joke among the Fab Four.

Despite being inapt for the monsoon season and a public beach, it felt right to wear it that evening.

'Bawi, you are the first one I'm telling…' he began.

Of course I am, who else would it be you adorable gadhera?

The flicker of hope in my heart multiplying by the second.

You have died a thousand times thinking about me, every minute, every hour, every breath and my absence has made your heart fonder and your denial weaker. Admit it.

He took a slight pause. The suspense was killing me.

'Umm, how should I put this? Bawi, I think I am in love.'

So, this is how it feels to finally get what one dreams of?

It felt amazing as well as nerve-racking. My heart was on fire. My entire body seemed to break into a nervous sweat.

*Tra la la. It's happening! Vacation cancelled. 25th birthday to be spent in Krish's arms. Sorry Coco and Aliya. Change of plan. You can f**k off to Europe on your own. I am going to be singing SRK love songs to…*

'So yeah, I met someone on this trip. She is cute as a button, wild-spirited and extroverted. Somewhat like you, I guess.'

He blurted out, a shy smile spread across his pinkish brown lips, words cascading out of his mouth like coins from a just-broken piggy bank.

'I must intro her to the gang. In fact once you are back, let's all do something together.'

He's pulling your leg Kai. Anytime he's gonna yell 'Bluff' and punch your shoulder! It's coming, it's coming…wait for it.

'Her name is Suzie. She is a choreographer. From our city that too; what were the odds of that, eh? I go all the way up north and she has been in Borivali all along,' he gave a chuckle, as he rambled on, 'and you won't believe how we met. I was on my way to this ashram and misplaced my wallet in a bus, when this girl from nowhere lands up in the same bus station I was at to report my lost wallet.'

One, two, breathe, three, four, Yatha Ahu Vairyo.

My mother had once taught me that if you want to hit someone hard across the face in a bout of uncontrollable fury, you must chant the most powerful Parsi *nirang* prayer. It was her tried and tested formula to keep a cool head and God knows how many times she would have needed it, bringing up her two rascals.

You got this, Kai. He has left this Suzie-Loosie thingy inside a cave to rot with venomous snakes or maybe she's tripped and fallen down a mountain and the climax is yet to come. Nothing to worry about. He met her only to realise that he is utterly and butterly in love with you.

'Talk about divine synchronicity, *haan*,' he gave me a hug, completely oblivious to my quivering legs and tingling hands.

Suzie the bitch, Suzie the slut, Suzie's so damn ugly even crows look like swans in front of her.

It was essential that I repeat that to myself, to keep myself from wringing his neck.

'Sorry, I'm being selfish, blubbering about myself and sidetracking you. But it's great to see you after ages, Bawi, you look awesome as always. And I am really glad you are taking a break with your new friends. Hope you have booked your hotels in advance.'

He seemed slightly unnerved with my rather antagonist reaction to his news, making me wonder if he had expected me to throw him a party? A standing ovation perhaps?

'And tell me what's the dope on you? Got that diamond ring? Is Eiffel on the cards?'

Krish was simply being Krish, a best friend to boot. The diamond ring was another old joke between us; all my friends knew that a shiny two-carat solitaire was something I would like to have flickering on my left ring finger in the near future.

'Nothing,' I replied matter-of-factly, trying not to sound as distressed as I felt, using a sneeze to smokescreen the sound of my teeth grinding to their roots in fury and despair.

All I had craved for was a bit of normalcy; a boyfriend—someone to love and be loved by.

Was that too much to ask? But the last couple of years had been a logjam. There were occasional flirtatious encounters with a fascinating stranger or two at nightspots and with an undeniably attractive passenger, who gifted me a Made in China-Breitling, but no breath holding-earth shaking kinda situation there. Not even close.

He placed a hand over my left shoulder as we both stared at the sun setting behind the grey waves.

'Your task is not to seek for love, but merely to seek and find all the barriers that you have built within yourself against it,' Krish whispered into the cruel winds that were stinging my watery eyes.

Rumi, this once, I do not like you. I do not like your musings. And I DO NOT need any more gyan especially from this chump's mouth.

'Don't worry, Bawi, you will find the one. After all, who can't fall in love with you?' he said, squeezing me tighter, making me want to throw up on him even harder.

Oh Khoda, tumhe maree band kai bajaoch? (Oh God, why are you beating my drums?)

How was I supposed to go on a wild girls trip within the next few hours with this shitty news? Why did he return? To knock the wind out of my sails? Sadist! I had foolishly assumed that Krish Aryan was so away with the fairies most of the time that he would not notice any other female energy around him and miss mine. I could easily overlook a fling with a two-plaited village bumpkin rearing sheep on the hills, but this bimbo was not only from my city but also only 40 potholes away from where he lived. That meant, a regular shrew bleating around him on a daily basis.

How dare you backstab me, God?

He had clearly moved on from the last time we had met and I was still in la la land.

Who is surrounded by hot goras and can pick anybody up if she wishes to? ME!

Who has a high-profile job and meets at least 10 potential guys to date in a month? MOI!

Who is the one who has this undying belief in soulmates and pays obnoxious parrots to flip tarots for her? MEEEE!

Not this dimwit, thick as a meatloaf, blind-as-a-bat-human excuse for a man. Then why has he WON?

I had trusted him to go and find nirvana but he returned as a *deewana* instead.

I soaked up the piercing pellets of a dark cloud that split over our heads as we began to walk back to civilisation. Krish hummed some awfully joyful tune in the rain and I was as gut-wrenched as I was drenched. Both forgetting in our intense happiness and misery that we had an umbrella left unopened between us. As my Paulo wisely quoted, 'At every moment of our lives, we all have one foot in a fairy tale and the other in the abyss.' This was definitely the bloody abyss!

XXXSCORE: 420 +6 (insignificant first base snogs of the foreign shores variety) =426.

14

Our Barcelona Catch: Hugh Grant, Brad Pitt and Colin Firth

Not wanting to spoil my birthday week or the trip to Europe for my friends, I made every effort to give all the *gaali galoches* of the world to Krish in my head and move on. I had to turn the page, before my inner joy and hope decayed like a bad cavity.

It began with styling my hair differently, snipping a tiny fringe across my wavy hair which looked a bit misplaced on my roundish face, but I managed to pull it off somehow.

Krish had done nothing wrong, had he? Except for making me crush on him infinitely with his beatific voice, his puppy dog eyes and his disarming smile. Maybe it was time to shove 'the love of my life search mission' out of the door and explore other avenues of sexitement and adventure, which included wild and wicked flings if any came along.

'Being Miss Goody Two-Shoes hasn't earned me any brownie points until now, has it?'

I questioned my old pal Delna over the line who seemed to agree. She had just taken up a new job in Manhattan and was super excited about it, which meant she would give a nod to just about anything.

As Aliya's famous break-off slogan went, 'Sweetheart to get over someone, you gotta get under someone else.' (Not her original thought though.)

Made perfect sense. Krish was living rent free inside my head for way too long and I needed to terminate that lease with immediate effect.

Our first halt was España. We had booked ourselves in the heart of the city at a three-star hotel next to the famous La Rambla in Barcelona for four nights. Oh beautiful Barcelona, with walkways that appeared like rippled water; talented street performers; street traders, including several Indian sellers (Is there even one place in the world that we have not planted our flag on?); open-air cafes and vibrant bars; all buzzing with character and energy with a striking contrast to historic buildings like the Virreina Palace and the Liceu Theatre.

As we ambled through the 1200-metre tree-lined pedestrian street, we fell in love with both the vivacity and the laidback culture of Barcelona. Aliya was making the most of the sun city and freedom by refusing to wear anything but a bikini top with a pair of shorts that barely covered her butt. Coco followed suit and they both looked insanely sensual. I basked in their hourglass glory, relishing the attention they were drawing. The city made us feel so alive.

Physically, the three of us could not be more different. Coco the tallest had rich reddish brown hair and was contoured in all the right places; small-framed Aliya had a firecracker body of her own with curls to die for; and I was alternating between natural frizzy to straight hair, covering up my broader bits waist downwards, switching between my comfy denim minis and deep-slit multi-hued sarongs.

Simran and Zoya would have been green with envy if they saw me then. Simran was somewhere near the Indian border supporting Army widows and simultaneously dealing with a freeloader boyfriend who had dried out her bank account and Zoya was entwined into family obligations.

As for Krish, he probably had his tongue in that foul-breathed Suzie's mouth. Sometimes I fantasised about casting a voodoo spell on the *kutri* (bitch). I had seen a movie once where this young witch had assembled a rag doll out of straw and silk and then did some pretty questionable things to it.

But all in all, I was having a gala time with my super troupers. On the penultimate day of our holiday, we headed to the beach where after parasailing we flung ourselves on the sand with a tiny picnic in place. The pier was studded with travellers and locals enjoying the breeze, the sun, with drinks in hand. We chose a shady spot to avoid uninvited dark patches on our skin.

'Let's not forget our ulterior motive for celebrating my birthday week abroad—a sincere scout for cute and hot "firangi guys",' I reminded them, checking out our vicinity, 'and honestly we need to click better photos than of just scenery, ya. Who wants to look 20 years behind and see cathedrals, statues and hop-on, hop-off buses in our photo albums? What we should carry as a memory is a moonlit boulevard walk with a Mr Unforgettable or a twilight kiss with Mr Right or Wrong whoever comes first.'

'Agreed, need to make some sensational Kodak moments,' Coco nodded, as she applied sunblock over her honeyed body.

'But, I can only see potbellied uncle-types here,' I said, 'where are our potential hot dog men?'

Coco quickly removed some dating rule book which she had been carrying around like the Bible all throughout our trip. Aliya pulled a face as soon as she did that.

'Shut that silly thing, Coco, no book can tell you more about boys than I can.'

Coco did not pay Aliya any attention and read out from it.

'Commandment 2: Meeting men of both character and thrill is a hard task but not impossible. You have to really put yourself out there with dignity yet …'

'Coco, is there a page on how to do a doggy under a shower without slipping?' I asked with a straight face.

Ufff! Coco and her maps, her love manuals, her compasses and her dictionaries.

Aliya snatched the book from Coco's hand and whacked it on her head before sprinting topless into the greenish-blue Mediterranean and shrieking like a *junglee jaanwar,* without a care in the world.

'Yoooohooooo! I'm free. I'm sexy. I'm happieeeeee!'

The city had a couple of nude beaches but this was not one of them. Happy hippy Aliya had conveniently forgotten that. We were so busy pulling each other's legs for the next 15 minutes when Coco suddenly alerted me, 'Ooh la la! Do I see boys in uniform, north east?'

She quickly substituted her long-distance glasses to cooler Ray-Bans, making it rather obvious that we had seen them.

We spotted three firangi hunks surveying us from a distance. All of a sudden, I was body conscious. My four-layered abs were hanging out of a one size smaller white Levis t-shirt and the boys were honing in on us too swiftly to get my beach robe out of my beach bag and save myself.

'Be cool, casual, non-committal,' Coco whispered, quoting once again from that nonsensical book.

Hotties! Finally! The perfect opportunity for hanky-panky.

I wanted to whoop with joy, but I settled for a coy smile. Aliya, who probably had enough of shaking her pots and pans had now arrived on the scene of hope, thankfully with her blue and orange-striped bikini top back on, showing ample cleavage. This reminds me of a quote from Marilyn Monroe, 'The trouble with censors is that they worry if a girl has cleavage. They ought to worry if she hasn't any.' Trust her to always put things in perspective.

We soon found out that Nicolas, James and Peter were sailors in their late-twenties who had anchored at the Port de Barcelona for the weekend.

'See those three babies docked there. You can't miss them,' pointed out burly Nicolas with spiky ginger hair and a strong Kiwi accent, making direct eye contact with me.

Was this an open invitation for the ecstatic night we had been waiting for? Sure, we had flirted with strangers but this was like having Hugh Grant, Brad Pitt and Colin Firth in their late-twenties, at our feet.

'Ours is the one in the middle,' Peter, the darker haired one with more facial fur than the others and a slightly stiff upper lip à la Colin Firth educated us further, '*Millennium Cruiser*. Sounds like a luxury liner but it ain't so. It's all serious stuff.'

James interrupted him hurriedly, pushing back his smooth silky blonde hair, 'But it's not all that serious as it's our last night here. We set sail tomorrow. So would you gorgeous ladies like to boogie with us tonight? There's an open bar just for today and you could even take a dip at the casino if you feelin' lucky.'

(As if he needed to sell us the offer. Their drooly smiles and promising physiques were enough to get us crawling over thin ice to get to that ship, if we had to.)

'We'll think about it,' Coco reverted, a little too enthusiastically, making an obvious beeline for James, who was definitely the long-lost twin of Brad.

We broke into overlapping chatter as soon as they were out of earshot. Aliya and I were vaulting up and down.

'Yoo hoooooo! Open bar in Barcelona, better late than neverrr!'

'*It's raining men, hallelujah, it's raining men, Amen*!

'Cause tonight for the first time, just about half-past ten,

For the first time in history, it's gonna start raining men…'

I began to skip and sing. Nick, the one vibing with me, could easily be mistaken for Hugh Grant's sibling with more intensely tinted hair.

Maybe a bit too loud as three middle-aged women passing by, bearing an uncanny semblance to us 30 years into the future, matched our beat, but in Spanish.

Salud Barcelona!

Coco started again, 'Hey listen up, remember what the commandments advice. Numero 4, clearly states that when you bring out his masculine side by playing a damsel in distress, the dude will come to your rescue. Guys get put off by super alpha women. Extra servings of enthusiasm kill their interest.'

'*Bhaad maan gayu taru* rules *ni* book! (Let your rule book go to hell!) The women who write such books have married their pet hamsters. Hence, they want us all to end up like them.'

I was hopping around like a lovesick teen on the eve of turning 25, full of rejuvenated beans, almost pissing myself with anticipation. It was not like I was desperate for intimacy; I just wanted to feel good about myself once again.

'Stop brainwashing us, Coco,' Aliya said, kicking sand all over us, charged up like an AAA battery, matching my frequency, 'The only mandates we need to practise are fun, flirt and freak out. Stop being such a hypocritical prude. Like we didn't notice you giving that delicious blond package, what's his name, James Bond, a BJ in your filthy mind!'

Coco blushed as she stood up and lunged at us both.

'You vulgar cows!'

'Come on,' I pushed them to hurry up, 'we need to get back to our room and transform into sex bombs for Sailor Night.'

A very desirable dude was on my radar and I was not going to let that ship sail for anything in the world.

***

Back in the room that we shared, I could not stop obsessing about Nick, the chiselled bronze-faced wide-chested seafarer, as I tried on a short, black leather skirt, realising it had been a while since I had felt so attracted to someone and suddenly I found myself wanting to kiss him 'oh so urgently'!

'Earth calling, Kai,' Coco shouted in my ear, bringing me back to our personal fashion parade.

'Lost in Nicky, are you? So how many times did you seduce him and how many babies did you guys make?'

Aliya burst into laughter.

'Two! A bawaji and a gora. Porus and Morris.'

'*Kaminis,* you know I can't stand smelly babies.'

I hurled a shoe between them, good-naturedly.

'Can't help agreeing with Coco on this one. First whiff of single guy beef and you will be dreaming of that proposal atop Eiffel Tower and making kaleidoscopic rainbows out of toilet paper.'

'No, tonight I want to keep all possibilities open without overthinking it.'

I went on to explain, dabbing my glitter eye shadow after wearing a set of oxidized silver bangles. And I meant it.

'Liar, liar, your chuddies are on fire… the sparks between you and the Kiwi seaman were sizzling enough to create a short circuit,' Aliya quipped back, exaggerating as usual. 'And you are hardly the one-night stand type, Kai. You have worn your chastity belt ever since I have known you. And for the record, kissing doesn't count as doing it.'

'Just you wait ladies. I'm gonna be all out there like a freakin' porn star.'

I spoke with great determination, adjusting my B-padded cups from under my mauve lycra top, to aim for a more impressive lift before changing my transparent lenses to cobalt blue contacts.

'Beware Aliya. Our loyal Charlotte is about to transform into smutty Samantha for the night,' Coco enunciated, as she zipped up her tiger print bodycon dress and spun around for approval.

Comparing ourselves to the powerhouse quartet from the *Sex and the City* was one of our preferred pastimes.

'So long as he passes our L-G-W test, we don't care whose finger is in your well, sweetheart…' Aliya said, checking herself one last time in the mirror before we left.

Clad in an eye-catching bra-less bright green halter neck and skin-coloured shorts, she left very little to the imagination.

(L-G-W stood for length, girth and width of the male junk. And FYI for the men who are reading this, you are not the only ones who discuss multiple assets of the female anatomy in locker rooms. We do too and we can get pretty GRAPHIC.)

Our easygoing camaraderie, emblematic rawness and similar tongue-in-cheek humour were a cause of envy for many of our acquaintances and colleagues. In the bitchy and competitive world of the twenty-somethings, we had managed to remain the mad hatters.

The minute we jumped aboard the M.C., we were greeted warmly by our love interests.

Nick showed up with plastic injections which he aimed straight into our mouths. It tasted as sinful as the kamikaze shots from Gusto's back home.

Maybe it was the effect of the shots but Coco seemed to have shed all inhibitions and her 'hard-to-get' façade, as she dug her claws into James, who seemed to be easy game. She had braved through tonnes of personal crap the year before and deserved a digression.

Meanwhile, 'recently single and ready-to-mingle Aliya' was ignoring poor clingy Peter who had started to hover around her more than she could tolerate while Nick took the lead in showing us around the liner. During our mini tour, he slipped his arm around my waist and I felt a cold draught run down my spine—a sign that I was right on track. I needed a solid distraction from the *ulloo* I had left behind and the steamy Kiwi was the answer.

After listening to Nick describe the technicalities of the ship with little interest, we carefully trooped down a steep flight of stairs. I could hear Aliya huffing behind me.

'I'm wearing heels. If I fall and break my head, I will file charges. Now can we please have some fun?'

Aliya clearly had enough.

Nick pushed opened a tiny door to the deck on the landing to what seemed like a shifty underground den. As we stepped in, we were soon drowned by deafening music, hoots of merriment, flickering disco strobes and the waft of booze. Lo and behold we were at the ship's huge discotheque!

'WTF! They have this on these kinds of ships too?'

Aliya screeched in excitement.

Handsome liquor smashed officers, a few bawdy seamen and young plastic women who could neither hold their cocktails nor their boobs inside them, littered the place. Some were doing a drunken version of the '*Lambada*', others were faffing away while a small group shared joints on a corner table.

A tall, wormy-looking guy was doing a MJ moonwalk on the bar top and the smell of smoke and dope overrode Chanel No 5 that I had rubbed all over my 'sensual points' as instructed by Coco. (Commandment 9—always smell irresistible.)

Nick pulled me to the floor in one sweeping motion, his blue eyes blending into my fake blue ones, as George Michael's '*Faith*' thumped across the room.

'You need to loosen up, Kai, come on shake it up, live a l'il.'

My steamy Kiwi stated.

My limbs turned a little wobbly and my heart flapped and fluttered as he leaned closer to me, his hips swinging like John Travolta's, his one hand boldly wrapped around my waist, crushing my lycra and the other sliding brazenly over my butt, which was resting snugly under the tight black leather skirt. Everything he breathed into my ear and slid his hand over had a sexual innuendo to it.

Am I going to have a mini-climax in the heart of a ship's watering hole?

His kamikaze and weed-soaked breath over mine, added to his allure. I half-shut my eyes. The unconcealed anticipation was driving me wild. When nothing happened after a few seconds, I opened my eyes slowly.

No, no, no…NAHINNNNN!

Nick was gone and I was standing alone, literally and painfully moving my lips like a goldfish in the middle of the dance floor.

This can't be happening. My guardian angels can't be on chutti, just when I need them.

My heartbeats accelerated in sheer panic mode and I did not dare look around to see who had been privy to my humiliation.

What was supposed to be a night of unending escapades was turning into another ghastly conspiracy of the universe to make me feel shitty.

Why Khodaiji, why! Am I not good enough for him?

I could have sworn from the extremely warm welcome I had received from his skintight jeans that we had been on the same page unless he had stuffed a carrot in there.

Why would he? *Should I simply jump over the railings of this dinghy and plunge to sweet death*?

I quickly began to look around for an exit to some deck. Anything was better than being the world's biggest loser. And as luck would have it my gals were nowhere to be seen, they had clearly better things or people to do than babysit their *bechari* friend.

Oh Dadaji, send me to my cardboard box again—gotta crawl in there and dissolve.

'I've been meaning to tell you
I've got this feelin' that won't subside
I look at you and I fantasize
You're mine tonight
Now, I've got you in my sights

With these hungry eyes
One look at you and I can't disguise
I've got hungry eyes
I feel the magic between you and I...'

I kept tapping my feet and mouthing the words of '*Hungry eyes*' to keep up the sham of enjoying myself, with or without a dance partner.

And then, like a beacon of light at the end of a very dark tunnel, Nick re-appeared with two glasses in hand.

'Sorry doll, thought we both needed another trip,' he carefully handed a tipple over to me, 'before we smash it with some LSD.'

Surely, he meant LCD. It was this new technology for television, I had overheard my Dad talk about it with Mom. But I was so relieved upon seeing him that I did not bother correcting him and hauled myself straight on to him, shooting a wet smacker right across his ruddy lips.

After a substantial amount of guzzling, necking and tonguing on the floor, I noticed that Coco and James had reappeared from somewhere and they were going at it like starved woodpeckers Coco's, whose legs were around James's manly torso like a python, was getting her neck fiercely bitten by him, giving an overgenerous view of her vag to the entire cadet squad.

'Get a room, guys!'

I shouted across the room afraid they would both combust like two shooting stars.

All of a sudden, we were interrupted by loud cheering, thumping and hailing on the starboard side of the outer deck overlooking the harbour, making Nick and me dash towards it, with Coco and James following us.

'Me me me…'

I heard voices.

'Indian invasion.'

I heard another.

'Oh for the Luv of Pirates, it's your sexy friend Al-eee-yah and she is topless!' Nick shouted and began to excitedly jump up and down, applauding with the crowd; with the music merging into the milieu. I craned my neck towards the direction he was pointing.

What the hell is he talking about?

I could not help letting out a huge gasp when I saw my 'sexy friend' balancing on two bar stools, legs apart, pouring different liquors from a wide array of bottles she had managed to procure, into the beakers of overzealous sailors who had their mouths open wide enough for the entire country of Spain to pass through them.

'Now, that's one nasty chick. I bet you can't beat that!'

My squeeze for the night challenged me.

Maybe I was destined to do the walk of shame a few minutes later but I was not going to be a stick in the mud and just stand there, get poo-poohed by my date and not have some juicy anecdotes to take back for my friends and family (excluding parents, aunts, uncles).

Enough of being Krish's 'Fun-loving bawi', enough of being everyone's 'Bubbly Kai', enough of posing as Granny B's 'Perfect Princess'.

As plastered as I was, Coelho as usual, always came through for me—'Everything tells me that I am about to make a wrong decision, but making mistakes is just a part of life. What does the world want of me? Does it want me to take no risks, to go back to where I came from because I didn't have the courage to say "yes" to life?'

'You asked for it cupcakes,' I winked at him seductively before kicking off my heels and marching towards Aliya, who gave me a cheery 'hey Kai' and liberally pumped some awful-tasting liquid into my veins.

Now that I was sufficiently stacked, I was ready to notch it up. I drink not only to make others more interesting, but also myself.

Grabbing on to the nearest long pole-like structure that held some sort of cloth at its apex, which may have been a maritime nautical flag, I tried to outcry the noise around me, 'Let's get the show on the road baby…'

Not sure what my next move was, other than trying my luck with amateur pole dancing, I circled around its narrow circumference, determined to finish what Aliya had started. I could see Coco's horrified expression at a distance; she was pressing her nose into James's hard chest probably wishing the vessel to be capsized instead.

'Go go…'

I could hear the swarm of male testosterone chant in unity. The music from the discotheque got louder and was now spilling over the deck too. The audience got divided into two halves. On the one hand, Aliya was doing a shimmy with her perfect pair of hooters and on the other; I was dangling on a pole as if it were the last thing left on planet earth.

Whoa! Are they applauding me?

Encouraged by the sudden boost of adulation, I wriggled my right hand inside my tight top and (after a bit of struggle) just like a magician who cleverly pulls a rabbit out of his hat, off came my own purple M&S balconette bra.

'Ahoy! Anyone here thinks I'm boring?' I asked, spinning my balconette like a lasso.

The crowd went berserk.

'Hear hear! Give us a souvenir to take home.'

'Aye aye, pour some sugar on us ladies. Encore!'

'Girl-on-girl action, bring it on!'

But my satin underwire bra had a mind of its own. It slipped out of my swirling palm and landed straight on a bearded man's head, who promptly stuffed it in his shirt in immense gratitude and rolled himself a fatty as a prize.

The title track of *Full Monty* blared in the background and inebriated crude voices filled the air, 'Bullseye Captain'.

There was boisterous tooting and whistling from everywhere. If there was ever a moment in time that Granny B would disown me, it would surely be this one. And just as I was milking my Chippendales moment, there was a frenzied ovation on the other side which made my spectators to move away from me.

God save the ship!

Aliya was twerking and the only thing between her and her fans was her shimmery g-string. She was the winner of the night, fair and square but I got my reward too.

Nick rushed towards me, crushing himself into me, claiming his territory with an urgent kiss.

'You were burning it up there baby, I almost messed my pants,' he said, triumph written all over his face.

He began to gyrate all over me now, inhaling and exhaling in uneven breaths, as though a furnace had ignited inside him.

'So what say peaches, how 'bout we take this to my private cabin? Got a stash for us. You ready to ride a spaceship tonight?' Nick asked in-between licking my face like a hungry mongrel.

But as piping hot from the oven my red velvet cupcake was and as buzzed I was on passive weed and alco slugs, Nick's last line threw me off balance.

What the hell is he talking about? *Stash*? *Space-what? UFO*?

And then it hit me!

Sure I would have liked to gloat to my buddies back home about a summer fling or my recent act of bravado but manifesting into a junkie was not part of the grand scheme of things.

'Hardcore drugs? Over my dead body!'

I exclaimed loudly and stepped back.

'Go lick the marijuana off the floor instead.'

A befuddled and furious Nick returned it with a very vocal, 'You third world cock-teaser.'

There was only one thing left to do before I called it a night. And so with my head held high, though every bit woozy and uncoordinated, I gave him a middle finger in front of his mates.

'Nick, you are just another prick!'

I heard myself scream as I stormed out of the barge.

***

The 20-minute shortcut to the hotel took over an hour and was more eventful than it should have been. It included throwing up thrice on the way, kicking an empty can (unintentionally of course) on a tramp who chased me all the way down the road and forgetting my room number. By the time I hit the sack, I was exhausted, dehydrated, famished and distressed. I needed a hug, some TLC (tender-loving-care) and a shoulder to cry on.

I hoped the gals would make it back in time for our flight to Italy the next day or else I would have to call and remind them on their Indian numbers, which we kept with us for emergency situations.

It was almost 4 a.m. back home. Using my global calling card, I tried Shanaya first. But afraid my aunt or uncle would answer and give me a sermon on manners, I quickly cut the line. Simran was too busy saving the world and Zoya's husband would have a fit if I bothered them that late.

Should I try Krish?

His bedroom was at the far end of his house. Of course, I could only tell him jiffs of it—Nick would be mostly eliminated from the chat.

Don't do it, Kai. For once, listen to your mind and not your heart.

What I had expected was a sleepy hello. What I got was a crisp, female voice, 'Yes, Krish's residence.'

Who the hell was that? His mother or sister would never say 'Krish's residence' and that too at that hour, and *that too* in such a chirpy voice. And then I heard that haunting voice in the backdrop which I would recognise even if I had dementia, 'Whozaat honey buns?'

I instinctively slammed down the receiver, wishing the phone cradle was her head.

Suzie boyfriend chor!

She had moved in with my Krish lock, stock and barrel.

Kasam se, I will make Saali Suzie Floozie regret the day she was born.

I started squeezing and pounding my pillow pretending it to be the bimbette's wiry neck, until the feather and cotton stuffing started falling out. I passed out without changing into my jammies, the pungent pot smell still integrated into my hair and clothes. The last thing I remember uttering was something on the lines of, 'those tarts are getting lucky and my life is just yucky'.

XXXSCORE= 434

15

A Very Happy Birthday to Me

'Chillax. Shaddup. Stop overdramatising it and busting my brains out. Right now, I have a massive migraine from a crazy hangover...'

Aliya actually had the audacity to reprimand us as our aeroplane took off for Rome on a late July afternoon. We did not indulge her *ghela gaada* (nonsense) this time. Her latest revelation had us worried.

On the way to the airport, Aliya had spilled some beans about the previous night. She had pitched her tent in the second-in-command's suite along with two middle-aged first officers and a young second officer. She remembered little else though, apart from a contingency of a Turkish woman in the mix.

It was all very well to go overboard with one random guy but two or three, maybe four nameless faces and that too without protection? It was the epitome of foolishness and unsound judgement.

'Were you blasted? Buzzed on coke? Date raped?'

Coco and I were very concerned about the repercussions of these erotic escapades that Aliya continued to be nonchalant about.

'Don't be such sourpusses! We just sparked some doobies and I explored my options at the sausage fest. The more the merrier they say, right?'

We looked at her, not sure whether to slap her or kill her, or both. Coco and I had decided to call an intervention for her as soon as we reached Mumbai.

'All pretty well-hung I must confess.'

She was clearly taking great pleasure in psyching us further.

'*Gheli che ke*? What if you contract some disease?'

I was almost yelling now, paranoid that her reckless rebound would cost her more than what it was worth. Aliya was going through a challenging time with her on-off philanderer toolbag of a boyfriend back in India. I understand that, but last night was as irresponsible as it got. We all seemed to have a dating pattern, the introduction passage in Coco's rule book was turning out to be right.

Like Aliya was a bad boy magnet; Coco usually had them falling hook, line and sinker for her; Simran, like me, attracted the losers and dingbats of all age groups, moulds and sizes; Zoya one could not really say, she had barely experienced more than one and a quarter of a man though she had hit upon a goldmine nevertheless.

That morning, Coco was decorated in 15 love bites (yes, we counted) though she had not gone 'all the way' with her Australian find James Donahue and all they did was exchange life stories right into the wee hours of the morning; he then bought her a coffee and a warm bagel and cream cheese breakfast at the pier and dropped her back to the hotel like a thorough gentleman.

As for me, my birthday was hardly a day away and our plans were up in the air, what with Aliya giving us cardiac arrests and I, having to deal with my recent disappointments in the form of a stoned seadog and a kamini playing house-house with my best friend (eternal love interest).

The seatbelt sign flashed over our heads and the crew prepared for landing at Rome's Fiumicino Airport, but my thoughts were all over the place and then it hit me. I had rarely celebrated my birthday without my family. It was a tradition to start the day with sweet sev (sweetened brown vermicelli) or ravo (sweetened semolina) loaded with dry fruits followed by homemade lunch where mommy dearest would whip up the auspicious dhun daar (dal rice), tikho mitho patio (a sweet and spicy gravy prep) and chutney eeda na pattice (egg chutney pattice).

Dad would rise at the crack of dawn and go to Tata Agiary to be part of the *maachi* (a prayer ritual conducted by a priest). Mom would hang torans on every door of our house for good luck. Ash would rib me about growing another year older and stupider. Granny B did her usual *dhoom dhaam* on my *roj nu* (Parsi) birthday by insisting I bathe in *doodh phool* (rose petals milk), which was a tradition only for young children but she did it nevertheless.

The Parsis celebrated two birthdays—one according to the Parsi calendar which is the '*roj nu birthday*' and one according to the Roman calendar. So double the fuss and twice the *dhamaal*!

'Let's find out if the myth about Italian fellas being unstoppable jaguars in bed is true.'

Aliya's shrill voice crudely broke through my delicate reminiscing, causing a sleeping infant behind us to wake up and break into distressing cries.

Miss Sood's temper seemed to have cooled off and she was smiling at us once again.

'And let's have another orgy! Who's in with me this time?'

She announced grandly just as the flight touched down, unnerving the old rabbi and his companion seated in the diagonal row so much so that they grabbed their belongings and scurried out of the aircraft as soon as the doors opened before we had a chance to say 'Amen'.

***

Our room in Rome was far more sophisticated than the matchbox in Barcelona. It had a bathtub, a complimentary breakfast spread of butter croissants, eggs to order, French toast, seasonal fruits, a camembert, edam and cheddar cheese platter and fresh orange and pineapple juice.

After rambling around the ancient city to get a feel of its rich history, Aliya and Coco took me for an exclusive wine and dine session at Buon Pranzo, a swish Italian joint to usher in my birthday.

They were big on birthdays in Italy and the restaurant had not spared any effort in making it memorable for me, by sending us an array of their specials—a 16-inch quattro formaggi, pumpkin and ricotta ravioli, gnocchi alla romana, creamy mushroom linguine, seafood risotto (which I skipped of course) garlic dough balls and focaccia with olive drizzle. A feast for a queen!

An hour to midnight, we opened our second bottle of Rosé champagne, courtesy two hunks on the opposite table smiling encouragingly at us. The gals presented me with a small satin box. It had an elegantly cut Swarovski-embossed cherub popping out from it.

'May the next little package you receive have that much desired ring inside it,' I read out aloud from the tiny lavender card stuck on it.

And just when it could not get any more heart-rendering, they began to sing happy birthday at the stroke of midnight, with three cute *camerieri* (waiters) blending into our intimate affair—one thrumming a banjo, the other jingling a tambourine and the third carrying a tiramisu cake, lit up by a thin red candle.

And just as I was counting my blessings while blowing my candle, a huge hand caressed my shoulders gently from behind, almost startling the chuddies off me. A beefy, muscular, chestnut-haired man wearing an unbuttoned, striped waistcoat and a crotch-hugging black leotard began to circle around our table. The tempo of the triad switched from a regular happy birthday to a local track—upbeat, perky and from the sound of it, slightly raunchy too.

But there could be nothing raunchier than a stud dipping his index finger into the whipped cream atop my cake and smearing it across his chest, before slamming himself closer to my face; gyrating all around my chair and then turning around to lightly balance himself on my knees.

Whoa! Whoa! My very first lap dance!

I covered my face in embarrassment as few of the late-diners and restaurant staff gathered around to be a part of my birthday gig. Coco and Aliya were almost falling off their chairs in hysterics, holding their stomachs hard; pausing only to take snapshots on their cameras and shrieking their lungs out, 'Come on, Kai, grab your birthday gift. Unwrap it. Go, Bawi, go! It's your lucky night.'

***

There was a light drizzle as we wobbled back to our four-star suite, holding hands to keep from toppling over under the effect of Prosecco and an overdose of laughing gas. The big drops falling on my head reminded me of the Mumbai monsoons that I loved so much. So did Krish. He always said that a sudden sprinkle was a good omen, a sign of new beginnings. Aliya was finding it difficult to find her balance, hyperactive as ever; Coco was supporting her with her rather unstable arm.

'We promise we didn't know that they brought in birthdays like this, 'twas a shock for us too,' Coco tried explaining, she was glowing.

I did not believe the two *mastikhors*, at all. But I would never forget the efforts they had gone through to ring in my 25th.

As we reached our room at half past one in the morning, I made a dash towards the blinking light of the answering machine to check for birthday messages. Before I had flown out of India, I had distributed my hotel details in advance to those who mattered.

12:03 a.m. IST: Mom and Dad (they said they missed taking me to Gallops at the race course for dinner)

12:17 a.m.: Pari and Jimmy (rapping a combined uncoordinated happy birthday song)

12: 25 a.m.: Brother from Australia (an accent already?)

12:40 a.m.: Simran (tipsy and giggly)

12:50 a.m.: Shanaya (very yawny)

I replayed them in case I had skipped Zoya's or Krish's. Krish never forgot my birthday perhaps because closer to the datc, I always reminded him, indirectly. He found it amusing but took it seriously and always bought me an Archies card, pink and white carnations and some out-of-the-box gift though it did not matter to me if he brought me a cookie or a crumb, so long as he remembered to wish me on my birthday.

I bet this year, the conniving shrew from Borivali has erased his memory chip, I thought to myself, wishing some voracious animal from the local national park would escape, hunt her down and chew on her slutty bits.

That night, I had dreams of chasing Suzie the Floozie with an axe. And just when I was about to chop her head off, she transformed into a *naagin* and hissed at me. I almost kicked Aliya out of the double bed.

I woke up in a cold sweat way before sunrise, hardly feeling geared up for a birthday outing in Rome. There was only one way to get out of the rut of feeling sorry for myself. I needed to meet a 'real man' with iron balls to match. A torrid affair that would un f**k my f**ked mind.

So I decided to drill a few strong words into myself while sitting on the potty seat, 'I, Kai the Persian Princess, is now a magnet for a "hot as a shashlik sizzler Al Pacino-type of Italiano". I am prepared to welcome him into my life with open arms. Krish nikamma Aryan on the other hand, can go take a flying f**k.'

I was told incantations work. And with that being said, I crapped him out of my system, pulled the flush, turned the lock of the bathroom, pushed the door and let out an earsplitting screech, 'Good morning, you lazy bums. Wakey Wakey. It's my b'day! New day, new adventures...new guys!'

***

When we reached the Colosseum at 11 a.m. after a heavy brekky, it was already speckled with tourists, mostly Japanese and American and a group of Gujaratis not shying away from giving their two bits.

'*Colloosum maan Tom Cruise dekha she ke*?'

'*Su boloché, Kanti ben. Tom naa. Gladiator filum nau hero Russell* Crowe *che*.' (Will we see Tom Cruise at the Colosseum? What are you saying sister, Kanti. Not Tom. The hero of the *Gladiator* film is Russell Crowe.)

We tried keeping a safe distance from them. Just as we finished buying our entry tickets, a rather tall person in a gladiator get-up came striding towards us.

'Photos, pretty ladies?' he asked.

We politely refused. It seemed a bit too gimmicky. But then on our way to the entrance of the historic site, Aliya had a change of mind and did the unimaginable. She approached the man in the armour, pulled him by his left hand and brought him over to us, 'Russell, have you met Kai Juicewalla? She belongs to the smallest yet a very prominent community known as the Parsis. If you are single under that metal hat, you could buy her a coffee for her birthday.'

Oh, why doesn't the Colosseum just fall over us and bury us alive?

She was sure going to get a mouthful from me.

What if behind his little masquerade, he was a sexagenarian old *thadki* or worse still, a woman dressed as a man? Sure, I swooned over older chaps but only if their names were Richard Gere or Harrison Ford. And this guy was neither though he had a robust, well-built frame and unusually large feet.

And you know what they say about men with big feet? Take a guess…

My fears diminished slightly when he spoke in a seductively husky, youthful voice, 'Hi Kai. Me Gabriele. I am on break in five minutes. We get a caffè together, what you say and then you tell me more about your beautiful *nazione* (nation) you come from.'

The magnetic aura of Italian fellas is not a fabrication of over-hormonal women. Right from the *AlItalia* crew at the airport to the cabbie to the hotel staff—our tongues had not stopped hanging out. And our eyes were as sore as over-ripened plums, from all the ogling at these Italian studs.

'Italians are like yummiliscious Merwan Bakery's mawa cakes. Wanna just gobble them up.'

I had emphatically stated the previous night to Coco and Aliya who nodded in agreement.

I kind of wanted to say yes to Gladiator *saab*, but that would mean missing the iconic monument tour. And how can you be in Roma and not explore the Colosseum? But then again, it was 'my day' and I had promised myself that morning to get out of my sufferer mode and have a blast.

Choices, choices.

As I stood confused, the two stooges made up their minds for me about what my modus operandi should be.

Suddenly, I found myself almost toppling and diving straight into his unusually solid pecs, and apologising for it. Coco and Aliya literally threw me into the arms of the stranger, and marched off in the opposite direction, leaving me shuffling my feet, wondering what to expect next.

'She is all yours, Russell, but have her back by 2 p.m. We'll understand if you don't want to bring her back at all. Ta ta. *Arrivederc*i (goodbye).'

'Luvvv you, Kai. Blow your candle hard. Really, really hard.'

I could sense him smiling under the gear. Not wanting to torture me any more, he removed his helmet and let out a loud exhale. Phewwwwww!

I drew two sharp breaths, almost falling over him again, *Oh Khoda*! *Throw me smelling salts, I am about to faint*!

The most rugged, jaw-dropping creature I had ever laid my eyes on, akin to a succulent extra-large pizza dripping with smoky scharmoza, dotted lavishly with all my chosen toppings, was in front of me, dabbing his sweat with a towelette and staring at me as if I was the only girl on this planet.

The next few lines he spoke might as well have been in Italian, Latin or Urdu for I could not see, hear or feel anything beyond those stormy eyes, rich brown hair tied back into a small ponytail, distinct dimples over angular cheekbones and to make matters even more complicated, a God-awesome physique. I gaped at him dumbstruck. Why did they not make them like these back home?

After all the years of enduring washouts and snoozers, I have finally found my match, right here in the heart of Italy. An Italian Adonis in flesh and blood. If this isn't Khodaiji nu chamatkar, then I don't know what is?

'*Ti desidero*.'

I finally managed to blubber, hoping to start off on the right foot with my bite-sized Italian I had mugged from Coco's pocket dictionary.

He had a naughty twinkle in his eyes which meant that I had goofed up the words. I meant to say, 'You are handsome.'

'Bella, tonight I will show you my beautiful Roma, we go to all the great places, your birthday we celebrate in big fashion, *si*?' he declared, stretching out both his hands midair, instantaneously making me draw parallels to SRK's famous stance!

Is this a sign from the universe?

Not wanting to waste a single moment in contemplation, I took a leap of faith. Because taking a leap of faith is better than taking a leap of doubt, any day. After what seemed like the world's longest hug, he disengaged reluctantly and said, 'I go change into my own clothes, then we get an espresso and biscotti and talk about tonight.'

We crossed the street, arm in arm, and made our way into a small but chic cafe overlooking the Colosseum. It felt as if we had known each other forever, in spite of the different accents and language.

I soon found out that Gabriele Sorrentino and his six-pack abs were in their mid-thirties and never been married. Apparently, Gabs had another proper job but worked part-time at the Colosseum twice a week.

'You come to my home eh, later tonight? We shake it up a bit, eh?'

He pulled his chair closer to mine, kissing me demandingly on my lips, as if he were entitled to my time and my body. Not that I was complaining. My sleeping loins needed a thunderous wakeup call.

A holiday fling with an enthralling foreigner is a silent prayer answered. If this won't get that rat in Mumbai out of my system, nothing will.

His sensual fingers flirted around the buttons of my bright red shirt, smoothly caressing my moist neck all the way down to what was usually restricted territory on a first date and then using his remaining five digits, he stroked my curvy thighs which were calling for attention under my knee-length beige cargos, as he manoeuvred his pink tongue into my left ear making continuous rotating movements that transported me to a different kind of zenith than I had experienced before.

'*Ho bisogno di te* (I need you),' he whispered in a buttery tone that took my breath away and threw me into thresholds of heart-pounding ecstasy.

Full blown PDA!

I am going to get deported for fooling around in public. He is a stranger. Does he prefer vanilla or chocolate? That middle-aged lady on the next table, minding her own business behind a newspaper is actually a butch cop in disguise and her job is to sit in cafes like this and nab horny couples like us.

I will be tossed into a cell filled with real criminals, my passport confiscated for good and become the next hot headline in India: 'Parsi tourist sent to the gallows for flashing in public'.

Then reminding myself that this was not Mumbai where law-abiding *pandus* emerged from hidden bushes with their wooden lathis yelling, '*Choo choo, phurrrr phurrrrr, hutt hutt*' at canoodling couples, I let myself go with the flow.

'Bad news, my break is over.' The Italian hunk informed me in-between our jaw locking session; half-heartedly drawing himself away from me, glancing at his watch and adjusting his navy trousers as he stood up.

'But good news is that I see you soon at Fontana di Trevi, 7'o clock. We then raise a glass to your big day after that in Lucia's. Is this sounding all right for you, bella?'

I simply nodded in awe, trying hard to not gawk at a rather obvious package hitting me at eye level. He made me an offer I couldn't refuse. (Nod to the *Godfather*.)

Plopping a slurpy 'mwaaah' on my burning lips, he strode off like a knight in shining armour, back to his touristy-duties, leaving me gasping for air.

A fleeting night of unbridled passion with a bare-chested perfect tushy Sex God who warmed the cockles of my heart and set me ablaze with excitement? A verrryyy Happy Birthday to me.

'I don't know the question, but sex is definitely the answer.' Woody Allen, thank you for articulating it for us.

16

A Trip down Gangsta Paradise

Back in the hotel room, the girls were *maha* thrilled to hear about my high-charged action plan on my special day. Aliya handed me a razor to shave my underarms and Coco blow-dried my hair. I was trying to live in the moment and so far it was working out pretty well.

Still no birthday message from Krish. Whatta scumbag!

The size 12 River Island bell-sleeved, knee-length, wrap around black dress seemed to have transformed into a size smaller as Aliya tried zipping me up from behind, commanding me to hold my breath in. Holiday weight was what I told myself, as Coco helped tuck in some of the extra meat around my waist, inside the garment.

'Silver thongs, hmm hottttttttt! But have you mowed the lawn?'

Aliya's concern made me smile.

'Yup, twice over, do you wanna examine it, Chachi Sood?'

'And girl don't you dare come back until you've measured the L-G-W of the gladiator for us. Please borrow a tape at the reception on your way out.'

Aliya was quick to remind.

'You gals are sure my arms don't look like a sumo wrestler in this?' I asked.

I had recently started taking thyroid tablets, which was not a good sign.

'Not at all. You look stunning, baby doll.'

Coco pacified me, placing a protective peck on my right cheek, 'and in case you plan to spend the rest of your vacay between his legs or on a gondola, or both, do keep us in the loop. Remember we fly back home on the 24th at noon'

***

Quarter of an hour later, I paid the cabbie and trampled the cobbled path leading to Trevi, unsteady with excitement to meet my 'lust at first sight' in my new black patent leather wedges, which surprisingly gave me no shoe bites.

His ponytail had altered into a flowing mane and he looked dashingly deadly in sleek white pants and a long-sleeved pastel peach shirt that enhanced his kadak as gootli pau (hard as bread) arms. If the stud muffin had been a real muffin, I would have relished him up in a tick.

'*Ciao amore mio*! (Hi, my love!)' he exclaimed, grabbing me to give me another taste of the morning but this time he lifted me up from the ground and swept me off my feet, literally.

After what seemed to be the most passionate smooch of my life accompanied by saxophones, a belly bursting with fluttering butterflies and the works, Gabs led me to the famous fountain and arranged three coins across his palm.

'Close your eyes and throw these one by one with your right hand over your left shoulder. Legend says, your wishes will come true. If you toss one coin, you will return to Roma. Two, you will fall in love with an Italian. Three, then you will marry him. Your choice…'

I stared at him, suddenly wanting to skip the night out and beg him to take me to his house.

Marry? Did I hear correctly? Nah!

Whoa! Could Gabriele Sorrentino with these brown leather boots and the sexiest booty in history be the MAN OF MY DREAMS?

'*L'amore domina senza regole.* (True love is unconditional.)'

I took two of the silver and followed orders.

'You hold on to the third for me Gabs,' I said, winking at him, 'let's see how it goes. We can always come back in the morning.'

'Your wish is my command, Kai. Come now, let's go, we are late already. I have a special surprise for you,' he said, stroking my head affectionately and then in a grand romantic gesture removed a red rose from his back pocket, touched his lips gently to my right hand, and chaperoned me to a swanky set of wheels with doors that opened upwards and an engine that would give my humble Maruti back home a strong inferiority complex.

As we entered the moderately lit Lucia's, the first thing that drew my attention was that it was flooded with cigar-blowing gents, busty waitresses and psychedelic lights. A few heads looked up as we entered, giving us a twice-over, and then returned back to minding their own business. I may have even heard some muffled low voices but that could just be a coincidence.

Am I looking awful? Am I looking too chubby-tubby in this? Is Gabs too hot for someone like me?

Self-doubts, self-doubts, self-doubts.

But Italian women were rather well-built themselves and unlike India, most of Europe was not that body biased; their policy was more of a live and let live; something that made life so much easier and bearable.

Engaging his arm possessively around my shoulders, he led me to a large round table surrounded by affluent-looking men in suits and semi-formals, seated on enormous worn-out divans. Gabs's buddies stood up at once to seal their smoky lips on my glossy ones. By then, I had gotten the idea that in parts of Europe, a lip-to-lip greeting was no different than a handshake.

The lads at our table were boisterous and intimidating and I felt slightly left out as I sat there for almost 20 minutes without a drink, nibbling nuts and corn chips from their table, listening to them crack jokes in Italian, as they puffed on beefy Cubans and guzzled from wide-bottomed crystals.

'Sorry Kai, I am being so rude. When we meet, we always forget everyone. Just macho men, you know?' Gabs said apologising, rubbing his hand up and down my right thigh.

'But don't worry, I will give full attention to you and your secret friend here.'

Finding his way up the front slit of my dress with ease, his fingers touching my thong oh-so-lightly, he kissed me deeply, his tongue reaching the back of my throat, making me suffocate slightly yet enjoying the novelty of it, all the same. Unabashedly placing my hand around the seams of his trousers, he asked me gruffly if I would return the favour after he had finished exploring.

All of a sudden, I felt breathless and bare.

Were his friends judging us?

Nope.

Did we have spectators from the other tables, condemning our actions?

Nope.

All of them seemed too self-involved to care.

God! I love this country. Maybe, it would not be a bad idea to consider packing my boria bistar and camping here for a while.

After 15 minutes of intense foreplay and breaking every barrier possible with hundred other foreign souls present in the room, my hot-blooded Adonis waved to a blonde hostess. She came over at once and winked at us. They seemed to be on first-name basis.

Hmmph!

Emerald-coloured drinks arrived within four minutes, swirling in hand-blown glasses with an olive and a cherry swimming in each of them.

'It's the best one here, so bottoms up, bella. You look so sexy tonight, si,' he rasped in my ear, the whiff of Hugo Boss adding to his raw appeal, '*Me casa, Amore Mio, presto.* (My house, my love, soon.) After we finish this work, I will fling you over my bed and eat you like a big bowl of meatballs.'

I wanted to savour every moment of this EPIC vacation. Which was now 10 out of 10 in my book!

Life is ekdum super-duper. Thank you Khodaiji. Best birthday ever! Thank you, Univ!

The man sitting on Gabs's right, clad in a long coat, leaned over to whisper into Gabs's ear.

'Si Si. My bad.'

Gabs staggered up and gestured towards the quartet.

'I haven't done a proper introduction. These handsome men, he is Big Papà *Uno* Antonio, you can call him Tony if you like and Big Papà *Deu* Eugene. And this is my eldest brother Stephano and his partner Warren from New York.'

They were family? Oooh, I didn't see that one coming. I would not have kept my legs wide open like London's Tower Bridge, had I known.

Speaking about bridges, the first thing that came to my mind was a line from one of my fave books of all time, *Bridges of Madison County*, 'It seems right now that all I've ever done in my life is making my way here to you'.

And that was exactly how I felt that night for Gabs.

I smiled at both the papas, graciously.

Arrey! Keva bhi mitha che eleko (so sweet they are).

I have always felt kindly towards the elderly. I renamed them Naushir kaka and Merzi kaka, respectively, in my head.

'We Parsis say *maara Puppa*!'

I explained, beaming at them, feeling very much at ease now. Neither of the *naalayaks* I had dated back home had introduced me to their families.

Wowzers! Does this mean anything? Like wedding bells in some distant future? Ding. Dong.

They say love happens when you are not looking for it. I had come to Europe to create a few exotic memories, not a new set of family members. But then when God proposes, who am I to dispose, eh?

Gabs's voice interrupted my delightful daydream, 'Papà Uno owns half of this country.'

Oh, Naushir kaka is like some sort of a nawab saheb. Remarkable.

My folks would be so proud if I settled into an A-list dynasty. Relatives would be green with envy. Stouter and balder Papà Deu, Merzi *kaka* offered me a fag, which I politely refused.

They all seemed to be wearing some sort of an engraved metallic ring on their middle finger.

'It's nice of you to make me meet your loved ones Gabs, you all seem so close.'

I communicated my pleasure into my new boyfriend's ear, straightening the hem of my dress which was nowhere near my knees, 'quite similar to us Juicewallas'.

Whoopie! There was so much to tell Simran and Zoya when I got back home. They would be so proud of me and might even throw me a party.

Gabs's fingers ran through my hair tenderly, his eyes not leaving me once, 'Si, bella. Family *bondage* is very important to us Italians. Now soon you become one of us. Perhaps tomorrow I take you to meet *Nonno*?'

Surely he meant bonds?

'Oooh yessss, I would love to meet Nonno.'

I guess he meant Nunno. Must be his accent. Dellu used to have this mangy, fuzzy, cute pup called Nunno before she shifted base.

Gabs seemed so chuffed at my keenness to meet his dog that he made a hip hip hurray gesture and announced to his brood, 'Kai says si. Kai says si. *Ti amo* (I love you), Kai!'

Actually, I was super dog phobic but I did not want to steal the joy from all the optimistic faces around me, so I played along. Maybe I could talk to his beloved pet, through a window or kennel.

Sure enough, the choir on the table stood up and began rejoicing too.

'*Cin Cin, alla nostra salute*! (Cheers to our health!)' they recited unanimously and his brother even congratulated me.

Was animal consent that important to tie the knot in Italian culture? And I always thought we Indians overdid it.

Overwhelmed with the shouts of approval and adoration, I ran straight into the arms of the big papas to take their blessings.

Big Papà Uno, with a mole on his chin bigger than his nose, returned my affection with a terse snap of my bra strap.

Ouch, Naughty Naushir. Not too paternal I must say! And then it all began to heat up, but not in the way I would have expected. He reached inside the inner lining of his coat and handed over a hairdryer-shaped object to me. I took it shyly thinking it to be a token of sorts—an Italian tradition to confirm a partnership, like Hindus have the *roka* and we have the *rupiya pehervanu.* When I inspected it closely, it looked so much like a Holi *ni pichkari* (water gun used on Holi) though it seemed to be darker in colour and so much heavier.

Is it some sort of a family heirloom?

Papà Deu removed a similar toy from his trousers and holding it up to my face where I could see it much better, he questioned in a crusty voice, 'Which one you prefer *dolce signora* (sweet lady)? *Di Tony o mio*? (Tony's or mine?)'

I almost choked on the salty almonds I had just bent over to grab and stuff my face with. (In happiness or sorrow, I shall never stop pigging.)

Was this some kind of inside joke? Or perhaps a big, fat misunderstanding? Gabs and I were on a romantic date. Nothing controversial about that.

I have it all under control.

Five pairs of eyes were gaping at me in anticipation of a response. Adamant and proud Papà Deu shoved the pichkari in my right palm. I refused to call it anything else, hoping that if I denied what it really was, it would simply vaporise. Or at least I would.

*Bhen**od*! *La*da per eeda*! These ain't *bachche ke khilone.* They are f**king revolvers! *A sinister set-up! Aaje taari waat lagwani che, Kai.*

I am not sure if I screamed all that aloud but I had wanted to.

Gabs placed his hand over my trembling ones that held the weapons, glowing at me in pride. He then took the second one and handed it back to his Papà Deu.

'You belong with us now. From this day until the day you die.'

Grabbing the nearest edibles off the table with my other quivering hand—honey peanuts this time—I crammed them all together into my mouth, just to buy time and process the nightmare. It was one too many and soon I was spluttering them out.

Naushir kaka stepped forward and snatched his weapon away from me straightaway, and I felt a resolute palm slap my back twice. Three peanuts shot out, straight into Merzi kaka's left eye. He yelped and then took two menacing steps towards me, snarling at me like a rabid beast, making me almost shit in my pants.

Is he going to blow my head off? I am glad that Coco and Aliya have clicked enough pics of me on this holiday to share with my family, so at least that's sorted. Bye, bye unfair world. Maybe next life, you will treat me better.

I felt nauseous, but this was no time to have a blackout.

Okay, calm down, Kai, say your Ashem vohus...These prayers have always been effective.

I needed to recite them with utmost dedication unless I wanted to be Ajit's Mona darling and perform cabarets or pour drinks or both for the thug-squad for the rest of my life.

But desperate times call for desperate measures. Flopping over the nearest futon, holding the left side of my chest, I began to squirm.

'Heart attack!' I heard an unfamiliar voice rumble above me.

'Call a doctor. CPR.'

'Kai, let me take you home,' Gabs was trying to kiss me again. No more of that, please, you psycho!

'Toilet, toilet, vomit…'

I managed to fumble, feeling faint, muzzy and petrified all at once; this was not how my version of *Romeo & Juliet* was supposed to play out. Chanting three Hail Marys (it was a Catholic country, so I assumed it would bring help faster), I pitched myself forward without a plan. All I knew was I had to run faster than PT Usha.

Alas, my attempt to scoot did not last too long and I collided with the rounded bosom of a young waitress, head first, who understandably let out a high-pitched shrill. Ignoring her and pushing her off me, I propelled like a turbo jet into the first available gap I spotted in the sardine-packed room.

*It's now or never, you gadheri. The maha h*r*mkhor goondas will make kuchumber out of you.*

I could hear the sound of those dreaded footsteps on my trail.

'*Amore mio* (my love), oh Kai…Kai.'

Panting and puffing, I almost broke open a closed door and rammed straight into a chef holding a bowl of bolognese. The sauce spilled all over his uniform, but there was no time to apologise. Who knew, he was probably some thug-chef with a pistol in his pocket.

I quickly dashed out of the backdoor of the kitchen and darted out of Lucia's swifter than a buckshot (ironic I know) jumped into what looked like a taxi parked in a dark alley and pleaded to Jesus with all my heart that the cabbie was not one of the mafias too.

***

The next day, we hopped on the first available flight to India. The plane was chockablock and all that remained for us was a single row in coach class. A stark contrast to the premium upgrade we had got on the plane to Europe, less than a week ago.

'How hard the mighty have fallen,' Coco said, sighing.

'From an unlimited supply of impressive labels, scrumptious hors d'oeuvres and a selection of the latest blockbusters on our way in, to cheap cava, a bag of oversalted pretzels and four-inch tv screens on our way out,' Aliya said, groaning.

Being the tiniest, she was squeezed between Coco and me and had not stopped complaining since the time we boarded. I was feeling terribly guilty and had profusely apologised to Coco and Aliya for ruining our vacay.

'You girls missed seeing everything because of my idiocy. The Sistine Chapel, the Pantheon, the gorgeous piazzas…I'm sorry.'

Secretly, I was relieved that we had chosen to flee. Not only was I done with paellas, tacos, frittatas, pastas, calzones and mascarpone cheesecakes but there was no way we would be safe in case the mobsters still had unfinished business with me.

'It's fine, chill. I will ring the Pope and arrange a date for your next birthday. At least there won't be gang lords and guns then, just the good Lord and nuns,' Aliya said, giggling.

My squaddies had enjoyed themselves thoroughly at my expense, all the way from the hotel to the aircraft. I deserved it.

'Look at the bright side, at least you got to meet the original "Godfather" up, close and personal.'

Coco kept the crazy momentum going, trying to adjust her long limbs into the minimum legroom we were stuck with.

'Sure, but meeting one was not part of my itinerary or bucket list.'

'As I walked through the valley of the shadow of death I took a look at my life and realise there's not much left...' I could not help humming rapper Coolio's song.

I could see the funny side to it, now that the plane had kicked out of Gangsta Paradise and I could breathe again.

'Actually, the skull and cross-embossed rings on all of them should've been a dead giveaway. I watched a biopic once in which several such cartels operated in various cities. Each one had a unique symbolic identity. '

Coco was shaking her head and shoving a sour cream and onion potato chip into her mouth; as if we were expected to have done a diploma in Mafia-logy before we decided to go on our fun break.

But Aliya simply could not get over the fact that I had confused an Italian grandfather for a doggy. Not that she knew any better but she would do anything to avoid the impending Spanish inquisition that Coco and I had planned for her on our return journey. She was desperate to shift the focus to something else and save her ass.

'Come, Nonno, good boy. Give your ashirvad to the blissful couple with your right paw.'

Aliya was relentless.

I shoved my ear plugs into my ears and shut my eyes, blocking out their incessant chatter and Aliya breaking into woof woof now and again, for my benefit.

Orgies, pole dancing, lap dancing, underworld sharks! What else was left? A Martian encounter?

Sigh! So much *saza* for a little bit of *maza*?

Seriously Khodaiji. Why can't you just leave me alone ya?

XXXSCORE = 444

JOYRIDES AND PARACHUTES

17

Met My Knight in Shining Convertible

2010

Soon after my trip with the gals in July 2009, I suggested a Fab Four catch-up sesh, mainly because I wanted to gift them souvenirs that I had bought them. There was rarely an occasion when either of us called and the others did not show up, no matter how neck-deep we were in our respective lives. Except that day, when Krish was unable to make it because it was Slimy Suzie's parents' anniversary.

He had also called to apologise for his lapse on my birthday. 'Apparently' he had been a patient of severe diarrhoea and was incapacitated for the day.

'Sure, you *nuffat* (thick-skinned)! Incapacitated in her arms, I bet.'

I was on the verge of screaming over the instrument but held myself together.

Slamming the phone down instead, convinced that thc dayan had done *jadu tona* on him and had chained him up before throwing him inside her secret dungeon, I swore never to speak to him again.

To make matters worse, non-purposefully of course, Simran and Zoya rubbed salt over my wounds during brunch at Gaylord, Churchgate.

'How is it possible that you still haven't hooked up with your Mr Right?' Zoya asked.

'Love-jinxed, stars-afflicted, cupid-cursed, need I say more?'

But I was not being a martyr, these were slowly becoming stone hard facts, even though they were clueless about my Krish fantasy. If they did find out they would either die laughing or be too astonished to react.

I went on to tell them about my trip and entertained them thoroughly with our adventures in Europe.

'Zoya, we have competition and alas, we must accept that we will soon be replaced by this madcap Aliya and a very classy Coco,' Simran said, fisting the table in mock anger.

'Hmm. But at least she has good taste in friends, if not in men,' Zoya agreed, 'so that's a relief.'

'Arrey, don't be silly, old is gold na.'

I assured them tunnelling my spoon into the cheese soufflé greedily.

Simran had an announcement to make—she was moving in with a guy twice her age.

'Hope you are not being rash and reckless again. I don't think this is the way to resolve any daddy issues you might have.'

Zoya scolded her.

'No Aunty Z, that ship has sailed; Dad is super proud of my achievements.'

Simran defended herself looking every bit infuriated.

As always, sensible Zoya was dampening the newsflash with her own objective analysis.

After hearing Simran prattle about her selected flavour of the season, we were not convinced that Shashank Veerkar a PETA activist and a jobless bum, had any good intent with our friend but nobody dared contradict Simran Khanna's choices, unless they were okay about not seeing another sunrise ever again.

Simran hopped from one serious relationship to another; not her fault entirely for she was a dickhead magnet, pretty much like me.

But that afternoon, my non-existent sex life was the hot topic of discussion.

'No golden goose yet? You must be such a showstopper in your glamorous attire, pencil heels, that wavy ponytail of yours, shiny smile.'

Simran began to shower tons of lavish praise on me.

I was grateful for the compliments, but I did not have the heart to mention that I had recently gained a stone and a half and had broken skirt zips and ripped blouse buttons to my credit.

What most people having regular jobs do not realise is that even though we make fantastic hostesses flying across cities, we do not come with 'Available. Free for all, let's have a ball', signboard.

Working on long-haul flights and standing for hours to end is physically demanding and mentally taxing. Challenges that range from potential hostage threats in rarest of circumstances to calming down a disgruntled passenger who did not get his choice of meal.

It is not that the hush-hush one night stands did not happen at 35,000 feet above sea level but as open-minded and fun-loving as I was, 'wham-bam-thank-you-ma'am' had never been my scene.

I was running 26 and needed a stable, loving partner who knew where he was going in life. (One of us needs to.) Not a fumbling boy crush who did not know the difference between a Persian enchantress and an evil sorceress.

Was I asking for a Bharat Ratna? No, right?

Just an Eiffel Tower proposal overlooking the magnificent river Seine studded with the prettiest of lights; a talented European violinist playing in the background and a two carat rock (I would even settle for one) as my lover went down on his knee and promised me the sun, the moon and the stars, while I pretended to be caught unawares, clasping my right hand over my mouth and shoving my left palm over his face, to slip the sparkly without delay, lest the tower collapsed to the ground and fudged my plans.

***

So when six and a half months down the line, on the widely celebrated day of 14 February 2010, on a Mumbai–Dubai flight, Rahul Indur Oberoi, a chocolate boy with a heart-melting smile, bearing a vague semblance to SRK from his *Fauji* days, boldly handed me his visiting card, I accepted it readily.

For those who are SRK-illiterate, Rahul is Mr Khan's most used screen name. I dashed into the business class galley and broke into a mini-victory dance. When one of my Scottish colleagues asked me what the brouhaha was about, I showed off the card.

'Ooh impressive, right side of the curtain (business class) too. Make sure he buys you some expensive jewellery on the first date,' she said, smilingly, 'and if he's a player, then go get yourself the best shag of your life, if nothing else.'

'I usually don't accept cards,' I found myself explaining to the young Mr Oberoi when I returned to pour him his third glass of single malt.

He asked me cheekily if I was as single as the Glen I had just served.

'I'm on my way for a business tour to the USA but will be back in Mumbai around the end of April. It's for a work trip—taking care of Dad's business affairs as usual,' he informed me, casually.

Was I supposed to know his father?

'Indur Oberoi' he added, nonchalantly.

Nooooooo! *Hold on sister. Don't jump on the trampoline yet. Did he just say INDUR OBEROI*?

Who did not know the flamboyant Mr Oberoi? He was a VIP and privileged cardholder of our airline and the owner of one of the biggest pharmaceutical companies in the world and travelled in nothing less than a first class seat, with two man Fridays in tow.

Known to hit on anything with breasts, the business magnate was infamous for *pataoing* firangi air hostesses on his stopovers and the grapevine had been rife with rumours about his many extramarital dalliances.

A red flag?

On seeing my hesitation, he gently touched my palm. Not in the mood to lose my job over inappropriate in-flight behaviour, I retreated slightly.

'It's Kai, right? Well it's Valentine's today. Maybe I was meant to sit here in your section and nowhere else. Not sure if you believe in soulmates and divine intervention, but I do.'

Oh Khodaiji, of course I do! He had recognised my soul. As Rumi said, 'Lovers don't finally meet somewhere. They're in each other all along'.

'And you can call me Rio for short,' he said, winking naughtily and I was sold.

I kind of dug Rio. *Mitho che* (cute types)! But I had to play it cool or *at least* try.

What was the harm in dating someone new? Krish was passé; the Fab girls had their own lives; James and his Lady Love Coco were inseparable, he had even visited India twice since their tryst; Aliya had scrammed back to the asshole Amrish despite several warnings and Shanaya was busy with her first job in a law firm. And Simran was kept busy by that creepy Shashank. I was pretty much on my own, on my days off in Mumbai when I was off flight duty.

'I would love to take you out for dinner to Mikasa, Traṭs, or anywhere else your heart fancies. I promise, if you get bored, you can fake an emergency and leave.'

I had only read about the swanky Thai restaurant Mikasa in the *Mid-Day* and I was desperate to visit it. The way to my heart was food, food and only food and if he had sensed that, then he was worth taking a stab at.

'What say, beautiful Kai? Shall I start getting excited about your call, two and a half months from now, 29th of April? Shall we save the date?'

And in the worst-case scenario, even if he turns out to be as boring as a donut without sprinkles, at least I would get free dinner. Ask not what you can do for your country. Ask what is for dinner (to distort Orson Welles's quote).

I thought to myself before accepting his suggestion with a subtle nod.

***

A month before Rahul was supposed to be back, Coco and I received some disturbing news. Our third musketeer Aliya Sood had resigned overnight and had left with no forwarding address. The company had accepted it quite willingly for they had recently recruited a new batch of eight newbies, all-male crew this time, which they believed was the current need of the Indian aviation market. They had also marginalised our flying sectors to London and Dubai. Breathtaking Switzerland would now become just a bewitching memory.

All efforts to reach Aliya's personal number were reciprocated by a prerecorded voicemail in an unrecognisable language and when we finally did reach her landline number, her mother hung up on us abruptly after hearing who we were.

We were too shocked to understand what exactly was going on with Aliya because although she had gone a bit out of touch with us in recent times and we seldom got flights rostered together; we had assumed her temporary detachment and need for space was because of her messy love life with Amrish. But we had always believed her to be quite a trouper and have it all under control, so we had not probed further.

Apparently, we were wrong, for she had disappeared from our lives as mysteriously as airplanes do over the Bermuda Triangle, leaving both Coco and me groping for answers in the dark about the whereabouts of our beloved partner in crime and wishing we had been there for her instead of working on our presumptions.

Well, at least Coco and I have each other. (Fingers crossed.)

Alas, my complacency was short-lived. A few days later, Coco dropped another bombshell when we were casually hanging out at Gusto's enjoying the happy hours—James asked her to move in with him to Sydney. He was finally quitting his marine career.

He wanted stability, marriage, family, babies, pets, a house with a white picket fence; a blossoming garden of lilies and he could not visualise any of that without her. And she refused to do long distance forever, stating one of her own made-up commandments this time, 'Absence makes the heart grow fonder and then it goes yonder'.

'So you are leaving me too?'

My eyes welled up.

'I know, Kai. I'm sorry, but what would you do? If you met the love of your life?'

Coco looked down, not meeting my eyes.

'I wouldn't go!' I said, screaming at her over the table.

They should call it Unhappy Hours. Dammit!

I stormed out of Gusto almost flinging the cash at her.

That lucho, James Donahue! Scoundrel! Fancy swooping in this way and taking my friend away without even asking me. I will never forgive him. I will make kheema out of him when I see him next.

I refused to speak to Coco for the rest of the month.

But as they say, change is the only constant in the world and everything was changing that year.

Zoya was two months pregnant much to her delight but it was a difficult pregnancy and she was mostly on bed rest.

I refused to take most of Krish's calls.

Poor Simran was nursing a broken heart yet again, no thanks to 52-year-old Shashank, *saalo* cradle-snatcher who had the gall to assault her in a lovers' spat. She had filed a police complaint too but he had them wrapped around his finger. I had intervened then and solved the situation in my 'own way', and it was safe to say that Shashank would not lift so much as a finger on any woman ever again.

After all, Simran had saved me once from myself. Even Shanaya was leaving soon for a year-long stint to Hong Kong as part of the legal advisory board of her company.

On a weekend trip to Pune with my cousins, Jimmy had announced that he was setting off to Andaman to learn scuba diving and Parizad declared she was tying the knot, end of the year. (Thankfully, it would be a destination wedding with only 75 close family and friends as attendees, which meant none of the dreaded Parsi predators would get invites.)

Almost every person I cared about had something going on in their lives except me. I was doing the same job, pining for the same things, eating like there was no tomorrow and complaining and blaming others for everything that was going wrong in my life.

I object. All of my near and dear ones should infinitely stick to me and stop growing, progressing, evolving, moving on, falling in love, marrying or worse popping babies.

Objection overruled. Suck it up, Miss Juicewalla.

Sigh.

And when 29 April came at last, I hammered straight to the point over the line: I could not wait to see him at Mikasa over the coming weekend. Rahul seemed delighted.

Fortunately, I did not have a flight rostered that following Saturday and I was looking forward to a night out in town. It had been centuries since I had been asked on a proper date. The dinner spot was on the other end of town towards Cuffe Parade and I was slightly disappointed that Rahul had not suggested picking me up or at least sending a car when he had a fleet of them.

My driver had his day off, so I was left with no choice but to hail a cab. But I tried to not let the minor oversight cloud my judgement so early.

Earlier that evening, Zoya had some gems to share over the phone, 'Be as cool as your Mom's *thanda* rose Falooda. No giving details of past bawi escapades—flashing, lap dances, are defi no-no subjects. And most importantly, no making out on the first three dates at least. Be enigmatic, out of reach and keep him guessing.'

But mind games were not my thing at all. Did she not know me *at all*? I am as subtle as a lit up billboard when it comes to expressing my interest and no matter how hard I have tried to be bashful or mysterious on dates, my over earnest body language always gives me away.

After I hung up with Zoya, Krish rang me.

Perfect timing.

He wanted to share some news with me and asked if we could meet at The Shack.

Why? Do you want to RDX me? Do you think I am at your beck and call?

'No, I can't, I have a date tonight. With a Richie Rich-type of a guy. Not some arty-farty loser type.'

I snapped in a high and mighty voice.

'Achcha. That's lovely Bawi. Have a nice evening, we can always meet some other time, I guess.'

I had not meant to sound boastful or spiteful but the *kam*no* had it coming. Though as usual, he was being an oblivious buffoon about it.

A few months ago, he had introduced the swine Suzie to Zoya and Simran. They had certified her to be quite a hot number. Wasn't that peachy?

The scheming wench!

I had avoided that lunch meet; I did not want to be put in a situation where I had to pretend to be *maha* happy for him.

I was not happy for him at all. I wanted to throw him and his hot property out of a fast train. To put it mildly.

***

Granny B was over at my place for the evening and was complaining about her *aalsoo gangubais* (lazy maids) to my father when all of a sudden she took out her prayer book from the inner flap of her wheelchair and started murmuring under her breath while I pranced around the room getting dolled up for my date with Rio.

'I am only praying this works out, though I would have preferred someone like a Shiamak Davar for you. Even if he is much older,' she said, clearly unaware about the agonies of dating in this day and age.

'That's your crush, not mine. Not any more at least,' I said, smiling.

I quickly planted a wet kiss on her right cheek, closed the main door of my house behind me and left.

As per Zoya's counsel, I had chosen something that was sexy, not slutty. A dark blue A-line skirt with black motifs and a lightly sequined black off-shoulder top that hid my love handles well and played down my puffy arms. I had progressed a whole dress size in the last few months and even though it was not half as bad as it had been in my pre-flying days, I remained conscious, hoping that my date was a 'curvy-bod worshipper'.

I was about to seat myself inside the air-conditioned cab, when I heard some noise. I looked out of my cab and witnessed the funniest yet most precious sight I had ever seen.

The love of my life, 96 years old and a bit in her white *mathabanu* and gold-rimmed glasses that were almost falling off her face, was trying to balance out of her wheelchair, half-standing, half-holding the parapet of our old third floor balcony, as she waved me goodbye and wished me in the loudest voice she could muster, 'Good luck, princess! *Maja karje,* kiss *karje,* photos *leje. Ne bhooki na rehti.* (Have fun, kiss him, take photos and don't remain hungry.)'

That was enough to bring in a zealous audience.

Sherlock Holmes nee Soli Homi Hansotia of ground floor Flat B was poking out his inquisitive head from behind his burnt orange curtains; first floor flat resident Mr Khoobchandani's pupils were popping out of their lecherous sockets and his neighbour 50-year-old bachelor Joseph Gomes adjusted his binoculars. A pair of arms appeared from behind Granny B, guiding her away from the ledge of the balcony.

When I related this hilarious episode to Rahul over dinner, he was in splits. He looked dapper in a suave raspberry coloured blazer and khakis.

'That's why I love bawas ya and I always wanted a bawi girlfriend. I admire their philosophy of life, "*khao pio mast raho*"! Imagine how much *paatra ni machchhi and sali marghi* I would get to eat every day. Have I pronounced them correctly? In fact, my favourite dish in the world is berry pulao from Britannia,' he declared, sounding like an excited teenager.

If this was a hint, then he was certainly not being subtle. Soulmates in the making? Could be, could be….

'Most of what you said is made only for special occasions.'

'If we were to get married, would you be cool about a non-veg spread like with the works? Or would it be against your vegetarian ethics?' he asked so matter-of-factly as if planning a wedding had been a part of the evening agenda.

This was going faster than a rocket ship.

Choking on a portion of crispy noodles that came on the side with our hot and sour soups, I quickly changed the topic to his hobbies but he steered back to me, making it evident that he was pursuing this seriously, 'Tell me, is it true that Parsis polish and shine their vintage cars every single day but rarely drive them?'

I shook my head, amazed how many such myths about my community were floating around.

'Are you by any chance related to JRD? And do you also have like this large inheritance of hidden treasures tucked away in your Godrej steel cupboards and bank lockers, unused for generations?'

That ignorant, eh?

He was so awestruck about us bawas that I could not help playing along, 'Oh yes of course, JRD was my great grand uncle. Also if I haven't mentioned already, Prince Willy is my cousin and I travel without a passport. And yes, we all eat dhansak for breakfast, lunch and dinner.'

We both chuckled, it was obvious we were already relaxed in each other's company and shared a similar sense of humour.

'Uhhh…now if you have finished your court martial, should we order the mains?'

As much fun Rio was, I was famished.

He requested the attentive waiter for the menu.

I soon found out that Rahul Indur Oberoi was 29 and a bit of a Mr Know-It-All. He had a jovial disposition and a chilled out air about him. In his short life span, he had trotted half the globe, spoke four different foreign languages, held a fancy business degree from an Ivy League college and loved driving his daddy-owned imported cars all around town.

Boys and their toys.

I generously helped myself to the measly portions (expected of gourmet places) of spring rolls, pad Thai noodles, green tofu curry and jasmine rice as we chatted away. I wondered how a guy like him was not taken by some gold-digging chick already. I did pass that by him and he simply smiled as he held my hand across the table, a bit too earnestly, almost knocking down our dry martinis, 'I suppose, I was waiting for that one cute Parsi gal.'

Throughout our cosy dinner Rio continued to shower me with compliments and by the end of the night, we were fawning over each other like smitten kittens.

When the server brought us the bill and placed it in the centre of the table, out of impulse I started digging for my wallet.

'Please Kai, don't be silly. Never.'

It felt so damn good.

Masterstroke Dadaji! *Not bad at all.*

He then placed his hand in his right trouser pocket; then his left; then the hidden one in his blazer, feeling himself up and down.

'Oopsie, I seem to have forgotten my leather on my dresser,' he said, shifting uncomfortably.

I knew it was too good to be true. Crappity crap, is he bumming around?

Turns out he was not.

'Oh it's all righty then,' I slid into my purse, reluctantly this time, 'I'll take care of it.'

'Are you sure?' he uttered sheepishly. 'It's never happened before. I must look like a complete twat. And here I am trying to woo you. I like you soooo much.'

Throwing Zoya's 'play-it-cool mantra' out of the window, I leaned in to kiss him lightly on his lips for his candour.

'I am going to drive you to Bandra, Kai, only so I can savour more of these "mouth-melting desserts".'

Uhh, wouldn't you otherwise? Considering it is almost midnight and somebody can abduct me, for my empty wallet, lip gloss and tooth comb?

The waiter hovering around us cleared his throat impatiently and I hastily reached for the bill. I almost passed out.

Baap re baap! Su karyuch paap? 10 grand!

*Maari g**nd faati ne godown thaigayee.* (My ass ripped apart.)

I had no choice but to pay up. I do not fancy washing utensils, that too at restaurants.

Luckily, I had gone to the bank the same day to deposit some cash for Mom but I had been three minutes late. That 15,000 rupees was still in my wallet. Heart clenched, I was forced to unclench my fists to count the moolah—500, 100, 1,000, until I reached 11,000, assuming a heavy tip was also in order.

'I'm going to make it up to you, sweet lips,' Rahul said, hugging me as he revved his shining silver convertible.

Being a convertible virgin, I should have been feeling majestic in one. But all I felt was 11,000 rupees poorer and a bit sullen.

How I regretted not having my mother's papeta per eeda (eggs over potato) for dinner. No one can separate a true-blue Parsi from their eggs and I hoped there were some leftovers in the fridge. Thankfully, there was and I sat on my bed well past 1 a.m., relishing my gher nu bhonu (home-cooked food). Nothing came close to Mommy's cooking.

And the same went for her wrath too when the next day I had no explanation whatsoever as to where I had blown her 11 grand. Not even the soppy smooch that Rio had bestowed upon my fuchsia lips before I got out of his plush convertible made up for all the brouhaha.

***

Having Rahul as my committed boyfriend felt like receiving a lifetime achievement award. *Ekdum jhakkas*!

He made up the first date botch by taking me anywhere I wanted on our next one and footed a handsome bill. As I saw more of him, I realised he was simply absent-minded and over time, I found his 'forgetting this or losing that' quite endearing.

Rio was attentive, fun to hang around with and kept me in splits most of the time with his corny Parsi jokes and his easygoing nature. His sunroof cars added to his interest value and I spent many a late evening kicking off my heels and popping my head out of a roof as we sped over the newly built Bandra–Worli Sea Link and the Marine Drive stretch, with the wind passing through my hair and enwrapping me into a much desired feeling of utopia. Sure, we got fined for breaking speed limits once a while, but Rahul was a natural sweet talker (like SRK) and charmed his way out of any bad cop issues. I was a free bird in love with the guy of my choice who let me be myself.

Could life get any better?

Nope! Maybe the third time was the charm. *Officially* third.

Rahul adored my quirkiness and his beguiling eyes followed me everywhere. He even travelled on some of my flights to Dubai and London on my staff discounted tickets, mixing business with pleasure. It felt good to walk hand in hand in Dubai malls, sample different cuisines, browse through high street shops, or just stroll around Oxford Circus and the West End and do Londoner things together. He called me his 'va-va-voom gal' and was always generous with flattery. My kiss score boomed through the ceiling, bearing witness to our passion-filled lovemaking.

Our relationship thrived on innovation and extremities in the kinkiness realm. From role-playing to shopping together for adult toys, naughty props and games in the funky back lanes of Piccadilly Circus, to some serious dirtttyyy talking in bed to keep things interesting—young Mr Oberoi was insatiable between the sheets and I was unstoppable.

How I missed Aliya then. I wanted to share all the gory details of my sexual discoveries, adventures and dark confessions with her as I knew they would resonate only with her.

My self-confidence was at its all-time peak and I soon forgot what it was to be miserably single. I happily expanded to a size 14 on the threshold of a 16, at an alarming pace. But it did not seem a big deal to Rio at all. He swore he revered every inch of me, including the part of my tummy that wagged over him whenever I was on top. Unfortunately, old fears like memories do not just go away and I would recoil or hold my breath in whenever I felt less than my best self, which made him reach out at once.

'Shhh Sweet Lips,' he would then placate me sensitively, his soft lips over mine, making a huge fuss over me, knowing how happy it made me. 'I love you just the way you are. I wouldn't trade a thing. Now go try on that black slinky negligee we picked up at Ann Summers last week, I can't wait to sink my teeth in it.'

Until Rio, I had by and large been that girl who turned up her nose at other women who gave their men priority over their friends. I had even given Zoya and Coco hell for it.

But *love* changes every damn thing. So when I chose a romantic weekend getaway with Rahul in Ko Samui over Zoya's birthday, she was hopping mad at me.

But Kai Juicewalla finally had a boyfriend. A Prince Charming nonetheless and this time he was not the fictional tall, dark and handsome from the pages of a Jackie Collins novel, he was my true-blue bonafide connection, and my boarding card to bliss.

And I would be damned if I was going to give that up for anybody including a personal invite from SRK (unless it was a private tour of his room or something).

Checkmate Krish Aryan. *Check f**kin' mate*!

XXXSCORE = 777

18

I saw someone Kissing Santa Claus

2011

On our first anniversary, Rio and I went back to Mikasa, nostalgically talking about our first date and laughing about the fiasco of the forgotten wallet over a cosy candlelight dinner and discussing how time had gone by so fast. Just before the dessert arrived, I received three missed calls from Simran, so I excused myself and took it privately.

The breaking news was that Krish had called it quits with Floozie. She had cheated on him with her ex. Simran emptied the entire dictionary of gaali galoches she knew over the phone. She sounded beside herself and furious, making me realise she cared a great deal more about Krish than she showed.

'He caught them ramming each other on the eve of his first album launch, that too. Just imagine. Poor Krish. He looked worse than a train wreck at the biggest moment of his life.'

'Gosh, I didn't know...'

I was at a loss for words.

'If you had made it this evening, you would.'

I ignored that. She had every right to tick me off. I had purposely avoided the event, though not completely sure why. Besides it being my anniversary with Rio, my ego had got the better of me.

But now my blood was boiling, the besto in me taking over.

*That slutty vamp! Screwing my best friend over like this! Suzie taara g**nd maan keera ne chipkalee naa chodoo, tau maru bhi naam Kai nathi. (If I don't put insects and lizards up your arse Suzie, my name is not Kai.)*

'Let's feed her to hungry wolves.'

Spewing words of venom came naturally to Simran too.

'Yeah and drag her through the city by her hair tied to a donkey.'

Though in retrospect supporting my best friend Krish on his big day and letting go of any grudge would have shown some loyalty and maturity.

'My bad. I wish I had been there. Glad he had you and Zoya to take care of him.'

I expressed regret and hung up. Rio was waiting.

I went back to my table, strangely mixed up. I never wanted to see Krish hurt, so then why was I getting a teeny-weeny bit of sadistic satisfaction that he was suffering? *Karmo ka phal mitha hota* hain type?

I am a horrible person. Maybe I need a therapist. Or a tight slap. Or both. I don't deserve his friendship.

Guilty about leaving my boyfriend in the middle of our last course, I leaned over to kiss Rio, forgetting about the bowl of chocolate soufflé in front of him. It ran all over the table and splashed over his new Massimo Dutti linen shirt.

The good-natured guy that he was, he did not complain about the mess but simply asked for wet towels to wipe it off before kissing me even harder.

Rahul Oberoi was a great catch and there was no two ways about it. And to top it all, the Juicewallas could not get enough of him. Sunday brunches with the fam; elegant brooches and handpicked curios as gifts for Mommy from his travels; Yardley soaps and 4711 Eau de cologne bottles ordered from a specific shop in Munich for Granny B; spinning Dad in his latest wheels, had become my boyfriend's 'thing'.

'He is a good boy, marry him soon', my mother would often advise.

She had developed a soft corner for him thanks to his well-bred disposition, which was a deal-sealer for my mother.

'Yes, but first try some *chana nau aato* that will make him fairer,' Granny B started, pursing her lips as soon as I gave her a disapproving look.

'Have you met his parents?' Dad would enquire every other day.

Though open-minded, he reminded me often that in his days a Parsi boy asked a girl's hand in marriage as soon as they started a formal courtship. Mommy disagreed.

'I had to propose to you; if I left it to you, you would have been a bachelor married to your old fiat,' she chimed in.

Dad was well within his rights to be concerned. Rio had not introduced me to his family, not even his half-brother and that made me slightly uneasy. Was I not worthy enough to be considered as a daughter-in-law of the Oberoi fam?

I brought up these apprehensions with Zoya and Simran over a coffee reunion at Taj Lands End, a week before my 27th.

Hot Mamma Zoya donned in an Indo-western ensemble had brought her pooping and yowling son on our outing while his two nannies were made to hang around in the lobby of the hotel. I did attempt to hold him to keep her happy but she yelled, 'He's not a football Kai', and I promptly placed him back in his pram.

Krish had retreated into his shell, still reeling under post-Suzie trauma. I had spoken to him a few times over the phone, but he had sounded distant and aloof. He had not even called me Bawi in his inimitable style, making me realise that he was much more affected than I had thought he would be. Being the artistically sensitive soul that he was, he had probably fancied the two-faced tramp a bit too much for his own good.

'I don't know how long I can endure any more of the *gadha mazdoori* on these flights. My bones are creaking. And in the last six months, five passengers have asked me, "Miss Juicewalla, some freshly squeezed juice, phuleeze?" Even if it is an innocent question, it just sounds so vulgar.'

I whined to my besties.

Simran grinned saucily, she looked as tomboyish as ever, her trademark dimples intact.

'Just tell 'em we got ripe oranges and juicy melons baby!'

Zoya rolled her eyes.

'I wouldn't call it bonded labour. You party in London every second week ya, c'mon.'

'Look who's talking! Mrs La-di da who can afford to go there every weekend. Snapping your fingers at poor crew like me who have to endure your starry *nakhras*, make your bed and pick up your smelly socks whilst your personal valet fills up your immigration forms and fans your butt.'

'Touché,' she said, laughing, 'My hubby is certainly reeking in wealth. And making some serious dough in real estate, enough for 10 more generations at least.'

'What a show-off you are Z,' Simran said, 'and here I am, still paying EMIs for some asshole ex who has gone underground.'

'But if I were you Kai, I would turn up the gas stove on Junior Oberoi and ask for an explanation,' Zoya said, finally touching upon the sore subject.

Simran did not seem to agree with her.

She had met Rio once, over a drink, and she thought he was decent enough but then again, her judgement of the male species was as abysmal as mine, if not worse.

'Going out with someone and getting them to slip a ring on your finger are two different things and it takes both skill and tact,' said Zoya who had banged only one man in her life, but somehow seemed to have a PhD in Romance-ology.

Maybe that is the secret. An arranged marriage where one has no choice but to make it work.

Simran was smirking; she had read my thoughts—we rather eat our arms than have our parents choose our life partners.

As the conversation flowed over finger food, biscottis, herbal teas and café lattes, I happily blabbered about the number of presents I had showered on Rio, which included designer shirts; leather jackets; pricey car accessories; premium belts, perfumes, gym wear, watches and whatnot. Not leaving out the umpteenth number of times he travelled premium class on discounted tickets.

'For a man who is rolling in money, don't you find it a bit peculiar that he is quite a *muffat-chand*?' asked astute Zoya.

I jumped to his defence.

'Not at all! We have an equal partnership and I am not a girl who wants a man to pay for my facials and pedicures. Besides, he just bought me this Coach bag.'

I flung my lilac and beige handbag on the empty chair next to her. Not that Coach would remotely impress my posh friend who endowed her house help with Michael Kors watches and Longchamp totes on special occasions and various festivals.

'What do you think husbands are for?' Zoya snapped back.

'What does your Parsi *pakshi* have to predict about him?' asked Simran, giggling.

I had not consulted Rusty and Sohrab since forever. I did not need to. I was finally in a good place, touchwood. Moreover, almost everyone I knew had a dysfunctional relationship with their partners; it was not anyone's place to judge me.

'I think you are just being unfair; going Dutch is the norm these days.'

'But this ain't Dutch, these are freebies.'

Zoya continued to nag. But she knew from experience that when it came to relationships, neither Simran nor I paid any heed to her advice.

So she simply changed the milk bottle for Baby Naseem, shoved it in his mouth, looked up and smiled brightly, 'Okay, your call.'

'So long as he makes you meow…who cares?' Simran added with a shrug.

'Oh, he makes me roar.'

I assured them both adamant to prove grandma goose Zoya wrong and then turning to her, I said, 'If I don't get that Cartier ring I have my eyes on by the end of this year, you can change my name.'

'To what? Sucker-wala?' she quipped, breaking into a grin.

I picked up the black olive and gouda crostini and chomped on, appearing unaffected. I did not want a heated argument with my BFFs about whom I chose to love. Besides, Simran was crashing over at my place that night and I did not want either of us losing sleep over something that trivial. So, I let them blow on.

I was getting love, sex and companionship, and fantasising about SRK, Krish or Gerard Butler was no longer a necessity. It may not be a love so powerful, so boooooombastic that the dusky midnight sky turns into one massive rainbow, but my mind did break into SRK songs when Rio and I kissed and that was plenty more than I had ever got.

My perpetually sore lips said it all.

***

I discussed being Mrs Rio Moneybags with Danesh Camelia Khambatta, a new male purser who had become some sort of a friend-substitute for Aliya and Coco. Dan, half-bawa and half-Catholic, was openly gay. Good-looking to a fault with a sharp long nose inherited from his paternal side that suited him just fine, he would proudly state often, 'Longer the nose, bigger the knob. It gets me into places.'

I did not dare ask him 'which places?'.

Dan was the breath of fresh air I needed; a real mastikhor with heavy sarcasm and exaggerated gestures to match. I was glad my airline had finally opened their wings to hiring Indian boys too. Having a bit of brawn always helped, even though in this particular case, Dan was more beauty than brawn whose immaculate skin-care routine of applying moisturisers, skin-tightening serums and lip balms could give any model a complex.

We got along very well. Dan had kept his mother's name as his middle one and claimed that it enhanced his exquisite femininity, which he prided himself on.

His mantra was 'I am too glam to give a damn!'

'Why hasn't he discussed any future plans with you yet? Sounds a bit commitment-phobic if you ask me. And if he is, then you need to toodle-oo him really quick, honey,' Dan said one day over high tea at the Orangery, Kensington Gardens, London.

'Dan, how about if we are 40 and still single, then you and me…uh you know, uh get hitched?'

In most romcoms, the protagonist always has a backup plan like this. Usually it is her straight male best friend, but in my case my bestie was the MAIN PLAN!

'Are you insane? Even if I were 70 and senile, I'm not living with a woman. And why would I still be single at 40?' Dan said, offended that I had slotted him in the category of 'forever boy-less'.

But after speaking to Dan, I decided to take up the issue with Rio post-New Year's. 'If it ain't broke, don't fix it', I kept chanting to myself to keep going. But the truth was, we were both not getting younger and we were exclusive; we had this instant organic connection between us and we did not have to pretend to be anyone else other than ourselves around each other. So, the next step only made sense.

Moreover, Ash was returning to Mumbai the following year for good this time, with his pregnant wifey Aarti. And my mind was not exactly doing a hip, hip hurrah! Having a weepy wailing tot under her roof had never been on Kai's agenda. (Thankfully, Dan shared the same dislike for leaking toddlers.)

***

It was Christmas morning and I was still struggling to open my eyes when I heard the doorbell ring more than once.

'The *bhajiwali* has no manners, really,' I murmured, turning to my other side.

I was in a good mood so it did not bother me that much. I was home for the festivities and that is all that mattered. My family celebrated all festivals with great ardour—hearty meals, perfect table presentation, Mom's finest silverware and glassware and all the works.

But that year it was not just another traditional Christmas Eve buffet. Mommy dearest had outshone herself with ingredients, sauces, proteins and exotic legumes traded in from London by her one and only daughter. So we had a tempting spread of roast duck with orange jus and root veggies, avocado couscous feta salad, chicken roulade, cold cuts, mashed and rosemary potatoes, a three-layered giant asparagus and leek quiche, mini-cheese eclairs, a surfboard-sized spinach and parmigiana cannelloni, Russian pattice, vegetable kiev, chicken vindaloo, rogan josh, rogan soya, garlic prawns, chilli paneer, vegetable moussaka, two kinds of velvety bakes, egg fried rice, schezwan chicken/paneer, sweet honey noodles, Christmas cake from Marks & Spencer, UK, and brandy-infused hot puddings from a luxury *boulangerie* near Carnaby Street, London. If there was a contest for the best home chef in the world, she would win hands down.

Exotic hampers brimming with delectable sweets and marzipans (from the sweet sellers at Hill Road in Bandra) were opened; gifts were exchanged and a colourful eight-inch bauble with an angel floating in it that Rio had bought from the Selfridges' Christmas market for our Xmas tree, dangled alongside the customary golden star, right at the top.

Nostalgic stories were shared with Granny B enthralling us with tales of ancient Persia, the mystery of our holy Mount Damavand and general *gupshup* dating back to the 1920s. Shanaya was back from her Hong Kong stint and her new boyfriend Gary had joined us. Jimmy had dropped in with his new flavour of the month on his way to a 'cooler party'.

Rio had kept his arm around me the entire evening, whispering into my ears, two 'I love yous' a minute, making me extremely happy. He thoughtfully slipped out a wee bit before midnight because he knew it was our family tradition to bring in the 25th with only the immediate members of kin. He had always been so non-fussy, and that had made me fall for him even more, since day one.

As I was lying in bed and reminiscing about last night, my bedroom door burst open. I was about to throw a fit at whoever had broken my morning code of privacy when I saw a familiar face standing over my bed.

What in Khodaiji's name is Dan doing in my bedroom? That too in eye-stinging fluorescent yellow trousers and a jarring orange creased shirt? It's probably just a dream.

But it was soon to turn into a nightmare.

I rested my head back on the pillow, half-shutting my eyes again.

'What's with the elf pyjamas?'

I heard a whiny voice above me, followed by an impatient push.

'Move your big bum, sis. I need to sit down and catch my breath.'

'Has a bus run over you, charsi?' I asked, covering myself with a blanket, watching him rock to and fro, his face as white as a sheet, totally wrecked.

I then took a glass of water from my nightstand and sprinkled some drops over his face and hair.

'Are you sleepwalking? Did something happen last night? Why aren't you in bed?'

'I haven't slept at all.'

I had been to one of those rough thrashes with him—shots, snorts, sniffs, drag queens and frantic socializing. An overwhelmingly rigorous affair although his gang was pretty chilled out.

So, I was not surprised with that but there was a chill in his voice.

'Kai, I am not going to beat around the bush.'

I sat up and peered into Dan's face with my bleary eyes. Dan suddenly looked much older than usual as he sat up straight, pouring some water from the jug into the glass I had earlier used on him.

'So you know I was at Faiz's place last evening, right?'

I nodded unwittingly, not sure I wanted to hear what was to come.

Faizal and Dan called themselves sisters (a gay code for platonic love) and were the closest of friends.

'So I am ready to get with this beautiful boy on Faiz's terrace, right?'

'Too much info Danny Boy, but whatever...'

My vision was still hazy. I needed my chai. Despite that I managed to roll my eyes.

'And then around midnight someone I never expected to see, like *ever*, *ever*, ever walks in.'

'Who? Who?'

*What the f**k is he talking about?*

'I can't, Kai. It will destroy you.'

This boy was stressed.

'SSS R.K? Yikes! Oh Dan, please don't do this to me. I will jump off the 35th floor of The Shard. (If I have to kill myself I might as well die in style).'

SRK at a gay X'mas party? *Why OHHHH Why*?

'Focus, Kai, please I beg you.'

Dan shook me slightly.

'So he doesn't realise I'm there, and then he heads for Faiz's bedroom. Faiz is dressed as Santa, cute na?'

'Are you still talli or what?' I enquired, wondering if I should lay him flat on my bed and lullaby him to sleep.

Dan began stroking my hair in a strange way; he seemed to be buying time and consoling me at the same time. I was this close to biting his hand in frustration.

'Who was it, you gadhera? *Bolse*? *Ke maari maree java ni vaar joich*? (Will you tell me or are you waiting for me to die?)'

I raised my voice at him now, tugging at his shirt too, irritated with the dreaded migraine rising. He looked me straight in the eyes then and stammered slightly before breaking my Christmas bauble of trust, happiness and joy, over my head.

'Huns, I am sorry to be the one to tell you this and please don't start digging your hideous golden nails into my sensitive, soft skin but…I swear on every label I have ever purchased on Bond Street… Oh Jesus, have mercy. Kai, oh my Kai, it was your boyfriend!'

19

Kamasutra to Karma-sutra

'Kai Kai!'

I may have blacked out for a few seconds because the next few moments were so distorted.

And then, the next minute, I may have sounded bat shit crazy.

'Rrrrrahul, Rio...was with us until 11:15 p.m. last night. He even called me up when he reached home to thank me again for the wonderful evening with my "cho chweet family" as he addresses them.'

Maybe Danny Boy has not recovered from last night's buzz. That's the only explanation to this madness.

'Luv, it's 2011, we all have cellphones,' Dan stated quietly, 'which could be used from anywhere, right? And I recognised him from all those snaps you have *pakaoed* me with. And I think we had met twice too, once in passing at our hotel lobby in Dubai and the other time around Diwali at some party.'

I was shifting uncomfortably. Why was my friend destroying my favourite day of the year?

'You must be mistaken, Dan. Rio is not gay, in fact, far from it. You can't just crash into my house and fabricate stuff like that. You are just jealous of my raging sex life or hammered or both.'

My voice hit crescendo and my knuckles threw punches over his rib cage.

Dan leaned over and shook me firmly.

'Oh dahling, let's avoid getting tantrummy and causing a scene at this criminal hour of the day. I'm nastily hung over and can scarcely keep my eyes open. Now listen to me carefully. You know that I have been a fag since I was in my baby pink chuddies, right? I know a swinger when I see one, especially with his pants down.'

Danesh Camelia could be an explicit, ruthless and a coldblooded diva sometimes.

'I had a feeling all along. Too branded, too perfect, too anti-homo, you know? Barely spoke a word when we met. Afraid of being unmasked I suppose. There was always something very fishy there.'

And the diva kept digging in her claws. I knew he did not mean to be hurtful but at that moment, I would have appreciated some diplomacy, some empathy and a tight hug.

Had I seen the signs too?

No.

He was the perfect BF. He treated me really well. He was doting and kind. Yes, he indulged in high-end designers, filed his nails more than me, always smelt like a bouquet of flowers and wore snazzy socks but so did plenty of metrosexual men. Above all, he was respectful to all the people I loved.

Though of late, he had been taking phone calls privately but these were 'purely professional', he had reassured me. There was a Mohit Ahuja from his Delhi office, Shailesh-something from Ahmedabad, Anton from Sweden and more recently a Mr Faizal Merchant, his new manager.

Faizal? *Faiz*?

I shut my eyes.

'I am calling him up right now. *Doodh ka doodh aur pani ka pani ho jayega.* (To get the facts right.) Only to prove to you that you have lost your marbles.'

You know that feeling when you are fuming and sinking all at once?

'Christ, Kai, get a grip.'

He squeezed my hand as I started searching under my throw for my phone.

'I wouldn't just come here and jack up your mind, na? The last thing I wanted to do is to be the bearer of such bad news but I'm afraid there is more.'

What? That Rio is not only bisexual but an alien cross-dresser with a secret mistress tucked somewhere as well?

'Rahul Indur Oberoi ain't the son of Indur Oberoi. He actually works in his office as his PA, travels for their *chota mota kaam* here and there and swindles accounts to pay for his expenses. The only thing your lover boy has in common with the Oberois is the surname.'

'Are you freakin' nuts?'

Now I was screaming.

'He drives the best cars, owns properties everywhere, gifted me an LV just recently.'

Well actually, I had gifted him 10 times the number of gifts he had. And his passport had a different middle name which he said was his Hindu name according to numerology or something to that effect. Okay, so I had never seen the houses which he claimed to have in every corner of Mumbai except the one near Kemps Corner, which was not much but I had not given it a thought.

I was flabbergasted.

'Faiz told me everything this morning. They have been bonking for a few months now. Faiz had no idea about you two. His undercover name on this new hush-hush website, which by the way is banned in India for its iffy content, is "Randy Rio".'

With that said, I asked the messenger of doom and gloom Dan to leave otherwise I would have shot him. I was hangry. I needed to binge because the tension-*wala* acidity was squishing my intestines and only food would save me from taking any drastic step. So, I yelled at Kamala tai to bring me tea and an omelette-toast as soon as Danny left. She brought it quickly.

As I sat gobbling my breakfast in my bed, waves of unimaginable sorrow and despair shot down my spine, causing every muscle in my body to contract and disintegrate into ash, as if it had been electrocuted by some high voltage device. Despite having eaten, I felt my bedroom spinning like a merry-go-round as I held on to the edges of my bed. So I could no longer blame gas. This was real. And 50 times worse than the scary and deadly serpent ride I took at Alton Towers on which I had a bladder explosion and did *su su* in my jeans.

I started to tear the walls down. Literally. My bedroom, my sanctuary of hope and optimism was now a grave; I was in mourning. I had lost my reason to live.

'The hottest love has the coldest end.' Now who said that? Socrates I think.

Flashes of Rio and Faiz appeared before my eyes, causing me to throw up my breakfast and I had no energy to clean up as I sat there as one big mess.

I thought of the small wallet card the f**ker had gifted me which glorified these lines, 'Love is patient, love is kind; love bears all things, believes all things, hopes all things, endures all things; love never fails. - The Corinthians'.

Does this include tolerating a bisexual lover, a liar, a moocher and a cheat? Is this the definition of love? No deal-breakers and no list of non-negotiables?

*Har*mi, vahiyat,* cock-sucking b**tard!

I threw my empty tea cup towards the window, it crushed into tiny pieces, one flying straight back and pricking my elbow. I let it bleed, wishing it would not stop until every drop of me had drained from my lifeless body. I did not know what hurt more, that he had lied about his identity or dumped me for a guy.

I was freaking out almost as badly as I had when I had found out about Jangu being hitched. But I was much younger then; there was *hope*. Now I had to start all over again with someone new who once again would be a shot in the dark. All my past efforts were null and void. Did I have it in me to go through the process of falling in love ever again? Well at least one thing was confirmed. There was a universal conspiracy against me. Just like I had suspected.

I needed to talk to someone before I removed any traces of Rio from the night before. I did not want to call Simran or Zoya and have the 'we-told-you-so' salt rubbed on my wounded pride and butchered heart. I needed a balm, cool and soothing.

As if on a telepathic cue, Krish called to wish me a Merry Christmas just then. His usual 'Ho Ho this is Santa Claus' gimmickry was cut short as soon as he heard my quaky voice; he immediately suggested we meet up the following day. It was everything I needed.

But before that I had some unfinished business to take care of…

***

I met Rio the same evening at his friend's empty flat at Breach Candy where we often spent quality time. He took me in his arms so ardently and warmly that for a flip second, I wondered if Dan had been too smashed and I had been an idiot to buy his story. But just then his phone rang and I could see a 'Sameer' flashing on the phone.

'Work call, but will take it later.'

He flicked a strand of hair off my oval face as he began to tell me how much he loved me, biting me impatiently across my neck.

Yucks! The last thing I need are his droppings in the form of teeth marks.

I returned it with a tongue-in-ear manoeuvre that always got him as aroused as a school boy watching porn. Every kiss, every embrace, every touch that followed and had once filled me with unconstrained desire, was now making me sick to the bone.

Shuddering to even think about where all his devious mouth had been the night before and many such nights, I wanted to break down and ask him for an explanation but I knew I needed to finish the game I had come to play.

And just when he got pumped up like he usually did after a brisk foreplay, I gave the fekuchand his well-deserved reward—a sharp knee-to-nuts attack, that threw him across the bed on to the floor with an earth-shattering scream as he groaned and gasped for air, holding on to his prized possessions lest they fall off.

Spitting over his gobsmacked face, I began to walk away, leaving him moaning in what I hoped was explosive pain. He had not only trampled over my heart, but also fooled around with my family's feelings. And that was simply unpardonable.

But I wasn't yet finished with him. So, I stood over him as he lay curled up on the cold floor like a ball of useless lard, whimpering, pathetic and begging for mercy. Holding between my fingers, his handsome face that lay under floppy soft hair that I had loved so much, I tunnelled deep into his bamboozled eyes one last time, before speaking my last words to him, 'You don't hang your stockings on two Christmas trees, buddy.'

Grabbing his garments, which had been strewn all over the bed in the earlier raptures of his hankering desires, I flung them out of the seventh-floor window.

Who have I become?

I could hardly recognise myself. From lovemaking to ball-breaking, the journey was short and eerie.

But every self-respecting woman has (and should have) two sides to her, one of a nurturing partner and the other a badass bitch. It all depends on which of her buttons you push. And this sleazeball had pushed the wrong f**king one.

***

Surprisingly, our 'shack' at Juhu beach was still around. It had been ages since our last visit. Krish was running late. As I sat waiting for him, I noticed a few bottles and soda cans littered up the place. Typical of most Indian beaches where people think public property is their personal garbage-dumping ground. I was no environmentalist but that day everything was irking me. The night before had been brutal to my broken soul, with recurrent nightmares of Rio posing for nudes with all his 'special' male-friends and goading me to shoot them in an orchard filled with black oranges.

Walking up to a group of teenagers who were cracking bottles nearby and bragging to each other about their drinking prowess, I shouted, '*Yeh tum logo ka baap ka jagah hain kya*? *Ghar jaake dudh piyo.* (Is this your pop's property? Go home and drink milk.)'

I had to yell at someone.

With my unkempt hair, which I had not bothered to comb that day and my matron-type bronze-rimmed spectacles falling over my face, I must have looked like I meant serious business because my *dhamki* worked and they scurried away from my spot. Lots had been taken away from me the day before, and I was not going to let a bunch of underage delinquents gain control of The Shack.

Krish showed up with a copy of his new music album, a mistletoe and a metallic photo frame which encased an old photograph of both of us that had been clicked a long time ago at Yoko Sizzlers, Santacruz. It was the last week of college and we had treated ourselves to garlic and pepper shashliks. Krish had his arm around me with a big, goofy grin plastered on his face. I seemed to be laughing at some joke, my head tilted, podgy cheeks enhanced, happiness written all over me. Simran had snapped us and then clumsily dropped the pocket cam in the mix of cabbage, peas and mash; Zoya had refused to be in it because she was having a 'pimple day' or something as bizarre as that.

'That's soooo cute. You still have it?'

I took the photo frame from him, my throat clogging up with nostalgia.

My besto held up the tiny festive branch that he had brought with him over my head and planted a kiss on my cheek which got a watery smile out of me despite my doggone mood.

'Okay Bawi, thou pour into thy cup.'

He had come prepared. He beckoned me to sit with him on the soft sand, placing a square napkin under me knowing how much I disliked getting dirty.

'*Gelch**yo. Jhootto. L**duchand. H**ami...*'

I ran out of breath, emptying the entire dictionary of Parsi cuss words into Krish's ears. He waited until I had finished, before speaking.

'Hell hath no fury like a bawi duped, huh? But on a serious note, it's the shittiest thing to happen to anyone Bawi. Who knows better than me?'

I nodded solemnly. Krish had gone through some heartbreaking f**kwittage of his own.

'I know this is the last thing you want to hear but from someone who cares for you so much, I can only emphasise how vital it is for you to reconnect with yourself. This entire quest for an elusive superhero with a diamond ring popping out of a champagne glass with moonbeams shining over your head is nothing but onscreen *kachra* and unhealthy codependency we have with our other halves.'

I pulled a face and said, 'If I needed a sermon, I would ask the girls.'

'Hmm. But what kind of a best friend would I be if I wasn't honest? First step, flush out that silly SRK out of your system, Kai, and put a lid on all those dumb Hollywood romcoms you watch. They should be banned for all women from 16 to 60.'

(I would like to lower the age and add fairy tales with equally dumbass drift.)

'Love and happiness like butterflies flit away when you chase them. Even Baba Tridev emphasises that we can find bliss only within our inner selves and not through external stimuli.'

There was finality in his tone.

I knew Krish was not criticising me because the concern in his voice was unmistakable. He quoted various sadhus, swamis and philosophers all the time and we were all immune to that. The great Rumi's sayings were still sensible, the others were highly questionable. But Krish had my best interest at heart; I never second guessed that.

Feeling exceptionally unguarded, I took his hand into mine and asked him all choked up, 'Tell me Krish, you know me the longest, right? Do you think something is wrong with me? Why is love so easy for most and impossible for me?'

Krish seemed to have swallowed a tennis ball as he sat there, mum.

'You know I should have caught on when the creep insisted on taking me to a male-strip joint in Soho…wanted me "to have a good time", so he proclaimed. I thought he was the coolest boyfriend ever. What a fool I was!'

I shook my head and laughed at my extreme gullibility.

Krish elbowed me affectionately and said, 'Look at the bright side Rudolph. At least, you both had something in common.'

He handed me a tissue to wipe my runny nose.

'Yes, but Rio was more like *kabhi pussy, kabhi bum.*'

We both fell on the sand, chuckling at my joke.

'Bawi, you know what your problem is?'

Krish finally found his balance as he sat up and dusted himself off.

'You are too good for all these sponge-offs. You just have to wait for the best, you know, a true alchemist who will change your life forever.'

'I thought you stopped believing in those things, Krish?'

'Ha ha! I still don't. I am spiritually evolving and away from such cravings. But that doesn't mean that I can't wish it for my Bawi who wears her heart on her sleeve and shoves her brains in her pockets and believes in others more than she believes in herself.'

No one could have said it better. Maybe because nobody knew me better. I rested my head on his shoulder, watching the eternal circle of time receding into choppy waters. I felt my trust, my belief and my faith in goodness sinking with it.

'Sun'll come out tomorrow
Bet your bottom dollar that tomorrow there'll be sun

Just thinking about tomorrow
Clears away the cobwebs and the sorrow 'til there's none

When I'm stuck with a day that's grey and lonely
I just stick out my chin and grin and say
The sun'll come out tomorrow...'

Krish hummed the popular number softly.

I still strongly believed that having someone who you were deeply in love with, sure made life bearable. The smallest things made the biggest difference—have someone to feed you with their own hands (Sid and Rio both did that), massage your shoulders when you are exhausted, play adult poker with you and then end the night with a sizzling 69.

'If only life came with a remote control where you could rewind your mistakes, fast forward to a brighter tomorrow or press pause on the nicest moments.'

I groaned again.

'Bawi, you are a masterpiece, there is only one of you! Now don't you worry, it will all fall in place,' he said, gently rubbing my knee with his hand.

'Hey, you haven't read what's behind the picture frame?'

I looked down, flipped the frame and read: 'All I want for Christmas is for my best friend to be happy. Luv, your Besto'.

I observed the photo closely.

'Will I ever laugh with such merry abandon again?' I asked Krish, 'I was only 19 here. Those days, my biggest source of pain was weight gain.'

'Listen. Don't you dare blame yourself for someone else's f**k-ups. Sometimes you have to just let go.'

He spoke this with such strong conviction that I wondered if he was talking about himself or Rio. I did not want to know this time.

'Men should come with instruction manuals or they shouldn't exist at all!'

Krish laughed.

'Chalo. Before the ants bury us alive, let's get outta here. How about egg club sandwiches and fries at Sun N Sand with steaming cups of adrak wali chai? My treat.'

He got up on his feet and helped me rise.

No matter what the crisis, food always made things right especially fries.

XXXSCORE= 911

20

Messiah Clooney to the Rescue

2012–2013

After the Christmas fiasco, New Year's eve was rather low key. I was nursing my scars and felt numb and emotionless.

'A bad relationship is like a horrific haircut, it takes time to outgrow it.'

(Thank god for chick flicks dishing out such great wisdom.)

I needed something or somebody to unbreak my heart; uncry these tears; undo this hurt. I felt spiritually disconnected with myself and even my guardian angels who always came through for me (however late in the day, the meanies) seemed to be lost on a seal-hunting expedition to the North Pole or perhaps given up on me.

So, there was only one thing left to do. I requested Sohrabji over the phone for a reading, as his wife had a slip disc and could not entertain guests at their home.

'Sheeeeet happens Sheeeeet happens. Last was a big mistake. New love, new love, coming.'

Thus spake the bird in the background when I called.

'He better be right or I shall make KFC out of him,' I warned *bechara* Sohrabji before hanging up. Though chances of falling in love with someone again after all the 'sheeeeet' were close to zippo.

'I don't need to be a genius to figure that love is not for me. Flings are not for me. Relationships are *definitely* not for me. And SRK is going to be in adult diapers by the time I ever get to meet him. So cut to the chase, nothing is for me. I think I have lost my touch.'

I found myself venting out to Simran on our Valentine's coffee date at CCD.

'I thought you mentioned that HE was on your flight a few months ago and you sniffed around him like a bitch on heat all night long while he slept in his first-class suite.'

'Yes, and that's all I could do. I was dating Rio then. What should I have done? Shaken him awake and professed my undying love?'

'Missed opportunities are worse than none. I bet you are kicking yourself now.'

'More so, because my so-called King of Diamonds proved to be the Queen of Hearts. Now I regret not slipping my phone number into SRK's vest pocket or shoe.'

'Regrets. Regrets. That's all we have...'

Simran sighed. She had just withstood yet another manipulative boyfriend, a tour director who had turned out to be discreetly engaged, so she was as exasperated as me.

'Valentine's disgusts me. An over-promised and under-delivered day made by corporate sharks to squeeze us out of cash and our peace of mind.'

'Exactly two years ago, Rahul had grovelled for a first date with me.'

I informed her flatly, wishing I could expose him to the real Oberois for identity theft.

'Why do you think all women-related problems have the word "men" in them? **Men**strual cramps, **men**opause, Coincidence ?' I asked, trying to lighten the mood.

'All men are bhen**ods. They should be garlanded with *chappal ka haars* and flogged in public with spiked belts.'

Thankfully, Simran's sassiness was intact.

She seldom minced her words, but I could see from the dark circles around her eyes that her last connection had taken a toll on her.

I reached out to hug her, remembering the first day we had met. Ironically, we had been chasing boys in college even then. But that day, we had converted into man-haters from man-eaters. Thankfully, we always had each other's backs especially when it came to matters of the heart.

Krish and I talked quite often on the phone but the only difference between us was that Krish was single by choice and I was not. His annual trips to the North East, Rishikesh, Burma, Ladakh seeking answers to life continued. Of course, they made little sense to me. I did not see any point in talking to Nature and deciphering cryptic clues from it.

'It's a part of self-healing and finding yourself. After all, what are we but tiny specks of flesh and spirit in the larger picture of life?'

He would say laughing.

I had found myself. Thank you very much. And it was in the middle of nowhere—part of no picture, big or small. There was no *picture abhi baki hai* for me any more. But the silver lining was that like old times, we were inseparable once again and I celebrated every small achievement of his. In our rollercoaster-like friendship, life had come full circle.

He had started getting noticed for his work in Bollywood films and I was excited for him. Best friends are kindred souls too. His mother was doing much better as of late and he had taken her on a few holidays. Ishika had broken off with the thug she had almost eloped with and had found herself a serious accountant.

Zoya was shortlisting schools for her kiddo already. Coco and James were to get hitched in July, but I would not make it to Sydney because my flying schedule had become even more hectic.

I felt I was stagnating in my job but on most days, it was a true blessing. Being busy and meeting new people every week kept me distracted from my heartbreak.

Besides, Air International had flight attendants of mixed nationalities and my colleagues were a fun, lively and carefree bunch of people who had the innate ability to smile through almost everything.

Fortunately, I did not hear from Rio ever again.

'Good riddance to bad rubbish', Danny would growl whenever I tried to play the victim card.

Granny B had moved permanently to her beloved Lonavala where she wanted to spend her remaining days in oneness with Nature—the clean air, her rose shrubs, rare birds that chirped on her window sills—her dogs and her beautiful memories.

The family understood that and one or the other of us managed to do the two- and half-hour drive from Mumbai to Lonavala as often as we could to pay her a visit.

Coco informed me that she had heard from a source about Aliya moving to Kolkata to live with her brother. An exasperating mystery we had not managed to solve yet.

Despite Dan's warnings of relationships being the biggest scam of the 21st century, I loathed being on my own. I was a couple of years away from the high pressure 30 and nothing was going according to plan. I had become an insomniac overcome by fears of being alone, not to rule out the fact that I had gotten more bitter than cough syrup about my love life. I felt aimless. Nobody even seemed to crush over me and vice versa. The restlessness and paranoia of being deceived all over again by some guy was overwhelming.

Though Krish recommended the Art of Living course to gain clarity, I hired a yoga teacher to show me some *pranayamas* and asanas instead, though it was no substitute for partnership and intimacy, merely a placebo. So, I turned to food with vengeance.

If I had to write about that phase I would have put it so:

'Kai Juicewalla has manifested into a raging foodaholic who eats and drinks to her heart's content, and has grown rapidly into a size and half bigger.

She cracks jokes on herself at work, hugs her parents to assure them that she is okay, goes to the fire temple and prays for normalcy, donates money to a secret cause, cries on her pillow all night and wakes up the next day and carries on as if nothing is amiss.

Sometimes she sedates her fears in alcohol and other times, with whatever carbs she gets her hands on. Her fridge is her new love interest and she cherishes the comfort it gives her in return.

She read about this thing called inner child-healing in some books borrowed from well-wishers but that meant digging from her own coffin of buried memoirs and burning it to the ground again. So, she burned those books instead.

Her uniforms are disintegrating from their seams and when one of her trousers split from its crotch, whilst she bent over a food trolley to serve a passenger his smoked salmon and trout appetiser, her tailor Shakeel at Elco Arcade, Hill Road, added extra material to discreetly make it fit.

It was then that she knew she was in big, fat trouble and needed a miracle asap.'

'I need help.'

I found myself telling Pari over a call.

(My only saving grace was that my brother had finally returned to Mumbai and as much as I had reservations earlier about sharing bathroom space and it being a tight squeeze, my adorable baby-nephew Rehu provided a welcome change from the dull, tedious and my borderline depressive status quo.)

Coincidentally, Pari's sister-in-law Farzin, who was a model, had spoken about one Dr K Qureshi who had helped her in her fight with bulimia. Pari suggested that I meet him.

I did not see the harm in paying a professional. Better than giving a *supari* to a hitman to eliminate Randy Rio.

So around the 23rd of October, on one of my days off from flying duties, I found myself squirming on a chair opposite Dr Kabeer Qureshi who could be correctly described as a 'mouth-watering, lip-smacking rasmalai'.

Why God? Why can't he be an ugly, old fart instead of being a silver fox? Is this a test?

'You are the heroine of your story, Ms Juicewalla, so you must never settle for a supporting role. Embrace those flaws, rehash the past if you must, wear those scars proudly.'

'This world will unlock countless doors, when you live each day with love, joy, courage and intensity.'

His pearls of sex…uh wisdom that bounced off my ears in our lengthy one-to-ones through the next few weeks, often made me wonder if he was simply a poet trapped in the body of a shrink.

Oh, cut the blah blah. Can I strap you to your desk and devour you like a lollipop instead?

Even though I cognized what he meant, that one should never settle being a sidekick in any kind of partnership and keep one's standards high, I could barely focus on his words. His heart-shaped lips, smooth chest, enticing persona, Morse-coded tattoo on his left wrist, impeccable dressing sense took all my attention and most of my breath.

How did the rest of the female patients survive this?

But the stints got harder by the week for not only was I killing myself resisting his sexiness, but I had almost emptied my pockets to pay for the extended therapy sessions so I could see more of him in the hope that I could show him 'more of me'.

'I ask this the utmost love for you—don't you ever learn woman?'

Pari was shocked, when she pinged to ask me how it was going.

'Kai, he's your therapist ya.'

'But have you seen him? I swear you will crush on him too. And I so need this. I mean 'The Lord of Small Mercies' up there finally realises how dreadfully miserable I've been and sends me this Messiah who has an uncanny resemblance to George Clooney.'

'And if I don't act upon it, I will never forgive myself.'

No, I was not going to get swayed by her lack of support.

For as soothing as Killer Looks Qureshi's husky voice was and he was undoubtedly a thorough professional in his approach, I got a strange vibe from him that I could not put a finger on.

Mid-December, Pari and Shanaya held a Saturday intervention for me at Candies, a popular fast food joint in Bandra. Seeing the giant red flag from a distance and recognising my pattern, the lawyer in Shanaya blackmailed me into cutting off my sessions.

'They are bound by law and they can't get involved with their patients. I could litigate.'

I was gorging on the awesome butter chips and veg junglee sandwiches, refusing to pay any heed to either.

'So according to both of you, I should get stuck with one man forever like Pari? Or then lock myself in a bathroom and cry over a *ch**tya* for the next five years? I rather risk a lawsuit in that case "your honour".'

'Get over it, sis!'

Pari was quick on the defence.

'Rahul was a jackass. But he's not the only one in the universe. There will be more. (*Jackasses*?) Better ones like my Cyrus. And every guy you meet won't be on Europe's 'most wanted' list.'

Shanaya and I broke into chuckles. I had almost forgotten Gangsta Gabriele.

What was so horrendous about flirting with my shrink? He was an all-rounder, mentally stimulating, easy on the eye and knew all my dirty secrets.

Kabeer Qureshi was a man of the world who understood every inch of my head space, that too in a short span of 7 weeks and 14 sittings only! Now all he had to do was explore the rest.

'Kabeer is like this lollipop. You just want to unwrap him and put him in your mouth. And he smells, oooh la la—sex on toast even from five feet away. Like fresh grass mixed with heady cologne. Wait, let me see if I can find a pic of his on Google.'

I could not believe I was so cheerful again. My self-esteem was back in order. It was all thanks to KQ. Mmmmuah!

'Aha, found it!' I exclaimed. 'Though there isn't much. There is this one that looks like he's in a conference or something, a group click with the medical faculty…oh wait and an award one too. Ooh, he lights up any room. Check this!'

I almost slapped the phone on Shanaya's cheek. Pari grabbed it, and I could see her curiosity pique slightly.

'Wow! I see where you are coming from. I mean ya hmmmm, it makes sense but still…'

I was certain she had forgotten about her darling Cyrus in those few seconds. But Shanaya was annoyed with us and refused to even entertain our oohs and aahs.

'Mental health is not to be taken lightly. Besides, didn't we both decide that casual romps were off the table?'

'Maybe your table. But what did "chasing a so-called fairytale romance" get me, haan? A wet (no pun intended) pillow and an addiction to sleeping pills? And men do it all the time. Why should there be different rules for us when it comes to lust?'

Of course, I did not tell them about the thin golden band on KQ's left hand, they did not need to know *everything*.

A deceitful slimeball had lied through his teeth and knifed my soul. Movie nights, endless drives (albeit in his stolen cars), airport pick-ups, strawberry and champagne baths had all been snatched away from me overnight. I had suffered enough and it was my time to take charge of my own happiness. I was now committed to myself and myself only.

'Illegal or immoral, I care a damn now! If I want some fun and enjoyment, I am more than entitled to it.'

I asserted, throwing them both a dissatisfied look and digging deep into my corn and mushroom baked dish. Shanaya held my hand firmly.

'We understand that you need closure after the Rio shamble. But there are better and more rational ways to move on than hooking up with your therapist, creating a scandal and getting his licence revoked. Give it some time.'

Whatever! Only the person wearing the shoes knows where they pinch.

I had to break free and feed my wild passions. Period. And it was fairly easy for them to preach. Shanaya was in a solid relationship with her restaurateur beau Chef Gary and Pari was already well-settled.

I had done all the footwork the therapist had recommended and I was now geared for new innings. And who better than the coach himself?

So on a day before Christmas eve after jet splashing half a bottle of Jean Paul Gaultier over myself, waxing my legs and arms, salon straightening my hair and dangling my chalk white thunder thighs from under my lucky denim skirt in front of his steady eyes, I mustered the courage to ask KQ out on a date, at the end of our final session. He did not seem surprised at all.

'You are a very attractive and intelligent woman, Kai. Wish I could, but I like to stay away from any controversy. Besides don't you deserve someone who is all there for you or then the purpose of all our conversations is lost? What do you think? What does your inner child tell you?'

I sighed, that inner child again! She was turning out to be quite a liability if you ask me. I gave him a half-nod. Well at least, he had not spoken about his wife and ruined the moment.

As I got ready to leave the cabin, for the last time, I hugged him tight. I knew this was not patient–doctor protocol, but I had to leave a part of me with him.

He placed a light peck on my cheek, wished me well and bid me goodbye. I let him go and began to turn the door knob.

Haven't you heard of the phrase, strike while the iron is hot?

No, Kai, no. Stop! *You just heard the man.*

Click. Click. Lock.

'Uhhhh, Kai, whaaa whaaat's going on…?!'

KQ's uncertain voice was barely audible, as I took a few steps towards him and ripped open his shirt buttons in a jiffy, kicking the chair between us aside. The tug-of-war between us must have lasted for a mere 20 seconds.

Flinging the paperwork from his desk on to the carpet in one clean swipe before pulling him into a passionate embrace of locking lips and biting necks, the rasping of the dark wood beneath us was submerged by our heavy breathing. As bestselling author Candace Bushnell puts it, 'Man may have discovered fire, but women discovered how to play with it.'

I walked out 35 minutes later feeling more empowered than a hundred bloodhounds. Kai Juicewalla's therapy seshes had been a roaring success and her inner child was jumping in sheer ecstasy.

XXX Score = 916

27

Fake It till You Make It?

'Okay I am ready to give online dating a shot.'

I said to Shanaya who had been insistent that I scan through some websites that have worked for a couple of her friends.

I loathed the concept of online dating or groom hunting. To me, taking the help of matchmakers, well-wishers and websites to find a life partner was the height of desperation. But beggars cannot be choosers.

So, somewhere in the beginning of 2013, I gave Shanaya the go-ahead to set up my profile on a wedding site.

'Just as long as it's not a hook-up site.'

I warned her. KQ had been a one-off (George Clooney *ka bhai* after all) and I was back on the Rajdhani train of hope.

Happy to oblige, Shanaya cancelled our karaoke night at Three Monkeys and instead came over to kick-start the hunt.

'Think of it as a lounge bar or one of your flights where you are just checking out random men,' she tried to sound convincing, 'except that these are safely tucked behind the screen.'

I nodded, giving a huge yawn. I was lying on my sofa, editing my second short story of my debut book

Guess what is the new way to get rejected? Algorithm.

'Sis, these sites are meant for f'ugly lovelorn case studies who don't have the confidence to find their equal in person. I am hot, sexy, gorgeous, yes, overweight still, but I can do better than this. Let's just drop this and go hit a club.'

'But you haven't done better, have you?'

She was not being mean but she had always been brutally straightforward.

'Well, I will give this online thing a chance and if it doesn't work, I will continue to write dark narratives around "frustrated women slicing shrivelled up willies", in my novel.'

I warned Shanaya who simply did not seem to care about my opinion or my half-baked book.

I glanced at the screen, reading profile write-ups and scanning photographs with no great interest.

'Why only bawas? You know what happened with Jangu.'

'That was a lifetime ago, Kai.'

I rolled my eyes.

'Besides, if we are looking at arranged marriage then we might as well try our own *namunas* first. Now stop daydreaming and pay attention. Check out this one.'

Shanaya was seriously on the prowl; the entire virile community of Parsi men was jumping out from her laptop. I yielded to her efforts by grunting and snorting and providing my two-paisa worth as deemed necessary.

'*Arre baba*! Too toothy.'

'Is that an egg or a head?'

'So thanda.'

'Ugghs, creepy.'

'Incestuous! Looks like my brother.'

'Nah! So bawaji.'

Shanaya shut the laptop.

'Don't you want to find a man, get him to propose to you and get Granny B to give you both her blessings on her hundredth? You have less than 12 months to go and it's not gonna happen if you're gonna act all high maintenance.'

'No, no, open it; I think I just spotted an interesting one.'

I nudged her, trying to sound more enthusiastic than I was.

She was right. I had to take a plunge into the unknown if I wanted to surprise Granny B on the occasion of her groundbreaking feat. Moreover, now my dream of finding love can be crushed in the privacy of my home.

Shanaya read out, 'Hello there! I'm Neville Forbes. Six feet tall and crossing over the border of thirty-five. Few times bitten, so much wiser but still not shy. A Zoroastrian man looking to meet his Earth Angel in India. If you are ready to be spoiled by a guy who will treat you even better than his 1935 vintage HMV gramophone, drop me a line and let's see if we rhyme. Only pretty Parsi gals may knock on my door. Knock knock!'

'Cheeeeezzzzzzzy. Meet his angel? Like seriously! What's next, his fairy godmother? And his nose, too hooked for my...'

Before I could complete my argument, Shanaya decided to call the shots and make her sales pitch. She ran into my washroom, punching some digits on her cell, and shut the door and for the next eight minutes I could only hear her muffled voice. I heard a giggle and an "ooh really" and an "aah how wonderful" and next I knew, Shanaya was out of the loo, looking as though she was about to have a mini-orgasm.

'You Kai have got yourself a date with a winner on the second Sunday of March at the JW Marriott. An investment banker from San Fran, an art dealer too. An Ivy league product. Double whoopee on that! Holds a full-blown American citizenship. Health junkie. Collects antique coins and *Tinkle* comics.

Scorpio, a star sign match for you. Loves opera, jazz and hiking. Hates Bollywood. I know, sorry, but you can change him. Has a slight American accent. Is a divorcee and shares joint custody of their 10-year-old son, but he's moving back to India alone, to be with his ageing parents and "enjoy his heritage" in his words. And also to make sure his younger brother doesn't plunder his property. He is visiting *apna* Bharat, end of next month.'

'Hmm, sounds like he is in Crawford Market shopping for brides.'

'You better make it work, Kai. Don't you dare make your *hazaar* excuses and fudge it up. And his name is so ta di da! I hope you don't have a flight that March weekend. If you do, tell them you are too sick to go.'

'I think all this is pretty sick, us contacting despos prowling for trophy wives.'

I was a bit vexed with her pushiness and mild threats, but at the same time impressed at her earlier display of superlative persuasive skills.

'You must be dynamite in court and a bit of a nuisance for the opposition.'

I was not even sure if I felt a mild spark for this Neville F with his goatee, sidelocks and silver-rimmed glasses under a rather broad forehead.

'Well I am a lawyer, it's my job to get them to crack. By the way, doesn't he look a wee bit like Prince Charles?' she asked merrily, pointing to his mug shot still lingering in front of us.

'Shanaya, *taru bheju khasee gayuch su* (have you lost it)? *Dhaap marwa band kar.* (Stop fibbing.) Next you will insist that your Gary resembles young Prince Harry.'

***

And so the second weekend of March 2013 with my auspicious underwear (animal print this time) under my lucky denim skirt, I made my way to the JW to give this addiction called love another chance and to also get Shanaya off my back.

The next few months, Neville and I spent almost every minute with each other whenever I was in town. My flying schedule had got lighter too, due to some new law about having more rest days in India between sectors. He had flown back to San Francisco twice in-between for not more than nine days at a stretch; it was mostly to wind things up, out there. With his experience, he had lots to choose from in Mumbai in terms of his career.

Neville Forbes owned a plush six-bedroom penthouse on Pochkhandwala Road, Worli. It also had a library, a wine cellar (it was not in a basement but adjacent to his guest rooms) with the finest collection of wines across various timelines, an artist workstation and a room reserved for old clocks and vintage showpieces from his great-grandfather's treasures that were worth a fortune.

We hung about at Bombay Gymkhana and CCI (Cricket Club of India) quite a lot, a very South Mumbai thingy to do. He played tennis and squash there while I read a book and acknowledged regular members. We went for piano recitals and classical theatre at the NCPA (National Centre for the Performing Arts) together and sometimes we borrowed his very wealthy uncle's yacht and sailed around the Gateway of India to catch sundown over a crimson seascape. It was all so mellow and sophisticated.

And lightyears away from what I used to be—standing on my seat in a movie theatre whooping on SRK's entry in a film, and showering the person in front of me with soda and popcorn unable to hold back my excitement or keep my balance or both. Taking it a step further with my colleague Sonia, another ardent King Khan fan who joined me often in circling countless times around the superstar's mansion in an autorickshaw or car (whatever was available that time) before mustering the courage to shout from outside his palace, 'We LUVVVVEEE you Shah Rukh Khan! We LUVVVV- you!'

'Perfect,' Zoya said, approving at once on hearing about Neville. 'Just what you need. A solid and reliable guy. Not some filmy garbage. And a groovy bank balance always helps.'

I did not mention to her that he kissed like a gentleman, made love like a careful giraffe and steered away from anything oral waist down. And I certainly did not update her about his friend, 'His Highness'.

That I would reserve for Dan's quota of weekly entertainment.

When I did, Dan almost fell off his bar stool at Gusto's. Stuffing two paper napkins in his mouth, he seemed to be having a hard time swallowing his catty comments. And I was not making it easier for him.

'Sometimes when he is on top—the only position he seems to believe in—I imagine my hot Italiano or KQ instead. Sometimes both. That is the only way to get through it.'

'Honeybunch, bless your heart but anyone who has a name such as that for his little boy-toy ain't the one.'

I could understand the hissy fit he had ruptured into, but I had burnt my hands way too often in the past to trust the dudes who had 'rocked my world', in every sense. Awesome lovers seldom made good husbands. And Nev provided me with the predictability and consistency that all former lovers lacked.

And most importantly, he had taken me home to 'meet the parents'.

'I want a gentle breeze now, I am done with tornadoes.'

I was not lying. Nev was mature and level-headed and prided himself for the same and I welcomed the change. He used Google maps to be on the cautious side and left a quarter of an hour early because he hated being a minute late, anywhere.

'You Indians really suck at timing. Kai, it's 6:35. You are a whole five late,' he once said, grumbling.

Wasn't he one too?

'Caught in traffic and then gave a lift to an old lady at the bus stop; your San Fran is a village compared to my city.'

'Kai, you are such an uncivilised maverick.'

He said in jest, his US-returned twang more conspicuous when he was making a point.

'Undisciplined but in a cute way, of course. Still, I gotta train you.'

***

Dan who was on another tequila rampage that night was behaving infuriatingly smug, disapproval written all over his blemish-free face.

'Yeah, as safe as a hat on a sunny day. And sounds a bit cocky if you ask me. Well, if nothing else, at least he's loaded and the unmarried uncle he sucks up to also seems promising. Date both. If you can ignore his 1970's sideburns and Uncle Crorepati's dentures, you might survive.'

'The good news is that Neville already has a son, so the paternal rush has been over and done with. And you know how I feel about having babies.'

Having heard my anti-procreation theory for the nth time, he pretended not to listen and shoved a lemon wedge and a triple shot in his mouth all at once.

'And it's not as if I have a squillion options either.' I concluded.

The great thing about Nev was that he had the next 20 years of his life figured out and was as predictable as two poached eggs. And I still did not know whether I preferred gobhi parathas for breakfast or puri bhaji. We were planets apart in many things.

Nev was a thoroughbred, he shelled out for every meal (never forgot his wallet or his tips), opened all doors I walked into, even the restroom ones at the fancy joints we dined at and was mostly a teetotaller except for his obsession with fine wine. A weekly visit to the agiary was mandatory for him and he did his *sudrah-kusti* sincerely, daily.

If all this did not make me happy, then nothing ever could.

When Nev and I attended Zoya's kid's birthday together on her open terrace, he even had the sceptic Zoya wrapped around his finger.

'He's a keeper. No whacko flags. Old school. Don't lose him.' She was quick to bite.

'I won't,' I said reassuring her, 'I think he could be the one.'

'*Mashallah*. I am delighted for you. Thanks to Allah, it didn't work out with Spongebob.'

Nev's flawless manners and gallant behaviour drew admiration from Zoya's family and her guests too for not only would he stand up from his chair and offer it to the elders present there, but also greet them with a respectful '*salaam alaikum*'.

Krish had skipped the celebration; he was dubbing for a friend's film and Simran waltzed in an hour late, though hitting it off with Nev almost at once.

'Yaar, Vicky and I are on a break, so if this one goes down the Kai-toilet, pass my number,' she said, jokingly.

It felt good to be with someone your girlfriends adored. It reaffirmed my faith in my choice. And it was not like this one needed any more affirmation. My parents loved him, his parents liked me and besides my one-and half-year-old nephew who bit him each time he saw him; everyone in the family was fond of Nev.

That was a relief because it meant I could attend social functions with my dignity unharmed, without playing hide-and-seek with the *daila seeplas* (goody two-shoes) of my community who made my life difficult in mostly all of them. Yes, it was almost too good to be true. It made me forget how hard love could be.

Coco had sounded super excited when I called to wish her for her anniversary.

'He must really adore you and his parents to settle in Mumbai, wrap up his life in SF and come back for all of you. Though he sounds like a bit of a control freak, if you ask me. Damn babe, I wish our *fadoo* chick was here to dissect him like a lab rat…'

Her voice trailed off. Like her, I would do anything to hear Aliya shout once again, 'Hot dogs for the three of us with extra spicy sauce please' and embarrass us in public.

Like Coco, I had tried her cell phone umpteenth number of times but it was obvious that she did not want anything to do with us at all. Somewhere Coco and I recognised that it was not personal but just something our junglee Aliya would do in life, only if shit hit the fan. And it had! Though we just did not know how and what exactly.

So besides Dan and Krish, the rest of my lot were supportive about my latest flame.

Krish's stance was along the following lines:

'I hope you are being mindful this time, Bawi. If you ask me, you need to stop jumping into relationships like a tadpole and complete that book of yours. It's Granny B's dream to see you as a published author first and foremost. You're wasting your talent. Stop leaving things half-way.'

Okay, so my book was on hold. But not my fault. Having a boyfriend was time-consuming. And energy-consuming.

For one, I had to pretend to enjoy the gym. (That meant paying for one, flashing a membership card and never making it through the other side of the door.) Like most guys who desire a well-toned woman with an ironed out stomach, Neville Forbes was no exception and had been quite vocal about it.

Being with Rio had been as easy as selling chilled lemonade on a hot summer day, but Nev was opinionated about almost everything. And I did not really mind that except when it came to my food habits.

And once a foodie always a foodie.

But for Nev oils, carbs and sweets were like cyanide.

'Look at our Meher Jesia. She's kept herself so fit even at this age,' he used to grumble whenever I poked my finger into anything that gave me a food-gasm, 'maybe you should start eating boiled fish or braised chicken. This way, you will get your proteins and also regulate your diet. It will help you get back in shape.' (When was I ever in shape? Tee-hee! The joke was on him.)

Of course becoming a carnivore again would never happen even if he left me his entire inheritance, but if I wanted to keep him interested then it was imperative to keep a close check on myself and get rid of the excess lard I carried.

Hence, instead of going with my impulse and pointing out his paunch too and then telling him to piss off, I forced myself to bid a heart-wrenching goodbye to all my divinities: Indigo deli's moist brie sandwiches and home potatoes; New Yorker's crunchy onion rings, homemade chilly cheese toasts; Nando's peri peri fries; Tibb's frankies; McDonald's hash browns; full-fat mayonnaise and crème fraiche, crème caramel, etc.

'Basically my life is over and I have to accept it,' I complained to Dellu whom I caught up with over FaceTime.

Luckily, we had never lost touch.

She had listened patiently but expressed very little except for 'make sure your creativity doesn't die with all this unnecessary pressure you keep putting on yourself,' before we disconnected.

Nev counted every damn calorie like a *kanjoos makhichoos.* But he was not completely guilty; even I knew that it was high time that I took my body seriously like most of my friends.

Zoya kept enrolling in different zumba and kickboxing classes to watch her waistline, Simran had a god-given metabolism, Coco had been awarded the Perfect 10 trophy by her set of guardian angels and Dan had recently lost oodles of flab with a deadly diet and a newly acquired badminton hobby.

But what was harder than chomping on leaves and force-feeding myself with wheatgrass and *amla* shots in front of Nev was keeping abreast on international affairs on a regular basis so that I did not sound dull or frivolous in front of him and his circle of friends who went by the ostentatious name 'The Ivy intellectuals'.

From NASA's latest discoveries to the stock market, from architecture to antiques to global warming and pricey caviar; I had to feign interest in every mind-numbing topic under the sun. I tried hard to look at the positive side. Really hard.

It will serve you well Kai, to get your head out of those Bollywood films, squally desires, fast food and pointless devotion to SRK. Jo tere naseeb main hi nahin hain.(Who is simply not in your destiny.)

I reminded myself each time I wanted to gorge on kaju katlis, sinful ghee ka aloo parathas, etc., or flee from Forbes and his SOBO chumps.

'He is the ying to your yang. Opposites attract.'

'His IQ is probably the sum of all your exes added together. About time babes.'

The Neville fan club consisting of primarily Shanaya and Zoya used to reassure me whenever I felt a little doubtful and they were smart girls so they must be right. So when Nev held out a heart-shaped Tiffany pendant and proposed to me on his birthday on the 7 November 2013, less than 10 months into our relationship, I gave him a resounding yes, half-afraid he would do a runaway groom on me if I overthought it.

'A ring would have been a better way and there is no rainbow bursting out of a midnight sky either when we kiss, but I guess that's all romantic BS.'

I expressed my disappointment to Simran when I stopped by at her new pad in Versova.

'Ditto Kai. We should just give up on these silly, immature dreams and notions about love and romance. *Dimaag ka achaar ho gaya.* (My brain is fried.) Just look at our history. My last one was a paedophile.'

Our Robinhood Simran was ambitious, driven, successful but doomed in love. From unrequited to toxicity, she had seen it all. At least, I had someone decent and cultured to take to Granny B's birthday fête on 4 January.

And deep down I knew that I was not going to do better than Neville Forbes whose assets were as sound as his mind. (I meant financial assets only.)

22

Birthday Bumps and Royal Dumps

4 January 2014

Granny B was over the moon on D-day. Her mischievous grey eyes still had that sparkle and she looked 20 years younger than she was as she brought in her milestone birthday with our entire family in full force alongside her admirers, four generations of people who had known and loved her immensely. And of course, the Fabulous Four who had driven down to Lonavala for the night.

What does one gift a 100-year-old miracle besides everlasting love and endless respect?

We had dressed up Granny B in a saffron yellow dress with a jade brooch clipped over a cream-coloured pashmina, carefully draped over her, on that glorious day, and she was shining brighter than the sun and looked even more distinguished than Aapri Rani, Queen Elizabeth II.

As Dad and Ash wheeled her outside her chateau in the evening, into her beloved garden that had come alive with assorted balloons, colourful streamers, tinsels, lanterns and fairy lights thanks to Mom's and Aarti's efforts, there were cheers, applauses and tears of joy.

That Saturday, Nev would be meeting Granny B for the first time. She had only spoken to him over the phone but it was usually a one-way chat as her hearing was slightly impaired. When I finally introduced her to Nev, she lit up with joy and I was euphoric. I was fulfilling one of her deepest wishes—the older gen began acknowledging me with a newfound respect.

Why?

Well, I had hit a jackpot by landing a '*ghano majano* Parsi *poryo*' (very good Parsi boy) wrapped around me like an anaconda, and he was 'phoren-returned' to the boot.

That made me the talk of the town. Some from Granny B's old entourage insisted we do a small *sagan* (ritual performed on a good occasion) and pushed money-filled *parikas* into our palms as *shagun*.

Everyone was not that benevolent though.

One 75-old Piloo Aunty from Pune who arrived with her two pearly white Persian cats, Princess Tinkerbell and Prince Garfield, began her characteristic *kaklaat maan gose* (meaty nonsense), '*Chalo Khodaiji ni Meherbani ke evun ne tanne koi bakro sodhee ne tau aapyo.* (Lord's grace that he searched and gave you a good goat.) Now get married jaldi jaldi before he runs away too.'

Ignoring her, I gave all my attention to Granny B who was sipping on a shandy (beer and lemonade) pleased as punch with the undivided attention she was drawing and mesmerised with the magical ambience we had created for her.

Dad was circling around her like a bee, Mom was sorting out last-minute glitches and supervising her scrumptious food arrangements with Zoya and Simran helping out as much as possible, while Aarti was trying to keep little Rehu entertained.

The upbeat energy of the guests was infectious; everybody was in great spirits.

Krish looked rather handsome that evening in a pair of navy blue slim-fit jeans, a loose-fit Chinese-collared black shirt and a leather jacket over his shoulders, although strangely quiet. Not that surprising, for he was a pro at masking his emotions.

Of course, he was his usual caring self with Granny B, holding her hand protectively and making sure she had her plate full with the varied selection of yummies but he seemed distant from the rest of us. It was only when Granny B whispered something into his ear that his smile reached his deep brown eyes and he gave her a hug before disappearing for 10 minutes, which I guessed was to have a fag.

I had been waiting for the right time to introduce him to Nev, but he always seemed to be preoccupied somewhere else.

Pari and Jimmy could not make it—one had a painful tooth and the other was globetrotting and making his millions. Shanaya was trying to keep up a brave front; her parents had caught a whiff of her Roman Catholic boyfriend and threatened to disown her if she took it any further.

I had witnessed the jealous stares that my uncle and aunt threw my way when I had turned up with Nev. They simply could not digest the fact that their overly educated, stable and pretty daughter was dating some parjaat restaurateur, while the so-called black sheep was bleating accomplishment.

I was so very grateful for my parents who did not care whom I selected or rejected, so long as I was happy. Touchwood!

Krish had forbidden us to arrange for any live band for he wanted to serenade Granny B in his style with her all-time favourites on his guitar.

It was close to sundown, after the second cake cutting (there were around five different cakes) the entire crowd pulled their respective chairs closer to my grandmother's, to feed their souls with the rhythmic beats of Krish's guitar and the joyous cadence of his bounteous voice that echoed all across the tiny town of Lonavala. Just like it had happened approximately 11 years ago under the same roof on our first holiday as the Fab Four.

The January wind was not being that merciful and Dad draped Granny B's shawl tighter over her shoulders, afraid she would catch a cold and placed another one on her legs, in case of mosquitoes, though we had earlier asked her helper to apply Odomos on them. Two bonfires on either side of us enlivened the heartwarming surroundings.

Everyone present there was completely engrossed in the rhapsodies and delights of the spectacular celebration and the devoted look on their faces spoke volumes about their admiration and attachment to the lady of the hour.

While a few rose to boogie-woogie with their partners, others hit high notes as they sang along. Then there were some who immersed themselves in the nostalgia of old English tunes whilst the rest encircled Granny B, holding hands and making a circle of love. Every guest, young and old, had their own special memories with my beautiful grandmother so the collective warmth of emotions was running high that evening.

Would most of the guests ever meet the birthday girl again? Perhaps not. That would be the last time they would hold her soft hands in theirs or hear nuggets of her unmatched wisdom that had been a guiding light to many a soul in their toughest of times. Granny B's reputation of imparting sagely advice was legendary.

Besto smashed out one gem after another, never tiring, never missing a beat, his voice as alluring as ever. For a brief moment, our eyes met and he gave me one of his lopsided grins. I looked away. Nev's hand was on my knees and he was humming along with the rest of the flock, '*Roses are red my love, violets are blue, sugar is sweet my love, but not as sweet as you…*'

Almost an hour into the sing song session, Krish announced, 'And this next one is a tribute to my best friend Kai and the love of her life, Granny B.'

Granny B's eyes ignited like fireflies and we both knew what was coming.

'When I was just a little girl
I asked my mother what will I be
Will I be pretty? Will I be rich?
Here's what she said to me
Que sera, sera
Whatever will be will be
The future's not ours to see
Que sera, sera
What will be, will be…'

I stood up and went over to Granny B; she on her wheelchair, and me half-squatting, half-bending, our cheeks touching as we waltzed slowly.

She then whispered into my ear so softly that I almost did not catch it, 'Princess, I think I am leaving you in good hands.'

I traced her expressive eyes, assuming she was talking about Nev. But she looked past everyone and blinked as her eyes fell on the boy who was enrapturing all of us with his bewitching vocals and whose eyes were moist as he watched the crowd clapping for us.

And just like Archimedes jumped out of his bathtub *nangu pangu* and screamed, '*Eureka, Eureka* ', I had unearthed the answer to my heart, which I had known all along.

I remembered my much loved passage from Coelho's book *By the River Piedra I Sat Down and Wept:*

> I've been in love before, it's like a narcotic. At first it brings the euphoria of complete surrender. The next day you want more. You're not addicted yet but you like the sensation and you think you can still control things. You think about the person you love for two minutes then forget them for three hours. But then you get used to that person and you become completely dependent on them. Now you think about him for three hours and forget him for two minutes. If he's not there, you feel like an addict who can't get a fix. And just as addicts steal and humiliate themselves to get what they need, you're willing to do anything for love.

Maybe it was time to go the Coelho way and lay my cards on the table with this enigmatic soul who made love to his guitar and who felt like home.

But first things first, I had to wind up a couple of things ASAP. I know, I know, my timing always sucked but then life is not life unless you make mistakes.

So just before dinner, I took Nev for a walk with the excuse of showing him the rest of our property, along the extensive backyard of our estate almost towards the far end (in case there was rona dhona) and told him that even though he ticked every box for me, I did not see us working out; that any wedding in the near or distant future would not be happening.

'It's for the best, Nev. You deserve someone who loves everything about you.'

I did not have the nerve to tell him that in my heart I never belonged to him, that no matter how outstanding his family was and how impressive his academic credentials were, he did not do anything to my soul. That in spite of him having crossed oceans for me, I could not even climb a treadmill for him. That kissing him was like tasting rubber and making love to him was much worse.

I expected him to be dumbfounded or even understanding given his maturity but instead, the eternally composed Neville Forbes manifested into an obnoxious beast.

'Gold-digger! I was leaving it all for you. And you were not even a virgin. I should've paid for skinny whores instead.'

Before I knew it, scrunched knuckles and a determined fist came lunging at me but stopped. He then began to shoot off obscenities at me, words that should never make it to any worthy writer's book.

I started to take a big step back and then another but I was trapped on the other side of a tree trunk and there was little room for exit. Even if I tried to run, he would catch me in a heartbeat. Besides it was so dimly lit that I could fall over a branch or a slithering snake, knowing my luck.

We were moderately away from civilisation and even though I could hear a few voices from the other side, I did not dare scream or cause a scene that would ruin the most important day of the most important person in my life. But my mind was numb with shock. Who was this rotten creature in front of me? I should have known better than to be impetuous when I could have simply waited for another day.

But the entire sacredness of those earlier moments had been so darn powerful that I had been lured to rise with the tide.

Maybe he would come around and I could explain. But Neville Forbes's temper only got shoddier as he tore away his *Star Wars* cartoon tie and threw it in the shrubs, edging closer towards me like an aggravated werewolf, foaming at the mouth, blinded with rage.

Even my prayers of help, failed my memory.

Mayday! *Mayday*!

I was in grave danger and would be kheema pau soon enough. Granny B's 100th would coincide with my funeral. It was too late to scream now. Even if I tried, I doubt a whimper would come out. So, I turned around in one quick swing and made a dash into the wilderness, it was the only choice left.

AGAIN? *First I run after men and then I flee from them*? *Barcelona, Rome, Lonavala...*

As I had anticipated, he picked up momentum and enveloped me roughly from behind. Dragging me by my wavy locks, across the muddy path, he pinned me to another tree and lifted his hand to strike me, his bloodshot eyes filled with bloodcurdling wrath. I let out a chilling scream, mostly because I felt a clump of hair lighter.

My precious cascading hair.

It had taken years of costly spas and scalp remedies to grow them six and a quarter inches below the normal shoulder length.

Tum kya jaano ghane baalon ki kimat, Devil Babu? (What do you know about the value of dense hair, Devil Babu?)

Wiggling under his powerful hold like a mouse, I targeted between his thighs (What's with me and kicking those nuts in every relationship, eh?) with my knee but it missed the spot by a few centimetres.

Damn! *Oh Shit*!

'*Saali,* thankless fat bitch, let me show you what happens to girls who dump me! You 21st-century women should be chained to a kitchen stove.'

No, Dadaji, bachao bachao, this can't be happening to me! This schizo is about to strangle me and bury me under our kaju nu jhaad. I promise I will never complain again about my body, my failures, my job…

'And what will I tell His Highness, eh? That you walked out on him, just like the rest?'

If I survived, then five years later that punchline would go down as the funniest sentence in this memoir I would write but just then it was anything but hilarious as his large palm came closer to my face. I had no time, energy or space to duck; alas my face was destined to become a chapati.

Bye-bye SRK. Bye-bye all. Forget me not. Sorry Granny B for jacking up the best day of your life.

What happened next was straight out of a Bond film. A long, muscular hand appeared over my left shoulder and punched Neville twice between his nose and mouth. He was not expecting it at all and fell over, his nose bleeding, his lips hanging open, abusing in the choicest of swear words, exhibiting the ughhhhhhhliest side that I had ever witnessed in any living form.

Krish and I left him there and floundered back to the jamboree silently. He quickly handed me a handkerchief to dry my tears. I was quaking from head to toe, but he did not hold my hand to soothe me or put his arm around like he would have, normally.

'How did you know I was in trouble?' I asked, zapped, dismayed and traumatised by the horrendous turn of events.

'I didn't, I had just come for a drag,' he replied in a detached tone.

I wanted to tell him that of all the people he should know the ill-effects of tobacco, but I could hardly afford to be preachy then.

'Thank you, Krish. SRK couldn't have done better,' I said gratefully even though *maari hawa ekdum tight thai gailee* (my breath had totally stopped).

He neither reacted, nor glanced my way. But from his body language and poker face, I knew that he was disturbed as well and saddened by my error of judgement yet again.

'Are you hurt?' he enquired, kindly this time.

'I will be fine,' I replied though my neck was a bit sprained. Luckily, I was wearing a long-sleeved open cardigan, so my arms were not hurting as much. Yet.

'Go into the house later and check for any wounds and cuts. Let me know if you need me to go to a chemist.'

As we blended back into the jollities and naach–gaana pretending the fisticuffs had never happened, we heard the furious engine of a Mercedes backing out of the exit gate, screeching its tyres in discontentment, crushing Granny B's precious flower pods as it disappeared out of sight.

Krish and I exchanged relieved looks. Neville the egomaniacal He-Devil was gone. The facade was finally lifted and I could eat, drink, burp, fart and freakin' live the way I wanted to now.

XXXSCORE = 998

23

From Man-eaters to Born-again Virgins

2014–15

Soft-spoken Neville who metamorphosed into a misogynist was not one to forgive injured pride so easily. His offensive and hostile messages hounded me for almost all of 2014, and he even sent various goons to pick up the few gifts he had presented me with. As they say, revenge is a dish best served cold.

I smashed the Tissot watch into tiny pieces and filled the Tiffany's box with pigeon shit (scooped from our windowsills by my loyal maid who volunteered to even go smear it on his face) and returned it with a note that read: 'Hope your earlobes turn into assholes and crap all over your shoulder, you petty *ch**tyo*'.

It was a line that I had overheard a colleague say (the last three words were my add-ons) and I had always wanted to find the perfect moment to use it. A little childish perhaps but well deserved. The narcissistic devil had camouflaged his serious rage issues really well and I could not help but wonder what the consequences would have been had I 'sold my soul to the devil' conjugally. Probably two years too late into our marriage, a band of detectives would have found my head inside a freezer alongside a Thanksgiving turkey.

Krish and I never spoke of the fiasco ever again and I appreciated his serene way of handling it.

'Karmic healing' was my new mantra. I even considered past life regression to see in which godforsaken century, I had cocked up.

'All the phonies that entered my life, were probably ex-husbands or lovers in various past lives whom I had used and spat out, or slaughtered in cold blood,' I found myself confiding in Simran one day, who was as stunned as I was with the whole ordeal.

The thought of being 30 and not married yet had been unimaginable and stressful. I was vulnerable. I had panicked. I was ready to settle for breadcrumbs and jaded chemistry.

'Get occupied. That's the only thing that will stop you from overthinking it,' she said, trying to make me feel better before hanging up and going back to the finger-painting class at an orphanage where she was volunteering.

She worked her ass off for every cause she believed in with so much zeal and dedication that no guy could ever come between her passion and compassion. I, on the other hand, was still stuck on the third chapter of my book, unable to come to a conclusion as to who the killer should be.

Shame on me!

I had to make a decision now which came from a place of self-awareness and accepting responsibility sans a therapist this time.

There was not going to be a fifth (or was it sixth?) inning for me in this game of love. I was done.

No more attracting the wrong men. (It appears that disillusionment makes one a 21-century Socrates.) I decided to follow Bridget Jones's philosophy to life: 'I will not fall for any of the following: alcoholics, workaholics, commitment-phobics, people with girlfriends or wives, misogynists, megalomaniacs, chauvinists, emotional fuckwits, or freeloaders, perverts.'

That meant almost every bloke from the planet was ruled out.

Neville the He-Devil had never been my type. He had always been derogatory in his own sugar-coated way but I had ignored it, too afraid I would end up in the single bin (or the shelf) if I did not keep silent and comply. I had been willing to compromise on almost everything, including my *shauk* for *khana, peena* and *jeena*. That in itself should have been the biggest "wake-up smell the coffee" call of all.

To recover from my breakup with Rio, I had partied with Dan and fumbled through; but this time around, getting sloshed and dancing on table tops was not my gig any more.

Though he managed to drag me to a nightclub for a *quiet* dinner on a less hectic weekday.

'Every straight member of the opposite sex I meet has their screws *dheela,*' I said to Dan at Athenos.

He rolled up his eyes, badgered me about 'boring him to tears' and then returned into the arms of his latest squeeze who I had been informed was a model by day. (I dare not ask him what his lucrative career was at night.)

Even chilling in crew lounges in London and Dubai and drinking until the wee hours with my funky bunch of colleagues was not appealing any more. It felt empty and worthless.

I was seldom alone but I was lonely.

I had gotten so used to making efforts, giving too much in relationships and changing myself for someone or the other and being outside my comfort zone that I felt incomplete and inadequate without it. *Who was I? The real me*?

I began to channelise my dissatisfaction into completing my book, seven short stories, each more psychotic than the other. But despite being occupied with the script of my first novel and lining up all the self-help books in the market I could get my paws on that directed me to embrace my 74.5 kilos with all the self-love I could muster, I felt myself slipping into old patterns and phobias where I battled nightmares and near-anxiety attacks, hiding inside the good ole cardboard box once again, shit scared of being the only one left out of the 'Happy Wives Club'.

With a 'back to square one' feeling pressing into me, I was back to square one in Panthaky Baug, soon after my 30th birthday. Rusty was so delighted to see me that he almost bit off my ear in delight.

'Kai, naughty naughty, you don't love me any more?'

He grumbled.

I apologised for being incommunicado for so long and presented my feathered pal with a gigantic pack of 5 Star bars and sour cream Pringles, which he grabbed readily. While Hooty fixed me some Parsi choi and rusk toasts with apricot jam, I waited on Rusty who now had a new deck of colourful cards.

'No man, no man.'

Rusty squawked, making my heart sink like quicksand, even though the information was hardly a shocker.

Sohrabji began to panic; he did not want me to leave feeling terrible.

'Nowadays, Rustom baba is on a sabbatical, Kai, don't take his words to heart. He gets his dates and days all mixed up, poor bachcha. Why, only last week, *aene motoo monu kholyoo* (opened his big mouth), and upset this dear couple, Minoo and Arnavaz Shroff.'

'Minoo *m***r ch*d* poking head in Chameli bai's sari.'

Rusty burst out, livid that his dear owner doubted his brilliance. But no matter how much Sohrabji covered up for his bachcha, he could not stop the latter from calling a spade a spade.

Disheartened that there was to be nothing much to look forward to in the near future but slightly comforted all the same, I took it as a green signal to shift my attention on a whole lot of other things I had been advised by friends, like meditation (zzz) detox (fat chance) and my book. I even removed the two ceramic white doves that were placed in the south-west corner of my bedroom which according to feng shui should have improved my romantic luck, concluding that even if I fostered real ones, it would not make an iota of a difference.

'I think I may have to make some serious lifestyle changes.'

I had shared my thoughts with Rusty who had completely lost interest in me and was chomping on his second chocolate; hinting at me to go home.

'Maybe towards the end of this year is when everything will change for the better.'

I confided in Dellu when I rang in to wish her on her new promotion as global sales head for the luxury chain she worked with.

'But to make that happen I have to stop playing Tom and Jerry with Krish in my head, quit dating half the gelc**diyas of the world and focus on enhancing the quality of my life rather than quantity of lovers.'

She was the only one who knew about my situation with Krish. The others were too close to home.

'Fingers crossed sweetie,' she replied, 'why don't you visit me soon? Manhattan is where the action is and who knows you may get some new ideas for your book too?'

Delna was one tough cookie who had worked her way to the top through sheer gumption and hard work. Like Shanaya and even Simran to some extent, her career was her prime focus and hence she was where she was. We all had our own paths to follow, mine was to be a bestselling author. Maybe it was not as lucrative as a regular 10 to 5 job, but it was still a dream.

Maybe once I had something to be proud of, the gloom and doom of the present reality would be put to rest once and for all. For that, I would need to not only change my mindset but also my habits.

'We can't become what we need to be by remaining what we are.' American businessman and writer Max De Pree could not have been more right.

***

When I refused to bring in 2015 at a rave carnival on the outskirts of the city with party animal Danny Boy and his crazy gang, he moaned like a disgruntled spouse.

'All work and no play, makes Kai Juicewalla a very dull girl. Going to break up with you!'

I did not expect him to understand. How could he? The biggest dilemma he had to ever face was when he had to choose between which of his three lovers he would be spending his Friday night with.

I had come to the realisation that finally we all walk alone and there were more important things than head banging and doping like caring for my well-being; strolling by the Serpentine; attending concerts and musicals; having a quiet picnic at Hyde Park or Windsor or catching breathtaking views of the Thames on a boat excursion with my parents, who made it a ritual to visit the U.K. often; writing my book; catching up occasionally with the rest of the Fabs and being genuinely interested in their lives for a change; watching my nephew build his first Lego; walking on Bandra promenades and breathing the good ole stale-ish Mumbai air.

Watching Dan and his buds pass around recreational drugs like canapes was not my scene any more. Invariably, I would be the only one sober at such digs and end up driving half a dozen stoned strangers home.

I rather eat real canapes. Food was my rush.

Dan had suggested a 'friends with benefits scene or no-strings attached sex and random hookups' as a break from my chaotic soulmate obsession, stating that he was very concerned about 'a possible snatch-rusting situation' (his words not mine) too early in life. He even assumed the role of my wingman and began to hunt guys for me (though I did not trust that it was all only for me). I found these options extremely irresponsible and wildly foolish because in such situations men get laid but women get screwed. Mostly.

'As human beings we come here to evolve, not dissolve; we have to rise above the selfish pleasures of the flesh,' I proclaimed, sounding annoyingly like Krish.

'Huns, if you gonna get all Mother Teresa on me and turn over a nasty new leaf, I will never give you make-up or fashion tips ever again. Your frumpy wardrobe by the way needs a rigorous and urgent revamp. Not having a guy does not mean you wear old bedsheets and walk around town.'

'Okay. Okay. Calm down Danesh Camelia Khambatta. I solemnly swear on your Christian Louboutin loafers that I will not remain this unexciting forever.'

***

Twenty months after executing her century, Granny B left us in September 2015. She had lived her life like the Queen she was.

My rock star was gone.

The love of my life was no more.

Our powerhouse of hope, positivity, gentleness and selfless devotion was demolished.

We had never known a world without her.

And I had never known a life away from her.

I knew no matter what happened or how far I got lost, her arms were my anchor and I would always make it home, safe.

She had a solution to every problem.

I had followed almost all of her advice except for one: 'Dikra, never run after a man or taxi because there is always another one coming.'

I should have. She always knew what she was talking about. She was a sturdy moral compass.

She was the calm after a devastating storm. The wind beneath my wings.

Countless others had benefitted from her fair judge of character and earthiness.

And now she was gone and so was her infinite wisdom.

My dear Granny B was a tower of unconditional love.

I had been insanely blessed.

I felt disappointed with myself that I failed to bring to fruition her dream of seeing me as an award-winning author. The book that I was in the process of writing was half-done—choked in the seams of my own laziness and complacency.

The Fab Four had popped by to pay their condolences. Zoya was fried and needed a break from her bossy mother-in-law. Simran was on the verge of another emo meltdown. This time, the short-term bloke in question had suggested they swap partners to 'keep their sex life thriving'.

'Where do you even find such shameful creatures?' Zoya asked while stretching her legs on the sofa and sipping on an Earl grey.

'You are lucky that your hubby isn't suggesting it. Haven't you heard? It's the latest fad of the rich and famous,' Simran said, stirring her hot chocolate, disenchanted with the dating scene and angry at herself for not being able to see through another debauched schmuck.

Krish was the only uncomplaining one that day, briefing us about the offers from big music labels that were pouring in from all directions. And with his new, intense cycling and swimming routine and the earlier stubble gone, he looked fitter than ever.

'Whackadoodles, how often have I told you gals, no guy-no cry, eh? Look at me, no woman-no stress and no headache—I sleep like a baby and I'm the happiest dude alive,' he said, munching on salted caramel popcorn and looking idiotically cute on my recliner.

'Yeah sure, we can see the halo orbiting like a space shuttle around your conceited head,' I said.

Simran then suggested we become like workout or diet buddies to wean ourselves off men and exchange monthly progress reports.

'I challenge you, Bawi Juicewalla and Sassy Khanna to boycott all boys,' Krish said, laughing and throwing his hands up.

'No guy-no cry challenge' did not seem all that impossible. I was so jaded with relationships that I was already sending flowers, cards and candy hearts to myself on important occasions; so I was almost halfway there. And what was the harm in showing a little TLC to myself rather than distributing it freely to thankless psychopaths of the opposite sex?

'Game on, Krish Aryan. Never challenge a mad bawi, you should know better.'

'You and your bawism,' Krish ribbed. 'If it was up to you, "Hindustan" would be renamed "Parsisthan" in which Mr Ratan Tata would be the PM and Field Marshal Sam Manekshaw the defence minister, if he was still alive.'

'Boman Irani the entertainment and broadcast minister; dhansak the national food; Freddie Mercury's "*Break Free*", our national anthem,' Simran quipped.

'Krish, have you forgotten you are half-Parsi too?' I asked.

'But that still makes me only half-whacko, na,' he said, adding, 'Zoya, won't we have fun watching these two hopeless cases crash and burn?'

'*Sau chuhe khaa kar, billiya haj par chali* (after eating hundred mice, the cats are going on a pilgrimage),' Zoya said, shaking her head, ready to bet her life that Simran and I would fail miserably, 'the odds of them winning a lottery are higher.'

'They're just jealous Simran, 'coz we possess the most active libidos and have years of experience behind us, while they had nothing much to look forward to except smelly diapers and a mosquito caught in some swamiji's beard.'

Simran and I reached for a high-five before settling down on our perch again, resolving to prove them wrong.

'Ignore them, Zoya. You and I are gonna have the last laugh. These clowns can't go without louvvvve for more than a day.'

Simran and I exchanged a knowing glance before jumping up and lugging Krish off his throne and pitching him on the soft couch, tickling him until he shrieked like a little girl.

Three-year-old Rehu who had been observing us from behind the curtain, came charging towards us like a cannonball and thinking it to be the best party ever, plonked himself on Krish's stomach and began showing off his newly acquired expertise of executing backflips.

We were creating such havoc and commotion that Mommy scurried from her bedroom to check what was transpiring in her living room. It was hardly the protocol for a sympathy visit.

But neither did she nor anybody else in the family mind it because we all knew that Granny B, wherever she was, was watching over us in great delight, relishing our *masti* like she always had and perhaps learning some new scrumptious recipes in heaven to overfeed us with when we all met again.

SMOOTH LANDING

24

Experiencing Joy Down Under

2016

With Granny B gone, New Year's Eve was quiet, pensive and empty with me staring into the mirror until 2 a.m., trying to find life's meaning all over again without my biggest cheerleader.

Hooty called me up on 21 March to wish me for our new year, impatient to update me on what I had missed.

'*Hud thaigayee aapra ghere* (things went beyond limit at our house),' she stated in her high-pitched voice.

My heart began to beat faster. Had anything happened to her boys? As much as Rusty had done a hotchpotch with my predictions, I still cared. But the news she had for me was even more bizarre. She and Sohrabji were now grandparents to triplets.

'*Oh tari, su vaat karoch*? (What you saying?)Wow!' I said, promising to drop by with some gifts soon.

But with back-to-back flights in the weeks following our conversation, it was only in May that I was able to make it to Panthaky Baug to congratulate the trio.

Rusty energetically flapped when he saw me, keen to show off his offspring—'Hatrick *maree,* hatrick *maree...*'

I could see that Hooty's tensions had multiplied in the last few months for she had gone completely grey. She then filled me in on what I had missed.

Sohrabji, who could never refuse his bachcha anything, had commenced his frantic search for a like-minded female companion for Rusty after he had expressed his carnal urges vocally by eve-teasing college-going girls of the colony.

Trying to do his best for his bachcha, he placed an ad in a Parsi tabloid but forgot to mention Rusty's breed. It was not long before he was flooded with prospects from parents of eligible candidates, including humans.

Thankfully, it all panned out well in the end. Sohrabji managed to find his frisky lad a missy called Freny, another African Grey that belonged to the well-to-do Kerawala family from Pune. Freny Kerawala was a slim, no-nonsense kind of bird with an exquisite set of feathers on her and our son-of-the-soil Rusty had gone *lattoo* over her from the word go.

The rest was history and Rustom Sohrab's legacy thereby lives on.

***

The other half of the year seemed to fly by and I was entirely devoted to concluding my novel. I spent hours in coffee shops of Bandra on my non-flying days working on its draft, impressing myself with this newly acquired discipline. It is amazing how creative one can be without any distractions especially of the romantic kind.

Krish had been travelling around India for his shows and once in a while when we did get to hang out, it was mostly touch and go. His no woman–no stress policy was going strong and music was his sole love then.

Life was hectic, college seemed like another lifetime and we were all trying to find a firm footing in our early thirties, which unlike the twenties, forced us to be accountable for the smallest of things. The good news was that my parents no longer forced me to attend those detestable community powwows. I was officially a 'grown-up' and I could not care less about upsetting others if it was to save my sanity.

Having stayed out of boyfriend trouble for over two years (a new record) yielded its own rewards—I worked hard on my novel, which eventually paid off. I found myself a publishing house willing to take a chance on a debutant author.

Around the last week of December 2016, I paid Coco a visit in Sydney. She had been coaxing me to visit ever since she had moved base. I finally relented because I thought spending Christmas in a new country might invigorate me.

I asked Shanaya to hop along for a change of scene. She had finally called it quits with Gary after her parents gave her a lot of grief. But she had recently been made a partner at her law firm, and was swamped with new projects so she could not get time off.

Coco had mentioned on one of our Skype calls that she had a surprise waiting for me when I got there and from her tone I assumed that she was pregnant. So, I packed my suitcase with presents for the baby in gender neutral shades.

James and Coco received me at the airport, and appeared as coupled up and cheerful from a distance just like I remembered them from his last visit to India before their big move.

Thank heavens for that.

With the number of strained and doomed marriages around me, I began to seriously doubt the credibility of the institution.

Coco had chopped off her long locks but looked as pretty as a picture in a blunt bob, faded skinny's and a festive orange Rudolph jumper.

I no longer minded being around happy couples as much as I used to, nor did I slander myself for it any more if I felt that rare pang of discomfort. It is only human to envy someone else for having something one pines for.

I am sure my Facebook followers were somewhat envious of my glamorous lifestyle when I posted photos of my 'typical week' on my Facebook wall—whether it was bragging about my gourmet dinner at a Gordon Ramsay restaurant or chewing on a delicate sundried tomato and basil sandwich and buttery scone at the Ritz in London, or clicking selfies with the theatrical cast of *Mamma Mia*.

Like many on Facebook, I too was showing off the 'happening' slices of my life for virtual accolades or just self-reaffirmation that 'I am doing okay', in spite of carrying the rock of Gibraltar on my shoulders.

As I drew closer to C and J who were waving at me near the entrance of the arrival lounge, with a pretty bouquet in hand, my feet faltered and my heart skipped a beat as I caught a glimpse of a familiar cheeky monkey popping out behind them.

'Aliya f**king Sood! You tart. How dare you!'

Dropping my luggage, I ran towards her and attacked her with the biggest cuddly bear hug and choicest gaalis. She reciprocated by bursting into giggles. Coco intersected our embrace and we almost toppled over each other, squealing in rowdy joy like the junglees we were, attracting odd looks from passersby while James quietly picked up my belongings and waited patiently until we had settled.

Aliya had landed from Kolkata the day before. Coco was not pregnant at all but had managed to trick Aliya by sending feelers through Aliya's mother that she had decided to name Aliya as the Godmother to her (unborn) child. Aliya could not evade her any more. She may have gone underground for the world, but she had to come through for her friend. We did not ask Aliya for an explanation, knowing she would speak when she wanted to.

'I have HIV. Please no drama, girls.'

Finally Aliya dropped a grenade on us a couple of nights later, in her usual *muhffat* manner.

The three of us were sitting in Coco's garden, sharing a nightcap of homemade passion fruit liqueur and gorging on sizzling chocolate brownies baked by James.

Coco sprung up from her porch swing and began pacing up and down like a restless animal. I retreated to my room to fetch my migraine pill. This was worse than the time when Neville the Devil had invited me to his house to test my culinary skills under the watchful eye of his unpleasant *bawarchi*. I had managed to conjure up a low fat omelette because that is all I could make then (and now) and several pieces of egg shells had got stuck in his throat, making him uncomfortable for the next 18 hours. I was subjected to verbal hell after that and until I promised to join Mrs Todiwalla's cooking classes, he simply did not shut up. (Yup! I should have seen the subtle aggro signs then, but all I did was swallow three disprins and push them under the carpet.)

Aliya's breaking news had clearly hit us hard. Though she nonchalantly helped herself to another bottle of Shiraz and mounted herself on a ledge while Coco and I continued to gasp for breath and clarity.

'Gals, I want to do something smacky and whacky, you know? For old times' sake,' Aliya said, looking at both of us hopefully.

'Anything.'

Coco and I chimed together, a bit too enthusiastically.

'Wow, having HIV is making you guys so much sweeter. But I am not dying tomorrow, hope you know that. But I still can't publicise it because they'll judge my family. I don't care a f**k but my parents in Bengaluru would not be able to handle it. So when I found out, I had no choice but to flee from everybody and everything.'

That night we booted James out of his own room and slept together, holding hands and talking till the wee hours of the morning about the good, old days. Aliya slipping back into our lives as though she had never gone at all was indeed one of the best things that had happened to me in a while.

Aliya's idea of 'smacky and whacky' was having her first sky-dive.

'There is something empowering about falling off a plane from 10,000 feet and going where the wind takes you.'

Coco and I were not sure about that but the following day all three of us found ourselves at the Sydney Flying Club, ready to jump out of a small yellow plane, clinging like koala bears to our respective instructors.

Once back home, we were reduced to tears as we watched our expressions on the video footage of the dive. Aliya had done the sport twice, screaming like the gheli she was, all the way down and Coco had almost soiled herself.

'And you Kai, was salivating all over your tandem dude. Shamelessly pulling down his pants on your free fall. Just look at the poor chap, he is squirming. Rewind it, Aliya.'

'I was scared okay.'

'If she wasn't on some self-inflicted sex famine, drooly Tim would be opening her parachute tonight.'

Aliya pitched in.

Aliya had been right. I had felt exalted. Not only because I had heaved myself out of a circling plane but the adrenaline rush that had emanated when the impressively sculpted, musk- scented blond Aussie had pressed himself against me, entrancing me midair with words like, 'Trust me and let go', 'You okay Miss, we almost there', was close to none.

'Got those familiar "hot dog" pangs, Kai?' Aliya asked, twittering.

'Tim had the whole package, if you know what I mean. He may be doing his job, but I am on holiday. And isn't Christmas the season to be jolly?'

'Yes, yes, jolly not horny,' Coco said. She was enjoying her third Tanqueray and tonic, pleased that she was hosting such an awesome reunion. 'But you might as well dust off your cobwebs soon, babe.'

'Lord have mercy, Saint Kai wants to leave the church! It's a Christmas miracle!'

Aliya who was clearly on a high was swirling faster than a dervish.

The pain of being separated for so long had now subsided. Coco was blissfully married and it showed. Aliya was still full of beans through dread and sickness like a true winner and had consumed five beers within an hour, validating that her health affliction had definitely not pulled the plug on her ceaseless capacity for spirits. I was on my way to creative stardom, fingers crossed.

If someone had shown us a preview of these moments in 2009, we would have never believed it; but there we were living our dreams, fighting our battles and still as thick as thieves.

In a way, nothing had changed. Nothing ever would.

James had sauntered in to replenish our snacks, pretending he could hear nothing through his headphones, but his smile said it all. He moseyed out after placing a quick peck on Coco's lips. Once we were sure he was way out of earshot, we both attacked her, 'What's James' L-G-W? Is he the biggest?'

'Shhh filthy bitches, that's my husband, stop prying. But if you must know, he's very well endowed and I have no complaints. But is he the Emperor of…? Hmm, I'm afraid not.'

'Spit it out, you *ra**i*' Aliya was prancing around, completely sloshed. She looked seriously *gaandi* (crazy)!

'You guys remember Marquis? The guy I dated on and off before I met James?'

'Ooh, that lazy son of a gun French cheesewalla from the farmer's market, who got you boarding trains from Zurich all the way to see him in Geneva and then ghosted you whenever it suited him? The one with the square jaw and uneven lips if I remember correctly?'

I tried recollecting Marquis's face from some photograph she had shown us.

'Her very costly booty call. He didn't even offer to pay for her travel fare,' Aliya reminded, never the one to forget easily.

'Shhh, keep your voice down. And just to be clear, he wasn't some cheese seller, he owned three dairies,' Coco countered, getting bashful all of a sudden. 'Well, so the few times we did get together, in spite of our volley of words being limited we used our lips for so much more than verbose.'

There was a slight pause before she added proudly, 'And yup, we kind of went all the way. Twice, uhh thrice—actually like twenty. Once inside a cable car, twice on the platform of his OCD mother's kitchen and six times where the cheese is…'

'Yikes! Stop! But we need the measurements.'

Aliya screamed, vaulting up and down on the bed, while I lay my head on Coco's lap, a bit worn-out even though Coco's hot revelation was slowly reviving my senses and making me wonder whatever happened to her rulebook on relationships that was stitched to her skin in those days?

Coco held up both hands in front of her chest and spread all her fingers.

'Hurrah! We have a hot dog champion!'

Aliya cheered, her infectious laughter untouched.

'But I knocked down three wickets in one strike. Shouldn't that make me the champ? Do the math.'

We did not know whether Aliya was serious or kidding for until then we had never broached the subject of that fateful night that had taken place over the dark treacherous (yet sentimental) waters we had once traversed together.

'I don't think it was our European expedition that f**ked me up,' Aliya said, almost reading our minds, 'it was Amrish my unfaithful ex who I went back to. The biggest blunder of my life! He had AIDS and never told me. May the selfish b**tard never rest in peace.'

I bolted up, my fatigue disappearing. Coco looked away, unsure of how to respond. We both were in complete awe of this wild child. She had walked through the fires and fought unthinkable battles but her spirit was unshakeable and feisty as ever.

Anybody else in Aliya's place would have given up on life, laughter and playfulness. This one had risen like a phoenix from the ashes. She reminded me of Eleanor Roosevelt's trenchant observation, 'A woman is like a tea bag—you can't tell how strong she is until you put her in hot water.'

Aliya was just that and more.

'But if there is a silver lining, it's that I have HIV, not AIDS, which is the last stage of the infection, and that's a bit different. In other words, I will still mess with you two on earth and not from hell. Not yet at least.'

We exhaled, as relieved as we could be in the moment. Realising that her declaration had created a disconcerting chill in the air, Aliya bounced off a few pillows at us.

'Now stop staring at me like two flat tyres and let's get back to our goss. Have I told you about my latest obs? The Rampant Rabbit. You can even choose your size, colour and speed.'

'I never related to vibrators,' Coco said.

'Me neither. I have never been intrigued by them. To me, it's like playing a game of chess without an opponent.'

'Got it from Hong Kong at some dealer's basement a couple of years ago. It was like a silicone *swayamvar* in there,' Aliya said, determined to increase our erotic knowledge.

'Come. Let me show you thakelas how much fun it is,' Aliya continued, grabbing an empty beer can near the waste bin and spreading herself on the carpet beneath us.

Before we had a chance to react or realise what was going on, she was throwing her head back and letting out soft mock cries and inviting moans, the cylindrical tin rolling in between her thighs, giving us a performance of a lifetime.

'Oh Aliya, this is effing epic!'

Coco was wiping her tears.

'Oh you like it, do you? Naughty girl Coco. Come hither. Let me spank you.'

'I want to record this C-grade film,' I said, standing over Aliya with my phone, determined to get a saucy click for keepsake.

Aliya suddenly lost grip of the object, making it fly out of her hand like a frisbee. I managed to dodge it but the wide-eyed-open-jawed invader at the door was not so lucky.

James had walked in innocently to ask us what we would like to order in for dinner. I do not think any one of us would ever forget the look on the Aussie's pale face as long as we lived. He immediately darted out of the room like a frightened squirrel with a blazing tale. James could not make eye contact with Aliya for the rest of the trip. And I am pretty sure he was off beer for a long time after that.

All in all, Christmas Down Under had been a memorable affair.

25

Margaritas and Matchmakers

2017–18

The year 2017 was a game changer for all of us.

My debut novel was released in stores on 26 June (same day as the first Harry Potter was published in the United Kingdom, exactly two decades earlier) and officially launched with dhoom dhaam in the fourth week of July.

On the day of the launch I was all nerves.

Aarti, Simran and Krish helped organise the action-packed event for the book release at the garden restaurant Out of the Blue (OOTB), Pali Hill, Bandra and made sure everything panned out flawlessly—from greeting the guests, to showing them to their seats, to satiating their taste buds and keeping them interested in the goings-on.

We were all in high spirits but I had this stomach knotting anxiety inside me that was simply not letting me enjoy the evening as much as I should be.

What if the zipper of my short black skirt popped open?

What if Granny B was the only one who thought I could do this and the actual readers hated my writing and ripped me apart?

What if the chief guest changed his mind and turned his car around and went home?

But soon I found myself on stage in gratitude and disbelief of the amazing ambience and the big turnout of 250-odd guests. The legendary Javed Akhtar graced the event as the chief guest and officially launched the book. SRK had been my first preference for the same but it was a long shot. We were simply not meant to be.

Over the years, I had brushed shoulders with several page 1/2/3 marvels on board. I had even exchanged pleasantries with Big B before making a faux pax by asking him if he was travelling to England that night on business or pleasure. Thankfully, he had been cordial about my nervy attempt to strike a conversation and there was no permanent damage.

Though the highlight of highlights had been when on a London–Mumbai flight in 2015, I gathered the courage to approach seat 1A where the future queen of England—the dazzling Duchess of Cambridge—was throned next to her equally illustrious and regal husband.

Much against the royal protocol, I indulged in small talk with the Duchess, which focused on increasing her awareness about our small and brilliant Parsi community and then took it a step further by inviting her to our 3-BHK for Parsi choi, cashew makrooms and shrewsbury biscuits. (Our version of English shortbread.) I even suggested a play date between George and my nephew who were roughly the same age.

Duchess K had come across as classy, warm and extremely gracious and smiled politely through my blunderings.

But on 24 July 2017, I was not complaining at all. I could not have asked for a more compelling, intellectually stimulating guest of honour than Javed Saab who captivated the audience for over an hour speaking eloquently about literature and the importance of reading books.

The Juicewalla family and their extensions were all there in full force and my heart did a *golati* (summersault) on seeing that people had taken time out from their busy schedules to turn up for me, including plenty of my social media followers.

I have fans! *Me*? *Piggy Pink Shoes*? *Humpty Dumpty*?

It was mind-boggling to say the least. Finally, the universe had orchestrated a few hours of privilege, fame and bliss for *moi*. Karmic respite for all the *g**nd per laats*, I had been lavished with, without any time-out.

Yes, I had arrived!

I was being chased for interview bytes. I was a living example that it was never too late to start on a clean slate. *What a crying shame that the Readymoneys and the evil sisterhood are not around to see it*. I could not help but think as I took half a bow and soaked in the adulation and applause.

We sold 200 copies in three hours! To celebrate, Zoya, Simran, Dan, Shanaya and I scurried to Olive Bar & Kitchen next door for the afterparty and the much-needed celebratory cocktails. Knowing how exhausted I would be in the aftermath of the affair, Krish and Ash were winding up things at the OOTB.

As we made ourselves comfortable within the stonewashed white walls of the restro, tanking up on margaritas and sangrias, Zoya and Simran got super nosey about my love life yet again.

'It's quite astonishing that our bawi has stopped playing catching cook with boys. Now don't you give us this poppycock about how busy you've been writing a bestseller blah blah…' Zoya said, refusing to accept that I had changed for good.

'Believe it or not, abstinence from love and all that crashes with it, smashed open the productive whiz in me,' I dismissed their doubts, pulling a face at them over my peach margarita.

The rest on the table began to snigger as well. They had each bought two copies of my fiction book but were not buying my claims and stories about my real life.

'Sorry to disappointment, all you Miss Marples, but there is no more fishing, hunting or stalking. Anyway, enough about my non- existent love life. We all wanna know the deets of how 'Harman met Simran', I announced, knowing fully well how excited Simran was to tell us about her brand new bait but was underplaying it, 'now spill the tea you bet–loser'.

'We used to play *chor police* as kids in the colony. Maybe those days it was puppy love. Then his dad got transferred to Chandigarh. I remember crying as if I had lost my full world. But I soon forgot. He came to find me 23.5 years and one divorce later. Could never stop thinking about his little *chor,* I guess,' Simran was blushing like a 15-year-old.

She had flunked our no-man challenge badly, but readily.

'Uhh, except now the handcuffs are real,' she added, in her characteristic sassiness, looking every bit like the satiated cat that had been served the 'extra cream'.

My eyes moistened up and so did Zoya's. The much-deserved fairytale we both had been waiting for, for our sassy Simran, finally came to fruition.

Three quarters of an hour later Krish rushed in sweating and panting. Bumming a light of Dan, he leaned on the backrest of his chair and closed his eyes as he took a drag. He was spent out.

Holding up my wide-rimmed flute filled with pink dancing liquid, I raised a toast:

'To every heart out here who contributed to my brilliance. Excessively indebted to all of you.

To Zoya, for always keeping me grounded with your canny perspectives even though you are infuriatingly correct most of the time.

Danny? I would've faded away like a washed-out Barbie if you didn't kick my ass from time to time.

To Shanaya, my cousin, my sister and my reality check, who always keeps me on my toes. To Simran, my co-conspirator and my very first saviour in college. You believed in me when I had stopped believing in myself.

Not to forget Pari who is on her third honeymoon and will return with good news again, I bet, for always being in my corner.

Last but never the least, Krish Besto for being the best friend in the whole wide world.

It is these close-knit bonds that have made me feel worthy, valuable and treasured in my darkest hours. You all are irreplaceable. My life would be nothing without each and every one of you in it. Absolutely nothing!'

Everybody hoisted their glasses, teary-eyed. I was completely overwhelmed that evening.

I conveyed my thank-yous to my family in person later. We ordered another round of appetizers and went back to our bantering.

Krish footed the bill of 25K at Olive, insisting that Queen Kai should not have to shell out a penny. Like a true-blue friend he had stretched himself and turned my moment into the biggest celebration ever. I could not help but be grateful to have him in my life in whatever capacity he chose to exist.

'This one is on me, Besto. Now go and get some much needed rest,' he commanded as he fed in the pin number of his credit card.

I smiled graciously, secretly wishing Krish's body, brain and heart came with a secret password too. If only life was that easy. Sigh!

I had an awesome book launch that most authors could only dream about then why was a small part of me still aching?

***

Towards the tail end of 2017, my happiness multiplied. Coco had her buns in the oven for real this time. Even Aliya was doing much better; she had become a doting and overbearing momma to two labradors and was overseeing a huge HIV campaign for the WHO; Krish continued to hobnob with Bollywood biggies and had been signed by two of the biggest production houses as the lead music director.

And Shanaya met her future husband. Finally!

Not knowing where to begin, considering all their known contacts drew a blank and their daughter flatly refusing to canvas her profile on a matrimonial website (wising up after my disarming experience), there were only a handful of options left for the Billimorias to choose from within our small community that matched Shanaya's requirements, which included a 'coolio Bawa' with solid educational qualifications, reasonably high on the social strat ladder, residing only in India and most fundamentally a 'non-mamma's boy,' and preferably not from a Parsi colony though that was negotiable.

'I don't think I can ever love again. It's almost a year and I'm still not over Gary,' Shanaya would vent each time we spoke. 'I will have to resign to my fate of being stuck in a loveless marriage, with a *mumma no buchko* (mamma's boy), no thanks to my narrow-minded and non-progressive parents. You are blessed Kai. No damn *shaadi ka* pressure.'

Touchwood. I really was.

I could not envision anything more torturous than sharing a bed, a bathroom, a commode or even a conversation with someone I did not love or respect or even like that much. I would rather fly solo forever, even if it meant adopting baby penguins instead. (Might need to shift base from Mumbai for that though.)

It was around late August, post *Khordad saal* (the birthday of our Prophet) that Shanaya's parents approached BBC aka Bepsi Berjorji Chotia from Cusrow Baug for urgent intervention in Shanaya's wretched singledom.

After pocketing an advance of a neat 14,000 rupees for her services from my uncle and aunt, Madame Chotia went to work at once, studying their daughter's portfolio under a microscope.

'*Oye*! *Bheja no bh**ro*! She is over 31 and still *kuari* (single)? Why did you wait for so long? *Aaj kal ni chokreeyo, marere,* I tell you, roaming around with these characterless parjats *aapru monu karu karva* (to make our faces black). On top of that, they overeducate themselves and then complain that *aapra chokrao maa koi kami che* (that our boys have something missing).'

After giving the Billimorias a rather harsh moral science lecture, Chotia shortlisted two boys for Shanaya from her Parsi-Iranian directory that was overflowing with personal resumes of lonely hearts of all shapes, sizes, ages and from various locations.

The first in the race was a Homyaar Irani, who answered quicker to Homzee. BBC raved about his sturdy middle-class values and of a great-great-grandfather who had been a childhood buddy of Dadabhai Naoroji, adding proudly that he also came with a Wodehouse Gymkhana membership and a sister who had been the runner-up of a beauty pageant organised by the World Parsi Org in 2016—as though all those were the sole essentials to conjugal bliss.

Sadly, Homzee had lost her when he suggested meeting halfway between her residence and where he lived, showing his laziness and lack of conduct too early in the day. Shanaya had rejected him in her head, almost at once.

Half an hour into the date, I received an SOS from Shanaya, 'A *seeplo sapal* (a goody two-shoes). Zilch social skills. And *pakauing* me about the history behind every Irani bakery. Gonna ditch the geek and c ya 4 an early drinkie. Okie?'

With his rather outdated pink and green checks short-sleeved shirt tucked into an unfashionable pair of high-waisted brown polyester trousers, oily hair and Gandhi glasses, Homzee was nowhere close to her ideal.

Gary owned two resto-bars in Goa and showed off three tattoos—Guns N' Roses on the left arm, Black Sabbath on the right and a brazen one across his butt which I had only heard about but never seen. Gary Shaw had been 'coolio' from the word go.

It is not fair to compare a fruit punch and a smooth whisky, but *bechara* Homzee Womzee would have never stood a chance with my dynamic, modish and hard-to-please cousin.

26

The Strange Case of Dr Jekyll and Mr Hyde

BBC exploded on hearing about the failed date and she spared no leniency whilst making ageist and abrasive remarks about it to the Billimorias over the phone.

'*Tauba, tauba, maara kaan barigaya.* (My ears are burnt.) So many *naatak-nakhras*! What does your precious daughter expect at this age now? Some *mitho* like Ranbir Kapoor? These girls don't want to adjust only. They think earning a fat sum and disco-dancing all night will give them relief in their old age. It will only buy them a nurse. Does your fussy dikri want to marry a nurse?'

Upon hearing BBC's lack of sensitivity, Shanaya made it clear to her parents, 'I will remain single and not compromise because of social pressure. See cousin Kai, I admire her for not …'

That was enough of an invitation for them to huff, puff and blow.

'That niece of ours! She is one *chaloo chapati.* An air hostess with her head in the clouds, changing boys faster than she changes clothes. She has always been a bad influence on you,' her dad said.

'My sister has not trained her children well, like we have. They follow no rules or regulations. Don't you remember how she dropped that *daayo* (well-behaved) Parsi fellow like a hot potato to write some adult *chaupdi*? *Ekdum bagdi ne dhoor thaigayeech* (she has become a spoilt brat),' said her mom.

Or something to the effect. It was safe to say that I was a tarnished blotch in their bleached white world. Though Shanaya did not mention the exact words, snips of their altercation slipped out of her mouth and it left me feeling more detached from my community than ever before. I could still get past judgmental strangers or acquaintances taking potshots at me for it was human nature to trample on one's joy and peace, but these were my very own people—it hurt ever so much.

So by the time Dr Burzin Doctor, a neurologist's turn came in Shanaya Billimoria's queue of potential grooms, she had almost given up. She had just returned from a luxurious spa break in Phuket with her school friends and was in no mood to entertain any more 'boneheads'.

I had to remind her more than once that he was a prominent doctor and probably far from the nerd she was imagining but Shanaya had stopped counting her chicks.

'Unbelievable. BBC said things like "they are an upper class family with high values" and "First Class *saras chokro che*". That clearly means I must prepare myself for another crappy date with another *dudh pao* (milky bread).'

She was blowing off steam the day before her blind date, in my balcony, where five-and-half-year-old Rehu was flying his toy plane over my foot.

'And with a surname like "Doctor" for someone who is actually a doctor, can it get any more pathetic?'

'You haven't played emotional roulette with a bisexual imposter and a psychopath have you? Nothing can be that bad. Now don't do your usual *peejan paatlu* (useless chatter), and give it a go.'

'An apple a day keeps the doctor away,' my little monkey contributed, making me smile, though my dear legal whiz of a cousin was in no mood to indulge him.

She had imagined a life away from her overbearing parents, lolling on the beaches of Goa, drinking feni and sucking on juicy crabs with the chilled-out Gary, helping him in his restaurant business and opening a nightclub. But life had other plans.

Hence, she wore her worst outfit (track pants on a first date with hideous green Crocs) tied her hair back in an unflattering greasy ponytail and stomped out of her house for her rendezvous with the surgeon.

'Will be waiting for your SOS', I messaged her on the way, 'chillax. You've got nothing to lose. If it backfires, I will buy you a classic mojito, your fave.'

But when her number did not flash, three hours into the meet, I hit the panic button. Her last-seen time on WhatsApp was several hours ago and she was not answering my calls either.

Has the doc misbehaved? Drugged and raped her? Stolen her organs? Is her phone misplaced in a tussle? Shall I call the CBI?

My mind was zooming in different directions.

Finally, at ten past nine, the phone rang.

'I am at his apartment,' she was barely audible.

'What? Why are you whispering? Has he taken you there against your will? I am calling the cops! Don't worry, Cuzz, I will send a rescue team. Just code word the exact location. Jaldi!'

'Calm down, NYPD; I just want you to cover for me. I've told Mom and Dad I am staying over at your place and we are having some sorta cousin bonding sesh with Jimmy and Pari.'

'But we are not, are we? Like, Jimmy is in Bali—'

And then it clicked. What a tubelight I was.

I disconnected at once not wanting to waste a second more of her playtime with the doc, super elated with the information, making up my mind to drive to Colaba the following weekend and rub the stinker on BBC's face.

'A harmless brew has turned into a screw, with your so-called *sojjo upper class Parsi with high values.* Is this what good bawas do, Bepsi Aunty? '

I even decided the exact words and pitch of my taunt.

Yes, it sounded childlike but I had a personal score to settle with the orangutan.

Here is why: On Shanaya's last visit to BBC, I had tagged along and experienced her bark and her bite first hand.

'Lose some weight if you want to have your lucky day too Miss Juicewalla, or you'll be left out too, along with one of those menopausal *dukhi aatmas.* It's a big, bad world. With your youth almost gone, your chances are getting lesser now. This stubborn defiance won't get you anywhere. I will even give you a five per cent discount on my fees if you let me try.'

Did she address all her clients with such insensitivity? Should she even be in this business?

The harassment did not stop there.

'Don't you want someone to make choi and rotli for and pay for your fancy-wancy beauty parlour bills? And don't forget that neither you nor your child will be accepted in our community or any agiary if you bring home a parjaat.'

That was it!

'Mrs Chotia, I am a self-sufficient 33-year-old woman and I work bloody hard every week, taking care of hundreds of strangers on flights. I have written a novel and I am not only a caring daughter, but also a good friend. I have no maternal instincts whatsoever and have no intentions of adding more pests to my overpopulated country. Last but not the least, I certainly don't need a *kaajwali* (matchmaker) to tell me how to live my damn life!'

Shanaya had to physically drag me out of there. But before I had a chance to return to the wicked witch's lair and mouth off my earlier practiced dialogue on nice boys and their so-called ethics, Shanaya blew us all away with an astounding announcement the following evening.

'Burzin and I are getting engaged. Right person, right time.'

Of course, Pari and I did not buy that and badgered her for the deets.

'Tiger in bed,' she gushed over an early dinner at a popular deli in Lower Parel.

'You sound as gaga as Lady Ga Ga,' Pari said humorously, 'but the truth is that it's all written before we were born.'

And there was no shortage of fault to be found amid my stars.

*Yup! You can't hurry LOVE. Even if nothing is written and you were dealt a blank page (like I was), it is what it is. Then no matter how many fortune cookies you crack open; or aromatic incense sticks you burn to attract a suitable, handsome as hell lover; or how many shrinks you buy to hear your sob story, love has its own f**king mind. No tantra-mantra-yantra can work if the good Lord has decided it's not in your best interest or worth his time.*

Wisdom had befallen on me late in the day but nevertheless a handful of lessons had been learnt.

Shanaya and Burzin had their *rupiya pehervanu* (pre-engagement ceremony) in 2018, a couple of days before our spring festival Jamshed-e-Navroz at the Turf Club, Mahalaxmi. Burzin, who was a national arm wrestling champion and loved the races too, often hobnobbing with Sobo's regular derby enthusiasts, threw an extravagant bash for the couple's nearest and dearest family and friends.

The Billimorias and Doctors visited good, old Rusty with a box of kesar pedas and sutarphani and he picked out a *shubh muharat* date for the lagan.

Dadaji ni Meherbani, it was finally happening for Shanaya!

'Seth Jeejeebhoy Dadabhoy Agiary', where most of the ritzy Parsi outdoor functions were held, was blocked for 17 March 2019.

We all saved the date gladly.

***

If 2017 was full of positive changes, growth and activity, 2018 was comparatively slow.

I was invited at the AIIMS to speak on body positivity and the effect it has on the young generation who seemed to be caught in a vicious circle of health supplements, gym mania and social media pressure apart from the regular peer pressure.

My own preoccupation with building my online community was taking a front seat with Danny pushing me harder and showing me some useful social media hacks that would keep me in the news until my next book.

'If you snooze, you lose.'

He put it in his inimitable style. So I posted, I blogged, I indulged. I blew my own trumpet. FB was giving me fruitful rewards. It was all travel-related mostly.

'Some women choose to follow men, and some women choose to follow their dreams. If you're wondering which way to go, remember that your career will never wake up and tell you that it doesn't love you anymore.' — Lady Gaga (*Cosmopolitan*, 2010)

So with this state of mind, no wonder my kiss score had been at a standstill since 2014. Of course, I had an understandable breakdown now and again but on the whole I was proud of myself. I had not been tempted with the propositions on flights either, which by the way had included a smooth-talking American billionaire and a rather debonair Dutch politician.

On my free time, I volunteered to spend time with the visually challenged and old age homes; after all, there were plenty of helpless and lonely people (in a different way) like me in the world, who needed affection and tenderness, so I decided to bat for their team instead of wallowing in self-pity.

'I miss the drama sometimes, it made me feel alive,' I confided in Simran one day. 'If you get some time off from grinding over the soldier's face, we could grab a drink and you can entertain me with some of your steamy accounts.'

Simran promised me that she would buzz me in soon, though I could not count on that at all. I had lost my partner in man-slaying. Simran was now addicted to Major Harman and we all know that love is that drug, far more lethal than cocaine.

KQ had once explained to me in a counselling session (one of the very few I had actually paid attention to) that making small changes every day that supported self-improvisation was the trick to prevent oneself from falling into old, destructive patterns of relationship enslavement. That the only way to create happiness is one step at a time by limiting time spent on self-defeating beliefs and surging forward with purpose and resolve. And that it was paramount to work on one's inner self as much as one does on their outer appearance.

As it turned out, sacrificing fast food and junk nosh was a lot harder than giving up on love, sex and all in-between. (Though I did get sober for 87 days, 8 hours to be exact.)

Figure-conscious Dan, who had recently got infatuated with pilates, water aerobics and some healthy mind–healthy body baloney to sustain his fitness levels, used to admonish me playfully whenever we spent a day out together in London or Dubai.

'A moment on the lips, lifetime on the hips sis.'

'Zip your lips then, bro,' I would splutter over my falafel roll or eggs Benedict (sans ham), 'and starve to death for all I care.'

'In my LGBT comm, gaining one stone equals to death of our sex life.'

'In case you missed the neon signpost, mine died ages ago.'

I would quip back, refusing to give up on my culinary debauchery and pay heed to his persisting commentary.

'Carbs' was my happy place—not Mauritius, not an African safari and definitely not pumping iron.

'You are lucky. Straight men are hell more tolerant of fuller bodies, I mean…healthier girls.'

Seeing me stew in his brash remark, he would quickly cover up, 'I didn't mean you at all, you are just a bit untoned. But drop dead gorg obviously.'

Early August, Krish proposed we meet at The Shack, as he needed to 'talk'.

Apparently it still existed. He passed it on his daily morning drizzly jogs at the beach. How he loved the rains! This time, I kept my hopes as tiny as a grain of sand or even tinier. As far as Krish was concerned, the biggest lesson I had learnt was never expect anything from him.

I was the first to reach.

The Shack's surroundings were not as tranquil as they used to be—there was a group of teenagers playing throw ball, a handful of urchins pacing up and down in the hope of making some money and a few transvestites lying on the sand, humming Sonu Nigam tunes. One could see Madh Island at a distance. As I waited for him, I could not help but wonder why Krish and I rarely met like two normal adults at a coffee shop?

Just as I began to reminisce on our several heart to hearts that had taken place on that site, I spotted him walking towards me, absorbed in his thoughts. Was it my imagination or had he become even more attractive than I remembered? I was rather tempted to whistle.

He had revamped his look once again with his hair cropped short, buffed arms enhanced by a slim fit, dark green V-neck T under a grey hoodie and pair of charcoal distressed jeans matched by black Skechers.

I am not sure if you all will ever get the pleasure to taste malai khaja from Parsi Dairy Farm at Marine Lines, Mumbai. The *mithai* is huge, square-faced, crunchy and crusty on the outside and oozing with rich malai on the inside and sinfully prepped in ghee. Pure ecstasy. No other words for it. And no it was not fair that Mr Aryan gave me similar yummiliscious feels as my favourite khaja.

Simply unacceptable. And super infuriating.

That trademark stud in his left ear was replaced by a tiny cross and a thin silver chain around his neck with a Sai Baba locket was a new addition to his look.

I hugged him happily. I cherished our friendship, in spite of everything.

'You look younger and slicker each time I see you,' I complimented him as he held me for extra 10 seconds before letting me go, 'and I seem to be expanding like a *phugga.*'

He sniggered as he slipped something in my hand—a pendant. At first I thought it was similar to the one he was wearing but on a closer look it was in the shape of half a dozen fries.

'Who cares? You would look amazing even if you wore a tent. Picked this up at a modern flea market ages ago in Paris when I went holidaying with Ma,' he said, grinning shyly at my flummoxed expression. 'It had completely slipped my mind and I found it in one of my old jeans, after all this time. Typical me, absent-minded. You still love your fries, don't you?'

That was the oddest, queerest and most thoughtful gift anybody had ever given me. And little did he know that he was my eternal bowl of crispy French fries.

'Thanks. Yeah, I still love them. Always have and always will.'

I took a deep breath, *had I said too much*?

'Anyway, I have given up on counting cals. Intermittent fasting seems to work for the entire *janta* but me. In fact, it went reverse and I gained a few more of those monsters.'

'Curvy is the new sexy nowadays, I read it on the cover of Ishu's *Cosmo*. So, count your blessings.'

Patting me fondly, he said, 'You are in a league of your own. Actually now that you have become comfortable with the "no guy–no cry" thingy, the next step is finding your life's purpose.

('Because a life without a cause is a life without effect'? Read that somewhere.) That means writing your second book which you've been procrastinating; some self-reflection and opening your chakras. Like me, you have a truckload of past demons to deal with and your own set of insecurities and revulsions. Aligning them will take time. *Om Shanti.*'

'Noted Gyani Baba,' I replied, bowing in mock reverence, 'but all these chakra-talks are giving me *chakkar.*'

'Laugh all you want, Bawi, but you will thank me one day. How do you think after all these tumultuous years, I have summoned the courage to confront my absconding father?'

I gave him a surprised look.

'I am going to do it, Bawi, but I needed to run it by you first.'

My heart felt a familiar twinge. I was touched that he had thought of my support as an invaluable part of a possibly life-changing decision.

Why can't you see that we blend perfectly like jalebi and rabdi? Are you blind to my amorous hints or in denial of your own?

Two perfectly valid questions that I wish I could throw his way.

How could it not have hit him yet that the meaning of the blah blah *moksha* that he was scaling summits for, existed *only* in my arms?

We Parsis have a saying for such thickheads: *Ena bheja maan bhoosoo che* (his brains are filled with sawdust).

Twelve years of one-sided fixation!

In that much time, I could have become the first Parsi President of India, if I wanted. But here I was dealing with a certified dummy destined to be a lifelong monk. A serial sadist who had taken the oath to torture me until my last day.

This isn't the time to lick my wounds but rather focus on standing with him.

I rebuked myself.

Confronting a father who had kicked him to the curb was impressively brave. A gamble. It could go either way.

'*Kabhi kabhi jeetne ke liye kuch haarna padta hai. Aur haar ke jeetne waale ko Baazigar kehte hain.* (To win sometimes, you have to lose. And the one who loses and then wins is called a gambler.)'

I buoyed him up in the way I knew best.

'Oh, Bawiiiii! You and your SRK dialogue *baazi.* I should sue him for psychological damage to my besto.'

Then pulling my right cheek, he asked, 'Feel like a nibble? You can give me some tips on how to approach my so-called father over some hot samosas at a coffee shop.'

We had coconut water each from the *nariyal pani wala* on the way back and then shared a plate of samosas and medu vadas at a hotel whilst weighing the pros and cons that the father angle would bring to the rest of his family.

I voiced my concerns about the fear of uprooting their lives especially his mother's which had just about settled, but he assured me he would not involve her in it. He had clearly made up his mind, so I wished him the best. After all, closure in any relationship was utmost to one's mental well-being.

Ask Me!

Krish too had sought out therapy at some point of time. With the help of that and a few ascended masters of the world, he had understood that most of his mood swings and life choices had been based on the foundation of a rocky upbringing. Retracing steps to our childhood often brings improved clarity and purposeful awareness to the choices we make in the present.

Krish had been trying to take the spiritual route, finding peace in his music and setting professional goals. I had been caught between dealing with what everybody was doing (and having) by a certain age and I wasn't; and being my own woman who refused to settle for anything less than the best.

Whatever it was, we both were trying to heal, trust and breathe again. The roadmap to soul restoration and heart reparation is anything but easy. In fact, it is a lifelong process for most of us. Maybe that is why we both felt that sense of kinship that evolved from being a member of the same lost soul tribe.

After we finished our feasting, Krish accompanied me to the parking lot of the hotel to see me off. When he opened the door of my car, I looked up into his dreamy puppy eyes, and a gush of protectiveness swept over me making me suddenly want to shield him from the big, bad world which was nowhere close to the idealistic one he had concocted in his head.

As I stood there, I dreaded the dire consequences of his father rejecting him once again. If that happened, I doubted he would ever be the same again. I hugged him tight. It was as platonic as it got from my side. He pulled me in a firm and strong grip and we both stood there clinging to each other, the intense fear of the unknown enwrapping us into a chilly cocoon.

Wait a minute. Am I imagining the slight graze of his jeans over my own? *Of course, I am.*

For a moment, I wished we were back at our shack rather than a car park, scattered with gawking drivers and leery valet guys.

I caught myself guessing what his weakest erogenous zone could be, other than the obvious.

With Jangu it had been the collarbone; the naval had been Sid's get-off point, Gabs had made sure his thighs got treated nice and Rio's man nipples was his G-spot. KQ was too spur-of-the-moment, but if I had to estimate, it would be his tush. And He-Devil had a thumb fetish.

I implanted a light peck under his left ear thoughtfully, it could be a hit and miss but my instinct told me I could strike gold. It was as if we had both been hypnotised into an electromagnetic field, unable to disengage.

*A rainbow so powerful, so midnight, so f**king, song kisses. Bloody hell*!

It felt like a game of scrabble in my head.

I heard his breathing becoming deeper, merging with my own silent cravings; and just as I expected it to all fall in place in one final swoop, he thrust me back assertively and slightly offensively, as if we were about to commit a sin as blasphemous as Adam and Eve. And there I was once again thrown out of the Garden of Eden, landing on my big, fat butt. I did not know whether to be insulted, puzzled, furious or flattered.

Either he had hated it or was simply embarrassed with the PDA or had gotten cold feet. Or did the ultimate realisation that he was human and not some saint, finally dawn upon him?

But I was not going to hang around a snuffle longer to find out.

Jumping into the car, I sped off, stumped, disarmed and fuming, resisting the temptation to bulldoze him once in for all. I did not have an inflated ego but I would be damned if I let the emotionally stunted chameleon with the mental bandwidth of a squirrel gain leverage over me and snatch my last ounce of self-respect. It had taken me blood, sweat, tears and years to unf**k myself and I was not going to let Dr Jekyll and Mr Hyde fling me into the eye of a cyclone of 'what-ifs' and 'why-nots' once again.

'Screw you, Krish Aryan. *Bailo. Beekangus*! (Wimp. Coward!) I will walk barefoot on hot coals before I let you play ping-pong with my heart ever again.'

I yelled above Tina Turner's unrestrained, '*What's love got to do with it*' playing on the radio.

'Oh-oh, what's love got to do, got to do with it?
What's love but a SECONDHAND EMOTION?
What's love got to do, got to do with it?
Who needs a heart when a heart can be broken?'

Tina was right. Love was indeed a secondhand emotion.

When I had watched the confused expression on Krish's face from the rear-view mirror, I promised myself that I was not going to let any weasel get under my skin like this, ever again. Even if he was the only mortal left on Mother Earth, I would never give my power away. EVER!!!

#IamsooveryouKrish*Kamino*
#ScrewyouAryan
#CelibacyZindabad

27

Kahani Mein Twist

12: 06 a.m.; 18 March 2019
Gusto

'I suppose it is a bit too late to cut a lengthy story short but you got the pic, right? Divine counterparts or divine counterfeits, they all sink faster than the *Titanic* when the ball drops.

I am this close to meditating with mountain goats and hermits,' I said, glancing around wondering how long I had chewed on the stranger's brains; Bryan was clearing the tab of one of the last customers.

But Mr Anonymous's tadpole eyes did not leave my glassy ones; he looked like a typical expressionless *putla*.

Just as well, for I may have finished my trudge down memory lane but I was not finished with bad-mouthing love just yet.

'But that's what love does, isn't it? Makes us putty in the hands of the beloved. It makes us throw caution to the wind and lose the last rational bone in our body.'

'We goad ourselves to take that leap of faith so that we can become somebody from a nobody in the eyes of a special somebody who makes us the apple of their eye. It may all very well be for a fleeting moment, a meaningful hour, a high-spirited evening, where every emotion is magnified and every sense heightened. Alas! The rose-tinted glasses wear off and we all end up either in a loony bin or a bar.'

'And trust me, I stayed miles away from the *ch**tyapa* called love up until the wedding today when these old-timers crossed all limits…'

I trailed off, moistening up as flashes from Shanaya's gig ran through my mind.

Mr Anonymous maintained his *maunvrat*, making me wonder if he was stoned.

'It's another story for another day but let's say you caught me here at Gusto tonight, right after a massive showdown. I f**king lost the plot. The aunties and uncles whom I had been avoiding since forever were at their villainous best. It's like *paap* to be single at thirty-five!'

He glowered at me and his glazed looks were beginning to cause me some concern.

'Sorry for the flowery linguistics, but if you were there, you would understand why. There's probably a meme of me doing the rounds already.'

Flagging for Bryan's attention before flicking across the table a credit card which he removed from a gold-plated card holder; it was almost as if he was suggesting that he owned my time.

'I got this.'

He spoke finally.

'But I need to confess something, I think I should tell you the truth about why I'm here. I need something from you actually.'

Voila! *There we go. I was right AF (as f**K)!*

'*Saalao matida ni jaat, ekdum luchao.* (All of you men are scoundrels.) Just can't keep it in your pants, can you?'

My hysterical voice thundered over Pavarotti over the speakers, and must have caught Bryan's attention because I could see him speeding towards us from the corner of my eye.

'Hey Mister-what's-your-name. You presume I'm some easy lay, eh? Just cause you now know me as well as my teddy bear, you think you can buy me off with five measly drinks?'

Springing up from my futon, I began thumping the table between us, dropping two coasters and a fork.

Just a few minutes ago I had been grateful for his timely intervention; after all, unloading one's emo baggage and reliving the most significant moments of one's life can be deeply therapeutic as well as profoundly liberating for one's soul. And there is always something untainted and authentic about ripping one's heart open to someone who has no vested interest in you or shares no past or future connection with you.

My heartthrob was bang on when he had mouthed in his sexy baritone (in *Dilwale*), '*Hum shareef kya hue, puri duniya hi badmash ban gayi.* (Just when I became good, the world became bad.)'

'And I've got news for you nut-jobs! Despite what I just told you and yes, I may have sounded sad and needy for most of it; I AIN'T FOR SALE! Gottttt it?'

Though I had a feeling I was saying much more than I should, the LIT was not going to let me off the hook that soon.

Mr Anonymous blew a long whistle before gesturing me with his hands to sit down again.

'And what gives you the idea that I'm going to obey you, you Sick Freak?'

'Kai stop! Pleeeeeze.'

I heard Bryan's frantic voice roaring over us.

'Bryan! So now you too are a part of this disgusting proposition. Do you get a commission for this?'

Note to self: Unfriend Bryan from FB as soon as I get home.

Bryan stepped back, his mouth hung open, his eyes popping out like a frightened deer.

'Hold on! Hold on! This is just a misunderstanding. Bryan, swipe my card and let me take over before we both get beheaded by our warrior princess here. I think there have been enough fatalities tonight.'

Mr Anonymous winked good-humouredly at the younger guy and began to stand up; surprisingly unoffended by my barrage of insults and raspy slander.

His last line extracted my suspicious antennas even higher.

'WTF! Am I being filmed? Is this a sting op by some jilted ex-boyfriend? Or a recorded exposition of my colourfully controversial life by my rival authors?'

(Okay, so I was not half as famous but someday I would be. *Inshallah.*)

I began to scan around the room for hidden cams.

'Calm down, dear Kai, and please take a seat. Let me reassure you that neither am I a spy nor a serial rapist.'

He spoke with steady leisure, as if talking to a child.

'I think it's time I introduced myself. I am Dez Zacchary. One of the creative directors at Astara Prime. My friends call me Zacky.'

He stretched out his hand and I had no choice but to reciprocate his formidable grip with my shaky one.

Who had not heard of Astara Prime? It was one of the top OTT and film production houses in India. In fact, they had recently been all over the news for a controversial documentary on freedom fighters.

'I kind of shadowed you from that Parsi extravaganza. Then I looped in my new friend Bryan over here, who made sure my intentions were honourable before he let me anywhere near you.'

Though he was coming clean, the smugness in his tone was confusing. Reading my anxious and disarrayed expression, he drove straight to the point.

'I was at the same wedding. Burzin's dad and my late father were the best of friends. I had just finished wishing Burzin and his pretty wife when I saw you, or rather heard you on stage. And jeez, you blew me away! So much so, that I missed out on grabbing my spot at the second seating too. And I have been fantasising about this Parsiliscious *lagan nu bhonu* (wedding food) since I got the invite; a much-awaited treat for us non-Parsis.'

Thank God there were three potato wedges left. I picked them up and stuffed them all into my mouth at once. Food for survival. At least he was a known suspect now. Small consolation there. But why tail me? And then he smashed into it with such fervour and excitement that I was worried he would leak in his pants.

'When I saw that impenitent madness and the fire in the belly, I was intrigued and got greedy. I wanted to know more. I needed more—straight from the mouth of the juicy and salacious Bawi Bridget Jones.'

Bryan nodded, smugly.

Me? Bridget Jones? She is epic. I am a simple Parsi girl with more jelly in my belly than fire; trying to hold my life together and flopping most of the time badly. So badly.

'I am pretty sure that I made an illustrious fool of myself.'

'Nah! You were sensational, ballsy and electrifying. A refreshing change from what we are used to.'

Pointing at the Marilyn Monroe poster, he stated in a gravelly voice, 'In case you missed what's written at the bottom.'

I squinted my eyes to read the illegible font.

'Imperfection is beauty, madness is genius, and it's better to be absolutely ridiculous than absolutely boring—Marilyn Monroe.'

'My plan was to approach you after your Oscar debut, which by the way will keep you on the Parsi hot seat for the next two years at the least, but you left abruptly.'

But it still did not add up.

I sighed louder than I intended to; he was right.

The repercussions of my bold feat would be anything but pleasant. I could see news flashes if not through the *Jame Jamshed*, *Parsi Times* and the *Parsiana*, then the Chinese whispers that found their way from colony *bageechas* to Parsi panchayat living rooms and WZO (World Zoroastrian Organisation) type of banquets.

Not to mention that the rest of the Juicewalla family after their return from their respective holidays would have more juice in store for them than a year's supply from Haji Ali Juice Centre.

It hardly mattered now, the damage was done.

Zacky had not finished yet, his Adam's apple throbbing, his froggish pupils more conspicuous than ever.

'I was compelled to follow your car. You very well may have gone home and I would have asked Xerxes, Burzin's father, to connect us tomorrow but my inner voice told me that your evening was far from over.'

But this was way too much for me to digest. I was not sure if I should feel flattered or spooked out. Dez Zacchary had gone through great lengths to stalk me. What did a biggie from Astara Prime want from a small-time flight attendant like me?

'I can't get you free tickets or discounts. That's only family privilege, so don't waste your time, or mine.'

He punched a fist over his forehead and shook his head vehemently.

'Lord no! You seriously have trust issues, don't you?'

Then taking a deep breath, he threw his head back, spread out his arms like a falcon and erupted like an inferno.

'Kai, you got one kickass story and believe you me, your life is worth exceedingly more than a stand-up stage show with a pathetic audience. You can't just be a one-book wonder. You are the whole screenplay! Don't you see that?'

'NO!'

'Your journey needs to be engraved up there with the stars. Not only will it stir others to follow their dreams but it will give them the courage to take risks, lead the way like shepherds, not just be part of the herd.'

He then pointed to the portraitures of Frank Sinatra, Queen, Madonna and U2 on the walls.

Su bukk bukk karech muo? (*What is he blubbering about*?) *These are pop stars, not sheep breeders. How plastered is he*?

Why was he creating a hype around me? Okay, so I had written a (in) decent novel and my breasts were still pointing in the right direction and I had an attractive enough face but that was it. I was no Shobhaa De.

'You give us your larger-than-life chronicles, exactly as it is and we will bring it on screen. We make it a bloody mega movie. These days it's all about hardcore original content. No fairy tales; no peddling roses, fluff and hearts to the audience; no false promises and fake narratives. The truth and nothing but the truth. For life is nothing close to a romantic SRK film, as much as we want it to be.'

My life—a film? What for? I haven't assassinated someone (yet) or appeared on Oprah (due someday) or Miss Malini (a local rage) or discovered life on the moon. I haven't even been able to keep my weighing scale in check.

'I can't. I mean I know nothing about scriptwriting and screenplays.'

I was completely awestruck by his unexpected proposal.

'You start with the first draft of the script; write from your heart and we will take it from there.'

I kept staring.

'Even if it takes you a year or two, I will wait. You know you can do this. It's time to tell your story, Kai, and share it with the world.'

'What's the catch?'

'There are no free meals, Kai, no free meals.'

As our wise Simran always said.

'Be right back.'

He vamoosed, to make a call I guess.

Kai can't have rocks hurled at her one moment and be enticed into a film deal in the next.

The universe didn't just cast webs of divine sparkles into her life without expecting a costly return gift. Okay so there's no denying that life has granted her exotic travel opportunities, decent money flow, fleeting glamour and bursts of fame which she is super grateful for but it's also robbed her of mental peace, a favourable metabolism and a steady heart and soul connection with that special someone.

So, being in the glass half-empty category, I drove myself nuts for the next 120 seconds, trying to figure out what new bombshell was about to explode on me.

Zacchary returned, looking even more magnified than when he had left.

'Had a quick word with my team. They're in.'

'Okay universe, *de taali teri muchi kaali*.' (It must be serious if he woke up the poor guys at midnight for this.)

Lifting my right hand upwards, I looked up to the amber-hued ceiling, imploring it to give me a fiver in return.

Suppressing their sniggers, Bryan began clearing our table and Zacky handed me his business card, simultaneously pulling out my phone number from my stammering mouth and nattering something regarding touching base soon, blah blah blah.

'One for the road' I yammered; knocking down the last few sips of my fourth or was it fifth LIT, I bid them both the loudest goodbye I could muster.

I strode out of Gusto, my head spinning like a carousel, making up my mind to pop a crocin once I reached home and stay hydrated.

Loads of uncanny things had happened to me in the past, almost sounding fictional if one did not know better, but this was in a league of its own!

Slamming the door of my car shut, I collapsed in the backseat and tried soaking up the events of the evening.

A film gig? My life, a potential movie script? Is this a dream or an out-of-body experience inside a dream? How sloshed am I?

Enchantment and wonderment akin to Princess Jasmine's as she flew across Agrabah on a flying carpet, embarking on her new journey, surged through my heart chakra, making me the happiest girl alive, even though I did not have an Aladdin backing me vocally, I crooned:

'A whole new world,
A new fantastic point of view
No one to tell us no or where to go
Or say we're only dreaming…

I'm like a shooting star
I've come so far
I can't go back where I used to be…

A whole new world,
with new horizons to pursue…'

And then the impossible happened.

I silently thanked every unkind kid who had caused me unbearable pain, every fella who had drilled a hole in my soul; every vile experience that had been a thorn in my side; every Nazi who had blown my self-respect into pieces.

For if it were not for them, none of this would be happening.

Someone somewhere under the sacred dome of one of our most revered fire temples had once upon a time illuminated it for me this way: 'This is a journey of faith and of victory, Kai. You have to chase your own dreams. Make your own mistakes. Trust the process, Kai, for everything happens for a reason. Life will change for you, but for that, you will have to first learn to follow your own heart and most importantly believe in yourself, even when nobody else does. You have just one life; own it Kai.'

28

Romancing King Khan

12:40 a.m.

The car speedometer was maxing at 130. Ram Singh hinted at weariness by a giant-sized yawn, and he simply did not care a paisa about my chirpy whistling or the speed surveillance cameras any more.

I had to share the *kahani mein* twist (plot twist) with someone before I burst into flames of joy.

Ram Singh, malum hain aaj aapke baby ke saath kya hua? Jab mein pub main thi na tab...(Ram Singh, do you know what happened to me today? When I was in the pub?)

No, that was not coming out right, nor did I want him to be the first to know. Krish was the obvious choice. He had mentioned pinging me later, but there was not a missed call from him, not even a measly text.

Must be kharata-maroing unless that TikTok Ho Ruby has lured him for a post-Goa nightcap at her pad.

The thought of it made me want to spew, but I managed to pull myself back to my blissful state.

For life is nothing close to a romantic SRK film, as much as we want it to be.

What Zacchary had observed was ringing in my ears. And it felt like an arrow in the dark; like a brick on the head; like an avalanche without warning; it was the writing on the wall that could not be ignored any more. And I needed real answers.

'Oh, *teri toh...*'I yelled.

Ram Singh jumped out of his skin.

'*Aap nahin.*(Not you.)'

It was one thing to marinade colourful LIT-triggered curses in your head and quite another to alarm an old, tired chauffeur.

'Bandstand *ki taraf lijiye.* (Take me to Bandstand.)'

Ram Singh did not fuss, for experience has taught him to expect the unexpected from our crazy family whom he has served loyally for over two decades.

A few minutes later, we parked outside the expansive property where my obsession resided. Even though Mannat was not even two kilometres away from my Bandra residence, it was unique just like the superstar was—an imperial crown that stood out from the rest of the neighbourhood, a mansion fit for a king.

And it was about time Queen Kai paid him a visit. So, I placed my handbag containing my jewellery on the front seat for safekeeping with my trustworthy driver and emptied over myself almost half a bottle of Givenchy that was hidden in the glove compartment for emergency situations just like this. Chugging down the last couple of drops from the carry-on flask to give my saturated palate a final rinse, I sprung out of my SUV and charged like a shikari towards my shikar. Because '80 per cent of success is showing up'. Right said Woody Allen.

My sari had become unmanageable and had acquired a skirt-like shape and one of my heels was in a critical condition.

Two sets of piercing eyes screened me suspiciously from behind the humongous iron gates of the superstar's property. But I was not afraid of them or anybody for that matter.

It was about time these actors took responsibility for the irreversible damage they caused gullible and die-hard fans like me. Like the rest of his gazillion fans, I had also been blindsided by this idea of romance and perfection that he brandished through his dialogues, songs, mannerisms in his superhit films.

Oh how I had also yearned for butterflies to smash into my stomach walls and rainbows to fall from the skies, like they had for his female leads in *Kuch Kuch Hota Hai*, *Veer–Zaara* and *Dil To Pagal Hai*.

Because all our lives, no matter where we are, no matter who we are, no matter what we have been through, where we live, what we chose to pursue, or what we are up against, there is one common desire that we all aspire for and that is our quest for true love. It has always been humankind's prime motive.

But we all jolly well know how far it had worked out in my case until now, right?

All I ever got was Jerkhead-Jangu, Sid-Break-Heart, Confused.com Krish, Nick Prick, Gangsta-Gabriele, Randy Rio, Killer Looks-Qureshi, and Neville He-Devil. I was done drunk karaoking to '*Another one bites the dust*' and '*I will survive*' post every heartbreak and romantic catastrophe.

I had also wrestled with the fact that I had never been enough for some of them and blamed myself for the disappointing results of all entanglements. When the truth was, most of them were totally mental and sapped out most of my confidence and faith in myself.

Perhaps even Krish would not have lived up to the hype, had we erased the Laxman *rekha*. I had stuck on to him like chewing gum because I was in love with the idea of a true soul connection despite the cold, hard facts staring at me. When in reality, as a boyfriend, he may very well turn out to be another average Joe.

Soulmates, twin flames, soul threads, *janam-janam ka saath* were the same old poison in a new bottle. A clever marketing strategy by devious minds who had been puppet-stringing the multi-crore film industry by selling fuzzy dreams on screen to starry-eyed idiots like me in exchange for *shauharat aur daulat* (fame and money).

SRK needed to be exposed.

'Eh you *ghelsappa*. Fekuchand. King Kong Khan, *bahar nikal* (come out).'

But it did not seem to cause much of an impact on the other side of the barricade, except for setting off a dog into a barking fit and stirring a few insomniac crows on trees.

'*Lucho*! Jhootto! How can you sleep peacefully in your swish castle while breaking the castles we made in the air?'

It was time to claim my power back. Seek closure. *Sunao* him properly.

A passing Honda City with a youngish couple inside slowed down.

'Hey are you okay? Do you need a lift?'

I heard a feminine voice call out.

'Yup thanks. Got a date with the King. Now get lost and let me do my job.'

They whooshed off.

Picking up a medium-sized stone and flinging it across with all my might, I watched it hit the bottom of the gate, making a distinct sound.

A burly, bearded man in a dark green attire appeared from behind the gates, and spoke to me sternly, 'Madam, *agar aap chup nahin hoge toh* police *ko bulana padega.* (If you don't keep quiet, we will have to call the police.)'

I began laughing hysterically. I had just arrived from a battle, so who was this *phooski* guard in front of me?

'*Bulao, lekin yaad rakho, "Taqt ki parvah, badshah se zyada, uske vazir ko hoti hai".*' (Call but remember that a minister worries a lot more about the throne than the king.)

I challenged them. The SRK dialogue from *Don 2* seemed to fuse perfecto.

I heard Ram Singh tooting twice; stumbling out of my car panic-stricken, waving his hand frantically and trying to communicate something desperately.

Though I could feel myself slowly slipping into the biggest hangover of my life, I gestured at him to take a chill pill.

This Ram Singh can be such a drama queen, sometimes.

The thick-bearded guard was joined by his slimmer counterpart and they took a step forward, menacingly. After surviving a narrow escape from being taken captive by real dons on my 25th birthday, this was not remotely intimidating.

I mirrored them. I would be damned if I let two gorillas with rectangular walkie-talkies sticking out of their backsides, come in between me and my object of desire.

I heard them hiss fiercely into each other's ears of what sounded like a Marathi-Hindi-English combo of '*Pagal hain, yedeee zaali,* ladies-*aahe.* (She is mad, become crazy, she's a lady.) *Shinde la phone karaicha ka*? (Shall we phone Shinde?)'

They disappeared once again behind their precious doorways, probably to have a discussion on what to do with me, when the powerful growl of an engine behind me brought me to attention. The headlights blinked brightly on my face making me flinch. I could barely see a thing.

Eve-teasers? Crappity crap my phone is in the car. I just told Ram Singh to get back inside and chillax. Now how will I alert him? Where is the doofus when I need him? I hope he has not snoozed off. I should've packed up after Gusto, gone home and watched some SRK flick for the endth time instead of inviting this type of trouble.

HONK! HONK!

It was the meanest, sleekest and shiniest sports machine in the city! And there was only one person I knew who drove this baby—my True Love.

I could feel the gaze of a solitary figure upon me from behind a heavily tinted window. I would have recognised that perfect silhouette even if I was in a coma.

I can't blow this. My heaven-sent rendezvous with SRK is finally here! It is the perfect time to unleash the pent-up anger umm lust. Maybe I had judged him too harshly. Perhaps it was time to call a truce and fulfil a longstanding fantasy. After all, isn't everything fair in love and war?'

Slightly nauseous with the overconsumption of an amalgamation of various spirits with a mind superlatively fogged with overwhelming excitement, I took a couple of unsteady strides towards the elegant beauty, half-afraid of falling unconscious on its bonnet or barf over myself.

Itni shiddat se maine tumhe paane ki koshish ki hai. Ki har zarre ne mujse tumse milane ki saazish ki hai. (I have tried to get you with so much intensity that every particle on this earth has tried to conspire to make me meet you.)

But thoughts without actions are futile. And so:

Plan A: Swoon. Kiss. Flee.

Plan B: Try opening the door. Jumping into his car. Making out.

Plan C: Lie across the hood. Force him out. Let the chips fall where they may.

But my body was simply unable to carry the weight of my unprecedented joy and unmatched happiness any more, and started to cave in. All I remember was walking on clouds (sorta) alongside melodic angels who were chanting in my ears, in their soprano voices, 'Hallelujah! It's now or never. Now. Now. Now.'

I felt possessed.

I opened my mouth to say something. Anything. There was so much to tell him; so much to share. But when someone you have pined for this long and so hard crops up in front of you without warning, appearing as enticing as a rich, creamy crème brûlée and as irresistible as a double-layered cheese éclair, words fail you. In fact, all rationality fails you.

Except perhaps when it comes to humming, '*Dil to pagal hain, dil deewana hain* (heart is mad, heart is lovesick)...'

The superstar probably used to overzealous fans parading and even courting him outside his mansion, was not paying much attention to me. Maybe, he could not hear me through the glass.

Hoping my Hindi did not sound too anglicised, I took another shaky step towards him and serenaded him with one more popular number, shriller this time, '*Tum paas aaye, yun muskuraye, tumne naa jaane kya sapne dikhaye...* (you came close and made me smile, you showed me so many dreams…)'

Okay, the art of seduction is not my 'A' game but the phrase 'try try try again until you succeed' seems as if it is made for me, what say readers? And then suddenly I had a very scary thought. What if my inebriation was playing tricks on me and I was serenading the wrong one?

The horn that followed sounded even more frantic than the first time. Maybe my attempts were a bit OTT (over the top), but as the kiddos say nowadays YOLO (you only live once).

Don't be scared darling, I'm not just a crazy Parsi, I am an author too. In fact, I just got an offer to write a film script, maybe you can be the hero in it? I can even play the lead…

I was barely two feet away from fulfilling my dying wish. The union of two long lost souls was just a heartbeat away. But before I could have a *dekho* into what the manifestation of my efforts may have looked like, I felt the strength of two hefty arms from behind, almost lifting me off the ground.

The predator exhaled short and intense breaths, their rough cheek grazing mine though their body scent felt familiar. Kicking the closest thing I could find, the shin, I began to scream, '*Bachao bachao* (save me).'

My film script was already in the making.

I was positive that my hero behind the shaded window would surely come to my rescue now. I was being abducted. King Khan would deliver like he always did on the silver screen.

But then several things happened all at once. Gates opened, my prospective 999th kiss skidded off and the voice behind me sounded all-too-known.

'Thank God, I had Singhji's number. Do you want to be served a restraining order?'

'Kkkkriiiiishhhhh!'

Still reeling under what had just transpired, I swerved around and began to fist punch his chest.

'Ouch! Crazy bawi, you hurting me! Stop it.'

WHACK!

'I've been trying your number for the past couple of hours to find out if you reached home okay. Stop you crazy woman! Not my hair.'

'Tried again at 12.30. Your damn cell has been unreachable for hours!'

THUD!

'Yeow, that's my weak shoulder. Kai nooooo! Have you gone bonkers?'

'What the f**k are you doing here Krish Aryan?'

I was screaming now. I had never been this mad at him. Of all the times I needed him next to me, this was the one time I did not.

The asshole had come in between me and my heartthrob. There was going to be some serious bloodshed now.

Yanking off the shoe with the rickety heel, I began to clunk him with it.

'*Gadhero, ghanchakkar,* you ruined my only chance. I won't spare you tonight.'

After dodging and diving all my angry missiles, he finally caught hold of both my palms in one of his firm ones and started to shake my shoulder with the other.

'*Chup*! Just *chup*! Enough. Do you have any idea what the time is? Such tamasha and *goondagardi* in the middle of the night!'

'Bbbut…'

'No buts. Shaddup. I was worried sick about you and then your chauffeur mentioned that you are standing in the middle of Bandstand alone. Though it didn't even take me a second to figure out where. Luckily, I had already left for your place to check on you.'

'Bbbut…'

His clasp loosened and my hands were free again though slightly sore.

'This is so typical of you man, your melodramatic bawism that's oblivious to everybody else's feelings. So long as you get what you want.'

'Get what I want? Really! Do you even know what I want Krish Aryan?'

Ram Singh who knew Krish very well and was smart enough to decipher that his role in the theatrics of the night was finally over, quickly got out of the car, handed over my belongings to my friend, avoided all eye contact with me lest I gave him one more sleep-robbing chore and then zoomed off full throttle to park the car back at my place.

Krish gestured me towards his Bullet parked against the ledge of the promenade on the opposite side of the street.

Soft water pellets assaulted us, just as we were crossing the road.

Dammit, it was raining in March!

29

The Wall Crumbles Like an Apple Crumble

'Good omen, eh?' I asked, as Krish and I sat and watched the panoramic seascape together, on the parapet of the promenade which was converted to a walkers track in the day and a chill-out spot by late evening. Not the best place to perch with an expensive inherited gara but I would dry clean it before my mom returned. There was not a soul in sight in that forsaken hour of the night.

'Sign of better things to come,' he managed to whisper, after a long pause, stretching out his left hand to catch a raindrop, placing his right one into my palm, my bag safely between his thighs. 'But it's almost gone. A passing shower I suppose.'

This called for a quick self-drilling.

No Kai, no. He's gaslighting your emotions. Someone up there is pranking you again. #heisjustnotintoyou

He looked awfully handsome that night, the baby blue T-shirt was bringing out his striking features. Or was it the Ruby Razzle effect?

'Where is Jiggleboobs tonight?'

I was trying to sound detached, but I could not hold my jealousy inside any more. Of course.

He frowned for half a second and then threw his head back and chuckled.

'Achcha Ruby! She dropped me home and went straight to her fiancé's. Why?'

I wanted to break into a cha-cha-cha, tear open my prickly sari and ride every wave; frolic with dolphins, but I kept a straight face.

'You know Sanjeev from Netflix? He is one of their business heads. Him,' he replied in a disinterested tone.

No, I don't know him but I like him already!

I filled him in quickly about the wedding and my collision with the stranger at Gusto. He tried listening in attentively though I could sense he was slightly distracted.

'You know for a woman who has travelled around the world countless times over, you're still quite a baby.'

He remarked, removing a bandana-like thing from his jeans and tidying up my smudged mascara.

'What the hell are you going on about?'

I asked suspiciously, not used to such odd behaviour from him at all.

Is the LIT still messing with me? *Was it really the 'King and I' a few minutes earlier*? *Is this buffoon actually holding my hand*? *Oh Khoda, I should really pull the plug on my alcoholism.*

'Nothing much except that I've finally realised that I just can't let you out of my sight and I certainly can't trust you. You suck at soul-searching and run away from anything that is good for you. It's pointless teaching you or making you even understand anything spiritual, gosh you are such a horrible student. A born rebel. And just when one would think that you were all drama'd out for the night, I catch you accosting a celebrity's vehicle!'

I nodded in agreement, wondering at the same time why his hand was now cupping my chin.

Who is this creature and what has he done to my Krish? *Tadan ajeeb thaigayoch muo.* (The dude is behaving really oddly.)

'But what's the freakin' point you are making you gaandu?'

My head felt 10 per cent better with the cool sea draft blowing in our direction.

His hand disengaged from my skin at last, but then moved to his left ear.

WTF is he up to now?

'Why are you scratching your ear? Oh Dadaji, are there insects here? Krish, let's get out of here!'

I leapt up and began to aggressively dust my sari, my skin tingling with imaginary creepy crawlies sneaking over it. Better safe than sorry. A swollen nipple was the last thing I needed.

'Calm down, Bawi, stop twitching, just relax.'

He pulled me back next to him, lightly massaging my tensed shoulders.

Is he on heavy duty medication? *Maybe procured some potent stuff from Goa suggested by one of his babajis*?

'So, I realised there is only one way of removing those *keeras* from your bum,' he continued talking, gently kneading his fingers around my nape setting off a cold shiver down my spine.

This was getting weirder by the minute.

And then he let go and once again began to fidget around his ear but this time he removed the tiny studded cross earring that he wore.

'Is it hurting you?' I asked, trying to gauge in the dim light if his lobe was red.

'I may be out of line here, but will you keep this? It's not even 0.25 of a carat but...' He squirmed as he spoke.

I shrugged.

Why did he want me to keep it for him?

'Yeah sure, give it. Will pop it inside the pouch with all my other jewellery. And apply some antiseptic on your ear when you reach home.'

'OMG Bawiiiiii!!!!!!!'

He stood up, his hands spread out, his cry loud enough to wake up sleeping mermaids. He then put back the earring in his jeans pocket, a resigned look over his handsome face, hands dropping to his hips.

And before I had a chance to process the bizarreness of it all, he yanked me up, pulled me into his arms and kissed me hard on the lips, hurling me into an orbit of puzzlement and elation, bringing me to my knees albeit metaphorically, to beg, plead and negotiate with every God of every creed and cult to not take this moment away from me, ever.

I could hear the gentle roar of the blustery waves hugging the rocks in front of us. The gusty breeze dancing in approval and amusement as it ruffled over our caressing shadows stained with heaving breaths.

Is this the end of a love drought? Am I on the cusp of a brand-new beginning of unprecedented bliss? Or is this another one of many intoxicated fallacies?

His lingering body fragrance of CK's Eternity brought back a very old memory of The Shack, driving me to an uncontainable frenzy. His sweet breath over my hybrid one; his strong limbs pressed hard against my trembling legs made me yearn for that oneness which had been long outstanding. There was not any part of me that was not tingling and jingling, including my toe nails. But above all, like never before, I felt the intimate presence of the love of my life. And its warm glow captivated my entire being.

It is not easy to explain your first kiss with your forever crush. First the heart lurches into full panic mode and then there is uncontrollable euphoria. There is a thin line between these two feelings, so it is hard to say when one spills over the other. Or perhaps they merge.

At first I thought the remnants of the daru was still screwing with my brains, but lips do not lie especially if they are as soft as Krish's. That was XXX999 done right and it had been deliciously unrestrained.

He then drew himself back carefully, his soulful eyes searching for my reaction, his lips begging for more, his voice hoarse, 'Why didn't we do this sooner?'

'Spoiler alert, you are the world's biggest duffer—I've been waiting for you until my last black hair turned grey,' I was tempted to shout back but instead placed my clammy tongue across his stubble, relishing its musky taste and whispered, 'just give me back my pretend ring.'

The 101 whip lashes and gaalis he deserved would be postponed for another day. For now, I was simply going to enjoy the pleasurable feeling of Krish Aryan's indestructible wall crumble like a sweet apple crumble.

I snatched the little cross back from his pocket, like an eager beaver, lest he change his mind or a night pigeon fly away with it.

'I don't want any gigantic declaration of love Krish, contrary to what you think. I just want love.'

He grinned back; there were no games between us any more.

I looked skywards virtually hearing my spirit guides exhale enormous sighs of relief and liberation, almost expecting sheening fireworks they had saved for a night like this, to crackle through the horizon.

Instead, I saw something equally beautiful—countless golden dots poking out their smug heads and the moon winking back in glee. They had held this secret of my relentless heart way too long.

But there were a couple of questions still pending. If he wanted to be Superman, he could have done so ages ago and saved me from a whole lot of outrage, disappointment and tears, so why had he not?

As if reading my thoughts he said, 'I guess over time, I lost my nerve. Besides, I would never forgive myself if I lost you…relationships have not been our strong suit, have they? Moreover, nothing is set in stone, feelings change over time; people outgrow each other. I didn't want to end up discarded like my mother was, lest you found someone better.'

Oh Khodaiji, who is the duffer now? How could I have not seen this coming? Of course, it all sums up now.

Krish the eternal overthinker had mulled over every permutation and combination until he had decided for himself that nothing can work out for him. Pretty similar to me. However, he had hit the nail. Love should make one feel good, complete, trusted and content akin to comfort food. But it had only destroyed us.

*Can two f**ked up morons cancel each other out and make it right?*

It was a long shot. But I had nowhere to go. I never did.

'But we can't run from ourselves forever, can we? Like your precious Rumi says, "What you seek, has been seeking you all along".'

He gazed into my eyes, impressed.

I grabbed him this time. Enwrapping him tightly into my arms, making sure that there was no space for even air to escape between us, I gently laid my head on his chest, something I had always craved to do. He was mine, all mine.

Bombarding him with kisses galore all over his cheeks, forehead and neck, the warmth of his body ploughing into mine; there was this undeniable fanatical intensity between us that I had never experienced before with anyone. It seemed to blow him away too.

But I still needed an answer to that one burning question, 'Why had he chosen that night?'

'When I saw you standing near the car ready to jump on his bones, my heart skipped a beat. In fact, it skipped quite a few. I felt territorial about you all of a sudden and went through this unexpected fit of rage, which isn't like me at all. What if you really strike gold with him? The other sods were no real threat, but this one is like my arch rival. Like I would absolutely stand no chance, if he, I mean if you guys...'

Krish thinks I have a chance with SRK? He must really think I am a goddess.

'True. If he had got to me before you did, you the Kingpin of Mixed Signals would've been in the kennel for good. For even though you are my satiating bowl of French fries, he is like sex on toast.'

'Okay got it! Can we stop there? But you could've given me an ultimatum long back,' he said, breaking into one of his lopsided smiles and making my heart prance again.

'Krish Aryan sometimes, soooo very rarely, you are the smartest guy around but mostly you are just a nincompoop.'

A flurry of wind blew into us and he delicately flicked the wisp of hair over my moony eyes with his fingers, his protective palm melting into my cool face. But my lips were far from satiated, my body equally famished, my heart overflowing with emotions, proving to me once again, that I had buried this truth far too long.

Weak knees and a fluttering heart were for commoners; for this was nothing short of a chemical dhansak!

So, I dug my fingers in his back, desperate to seal the deal, as I finally said those three magical words aloud, 'Wanna come over?'

Just as we were about to disentangle and leave, two *hawaldars* marched towards us, flashlights in hand and insisted we accompany them to a cop station.

Ending a passion-filled night like that at a slammer would be the worst anti-climax in the history of mankind. I had to act quick.

'Give them money for *chai-pani naashta*, quick.'

I stammered, tugging at Krish's t-shirt and frantically whispering somewhere around his neck.

'Oh *Maydum, kai bolte tumhi?* (Madam, what are you saying?) *Chai-pani che diwas gele; atta aaamchi bhi sataklee* (the days of tea and water are gone, now even we have lost it),' the tubbier one quipped while the other took out a ragged notebook and pen.

'Ratan Tata *ki bhatijee ko pareshaan karoge kya*? (Are you going to trouble Ratan Tata's niece?)'

With that said, Krish began fiddling with his phone, as though RT was on his speed dial. Though bribing was against his nature, telling a white lie clearly wasn't.

Fortunately, they were acquainted with Mr Tata's name and strode off, mumbling about a final warning or something to that effect; leaving us giggling our heads off until we developed stitches in our sides.

'Look, Bawi, look, a rainbow! Have you ever seen one at this insane hour of the night?'

Boy, he looked excited.

I ran my fingers through his hair affectionately. The seven vivid colours at a distance held the promise of a fresh start. Plunging for another yummiliscious kiss that took us to all the seventh heavens of all the immeasurable galaxies, I muttered under my breath, 'ONE THOUSAND.'

30

I Am Friends with the Monsters inside My Head

May 2022
(Three years later)
Lonavala

'Kai come no, let's check if our chillies and figs have grown?'

Rehu, all grown up at nine now, was standing over my head, trying to stop me from opening my MacBook.

'*Haan* coming, Chickoo, just finishing some important work and I shall be with you…'

'Do you know, I assembled parts and made my own mobile phone like an apple Iphone?'

He was a little busybody with the heart of an angel and obsessed with gadgets, specifically cell phones and speakers. Of course, being my one and only nephew, there was not a thing I could fault Rehu for.

Mom and Dad voiced together, 'Please go, before you upset your little fan.'

Earlier that morning as we drove into our picturesque driveway of the Château Juicewalla, we noticed the endless rows of blossoming rose pods, purple petunias, lilac morning glory's, yellow dahlias, leafy palms and pink bougainvilleas, which had bloomed effortlessly in pleasant hill station weather.

I had made a mental note of it—it would act as the perfect landscape for an alfresco session for my virtual celebrity chat show that I had kicked off over a year ago just for a lark (to chase lockdown blues away). It had begun to catch up in the digital space; achievers from diverse fields were interviewed by me; nothing that life altering, just a breezy tête-à-tête.

Rehu had been immersed in erecting a mini-fountain when we had arrived, enjoying the perks the lockdown brought, especially online schooling for the last 24 months. That was the main reason Ash and Aarti had set up base in Lonavala in the last couple of years; not only did it give their son more legroom to run about in the open air but the Covid threat may have been slightly less there. Mom, dad and I visited them occasionally and they had made a few trips to Mumbai on special occasions.

The years 2020 and 2021 had been a blend of happiness and stress; happiness because things were finally falling into place on the personal front, stress because covid had brought out the worst in people before making it better. The virus scare was not for the faint-hearted. The fear of death was looming large on all of us like a meteor ready to explode anytime.

Elastic blue masks had replaced sunny smiles; holding a loved one's hand or helping a disabled stranger to cross the street or opening the door to a needy soul had all of a sudden become perilous. Careers got axed, bank accounts dried up, a number of relationships/situationships were on the verge of permanent wreckage and many even collapsed.

Initially, I too went through all the higgledy-piggledy conundrums of the enforced lockdown, from "why Khodaiji why" moments to denial to anxiety to loneliness to developing new OCDs to paranoia to acceptance to resilience to exasperation to emptiness.

Pushing aside the churning of an unsettled stomach caused by the hullabaloo in my mind, I shifted my concentration back to my laptop and logged into my email account, going through my saved draft for one last time. There was no looking back now.

Who Wants to Marry Kai Juicewalla?

Chapter titles: Check
Chapters: Check.
Author bionote: Check.

With hands trembling, armpits sweating and three Yatha ahu Vairyos and two *Ashem Vohu*s recited, I gave my manuscript all the positive energy I could invoke within me before hitting SEND.

Bravo!

Penning my second book had not been easy. First of all, it had started off as a film script in 2019 under the guidance of Dez Zacchary over the phone. Unfortunately, Covid was not merciful to him and somewhere in the midst of the first wave of 2020 he crossed over to the other side, leaving me with a half-baked screenplay and nowhere to show it.

Second, the film industry had come to a standstill with a heavy backlog of old projects and nobody seemed interested in getting pitched by debutant script writers for new ones.

The travel industry had also received a huge blow and I was pretty much homebound; well, at least, I had a job unlike loads of unfortunates who had lost theirs.

I had not seen much of my friends for over a year and a half, though they seemed to be doing rather well in their respective lives.

The lockdown gave Zoya enough time to reconnect with the college-scholar in her whom she had left far behind. She was now building her own empire without the help of her hubby dear's wealth or contacts.

Simran and Harman both did their bit in the pandemic as expected. Whilst fearless Simran distributed household items and rations to those who could not get out or afford it, the *fauji* blood in Harman supported her by accompanying her everywhere while drawing personal safety lines for both of them.

Coco was her usual calm self over the line whenever we spoke, nestled in her own little family Down Under with two rottweilers to add to the party. My days of visiting her are over, considering I have both dog phobia and occasional kid phobia.

With several under-40 awards under her belt, Aliya had become quite a force to reckon with, rising to the challenge by embracing her setbacks. She is now leaning towards national politics, bless her heart. She joked it off by saying that this time, she would be dealing with men whose egos were bigger than their hot dogs.

With the rug pulled out from Dan's socialising feet, he admitted that he felt like a fish out of water in the real world. With plenty of time on hand, he had taken up stitching and inscribing his name on his designer shirts, sweaters and mufflers. He had even renounced bitching and gossiping for three months in a row. Enforced house arrest and celibacy did bizarre things to people.

Shanaya went into over hyper mode during the pandemic with Burzin having to show up at work and risk his life, day in and out. She asked me if I knew a good therapist to help her through her anxiety and apprehensions. I connected her to Kabeer Q for video sessions which made a huge difference. I am guessing his charm did rub off on her too. (So much for giving me grief about it, a few years ago.)

Pari had gone totally potty with the full *paltan* living under one roof 24/7 for the entire lockdown period. She was ready to give her kids up for adoption, divorce her husband and lock up her *kit kitee* (nagging) in-laws towards the end of 2021.

Navika my health farm runaway partner-turned-model was now a life coach too and an extremely successful one.

Rusty was doing just fine, a bit older but not any wiser. Sohrabji hardly slept at nights overcome with worry that his bachcha may catch the virus even though his wife constantly reassured him that animals and birds remained unaffected.

The idea to make the rough script into a book had been Krish's bright idea.

'You've been racking your brains for your second book and it's been in front of you all along.'

He declared one day and I never looked back ever since.

Writing a film script as opposed to a novel is a completely different experience.

Firstly, getting people to interpret words on paper is far more challenging than explaining the same through streaming scenes and montages.

Second, I had to start from scratch all over again and plough ahead with faith that my story was wildly unique and may inspire others in some way or the other. If nothing else, at the very least, it would give them a good laugh and that itself would be my reward. Maya Angelou knew what she was talking about when she said, 'If you don't like something change it. If you can't change it, change your attitude. Don't complain.'

But even then, once I was done, I went through my share of hell, with an editor who refused to deliver on time and a lit agent who seemed to change his mind every month about the structure of my novel. The ramifications of that had been unnecessary delays, which later turned out to be a blessing in disguise because not only did I get a much better team who believed in me, but also, it gave me the opportunity to supplement the final chapter with a twist that would not see the light of day, had it been otherwise.

The thing about a biography or a memoir is when do you stop? Life is ever-changing; gaining momentum, throwing one curve ball after another, showering surprises and presenting us with an opportunity every day to change our narrative, our perspective and our direction. And then there is the benefit of hindsight.

I had superstitiously waited to get to Lonavala, where a stronger Granny B connection prevailed, to e-deliver slices of my life story to my publisher. And that is exactly what I did a few minutes ago.

'Kaiiiiiiiiiiiiiii!' I heard another screech from the garden area.

'You better obey before he brings Lonavala down. He has a whole agenda planned for you, including a treasure hunt and a surprise.'

Aarti tipped me off.

Shutting my device into serious obedience, I ran over to where Rehu was and hugged him tight. We held hands and chatted nineteen a dozen. I was so proud of him; for a boy with such tiny and soft hands, he had done a superlative job of keeping Granny B's garden thriving.

My phone beeped, 'How's it going Bawi? Reached ok? Have fun with the mad Juicewallas and don't forget to bring back some choc fudge for me. Miss u already.'

My heart skipped two. Nothing new. He still had that effect. Twin flames always did.

'Kai no phone now, don't start your nonsense.'

Rehu snatched my cell away and dropped it into his pocket, making it very clear that he was the only one entitled to my undivided time and attention.

'Okay big boss!'

I said, laughing and saluting him.

He then led me to the backyard, which immediately brought back the taste of mulberries in my mouth. Skipping beside me in his orange shorts and a white singlet, carefree and joyous, he piloted me towards the mango tree. On drawing closer, I noticed a tiny shed-like structure assembled beneath the tree.

'Surrrpppprise!!!!!!!!!!!!!!!!!' he said, screaming into my ear. 'I made this for us. Welcome to our new home, Kai.'

He was pointing at a 6 feet by 6 feet barn-like construction, built out of a few tree barks, bricks, old sheets, cardboard slabs and thermocol blocks with dried palm leaves that acted as flowy curtains.

My throat went dry and a familiar twinge surfaced around my chest.

Seeing my downfallen face, he asked, 'You don't like what I made for us? We can play here, have our own picnic and share some secrets. I even charged my speaker.'

Flashes of a familiar cardboard box drew me to a halt.

'Come Kai let's go in, it will be super fun. C'mon!'

'Maybe after lunch?'

Wondering if there was any other way to get out of it.

'No! Now! What's wrong?'

'Nothing. It's awesome; so innovative.'

He had created it with so much passion, that I hated being a spoilsport.

Finally, I succumbed. Sunbeams penetrated through the branches of the huge tree above us, radiating their effect all around the box, making it brighter than I had expected. We huddled together inside it, cross-legged, the mud sticking to my linen pants, but it hardly mattered. I felt safe, strangely.

I spotted two pairs of eyes looking at us shyly from a distance with a couple of brown paper bags in their hands. (They were the gardener's children.) They seemed to be caught in a dilemma whether to encroach or stay away. In their short lives, they had already learnt that there was an unstated wall between privileged and less-privileged.

'Naina, Montoo, *aa jao.* Sit sit. Chalo, let's first take some selfies and then play together.'

I reached into the pocket of my nephew's shorts to reclaim my cell. They were stoked with my invite and entered willingly.

'Didi for you...' whispered the 12-year-old girl coyly, handing me the bags.

I looked at them gratefully, opening the parcels at once, to see what little gifts they bore.

In front of me lay an assortment of fresh garden produce of tomatoes, limes, beans, *jamuns*, hibiscus flowers, basil leaves, raw mangoes and various berries.

'We woke up at 7 today to collect all these for you. This was the second part of the surprise,' blurted Rehu, picking up a homegrown strawberry from the pile, and putting it in my mouth.

'*Wah*! *Bahut hi achcha hai!* (That's very good!)' I exclaimed, smacking my lips, making them all cackle.

'See Kai, now I will close the door but there is a spy hole,' Rehu explained, pointing towards the symmetrical incision he had carved into the thermocol that was supposedly the door; his tiny chest filling up with pride that he had made his Kai very happy.

I looked around, it had been a stuffy cubicle a few minutes ago but we had made it our cosy sanctuary, thanks to my wildly imaginative nephew. I guess it is in our genes.

'Abracadabra. Now from here, we can see outside but nobody will see us.'

'Hmmm. I guess so.'

'You know what this means, Kai?'

'Yeah. We are hiding from the rest, na?'

'No silly billy, that's obvious,' he sighed, giving me that, you-adults-can-be-so-dumb look.

'Oh then what cutie pie?'

'It means we can create our own magical world here, away from ordinary and boring people and live happily ever after.'

And when he put it like that, it all made perfect sense. He had just given me a different perspective to my oldest demon. If someone gave me a time machine, would I go back and do things differently? Perhaps not. Less rona dhona and self-sabotage perhaps, but some of us are meant to take the prolonged and insanely twisted route to self-acceptance and freedom.

I rarely sought wisdom in philosophy or read tomes on mindfulness or listened to transcendent discourses or well-meaning advice from friends. If one formula fit all, nobody would have problems. And there is no greater joy than squeezing the juice out of everything life has to offer, making your own blunders and walking down your own weird ass path to find your own distinct place under the sun. In life, you have to be your own hero and your own fan. If you can do that much, the rest will take care of itself.

My phone beeped again, seven message alerts in a row, this time. I smiled to myself.

They were from the Whatsapp group I recently formed of volunteers, whereby we visited old-age establishments, like sanitoriums, *dharamshalas,* hospices, and gave companionship and support to the elderly—the abandoned and the lonely in our community.

Our initiative, Be a Friend, was the brainchild of my father who had handed over the baton to me, with the confidence that if there was anyone who could get things done by getting people interested in the project, it was me.

Before Rehu went berserk on me and confiscated my phone again, I did a quick scan of the photographs forwarded by my super enthusiastic and highly capable team from their morning sanitorium visit, which I missed. But then my chest clenched, mortified with what was in front of me.

No, it can't be! Vam uh Veera Aunty? And Drrr Dolly. No way! *It has to be a big mistake.*

I zoomed in, rubbing my eyes in disbelief. They both appeared weak, weary, frumpy and worn-out. It had been only three years since…

How is it even possible? What are they doing there? What happened to their husbands and their children? Can fate turn so quickly?

I was a living testimony it could but for them it seemed to have completely spiralled in the opposite direction.

I posted on the group: 'The two ageing ladies in this particular pic, in the beige and cobalt blue. I would like you to give them extra attention. Please be extra kind and hug them as much. Whatever they need, I will bear the expenses. Just don't tell them it's from me. In fact, never mention that you know me.'

The team responded with a bunch of thumbs ups.

Past grievances were forgotten. Personal vendettas were buried. We are all humans and erring is our birthright.

The bachcha party in our tiny abode had now multiplied. Four baby chicks poked their heads through a hole, clucking away trying to find their voice with Mother Hen not too far behind; two tiny (thankfully harmless) puppies followed cue, scratching from the outside uncertain of their welcome and a snail ran across my foot.

Our bitsy box was spilling over with happiness, rhapsody, gaiety, egalitarianism and broken barriers.

Gadget guru Rehu showed me a small torch he had reconstructed on his own and then turned on the music on his JBL Flip 4 and began rocking and swaying with the other two children.

'EDM.'

'Wazzat?'

I must have sounded so foolish that he raised his eyebrows and shook his head in displeasure as he bespoke the forbidden words, 'Electronic dance music, Aunty!'

And did Krish officially propose?

No. And it does not matter any more.

I had survived a married parasite, a casting couch aspirant, a dope addict, a mobster, a bisexual with an identity crisis, a confused counsellor, a volatile devil to get here…

I am not going to spoil it just yet. After all, *shaadi ka laddoo kha ke kisko pachhtaana hai*? (Who wants to eat the marriage laddoo and regret?) I would rather have motichoor laddoos!

As of now, I am living the best version of myself, with my eccentricities intact and my eternal bowl of French fries and thunder thighs that will never desert me.

No animals were harmed in the creation of this masterpiece. Though I cannot say the same about the guys.

Acknowledgements

Thank you to the 6 F's for their valuable contributions

Faith

To God and my Zoroastrian faith that bestowed me with everything I could ask for and more.

And gracing me with a rich inheritance of eccentricity and humour which I take immense pride in.

To other faiths, for welcoming me with open arms.

Family

Without whom I would not have the luxury of pursuing everything my heart desires. For their consistent encouragement and giving me the freedom to do what I like, when I like and how I like but keeping the nest cosy, open and safe to return to. I am too possessive to mention any of them (and a bit superstitious too). Touchwood!

I cannot move ahead without thanking my young and effervescent nephew Rehaan who kept me on a strict schedule of edits and rewrites, making sure I completed what I started. Our stimulating conversations keep me youthful and inspired. He also kept me sane during the lockdown probably because he is the only one who truly gets me. He has given me a reason to wake up and smile and push myself to work and create some type of legacy, which maybe someday he can be proud of.

Forevers

My late grandmoms, Amy and Bapus, who are the soul of this book. There would have been no story to tell without both of them. I learnt forgiveness and humility from one; wisdom and unconditional love from the other. Super thrilled to fulfil their dreams of having me travel around the world and author books. If I could go back, I would hug them more and love them harder.

My late brother-in-law Burz who I know has got me covered. I sense it, I know it, I value it.

Bappu aunty who throughout my childhood reminded me where I needed to go with my life—'excel!'

Dasturji Dinyarji, Capt Desmond (Budgy and Sparrow) Rodrigues, Ronnie (Aslaji) Uncle and legend Dev Anand for making me believe that I was special and gifted.

Fighters

Prash, Kaizin, Dilshad, Porus and Richa for always having my back. For standing by me like gigantic rocks when the chips were down and all was dark and hopeless; for loving me fearlessly and for holding my hand throughout this journey and pulling me out of my struggles when I needed it. I could not have made it this far in the last few years without them.

Fantastic Team

My dynamic and impressive literary agent, the very witty and multitalented Suhail Mathur of The Book Bakers literary agency for seeing the potential in my manuscript and putting all his efforts to place it in the right hands. For always appreciating my work and consistently supporting me in the last so many years. Invaluable!

A huge thank you to Suhail and his team for designing the most enthralling and eye-catching book cover.

And my dearest Sanjeev Mathur for being a special and important part of this from the beginning.

The suave and charming publisher, Ajay Mago, for taking me on board and letting me be a part of one of India's biggest publishing houses.

The super intelligent and extremely knowledgeable Shantanu Ray Chaudhuri, chief editor of Om Books International, for gifting me an exceptional opportunity to know him, work with him and learn from him. And for having my best interests at heart.

My wonderful editor Jyotsna Mehta who left me speechless several times with her editing skills, comical timing, professionalism and sincere dedication to my manuscript. For drawing a fine balance between inspiring me to do even better and respecting my story enough to keep it authentic and giving me honest feedback when required. Can't think of anyone else who could have done justice to this book more than her.

So grateful to everyone who wrote such wonderful endorsements for this book. It makes me feel special and unique.

Friends

Who lent the outrageousness, excitement, sexitement and scandal to all my stories.

My Fab 4 and my travel gals. You know who you all are. My ex-colleague-friends and bosses from the airline who have shown immense interest in my work through the years and have been waiting for this book.

Close family friends, relatives, cousins, good friends, who have encouraged me every step of the way.

Diana and Ferzine for being with me since this book began ages back. Cyrus who has all the knowledge in the world, and is always ready to help.

Janhavi who started this author journey with me, believing in me blindly.

Kara (Tearoom) for listening to my ideas for this book over chai and cheese toast.

Julian for the awards he has envisioned for me.

My readers, my cheerleaders on FB, Instagram, YouTube who support me day in and day out, no matter what I post, blog or vlog. I can be myself with them all, which in itself says a lot.

All the above exist in the very heart of my writing. I have achieved because they believed.

Finally, to all my pain-in-the-ass ex-boyfriends without whom this book would not be so decadently delicious.

Every road planned or unplanned, straight or crooked, conventional or offbeat that I walked on has led to the making of this madly candid and insanely dramatic book; hence, I can be nothing else but GRATEFUL!